CATCH ME

The Donovan Family Series (#9)

MARGARET WATSON

ISBN-13: 978-1-944422-30-1

TITLES BY MARGARET WATSON

CHAPTER 1

Sam inhaled the aroma of leather, sweat and dirt. Smiled. All he'd ever wanted was right here in front of him. His for the taking.

He lingered in the late-night quiet of the locker room, basking in the scents he'd loved since he was a kid. He'd worked hard to get to the major leagues, to make it with the Bearcats, and he'd work even harder to stay here.

Slinging his suit bag over his shoulder, he paused at the door to wave to his favorite physical therapist, the only other person in the team locker room. "So long, Doc-ette. See you tomorrow."

Keara glanced at him and frowned. "What's with the jeans and sneakers? You're supposed to wear your suit to and from the park."

"Trying to blend in," Sam said easily. At close to midnight, there weren't too many men in suits hanging around Wrigleyville.

Surrounded by guys in flip-flops and cargo shorts, a suit stood out like a neon light. Everyone looked at him. A handful recognized him, and there was always a drunk trying to pick a fight with a ball player. He didn't want the hassle. So he carried his suit home.

Keara snorted. "Yeah, the six-foot-six inch golden boy of Wrigleyville just disappears right into a crowd." She returned her attention to the computer and said, "Just get your ass in here early tomorrow, Marini." Her hands flew over the keyboard. "Those glutes of yours need work, and I've got a full schedule."

Sam grinned as the dark-haired trainer continued to type. "Don't worry, Keara. I'll be here bright and early. My ass is all yours. And I won't tell your husband that you want your hands on it."

"Get out of here, Marini," she said without looking at him. "Try to stay out of trouble on your walk home."

"It's four blocks and a bunch of drunks. What can happen?"

Sam slipped through the door, walked up the ramp, through the gate and stepped onto Clark Street. Even at midnight, throngs of people crowded the sidewalks, bunching together and separating, flowing along either side of Clark like a multi-colored river. The muffled rumble of cars creeping along the street blended with the raised voices of the partiers and the too-loud car radios blaring out of open windows.

This was why he always walked home after games. The Wrigleyville neighborhood of Chicago was full of movement. Action. Fun.

It was alive, in a way few other neighborhoods were, especially in the evening after a home game. People having a good time, hanging out with friends, watching a game in one of the many sports bars in the area.

Walking home let him absorb that real-ness. Brushing shoulders with the crowds made him feel like one of them.

Even though he wasn't.

The crowds and laughter and noise in the bars beckoned, but he didn't go into any of them. He'd done that a few times and always regretted it. Too many guys who were sure they could help him straighten out that awkward swing. Guys who knew they had the answers to any problems he'd had at the game that day.

Too many cleat chasers who wanted a player as a notch on their bedpost. They were beautiful, willing women, but being a trophy had gotten old real fast.

No, he didn't go to the bars near the ballpark. He just liked to walk down the street, drinking in all the energy and excitement on the way to his quiet house on a side street.

As he waited at the crosswalk, jostled by a noisy crowd streaming across Clark, a group spilled out of the bar on the other side of Addison. They all wore softball uniforms -- white pants and red shirts emblazoned with 'Sports Circuit.' Sam raised his eyebrows. Teams were supposed to gather for drinks at the bar that sponsored them. That's how it worked. The bar spent their money on you. You spent yours at the bar. These guys were a few blocks out of their territory.

Another softball player stumbled out right behind them -- a guy in a green 'Seventh Inning Stretch' shirt. Okay. *This* guy was on the team this bar sponsored in the Chicago Sports and Social League.

The single member of The Seventh Inning Stretch team was jeering at the red-shirted group, raising his finger in the universal 'we're number one' chant. His face reddened as he yelled, "Stay out of our bar, losers!" Even from the other side of the street, Sam could hear the slurred words.

Drunk. Like so many of the other people on the street at this time of night.

Sam frowned. People were still streaming across Addison toward him, leaving the softball players alone on the opposite corner. The odd lull in people moving around created a bubble of solitude in the middle of the crowds.

The red-shirted players turned around to face the green-shirted kid, and suddenly ugly vibes filled the air. Keeping his eye on the softball players, Sam tried to elbow his way through the crowd to get to the other side of the street. No luck. Too many people surging toward him.

The melee developing across the street wasn't the usual

after-the-game, let's-get-hammered-and-have-fun bunch. For starters, it was one guy against a group. And that guy was a skinny kid who barely looked old enough to shave. His pants were too big and looked as if they'd been cinched tightly with a belt. His brown hair was shaggy, and his green shirt was wet -- as if he'd spilled beer on himself. He was pointing at the biggest guy on the other team.

Or maybe the guy he was shouting at had dumped the beer on him. To shut him up.

The light changed and cars streamed past him. Sam looked for an opening to dart across Addison, but the cars were bumper to bumper. As far as he could tell, no one was paying attention to the drama unfolding seventy feet away.

Across the street teeming with cars, the green-shirted guy was alone in a sea of red-shirted softball players. He faced a guy who was at least a head taller than him. The red shirted guy was twice as wide, too. The sleeves of his uniform shirt bulged over his biceps, and his pants clung to thick thighs. Either he did insane workouts or he had a really physical job. Or maybe he used 'roids.

Little Guy lunged toward the red-shirted group, both hands extended as if to shove Big Guy. He wobbled before he reached Big Guy, falling to one knee. Pressing his palms to the sidewalk, Little Guy slowly straightened.

Nothing good was going to happen here.

His heart racing, Sam pulled out his cell and hit 911.

"911. What is your emergency?"

"A fight. At the corner of Clark and Addison. Get the cops here. Now."

"What's your name, sir?"

"Just get the cops here."

Sam disconnected the call and started to drop the phone into his pocket. But some instinct made him open the camera app, hit the button and hold it down.

Sam held the phone above the heads of the people clustered around him, waiting for the light to change. Apparently, none of them had noticed what was happening on the opposite corner.

The skinny kid lurched forward again.

The big guy swung around to face his tormenter. Raising his right hand, he pulled his arm back, then let fly with a punch. His hand moved so fast it was a blur.

Little guy's head snapped back. As if he was moving in slow motion, his arms windmilled. He staggered backward. Crumpled to the ground. His head hit the curb with a hollow sound that Sam heard all the way across the street.

He lay there, unmoving. Blood flowed from his nose. His ears. Red soaked into the green shirt, turning it an ugly brown.

Why the fuck wasn't anyone else paying attention?

Sam waited for a break in traffic as the group of red-shirted guys across the street went completely silent. Frozen, all of them stared down at the guy lying motionless in the street.

Then they backed away and scattered like cockroaches in a sudden light. Some of them ran down Clark, some took off down Addison. Still holding down the camera button, Sam tried to get a photo of each of them.

The big guy, the one who'd thrown the punch, looked around wildly until he spotted a cab. He stepped into the street, practically in front of it, and the cab screeched to a halt. Just a few feet beyond where the skinny kid lay on the street. The big guy leaped in and slammed the door.

"Hey," Sam shouted, trying to chase after him. "You can't take off!"

The cab pulled away with the dick inside, and Sam zeroed in on the cab's number and license plate. Took a picture. Then, angry and pissed off, he stood and watched the cab head toward the lake. A few blocks later, it made a right turn down a major street and disappeared.

People had begun to notice what had happened. Some of them ran across the street, causing brakes to screech and horns to blare. They jostled Sam in their hurry, and even though he was using his elbows to move through the loud, stumbling crowd, it seemed like an eternity before he made it to the other side of the street.

He stood over the kid, unsure of what to do. How to help him. Blood still flowed out of his nose and ears, and its coppery tang swirled around Sam. The kid looked as if he was barely breathing. Sam had just crouched down beside the kid, trying to protect him from the flashing cameras and the crowd pushing closer, when the rise and fall of sirens suddenly registered in Sam's consciousness.

Thank God. He stood and spotted a Chicago PD squad car approaching to his right. It pulled to the curb in front of him, and a uniformed cop jumped out. He had a bristly grey crew cut and his vest was snug on a protruding gut.

"You the guy who called in the 911?"

"Yeah." Sam took a deep breath. "That was me."

"Driver's license, please," the cop said.

"Shouldn't you be taking care of this kid?" He nodded at the still figure, his green shirt now soaked with blood, whose head rested at an odd angle on the curb. The kid's feet sprawled in the street, trash fluttering over his legs.

"Ambulance is right there." The cop jerked his chin down Clark Street, where an ambulance was bleeping its siren to clear the way. "They've got him." The cop studied Sam with cool eyes as he drew him several buildings down the street, away from the kid lying on the ground. "You have that ID?"

Reluctantly, Sam pulled out his wallet, extracted his driver's license and extended it.

The guy held it between his fingers as he continued to assess Sam. "You try to stop the fight?"

"I couldn't." Regret was sharp and bitter on his tongue. "I was on the other side of the street when it happened. Too much traffic, cars going too fast."

"You know any of the guys involved?"

"Never saw any of them before just now."

"On your way to a bar?"

"No." Sam was beginning to get annoyed. Did this cop

suspect *he* was involved? "On my way home." He glanced at the cop's name tag. "Officer Dwyer."

"From where?"

"From work." Sam spoke through clenched teeth.

The cop tilted his head as his eyes took in Sam's jeans, the dress shirt he still wore, the suit bag slung over his shoulder. Then he looked down at his driver's license.

"You live a few blocks from here," the cop said.

Sam let out the breath he hadn't realized he'd been holding. The cop didn't recognize his name, so either he didn't follow baseball, or he was a Sox fan. Thank God. "Yeah."

"Can you tell me what happened?"

Keeping his eyes on the still-unmoving kid on the ground, who now had two paramedics kneeling on either side of him, Sam explained what he'd seen. He pulled out his phone and gave the cop the cab number. Recounted which direction he'd gone, and where he'd turned right. Then he pulled up the photos of the fight and showed the cop the sequence of pictures he'd taken.

A muscle jumped in the cop's jaw as he studied the pictures. "I'm going to need that phone," he said. "It has evidence on it."

Sam put it back in his pocket and let his hand hover over it. "What's your email address? I'll send them to you right now. This is my only phone. My manag... boss will be calling me first thing in the morning with my assignments for the day."

"Sorry, kid. Evidence is evidence. Even if it's on your phone. That was quick thinking, by the way, taking those pictures. We shouldn't have any problem nailing the guy who did this."

"Good. Great." Sam swallowed. They'd have his pictures. They wouldn't need him. His name wouldn't have to come up, bringing negative publicity to the team. "I'm happy to send them to you. But I can't give you my phone."

The cop's mouth hardened. "Not your choice, Mr. ..."

He glanced at Sam's license. "Mr. Marini. Hand it over. I'm not going to tell you aga…"

Just then a sharp whistle split the air. The cop looked over at the paramedics, and Sam saw one of them waving frantically at him.

"Stay right here," the cop ordered. "Don't leave." Insuring that he couldn't, the cop slid Sam's driver's license into his pocket. "I need to see what they want. Then I'll be back."

Sam watched as the cop jogged across the street. Crouched next to the paramedics. After studying the motionless guy on the ground, he stood up and pulled his radio off his vest. Spoke into it.

Dread crept over Sam. Why did the paramedics need Dwyer? Shouldn't that kid be waking up? His stomach clenched with foreboding.

Dwyer said a few more words to the paramedic, then jogged back toward Sam.

"Detectives are on the way. You need to stay and talk to them."

"What's wrong?" Sam asked, leaning to look past the cop to the paramedics and the still-unmoving kid on the ground. "Is he going to be okay? Why are detectives coming?"

"I'm not a doctor." The cop motioned him farther down the street. "I need you out of the way so I can block off the scene."

Still staring at the motionless kid, unease coiling in his stomach, Sam ignored the cop. "Shouldn't he have moved by now?"

"You need to step down the block, Mr. Marini." The cop grabbed his arm with an iron grip and tugged him down the sidewalk. Breaking the tight grip with a twist of his wrist, Sam shook off the cop's grip.

"Go sit in that bar," Dwyer said, nodding at a brightly lit storefront. "You'll be out of the way and we'll know where to find you."

Right. And have everyone in there staring at him and taking pictures as this cop escorted him to a booth. Because Sam knew he would. Shifting the bag to his other hand, Sam said, "I'll wait outside."

The cop shrugged. "Suit yourself. You could be here for a while."

"Mind if I go back to work and dump this? It's just down the block." Sam wiggled the suit bag. The hanger was cutting into his palm. Keara would chew him a new one if he went into the clubhouse tomorrow with a bruise on his hand. "I'll come right back. You have my driver's license. I'm not going to leave that behind."

The cop narrowed his eyes at Sam. "Toss the suit into my squad car if you like, but you're not going anywhere."

Sam frowned at the cop as he tried to stare him down. The cop widened his stance and stared right back.

"Look, buddy, I'm the one who called 911." Sam tightened his fist on the suit hanger. "I've answered your questions. Told you where the guy who threw the punch went. I even took pictures of the scene. You have my driver's license. So why are you acting like this? It will take me five minutes, tops, to get there and back. What's the problem?" He gestured toward the guy on the ground, who still hadn't moved. "You just said detectives were coming, and that you'd be here a while."

The cop edged closer, as if he was trying to intimidate Sam. "Only an idiot would let a witness to a crime walk away. It's procedure, *buddy*. Witnesses can't leave until they've been questioned. Especially one who's got evidence in his pocket. Which, by the way, you haven't given me." Dwyer held out his hand.

Ignoring it, Sam said, "And you've questioned me." Sam stared down at the cop. The guy was bulky, but Sam was a head taller. He wasn't about to let this jerk bully him. "I've told you everything I know. I said I'd come back."

Dwyer grabbed his arm and jerked him backward, so hard that Sam stumbled. The cop shoved him up against a brick wall. "I said, you're not going anywhere."

Finally pissed off, Sam clenched his fist. "Take your hands off me." His voice was low. Quiet. Sam stared at the cop. The cop stared back. "Right. Now."

"Is this our suspect, Dwyer?" A woman's voice. Low-pitched. Kind of sexy. Sam didn't look away from the cop who still hadn't released him.

Finally, Dwyer let him go. Turned toward the woman's voice. "No. Just an asshole witness who wants to walk away."

Sam took a deep breath. Then another. Stepped away from the wall and straightened his shirt. Took one final breath, then turned in the woman's direction.

Almost dropped his suit bag. She was tall. Slender, with legs that went on for a mile. Dark red hair. He couldn't see her eyes in the darkness, but he knew they were hazel. And gorgeous.

She wore dark pants and a white button-down shirt with a dark jacket, but she looked as hot as she had seven months ago.

She'd worn a swirly blue dress at his sister's wedding, one that emphasized all her assets. They'd shared several dances at Cilla's wedding, enough flirting to get him wound up and ready to rumble, and one smokin' hot kiss in the leafy privacy of the Garfield Park Conservatory.

Then she'd said goodbye and walked away with swaying hips, leaving him with nothing but her first name and memories he still couldn't shake.

"Jules?"

CHAPTER 2

Julia looked away from Dwyer to the witness he'd been manhandling. Stilled. Struggled to hide the sudden catch in her breath.

No effing way.

"Sam?"

"You know this loser, Carleton?" Dwyer interrupted.

"I've got this," she said without taking her gaze off Sam. "Get back to the scene and finish setting up the perimeter, Dwyer. Please," she added after a heartbeat. Dwyer was the type that nursed grievances.

Dwyer didn't move. "You sure? He needs to be restrained."

"I said I've got it," Julia responded, more sharply than she'd intended. "I need you at the scene," she said, trying to tone it down. "Maxwell and his rookie need help with crowd control. I know I can count on you."

With a dark look at Sam, Dwyer stalked off toward the flashing lights of two squads, her car and the ambulance. Julia watched him go, giving herself a chance to settle. Regain control. Finally, when Dwyer was out of earshot and Julia was certain she wouldn't embarrass herself, she turned back to Sam.

Unfortunately, he looked just as good as he'd looked seven months ago at Brendan Donovan and Cilla Marini's wedding. At six feet tall, Julia liked being able to look up at a guy. Liked being able to tuck her head into his neck while they were dancing.

And she'd done a lot of tucking with Sam at that wedding.

What was the chance he'd turn up as a witness at one of her crime scenes?

"So. Sam. Mr. ...?"

He cleared his throat. "Marini."

"Marini?" Julia frowned, studying his face. She'd met him at Cilla's wedding. Now that she looked, she could see the resemblance. "You're Cilla's brother?"

He sighed. "That would be me. You didn't catch my big speech at the wedding?"

"Must have been in the rest room." She narrowed her eyes. "I remember Cilla talking about you. You're a big deal baseball player. Somewhere in Iowa."

He shrugged. "That was a couple of years ago."

"Now you're living in Chicago?"

"Yeah. Have been for the past year."

She glanced at his suit bag, then pulled a notebook out of her jacket pocket. "What were you doing at the corner of Clark and Addison when our victim got punched?"

"Walking home."

She raised her eyebrows. "From... ?"

"Work."

"At close to midnight?"

"Yes." His lips tightened. "I went over this with that asshat."

"Indulge me, please, Sam. Can you tell me what happened?"

He draped the suit bag over a railing surrounding the outside seating area of a restaurant, then flexed both hands a few times. "I was at the stoplight on the other side of Addison from Seventh Inning Stretch," he began. "Waiting

16

for the light to change."

He recited the facts, then pulled out his phone. Showed it to her. "The puncher took off in a cab. This is the number."

"Did Dwyer call it in?"

"Not while he was talking to me. And he was talking to me pretty much the whole time."

Swearing under her breath, Julia reached for her phone, then tapped in Dwyer's number. When he answered, she said, "Did you call in that cab number our witness gave you? Get the drop-off location?"

"I didn't have time, Carleton. The guy wasn't cooperative."

She resisted the impulse to tell Dwyer that Sam was cooperating just fine with her. Maybe because she wasn't being a dick to him. "Call it in now. You have the number?"

A pause. "Yeah," he finally said. "I have it."

"Great. Let me know when you have a location."

Without waiting for an answer, she slid the phone back into her pocket. "May I see the pictures you took?"

Sam touched the photo icon on his phone, then turned so she could see the display. She watched without speaking. When it was over, she punched the icon and played it again.

Finally she looked at Sam. "Why did you record that? You started before the guy in red actually threw a punch."

Sam shrugged. "It was… off from the beginning. All those guys from one team, one guy from another team. The red team was in the wrong bar. The little guy was half the size of the guy he was going after." He rolled his shoulders. "I just had a bad feeling."

"You had a bad feeling."

"Yeah." He tilted his head. "Don't you ever know, in your gut, that something bad is going to happen?"

"Yeah, but I'm a cop. You're a… what are you? What do you do, now that you're not playing baseball in Iowa?"

He stared at her for a long moment, as if puzzled. Then

he said slowly, "I'm still playing baseball."

"Here in Chicago?"

He smiled. For a second, he looked like the guy she remembered from the wedding. All mischief, fun and sexy promises. "You're not a baseball fan, are you?"

"No, I'm not. I prefer soccer. And basketball."

He studied her, the smile hovering at the corners of his mouth. "I should have figured you for a basketball player."

This was not the time for flirty exchanges of information. "So. You're playing baseball in Chicago. You were walking home from work near midnight, carrying a suit."

She tilted her head, finally getting it. "You play for *that* team?" She jerked her head toward the ball park, still lit up on the corner.

"I do."

"Most of my friends are Sox fans." It was impossible to resist needling him.

"You need a better class of friends," he said immediately.

Thank God Dwyer wasn't here. Or any other cop, for that matter. As a female detective, she had enough problems being taken seriously without acting unprofessionally with a witness. Time to dial it down. "I'm going to need a copy of that movie you filmed. Can you come to the station so I can make a copy and verify the chain of evidence?"

Sam scowled. "That jerk told me he needed to take my phone."

"Dwyer's a little… old school." The older cop hadn't bothered to learn how to transfer the video and keep the chain of evidence intact. "We generally only confiscate phones if we find them on a suspect and we think they contain evidence of a crime."

"I knew he thought I was involved somehow."

"Why did he have you up against the wall?"

"You're not going to ask him?"

"Of course I am. But I want both sides of the story."

Sam rubbed his hands together in what she was pretty sure was an unconscious gesture. "He told me it was going to be a while. That suit bag is heavy -- I have shoes in there, too. I wanted to take it back to the ball park, then come back to talk to the detective. Dwyer didn't like that."

"No cop would," Julia conceded. But she'd bet Dwyer hadn't explained why. When Dwyer told someone to jump, he wanted them to ask 'how high' on the way up.

"I think you can go home, Mr. Marini. Can you come into the station tomorrow morning with your phone?"

"It would have to be early. We have an afternoon game."

"What time is early?"

"How long will it take?"

"An hour, tops. And that's if I have other questions."

"How about eight?"

Julia suppressed a groan. She wouldn't get to bed until three at the earliest. But she didn't want to let this go past tomorrow morning. She needed that video to identify the suspect and the witnesses from his team.

"Eight would be great. I'll see you then."

Sam picked up the bag and began to walk, then stopped. Turned around. "Dwyer still has my driver's license."

"Why did... ? Never mind." She knew why Dwyer had kept the license -- it gave him power over the witness. Dwyer was a burned out, cynical bully. He should have retired two years ago, but hung on because he didn't have a life outside of the force. "I'll have it for you in the morning. Unless you want to retrieve it right now."

"No, thanks. The morning is fine." The distaste in his eyes told her he didn't want anything more to do with Dwyer.

As he gathered his suit bag, he nodded toward the flashing lights. "How's the kid doing?"

Sadness settled on Julia's shoulders, heavy and tight. The kid lying in the gutter looked so young. So vulnerable. "Not good. The paramedics think he has serious brain damage. He'll be on his way to the hospital as soon as he's stabilized."

Sam's mouth tightened. "I hope you catch the guy who punched him. That poor kid never touched the jerk who threw the punch."

"And thank goodness you took that video," Julia said. "We'll find him, and we should be able to convict him. With that video and your eyewitness testimony, it should be an easy case to prosecute." She clenched her teeth. "He'll probably take a plea deal, but he should spend some time in prison."

A flicker of something that might have been uneasiness flickered across Sam's face. "Yeah." He cleared his throat. "I'll see you in the morning."

"The twenty-third district station. On Halsted," she said.

He nodded as he turned away and began walking. The suit bag flopped against his back with each step. Sam moved fluidly, with long, confident strides. The same confidence that had drawn her attention at the wedding.

She'd had fun with him that night. He'd made her laugh. He was a good dancer. And one hell of a kisser.

Not that she'd be testing her memories any time soon. The kid who'd been punched was in really bad shape, according to the paramedics. He might die. If he did, it was a murder investigation, and Sam Marini was her star witness.

No, there would be no kisses in fragrant, dimly-lit greenhouses with Sam Marini.

There would be no kisses anywhere. She had a job to do, and right now, Sam was a crucial part of that job.

Regret surged through her, making her ache. It was far too strong, she realized uneasily.

The fact that she had thought about him way too many times in the past seven months was irrelevant.

* * *

As Julia trudged up the stairs at the station the next morning, she heard footsteps hurrying to catch up with her. Hoping it was Sam, she turned with a tiny smile. "Hey…" She swallowed. Not Sam. "Hey, Jennings. How's it going? How's Gaby?"

Detective Alex Jennings grinned at her. "Gaby's great."

Julia smiled. He and Gaby had just gotten married, and Gaby was pregnant. "Are the girls excited about the baby?"

Alex shook his head. "Cece is over the moon. Bella is all sneering teen attitude. But I've caught her looking at baby stuff online with Gaby. So it's all good."

As they walked into the bullpen, he asked, "You going to my mom's benefit for Theresa this weekend?"

"Yeah. I'll be there."

He shook his head. "My sister would appreciate it, I know. But you're there every year. You don't have to do that, Carleton."

"I want to go. It's a good cause," Julia said quietly. "Helping people who can't afford it get into drug rehab is life-changing. That's why I go."

"Thanks, Carleton. I know my folks appreciate it."

"My pleasure."

She watched Jennings walk to his desk as she dropped her bag into a drawer in her own desk. Jennings didn't know that his parents were the only friends of her family who had stood by them during the time after her father's arrest. For that, she'd be eternally grateful.

She paid back their support by going to the Jennings' benefit every year.

Julia had barely dropped into her desk chair when the sergeant at the front desk rang. "Got a guy down here to see you, Carleton," Jacobs said in his raspy, too-many-cigarettes voice.

Her heart leaped in a completely inappropriate way. "Marini?" she managed to say in an even voice. "Send him up."

Julia hung up the phone and smoothed the front of her

pearly gray shirt. Made sure the pleat on her black Jones New York pants was even. She hadn't worn her favorite shirt and suit because Sam had been coming in. No way. It had just been the first shirt she'd grabbed from her closet that morning.

She rolled her eyes at herself. Of course she'd reached for her favorites. She was human, wasn't she? Who didn't want to look good for a charming, attractive guy?

Not her job to look good, she reminded herself.

Hearing footsteps running lightly up the long flight of stairs, she stood to greet him. No one ran up that steep staircase. Sam must be in really good shape.

Last night, even in the dark, she'd noticed the way his jeans clung to his narrow hips and how his wide shoulders filled out his dress shirt. Sadly, though, that would be the extent of her knowledge.

She wouldn't be exploring the long, lean body hidden beneath his clothes. Too bad, but Sam Marini was off-limits.

He appeared at the top of the stairs, and her mouth went dry. He wore a dark suit, and it fit his tall, lean frame like it had been custom made for him.

Which it probably had been -- Julia's practiced eyes knew a custom-made suit when she saw one. No off-the-rack suit made a man look that good.

His shoulders were impossibly wide. His thighs flexed in the pants that broke perfectly over his shiny leather shoes. And the light blue shirt he wore made his blue eyes as bright as the Caribbean.

"Good morning, Sam," she said as he approached her desk holding two cups of coffee.

"Hey, Jul…" He glanced around the bullpen and apparently saw the other detectives watching them. "Detective Carleton," he corrected smoothly, handing her one of the cups. "Thought you might need this as much as I do."

"Thanks." She took a sip and raised her eyebrows.

"How did you know I liked tea?"

He shrugged one shoulder. "Remembered from the wedding," he said in a low voice. "Before you left, I had a coffee and you had tea."

"I'm impressed," she said, and meant it. "That's a small detail to remember from a long time ago."

He gave her the crooked smile that had sent shivers rippling over her skin at the wedding. The smile that appeared too often in her dreams. "Small details are crucial in my line of work."

"That's good. I need to get a detailed statement from you, and then we'll download the video."

"How's the kid?" Sam asked.

She shook her head. "His family is with him."

Sam stared at his hands. "I wish I could have stopped it."

"That wasn't ever going to happen." She leaned forward and put her hand over his. His fingers were warm beneath hers. Hard. As if even his finger muscles were toned. "I could see from the video there was no way you could have gotten across the street. Too many cars going past. Too many people around you. Nothing you could have done."

She took her hand away and leaned back in her chair. "You did the next best thing. You got a video recording of everything that happened."

"Did you find the guy who threw the punch?"

"We got an address where he was dropped off. No one was there last night, though."

Sam frowned. "You think he gave the cabbie a fake address?"

"Possible. But, again thanks to you, we have the name of his sports team. We can get a roster with all their names and addresses and pull up their driver's licenses. We should be able to figure out who he is. Who the guys with him were, too."

She opened a drawer and pulled out Sam's driver's license. Slid it across the desk to him. "Here's your license."

When she'd asked Dwyer for it, he'd asked for Sam's phone. Gave her grief because she hadn't confiscated it.

The old-school cop had claimed it could be altered if it wasn't in police custody. Julia had gritted her teeth, but told Dwyer calmly that she'd seen the whole video, more than once, and would know if it had been altered. Thank God he was on nights -- she wouldn't have to deal with him again about this case.

"Okay," she said, pushing Dwyer out of her mind. "Let's get a copy of that video, then you can get to work."

Twenty minutes later, Sam stood up and shook her hand. "Good luck with this case, Julia. I hope you nail that bastard."

"If we do, you'll have played a big role in it," she said.

Without letting go of her hand, he leaned closer. For a moment, she feared… hoped? Sam was going to kiss her, right here in the bullpen. Instead, he murmured into her ear, "You free for a drink, or dinner, this evening?"

As his breath warmed her skin, Julia swallowed. Barely managed to conceal her shiver. Cleared her throat. "Sorry, I'll be working on this case."

"How about tomorrow?"

Heat washed over her face, and she tugged her hand away from his. Sam Marini was too damn tempting. She could still taste the kisses they'd shared seven months ago. "Thanks for the invitation, Sam, but I can't go out with you. You're a witness in my case. I'll be in touch if I need you for anything else."

He straightened and studied her for a long moment, his eyes focused on her with an intensity that made her want to squirm. Finally he gave her that smile again. The one that made her knees weak.

"I'll be here for another four days," he said, his voice deep and *so* tempting. "Then I'm out of town for a week." His smile became more intimate. More personal, and arousal stirred deep inside her. She knew her eyes were dilating. Her chest rising and falling faster.

Sam must have noticed, because he stepped closer. Close enough for her to feel his body heat. To smell the clean, outdoorsy scent of his soap. "Call anytime." His voice was a low rasp of heat and sex. "I'll always answer my phone for you, Julia."

His words sent that stupid shiver down her spine again. "Thanks," she managed to say. "I appreciate that."

He tapped the pocket of his suit jacket. "Day or night," he murmured. The way his eyes had darkened, she was pretty sure he wasn't talking about any damn phone call.

He held out his hand, and she took it. "Take care, Jules," he said. He held her hand for a long moment, rubbed his thumb over the back of her hand, then let her go.

He hurried down the stairs, turning just before he disappeared to give her one more of his crooked smiles.

After Sam disappeared from view, Julia dropped into her desk chair. Sam Marini just didn't give up. She sighed. Of course he didn't -- he wouldn't have gotten to where he was in his professional life if he let obstacles slow him down.

And in his personal life, he had quite the arsenal -- that long, lanky body, those expressive eyes, his surprisingly gentle hands.

And that damn smile. The one that made her clench her thighs together every time she saw it. The worst part was, she suspected Sam knew exactly the effect that smile had on her.

CHAPTER 3

"**I**'m sorry I can't help you, Detective. Our policies are in place to protect our members' privacy," said Celine, the pompous administrative assistant at Chicago Sports and Social League.

It was late in the afternoon, and Julia had already been at her desk for almost eight hours. She wasn't in the mood for Celine's bull. "Fine. I'll be visiting with a subpoena," she said, then carefully hung up the phone, proud of herself for not slamming it into its cradle.

She shoved her fingers through her hair in frustration, grimacing when she tugged some strands out of her braid. Tucking the hair behind her ear, she reached for her cell phone and scrolled through her contacts until she found a judge who'd given her a subpoena on a similar case. Five minutes later, she said, "Thanks, Judge Tompson. Please fax it to the twenty-third district station," and ended the call.

Instead of hovering over the fax machine, waiting for it to spit out her subpoena, she walked to the break room with her mug and fixed herself a cup of tea. Clinked her mug against the expensive, complicated and now battered espresso machine sitting on the counter as she took her first sip of tea.

"If there's any justice, Arnie, somewhere on the North Shore your Aunt Minerva is still griping about this damn coffee maker," she murmured. She greeted each new dent and ding on the no-longer-shiny surface with nasty satisfaction. "I bet your dear Auntie would have a fit if she saw it now."

Three years ago, when her fiancé had found out who her father was, he'd dumped her one week before their wedding. Julia had sent back all the gifts except this espresso machine, which had been from Arnie's Aunt Minerva. She'd meant it as a slight, Julia knew, because there was no espresso machine on their gift registry. And Minvera knew Julia didn't drink coffee.

From the moment Arnie had introduced her Aunt Minerva, the snooty old bat had been vocal about her dislike of the upstart Julia Carleton, a nobody who didn't belong with her nephew or in the north shore suburb of Oakvale. Julia had known that if Minerva had an inkling of who Julia really was, she'd be even more appalled. Her family tragedy had unfolded in full view of everyone in Oakvale.

After the scandal died down, Julia had changed her last name and disappeared. Seven years later, returning to Oakvale with Arnie, no one had recognized her. But Minerva was sure Julia wasn't good enough for her nephew.

So instead of returning the espresso machine, as good manners dictated, Julia had hauled it into the station, to the delight of every cop in the district. She'd sent a curt note to Arnie, telling him that since the coffee maker had already been used, he needed to reimburse his aunt for the gift.

Sipping the tea, she filled out some paperwork from her previous case while she waited for her subpoena. When the fax machine whirred to life, she gulped the last of the tea and shoved her mug into a drawer. She reached the machine just before the finished document fluttered onto the floor.

She scanned it to make sure it contained everything she

27

needed, grabbed her wallet and phone and ran down the stairs. The clock in the lobby said three-forty-five, and she gritted her teeth. That damn sports club had jerked her around for most of the day. She wasn't going to let this extend into another day.

As she drove past the ball park, a huge roar rose from inside it. Sam had said they had a day game, she remembered. Someone on the Bearcats must have done something good.

Had it been Sam?

As she slowed for a stoplight, her fingers itched to pull out her phone and find out. Instead, she kept her hands firmly on the steering wheel. She didn't care what Sam had or hadn't done in the ball game. His only importance to her was as a witness in this case.

She rolled her eyes. She was lying to herself now? Really?

She might not be able to date Sam while this case was active, but regulations couldn't stop her from thinking about him. And she'd thought about him a lot since she'd seen him this morning.

Maybe after she wrapped up this case, she could take Sam up on his offer of dinner.

Not that she was looking for anything serious. But she'd had fun with Sam at his sister Cilla's wedding. She wouldn't mind seeing him again.

With any luck, she'd have the name of the guy who'd thrown that punch in the next hour or two. They'd pick him up, book him, interrogate him, then hand the case over to the state's attorney. She doubted if the aggressive, violent guy she'd watched on the video would confess, but that recording was solid evidence. Twenty-four carat gold. A good prosecutor, like Sam and Cilla's sister Livvy, should be able to get a conviction.

Last night's victim, Nick D'Angelo, was in grave condition and on life support. Julia had spoken to his doctor, and the woman didn't expect him to recover. But at least his attacker would pay for what he'd done. And if Nick D'Angelo died, the charges would change from assault and battery to murder.

Pulling into the parking area of the Chicago Sports and Social League, Julia got out of the car and hurried toward the building. Remembering Nick D'Angelo, collapsed into the gutter on Clark Street, she yanked open the door and walked in.

Ten minutes later, holding the rosters of both the Sports Circuit and Seventh Inning Stretch teams, she slid into her car.

An hour later, she had photos of each player on both teams and had circled everyone in Sam's video. The perp was Derek Kirby. His address was a building in the Loop. Nowhere near the address he'd given the cab driver the night before.

"I guess you're not as smart as you think you are, Kirby," she murmured with satisfaction as she pushed away from her desk. Scanning the room, she saw Mia Donovan sitting on her brother Quinn's desk, laughing at something Q was saying.

"Hey, Mia," Julia called. "You want to give me a hand arresting a suspect?"

"Absolutely." Mia slid off the desk and hurried toward Julia. "Which case are you talking about?"

"That kid who got punched last night near Clark and Addison. I found the guy who hit him." Julia's fingers brushed the handcuffs hanging from the back of her belt. It would give her great pleasure to snap them onto Kirby's wrists.

"Good." Mia scowled. "I saw the video, and I'm gonna love helping you put the cuffs on that asshole. What's the guy's name?"

"Derek Kirby." Julia smiled as the syllables rolled off her tongue. Kirby had done his best to disappear, but thanks to Sam's quick thinking, they had him.

"Let's go get him, then."

* * *

Kirby lived in a fancy high rise overlooking Millennium Park. The place had been designed by a famous architect, Julia remembered. Won some prizes for her, too. As she and Mia walked toward the door, Julia studied the beautiful, graceful lines of the building and glanced at Mia Donovan, who was doing the same thing.

"Pricey address," Mia finally said.

"Yeah." Julia started for the door. "Let's go arrest Richey Rich."

Two minutes later, the doorman said, "Sorry, ladies. Mr. Kirby isn't available."

Julia held up her badge. "I don't really care if he's available or not. I want his apartment number."

The doorman cleared his throat. "He's not there."

"Where would he be, then?" Julia asked.

"At work, most likely."

"And that would be at... ?"

The doorman glanced at the other guy at the desk, as if hoping for some help. The other guy held his gaze for a moment, then shrugged. The first doorman said, "We're, uh, not allowed to give out that information."

"For anyone? Or just for Kirby?"

"For anyone." Another glance at the other guy. "Our residents value their privacy."

A lot of privacy-valuing going on today.

Julia leaned in. She loved being tall. There was nothing like a badge and a little height to make people nervous. And in her business, nervous was good. "You understand we're police officers, right, Mr. ..." She glanced at his name tag. "Peters. The rules about talking to people who are inquiring about one of your residents don't apply to the police. Where does Mr. Kirby work?"

Peters glanced at the other doorman again. Julia pressed her palms on the marble counter and edged closer. "I'm waiting, Mr. Peters."

Peters twisted his hands together. Swallowed hard. Glanced at Mia, as if she might rescue him.

"Mr. Peters?" Julia said sharply. "Where. Does. Kirby. Work?"

"His father…" Peters cleared his throat. "He pays us extra not to give out any information about Derek."

Julia curled her fingers around the edge of the counter to keep from reaching for the guy. "And that would be because… ?"

"Derek's a, ah, good-looking guy. With money." Peters swallowed and shot a desperate, 'rescue me' look at his partner, who was carefully studying the guest register and didn't meet Peters' gaze. "His dad said he sometimes has trouble with women following him home."

"Poor guy." Julia stared down at Peters, pleased when he eased his chair farther away. "You think we're a couple of spurned girlfriends?" She waited, and Peters' adam's apple bobbed up and down. "We're police officers. I don't care how much Mr. Kirby pays you. You can either tell us where his son works, or we can take you to the station so you can explain in more detail why you can't give us that information."

Peters took a deep breath. Glanced at the other guy, who was still fascinated by the guest register.

Mia strolled over to the other guy. "How about you? Or do you want to visit our station, too? I have to tell you, though -- it won't be fun. Uncomfortable chairs. We keep the thermostat turned down. Makes it chilly in those interrogation rooms. We do have really good coffee, though. If you like coffee, it might be worth the trip."

"Detective Donovan, you know the good coffee is for cooperative witnesses," Julia said without looking away from Peters. "I don't think these guys would qualify."

The second guy jerked his chin toward a video monitor that displayed the outside of the building. "Mr. Kirby is on his way inside. You can ask him yourself."

"Thank you," Julia said, clipping her badge back on her belt. She turned toward the door, waiting for Kirby.

He strolled in and walked toward the desk. Julia had seen the guy on Sam's video, but in person he looked even bigger than he had on the screen. Freakishly big. His arm muscles bulged in his dress shirt, and his dress pants pulled taut over his thighs. His neck was thick, and his chest broad. This was a guy who did some serious working out.

A guy whose punch could severely injure a person. Or kill him.

She and Mia watched him stop too close to them. Kirby nodded at the doormen, then let his gaze drift over her and Mia. Linger a few moments too long.

"Ladies. What brings you to my building?"

Cocky son of a bitch, leering at two police officers. "You do, Mr. Kirby," Julia said. She held up her badge. "I'm Detective Carleton and this is Detective Donovan. You're under arrest for assault and battery."

Kirby frowned. "What the hell are you talking about? I didn't assault anyone."

"You punched Nicholas D'Angelo last night at the corner of Clark and Addison, inflicting severe bodily harm. You have the right to remain silent…"

She finished the Miranda statement, then stepped behind him and tried to fasten her handcuffs on his wrists. Kirby slapped her hand aside and stepped away. As Mia moved into place on his other side, Julia narrowed her eyes at him. "That's assault and battery of a police officer. That'll add a few years to your sentence. Don't do it again, unless you think you'll like spending time in prison."

Kirby clenched his fists as Mia grabbed his right hand. Julia grabbed his left. He lifted his arms and tried to shake both of them off.

Julia nodded to Mia, who let him go and stepped out of the way. As Kirby stared at Julia, clenching and unclenching his fists, Julia stepped forward and used her right leg to sweep his feet out from under him.

Kirby landed hard on his ass and slid a couple of feet across the polished granite floor. As he was struggling to stand, Julia and Mia closed in behind him and got the cuffs around his wrists.

As they hauled him to his feet, he began to struggle. "Let me go, you bitches. You knocked me down. I'm going to sue you. That was excessive force."

Mia tapped the body cam on her jacket. "You're welcome to try, Kirby, but we've got everything on tape."

"Videos don't lie, Mr. Kirby," Julia said. *And the video of this asshole punching Nick D'Angelo wouldn't lie, either.*

"Let's go, Kirby," Julia said. She grabbed his wrist and tried to steer him toward the door. He didn't budge.

"I want my lawyer," he snarled.

"You can call your lawyer after we get you booked, printed and photographed." She tightened her grip on his wrist, and he tried to shake her off.

"I don't have to go with you."

"You're under arrest, Kirby. So yes, you have to go with me. Now move it."

When he didn't move, Julia narrowed her eyes. "Is that how it's gonna be? You're going to force me to use my Taser? I'm warning you, I'm going to be in a really bad mood if I have to drag you to my car and lift you in."

"You can't Tase me," he scoffed. "Do you have any idea who I am?"

"You're Derek Kirby, and you're wanted in connection with an assault and battery. You've battered a police officer and now you're resisting arrest. There are four witnesses here. So what's it going to be, Kirby? You coming peacefully?" Julia pulled a Taser off her belt and held it up. "Or do I need to knock you down?" She couldn't resist adding, "Again."

He stared at her, rage flashing in his eyes. She saw him consider running. Consider violence. But he wouldn't get far with his hands cuffed behind his back. The knowledge seemed to enrage him even more.

"Fine," he finally said, and anger shook his voice. "But you'll be sorry about this."

"I doubt it." She put her Taser away and curled her hand around one of his wrists. Mia took the other. Even his wrists were huge. Hard. Julia wondered if Kirby used steroids. That could account for his quick burst of anger, both last night and today. She made a mental note to get a subpoena for a blood test.

She and Mia had to use all their strength to maneuver Kirby down the sidewalk to the car. He didn't resist, but he wouldn't walk, either. By the time they eased him into the back of her car, Julia was sweating and her arms ached.

She slammed the door too hard once Kirby was inside, then exchanged a glance with Mia, who shook her head. "What a piece of work."

"Yeah. Pretty low flash point. I'm checking him for illegal drugs." Julia reached for her door. "Let's get him back to the station before he turns into the Hulk."

"Too late," Mia said, shaking her head. "He already looks pretty Hulk-like. Acts like it, too." She glanced into the backseat, then headed around to the other side of the car. "And seriously? What woman would find that attractive?"

"Takes all kinds, Donovan."

"I guess so," Mia said. "Me, I like a little more subtlety."

Julia grinned as she slid into the car. "You and me both. And you definitely have subtle." Mia's fiancé, Finn O'Rourke, was a movie star, but you'd never know it to talk to him.

Sam Marini was exactly *her* kind of subtle. Long, rangy, athletic. Sexy as hell.

Maybe she could get this case wrapped up tonight. The video had a few places where it wasn't quite steady. One or two spots where Sam had panned the crowd instead of focusing on Kirby and Nick. But it clearly showed Kirby throwing a punch. Nick's head snapping back. Nick falling. Lying motionless in the gutter. It wasn't professional grade videography, but Sam had done a good job of filming what had happened.

Even though there were a couple moments in the overall video that weren't as clear as she'd like, the overall picture was clearly drawn. As far as she could tell, there were no loopholes for Kirby to slither through. Kirby would be an idiot to try.

* * *

Apparently Derek Kirby wasn't an ordinary idiot. He was the complete package, with an outsized ego, off-the-charts arrogance and a sense of entitlement that barely fit into the building. Julia watched through the two-way mirror as he was processed.

"What am I supposed to do about this ink on my fingers?" he asked after being printed.

"There's a container of wipes on the counter. They'll clean it off," said a bored evidence tech named Dave.

Kirby ripped open two packages of the wipes, cleaned his fingers, then dropped them on the floor. "What's next?"

"Next is you pick up the wipes and put them in the trash can. Right next to you," Dave said.

Kirby scowled and didn't move. Neither did the tech, who towered over him by several inches.

Finally, Kirby picked up the wipes and put them in the trash.

"Thank you, Mr. Kirby," the tech said. "Now stand against the wall here so I can take your photo." He held out a card with Kirby's booking number. Kirby stared at him, making no effort to take it.

The tech shrugged. "I'm here until eleven tonight. Take your time." He set the card on the table and dropped into the only chair in the room, pulled out his phone and began to study it.

"I want to call my attorney," Kirby said.

Dave didn't look up from his phone.

"I can't believe this guy," said Mia, who'd joined Julia at the observation window.

"I specifically asked for Dave, because I've never seen anyone intimidate him," Julia said, allowing herself a tiny smile. "The way this is going, by the time Kirby gets over himself, his lawyer will be out of the office for the day."

"If he has enough money to live in that condo, his lawyer will show up no matter what time it is," Mia said.

Julia shook her head. "Go ahead. Spoil my dream of seeing this guy spend the night in a cell."

Another minute passed, with Dave apparently surfing on his phone and Derek Kirby glowering at him across the room. Finally, Kirby picked up the board with the numbers on it and stood in the middle of the room.

Dave didn't look up from his phone.

"Take the picture, asshole," Kirby growled.

"Soon as you stand where I told you to stand," Dave said, flicking his finger across his screen without glancing at Kirby.

Scowling, Kirby positioned himself against the wall with the inches marked off. Dave set his phone down and stood behind the camera. He took several pictures, telling Kirby to turn to the right, then the left.

Dave took the sign from Kirby and slid the handcuffs back in place before Kirby realized what he was doing.

"Hey," Kirby shouted. "What're these for?"

"I'm taking you to an interrogation room."

"I can walk without being cuffed," Kirby said.

"No, you can't." He tilted his head as he studied Kirby. "You need to get with the program, man. In here, we tell you what to do, and you do it. Sooner you learn that, the better it'll go for you."

"I'm not going to be here much longer." He stared at Dave's name badge, as if noticing it for the first time. "As soon as my lawyer shows up, I'm out of here."

"You watch too much TV," Dave said, opening the door and holding onto Kirby's arm. "'Cause that's not how it works."

He opened the door to an interrogation room, attached the handcuffs to a bolt on the table, then glanced at Kirby. "I'll send Detective Carleton in."

"Is that the bitch who arrested me?"

Shaking his head, Dave said, "You poor fool," as he closed the door.

CHAPTER 4

Sam loosened his tie as he headed toward the twenty-third district station. It was warm for May, and even at six-thirty in the evening, the sun beat down relentlessly on his dark suit.

He probably should have gone home before stopping at the station to see Julia. But home was in the opposite direction, and he'd wanted to find out how the kid was doing. He'd called the hospital, but they wouldn't tell him anything. Especially since he didn't even know the guy's name. He'd scanned the paper that morning, but only saw a small blurb about a fight near the ball park. The blurb hadn't included any names.

Had Julia found the jerk who punched that poor kid? Had he confessed yet?

He hoped so. Hoped that she'd found some justice for the kid and his family.

Sam refused to acknowledge his ulterior motive -- he'd been thinking about Julia all day. All last night, too, if he was truthful. If she'd closed the case, maybe she'd go to dinner with him.

He tightened his tie again, straightened his shoulders and walked into the police station. It smelled of stale coffee, alcohol and strong perfume. He glanced around the small lobby and spotted two people on a bench.

The man sat slumped against the wall, unkempt hair tangled around his shoulders and a dazed look on his face, as if he was still coming down from last night's high. Definitely the source of the stale alcohol stench.

A middle-aged woman sat next to him, shooting him exasperated looks every few seconds. She leaned over and murmured something to him, but he ignored her. The woman wore a stylish red suit, carefully applied makeup and an expensive haircut. And the perfume. Maybe she'd had previous experience with his stale alcohol smell.

"Can I help you?" the uniformed officer at the desk asked.

"I'd like to see Detective Carleton," Sam said. "About a case."

That was at least partially true.

The desk officer eyed him for a moment, then frowned. "Aren't you Sam Marini?"

"Yes." Sam braced himself. Was the guy a 'Cat's fan or Sox fan? "That's me."

The officer leaned over the desk and extended his hand. "Listened to the radio broadcast this afternoon. Nice game." He smiled. "Especially that walk-off double."

"Thanks," Sam said, shaking the cop's hand, relieved that he wasn't on the receiving end of a Sox fan's jeers. He was too wound today up to deal with that shit. "Everyone played well today."

The cop nodded. "Great bunch of players this year. Look forward to seeing you in the postseason."

"We have to get there first," Sam said, reciting a line he used at least once a day. "Wish us luck."

"You got it." The cop waved his hand toward the stairs. "You know where *our* bullpen is?"

Sam grinned. "Sure do. Hope no one's warming up in there."

The cop answered with a rumbling laugh. "This time of

day? Should be safe."

"Thanks," Sam said with a wave.

He took the stairs two at a time, only slowing when he reached the open space and its maze of desks and saw that Julia's was empty. As he stood looking around, wondering where she could be, someone called, "Marini. What are you doing here?"

Sam turned and spotted one of the Donovan twins. Connor. "Hey, Donovan," he said easily. "How's it going?"

The detective leaned back in his chair and grinned. "You're not sure which one I am, are you?"

"Of course I am." Sam scoffed. "You're Connor," he said, hoping he was right.

Connor gave him a thumbs up. "You're smarter than you look, 'Cat dog."

He'd forgotten the Donovans were from the south side. Sox fans. Ignoring the taunt, he asked, "How's Raine doing?"

"She's great," he said, straightening the chair. "What are you doing here?"

"I'm looking for Julia Carleton."

Connor raised one eyebrow. "Really? You found her all by yourself?"

Smiling, Sam lowered himself to a corner of Connor's desk. "Yeah, I'm smarter than I look." His smile dropped away. "I witnessed a fight last night. Julia was the detective who showed up."

"I heard about that case. Saw the video."

Sam must have given something away, because Connor said, "You took that video?" The detective leaned forward and punched him in the arm. "Way to go, man. That was a great piece of evidence."

"I wanted to check on how the victim was doing." He scanned the area again. "But it looks like Julia isn't here."

"She's here, but she's questioning someone right now. I saw her heading toward interrogation. Stick around if you like." He gestured toward Julia's desk. "That's her desk.

Her guest chair isn't totally uncomfortable."

"Thanks, Connor. Good to see you."

"Yeah, you, too."

Sam fidgeted in the chair, which *was* totally uncomfortable, as he checked his email and the news sites. Nothing much new, except St. Louis had lost their game today.

Any day that team lost was a good day. Sam knew St. Louis would be panting down their necks all season. The 'Cats were winning now, but stuff happened every season. Players got injured. Pitchers went into slumps. Every game St. Louis lost was a gain for the 'Cats.

Finally, after he'd been surfing the web for almost forty-five minutes, he heard the sound of crisp footsteps heading his way. Julia.

He looked up, a small part of his brain wondering how he'd realized it was her. Stood. "Hey, Jules," he said, noticing her clenched jaw and the strands of hair tucked behind her ears. Hair that had clearly escaped her braid at some point since he'd seen her that morning. "Tough day?"

"Don't call me Jules in here," she said in a low voice as she dropped into her desk chair. "Julia is okay. Carleton is even better."

"Carleton it is." He smiled. "I like the tough chick vibe."

Julia relaxed into her chair and gave him a faint, brief smile. "Men," she said, shaking her head. "What can I do for you, Sam?"

"How's the kid doing?"

Her smile vanished. "Not well. Still on life support. They've done some tests and it sounds as though he has massive brain damage and no chance of recovering. They're doing a few more tests, but the doctor told me they're expecting the worst."

Sam shuddered. Last night, the kid had been alive. He'd played a softball game, then gone to a bar to unwind and have some fun. Then he'd taunted the wrong guy, and now he was brain dead.

Julia's fingers danced over his. It was a quick, barely-there brush over his knuckles, but the sharp pinch in his heart made him want to grab her hand and hold on.

He raised his head to see his sorrow reflected in her eyes.

"That's awful," he managed to say. "I hope you found the guy."

Julia puffed out a breath. "Oh, we found him. He's sitting in holding right now, waiting for a ride to bond court. He'll probably be back on the street before midnight."

"*What?*" Sam scowled. "You can't keep him in jail?"

"He's entitled to ask for a bond hearing," she said, her jaw working. "As much as I'd like to keep him locked up."

"Did you show him the video?"

"Of course I did," Julia said, scowling right back at him. "Him and his lawyer both. The lawyer claims Kirby never hit the kid. Says D'Angelo was drunk and he stumbled and fell all by himself."

"And you bought that?" Sam reared back, unable to believe Julia would fall for that load of crap.

"Of course not." A muscle clenched in Julia's jaw, as if she was holding on to her temper by the tiniest of threads. "Anyone looking at the video can see Kirby's fist hit the kid's face. But it's not crystal clear. And that's all Kirby's high-priced, slimy attorney needed. He asked for bond court, and I'm heading over there soon." She shoved her fingers through her hair, showing Sam exactly how those strands of hair had ended up behind her ears.

"Will he get bond?"

"Probably." She sighed. "Most likely. He's got a lot of money and a slick attorney. No priors, which I suspect is because he's paid people off. He's got a nasty temper with a quick trigger, so I'm betting this has happened before. I'm going to search through old arrest reports to see if I can find something, in case this goes to trial -- a pattern of behavior."

She picked up a stack of papers on her desk and carefully aligned the pages. "I did manage to get a subpoena for blood work to see if he was using any illegal drugs. But that's minor compared to murder."

"Bond court. Tell me about it." He'd love to see Julia slice and dice this guy in front of a judge. Sam mentally readjusted his plans for the evening. "May I come with you?"

"Absolutely not," she said, shaking her head so hard that her dark red braid flew over her shoulder. "I want to keep you under wraps as long as I can. And I'm pretty sure *you* wouldn't want to be identified as the person who took that video. Even if you weren't a public figure, the media would be all over you. And you're the hot young baseball player on the north side's favorite team. Do you have any idea what that would be like?"

"You think I'm hot, huh?" He leaned a little closer. "For the record, you're pretty hot yourself."

Instead of fluttering, Julia slowly shook her head. "Really, Marini? That's what you took from my warning?"

Then one side of her mouth curled up. "And I was quoting some of the sports writers. You're the hot guy on the team." She tilted her head, and he saw the mischief in her eyes. "Sports-wise, I think they meant."

"So you read about me in the sports pages?" Before the words finished leaving his mouth, he realized he was an ass. Being the obnoxious star he'd sworn he'd never become.

Julia didn't seem to mind, if he was judging her tiny smile correctly. "If I've read everything else in the paper and want to waste some time, I might glance at a story about the 'Cats."

Playing along, Sam clutched at his heart as if she'd wounded him. "Mean, Carleton. Really mean." He liked kidding around with Julia Carleton.

"You got that right, Sam -- I'm mean as a snake." She picked up the papers she'd evened and shoved them into a drawer. "You don't want to go to bond court. Unless you *want* reporters camped out at your house and waiting outside the ballpark every day."

She leaned a little closer, and her scent of orange blossoms drifted over him. Orange blossoms? Or lemon? He wasn't sure. He needed to spend time soaking up her scent. Drinking it in. Analyzing it.

"Is that what you want?" Julia asked impatiently.

"Want what?" Of course he wanted to spend time with her.

She edged away, as if she could see his intentions in his eyes. "Sam. Focus. Do you want every reporter in Chicago chasing you for the story? Every person you see on the street asking you about that video?"

"No." The idea made him squirm. "Of course not."

"Then you need to get going, because I have to be in court."

"What time do you need to be there?"

"I'm not sure yet. Kirby is still in holding here. He has to be transferred to the court building on south California, then they'll put him on the schedule. A couple of hours, probably."

"Then come have dinner with me first. You can fill me in on what you did today, and how the kid is doing."

"I can do that here," Julia said.

"How many hours have you been here already today?"

"A long time," Julia finally said with a sigh. "But I'm not going on a date with you, Marini."

"This isn't a date. And I won't take you anywhere people will see us and assume it's a date."

"And where would that be? You know that, unless you pick a really bad one, there are other people in restaurants."

"We'll get takeout and eat at my place." Neither of them would have to worry about being spotted. And it would be a lot more private.

She narrowed her eyes at him. "I am *not* going to your place. Not for dinner or anything else."

"Nothing but dinner," he promised, holding up the three-fingered scout salute. "Scout's honor."

"You were never a boy scout," she scoffed.

"I might have been."

"Were you?"

"No. I almost was, though. In first grade, I had narrowed my activity choices to cub scouts and T-ball."

"Let me guess," she said, her voice dry. "You picked T-ball. And Chicago fans will be forever grateful."

"I think you're mocking me."

"That's because you're a smart guy."

"Come on, Julia," he said, lowering his voice. "You have to eat."

He could see it in her expression -- she was getting ready to say she wasn't hungry. Then her stomach rumbled.

Sam raised one eyebrow but didn't say a word.

"Fine," she finally said. "There's a place not too far from here we can go. I'll call ahead and see if we can get the back booth. Everyone will see you walk through the place, but once we're there, you'll be pretty hidden. And maybe there won't be many baseball fans at Oscar's. Or they won't be paying attention."

"Yeah, I know Oscar's. Love that place." He narrowed his eyes at her. "And I know all about that back booth, tucked away in a corner where people can't see you. You sit back there a lot?"

"My favorite spot in the restaurant. I like privacy." She took out her phone and pulled up her contacts list.

Sam scowled. Oscar's was on her contact list? And the back booth was her favorite seat?

He knew why *he* liked that back booth when he was with a woman. The dim light and secluded location made it perfect for a stolen kiss or some subtle fooling around.

She ended the call quickly. "We need to be there in ten minutes. Let's go."

Julia stood up and glanced around the bullpen. "Hey, Con," she called, and Connor Donovan looked up. "I'm going to get something to eat. Can you keep track of Kirby in holding? I need to know when he's transferred to bond court. Give me a call or text, please?"

"Sure thing, Carleton. Nice collar, by the way. You found that guy fast."

"Thanks, but I had lots of help." She waved in Connor's direction and headed toward the back stairs. Sam followed.

"So," he said after they'd slid into her car. He drummed his fingers on the laptop, sitting on a platform between the front seats. "Oscar's. In your contact list. You go there a lot?"

Julia backed the car out of its parking spot, then turned onto the street. "I like Oscar's." She gave him a half-smile, as if she was recalling good memories.

He cleared his throat. "And you usually sit in that back booth?"

"Yes. It's nice and private. Why?"

Private. Sam swallowed hard. "That's my favorite booth, too."

"Glad you approve of my choice." Her unmarked car was big. Heavy. But she drove it like she was comfortable behind the wheel. Confident.

He liked confident women.

He liked Julia Carleton, too. Too bad he didn't have time in his life for anything more than casual dates. A few casual dates with Julia, though? Oh, yeah. He still remembered the kiss they'd shared at his sister's wedding.

Still thinking about that back booth at Oscar's, and what she might have done there, he blurted, "Are you seeing anyone?"

She slanted him a glance out of the corner of her eye. "That was an odd segue."

"We're going out to dinner," he muttered, feeling like a fool. "I don't want to step on any toes."

The silence in the car quivered with unspoken thoughts. Tension tightened like a rubber band wound too tight. Finally, just as Sam was about to make some inane remark about the weather, Julia said, "Whether or not I'm seeing someone has nothing to do with going to dinner with you. Business, remember?"

"Right. Business." Sam sucked in a deep breath. "Just so you know, I wouldn't have asked you out to dinner if I was dating someone."

She glanced over at him quickly, then returned her gaze to the road. "Not even for a business dinner?"

"Not for a business dinner with you," he said, pleased when he saw her knuckles whiten on the steering wheel.

After a silence that stretched a little too long, he said, "You haven't answered me. Are you? Seeing someone?"

"Need to know information, Sam. And you don't need to know, because we're not dating. Kirby is part of an open case. A case where you're my witness," she said. She slanted him a look as she turned onto Broadway. "I have lines in the sand when it comes to my cases. Don't try to cross them."

He tugged at the tie that was suddenly strangling him. God! He felt like a fifteen-year-old kid asking for a date with the most popular girl in high school. "What about after the case is closed?"

"Ask me out then and you'll find out."

Sam relaxed against the door, feeling his confidence returning. "You're flirting with me. I'll take that as a yes."

Julia expertly whipped the car into a parking spot, straightened it out and turned off the ignition. "I repeat -- I can't go out with you while this case is active," she said. "Anything after that would be speculation. Not admissible in court. So let's go have dinner and talk about the case. I'll tell you about Derek Kirby, since you're the one who found him for me. As long as you don't repeat it to anyone."

"I grew up with two sisters. I know how to keep my mouth shut."

"Good." She stepped out of the car and walked around to the sidewalk, where he waited. "Let's go inside before I get a phone call, telling me I have to be in court."

She yanked open the door, walked in and paused at the hostess stand. Sam trailed after her, both turned on and intrigued.

He wasn't used to his dates taking control. The women he went out with usually fawned over him. Flattered him. Tried their best to please him.

And they bored him.

Julia Carleton certainly wasn't about to defer to him. It was a novel experience.

He wasn't sure he liked it.

CHAPTER 5

Sitting in the booth tucked into the corner at Oscar's, Julia watched Sam study the menu. She sat facing the door, Sam across from her, only his back visible to the other diners. All anyone would see was that he was tall.

So far, no one had bothered them. The waitress had been friendly, but all business. Sam would probably handle a fan easily, but Julia wasn't comfortable being scrutinized.

She touched her thumb to the cool onyx stone in her father's ring, resting in its usual place on the middle finger of her right hand. Every once in a while, someone recognized her. She got one of two reactions -- it was either 'oh, you poor dear' or 'I hope your father is burning in hell'. Both of them made her stomach churn.

Both sent her running.

That was why she liked the anonymity of sitting in the corner -- no one could see her.

Her mouth curved into a tiny smile. Although it *had* been fun to tease Sam about the reason she always sat here.

Sam closed the menu and pushed it away, then frowned. "You never looked at your menu."

She shrugged. "I know what I want." Tilting her head, she studied him. "You said you come here a lot. Didn't you know what you wanted?"

"Of course not," he said with that crooked grin that made her fingers twitch to touch his mouth. "How would I know what I felt like eating until I saw it on the menu?"

He leaned forward, setting his arms on the table. "Tonight I'm having a burger. But another time, I might have a taste for mac and cheese. Or their ribs. Maybe their trout," he said, and she watched him imagine all of those dishes. "Having the same thing every time would be boring."

Was that his dating philosophy, too?

Before she could ask, the waitress arrived to take their order. Sam asked for a Green Line Pale Ale beer and his burger, and she ordered an iced tea and mac and cheese with bacon and spinach. Julia handed their server the menus, then waited until the woman couldn't overhear them.

"So here's the story on Derek Kirby," she began.

As she told him about struggling with Kirby when she tried to arrest him, Sam scowled. "A guy like that, who uses his size and strength to intimidate and threaten? I'm surprised you didn't tase him as soon as he gave you trouble." He touched her hand, his fingers brushing over hers. "Did he hurt you?"

"No," she said, but his concern softened something inside her. "Just made me struggle enough to work up a sweat. And if I'd tased him?" She shook her head. "Mia Donovan and I would have had to drag his dead weight to the car. Then there's the paperwork." She shuddered, knowing how many forms she'd have had to fill out. "Much more pleasant to have dinner with you."

"Wow!" Sam widened his eyes and laid his hand over his heart. "I rank above dragging an over-developed muscle-head to your car and then spending the rest of the evening doing paperwork? Detective, you have no idea how flattered I am."

Julia relaxed back into the seat with a smile. Thank God Sam had talked her into dinner. His light-hearted teasing was the perfect antidote to a long, tiring day. He was the ideal companion when she needed to unwind.

And that was a very dangerous place to go.

Pushing the thought out of her mind, she said, "Wish you could have seen Dave, our evidence tech, deal with Kirby." Laughing as she described Dave scrolling through his phone while Kirby fumed, she ended with, "Kirby was like a spoiled little boy throwing a tantrum. And Dave was masterful with him."

"Give me Dave's full name," Sam said. "I'll send him a pair of game tickets."

Julia bit her lower lip to keep from laughing. "Go ahead, but I'm not sure he'd appreciate them." The laugh finally escaped. "He's a Sox fan. In fact, he was wearing his 'Sox Side Irish' tee shirt today."

Sam shrugged. "I'll still send them. He doesn't want to go? His loss." He leaned across the table, close enough that she could smell his fresh-air scent. "You should laugh more often. I noticed it at Cilla's wedding, too. You light up the room when you laugh."

His eyes were pools of sincerity. He meant every word.

She didn't get many compliments. Not the sincere kind, anyway. In spite of a tiny lump in her throat, Julia shook her head at him. "Really, Sam? Cheesy lines like that? The women must be falling at your feet."

"Only one woman I'm interested in seeing at my feet." He frowned. "Wait. No. That didn't come out right."

Julia burst out laughing. "You better watch it, Sam, or they'll yank your hot stuff card."

He just smiled at her. "Go ahead and mock. I meant every word."

Her laughter died. She saw it in the depths of his eyes that darkened to a tiny rim of blue around his pupils. Curling her hands into fists to keep from reaching for him, she took a slow breath.

She needed to get her head on straight.

"So the fun picked up when Kirby's attorney arrived,"

she said, aware of how awkward the transition was, but not caring.

Sam's eyes laughed at her, but all he said was, "Tell me."

"Kirby didn't say a word until the guy got to the station. Wouldn't even confirm his name and address, even though I already had his driver's license." Her mouth tightened. "Makes me think he's done this dance before. When the attorney showed up, I played them the video. The lawyer claimed the video was blurry and it wasn't clear that Kirby's fist actually hit D'Angelo's face." She curled her fingers around the edge of the table, then carefully relaxed them. "It was very clear. But he'll probably get bail. I'll make sure the State's Attorney asks for Kirby's passport and bond of a couple million dollars. We'll see what happens."

"Wow." Sam frowned as their waitress slid his beer and her iced tea onto the table. "What would happen if he'd been some poor slob who couldn't afford a high-priced lawyer?"

"He'd get a public defender." She shrugged one shoulder. "But not until tomorrow or maybe even the next day. He'd spend at least one night in jail." She took a gulp of iced tea. "Would have been nice to see Kirby's ass in a cell overnight, but that fantasy's not happening."

"*That's* what you fantasize about?" Sam's eyes darkened. "You need a better class of daydreams." He set his glass of beer on the table and leaned closer. "Or night dreams. Maybe I can help you with that."

She swallowed as she held his gaze. He could definitely help with her fantasies, because he'd already starred in quite a few of them. She opened her mouth to reply just as the waitress interrupted with their food.

Thank God.

"You guys need anything else right now?" the waitress asked.

"Another beer," Sam said. He glanced at her glass. "A refill on the iced tea, babe?"

Babe?

"Yes, please." She waited until the waitress was out of sight before she turned to Sam. Pressed her fingertips into the table until they whitened. "Don't call me that."

He shrugged. "Sorry. It slipped out."

He was *so* not sorry. His twinkling eyes gave him away. Time to finish her meal and get out of here. She'd give him a lift home, promise to keep in touch about the case, then put him out of her mind.

Grabbing her fork, she took a bite of her mac and cheese, then sucked in air as it burned the roof of her mouth.

"No rush, Jules," he said after swallowing a bite of his burger. "You have time."

She didn't have time. There was definitely a rush. The longer she sat here and flirted with Sam, the more trouble she'd be in.

She'd meant it when she said she couldn't date him while this case was going on. But even without this case standing between them, she knew it would be a mistake to go out with him. Being seen in public with a big-deal baseball player would bring more scrutiny. The inevitable photographs. People would recognize her.

That was the last thing she wanted.

She'd never dated a famous guy. Never intended to. At Cilla's wedding, Sam was a guy she'd flirted with. Danced with. Shared a smoking hot kiss with.

She'd figured she'd never see him again.

Now he was a witness in one of her cases. And not just a witness. The guy who shot the vitally important video. The guy who'd helped her identify the suspect.

Flirting with Sam at the wedding, dancing with him, hadn't been risky. That evening was supposed to be a one and done.

Flirting with him now? Double jeopardy. Getting cozy with Sam could endanger her case against Kirby. And being the woman on Sam's arm would expose her to a lot of unwelcome scrutiny.

Thank God this case was standing between them. Because Sam was tempting her enough to break all her rules and take a chance on being recognized as his date.

She took another bite of mac and cheese, hating that she wanted to reach across the table and touch Sam's hand. A quick glance across the table told her Sam had noticed the desire in her eyes.

Before he could comment, two young women approached the table, giggling and whispering to each other. They were in their early twenties, one blond, one brunette. Both attractive.

Sam couldn't see them yet. But he was definitely their target. Julia wasn't sure the pair had even noticed her.

As they edged into view, Sam turned and spotted them. Set his burger on his plate. "Can I help you ladies?"

The brunette giggled, then bit her lip. "Aren't you Sam Marini? My friend called me and said she saw you walk in here."

"I am," Sam said with a friendly smile. "Are you Bearcats fans?"

The blond nodded and said, "We think you're way hot."

Sam shot a quick 'save me' look at Julia, but she wasn't sure what she could do. Badge them and send them away? That would go up on two Facebook pages in about ten seconds. Hell would rain down on her from the Chicago PD ten seconds later.

She gave Sam a tiny shrug, ignoring his soulful gaze.

When she didn't say anything, he turned back to the two women. "Thanks, but all the guys on the team are hot right now," he said easily. "Have you checked out our batting averages? They're hitting everything that's pitched to them."

The brunette frowned a little. "She didn't mean that kind of hot." She slid a piece of paper that looked like a CTA ticket across the table. "I'm Ashley."

The blond added another slip of paper that looked as if it had been torn from a book. Julia scowled. She'd torn a page from a book to give Sam her number? Had she been raised by wolves?

"And I'm Crystal."

Each girl had written her name and a phone number on her paper. Sam looked down at them, then pulled out a pen and signed his name on each of them. Nudged them back in the women's direction. "Thanks for being a fan," he said, smiling at them. "Have a nice evening."

The brunette, the more aggressive one, frowned. "You're supposed to keep them. It's our phone numbers."

Sam glanced at Julia, then furrowed his forehead at the pair. "I'm sitting here with a woman," he said, sounding incredulous. "You think I'd disrespect her and take your phone numbers? Sorry, ladies, that's not going to happen. I'm not interested."

For the first time, the two women looked at Julia. She knew what they saw as they studied her -- strands of hair tucked behind her ears from her unraveling braid, her suit jacket wrinkled from her struggle with Kirby, and no makeup. She'd sweated it off during the arrest.

They turned back to Sam, and the shocked looks on their faces told Julia what they were going to say. *Her?* Instead of *us?*

Rather than making Sam defend her, she leaned closer to the women. Gave them her best cop stare. "Why don't you ladies leave Mr. Marino alone so he can finish his dinner. He needs to keep up his strength."

The two women glanced from her to Sam. Back to her. Their eyes narrowed at her innuendo.

Trying to intimidate her? Please. Julia stared back, resisting the urge to roll her eyes. These two weren't in the same universe as some of the murderers she'd faced down.

Finally, the two fans looked away. With one last regretful glance at Sam, they flounced back into the main part of the restaurant. Slid onto chairs at a table with two other women.

All four of them turned as one to look at her. Julia

resisted the urge to edge closer to the corner of the booth. Out of their line of sight.

Finally she relaxed into the seat. "Thank you," she said to Sam, leaning closer to touch his hand. Remembering at the last moment she wasn't going to do that anymore, she curled her fingers into her palm. "Telling them you wouldn't accept their phone numbers because you were with me was very... smooth."

"*Smooth?*" Sam looked as shocked as Ashley and Crystal had looked when Sam turned them down. "Only a total asswipe would accept a woman's phone number in front of a date."

"Like I keep reminding you, we're not on a date," Julia said, but her chest tightened. He was genuinely shocked at the idea, and a tiny brick fell from the wall around her heart.

Until she wondered if he would have accepted the slips of paper if he'd been alone.

"They didn't know this was a," Sam swiped air quotes, "business meeting." He reached across the table and took her hand. Tightened his grip when she tried to pull away. "And it wouldn't have mattered if I was alone. I was telling you the truth earlier, Jules. I'm... interested. In *you*."

Julia's stupid, quivering heart beat a little faster. "That's... that's..."

"The absolute truth," Sam said quietly. He raised her hand and brushed a kiss across her palm. His lips left a trail of tiny electric shocks over her skin.

Knowing she had to do it, she tried to tug her hand away. He didn't let go.

"You think this is some kind of game for me? That I'm a player and you're my next target?" He held her hand more tightly and leaned closer. "It isn't, Jules. I've thought about you since Cilla's wedding." His mouth curled into a smile. "I asked her who you were, but she pretended not to know. Don't know why she wouldn't want me to get involved with a cop, since she's a cop and she married one. Was she protecting you?" His smile made it clear he was teasing her.

"Is there something you're not telling me? Do you have deep, dark secrets?"

Julia eased her hand away from his. Cilla knew all about her father. Cilla knew she'd never get involved with a man who was high-profile. "She was probably just being a good friend," she managed to say. "Protecting me from your big, bad self."

"Cilla knows I don't have a big, bad self," he said, finishing the last of his burger. "Which means she was protecting you." He wadded up his napkin and tossed it on the table. "I'm going to have a lot of fun weaseling out all your secrets."

CHAPTER 6

Derek Kirby shot Julia a cocky smile as he walked out of the courtroom between his attorney and his father. She watched him leave, not allowing anything to show on her face. But she pressed her fingers into the soft leather folder that held her notes until her fingers hurt.

The outcome wasn't what she'd wanted, but it was what she'd expected.

Kirby was free to go on living his life until the trial, which probably wouldn't start for at least a year. That's what an attorney like the Kirby's could do.

Nick D'Angelo was on life support. Not expected to survive.

At least the video had been introduced into evidence. Kirby's high-priced lawyer had objected mightily, but the assistant SA had argued hard. The judge had agreed it was evidence, and it could be used.

Julia stood in the now-empty courtroom until the murmur of voices outside the door had faded away. Then she waited a little longer.

When she was reasonably sure the Kirbys had made it to the first floor, she opened the door and stepped into the quiet hall, heading for the bank of elevators at the other end of the corridor. The click of her footsteps echoed off the walls and bounced off the high ceiling, emphasizing that there was no one else around.

"Detective Carleton." A man stepped in front of her, stopping her in her tracks. His grey hair was brushed back in front and long in the back. Derek Kirby's father, Ronald. She'd noticed his bespoke Brioni suit in court, but even the meticulous tailoring and glittering gold thread couldn't conceal his girth.

She straightened, narrowing her eyes at him. "Mr. Kirby. What can I do for you?"

"Give me the name of your witness."

"Sorry, Mr. Kirby. That's confidential information." She stared at him, not completely surprised he'd asked. No wonder Derek was a bully. He'd learned at his father's knee.

Kirby leaned closer. "My son has the right to confront his accuser."

Like he confronted Nick D'Angelo? The words were on the tip of her tongue, but she bit them back. She was a detective. A representative of the Chicago PD. "The witness didn't accuse Derek of anything," she said, keeping her voice calm. "He simply made a recording."

"You know what I mean. Derek has the right to confront any witnesses."

"Yes, he does. In a courtroom. And he'll get that chance when his case goes to trial."

She attempted to step around Ronald Kirby, but he moved quickly for a man of his bulk. "You're not going anywhere until I get that name."

"Then I guess we'll be here a while."

He curled his right hand into a fist, showing off his manicured fingers, the nails coated in clear polish. He might get manicures like a metrosexual, but he was all thug. Even his fingers, thick and rough and brutish, belonged to a bully.

A bully twice her size, confronting her in a deserted courthouse corridor. Her heart began to pound, adrenaline flooding her body. Preparing her for fight or flight.

Not flight, she vowed.

He leaned closer, until his nose was inches from hers. She smelled whiskey on his breath and recognized violence in his eyes. "I know a lot of people in this town," he said, his voice a cold threat. "A lot of people who owe me favors."

"Are you threatening me?" Julia set her hand on the gun at her hip. Kirby's eyes followed her fingers. When she unsnapped the restraint on her holster, he stepped back.

"Not at all, Detective. Just asking a question." Out of the corner of her eye she saw his fist, curling and uncurling at his side. "A question you'll answer eventually."

"I've given you the only answer you're going to get." Keeping her hand on her gun and her gaze on Kirby, Julia stepped around him. This time, he didn't block her way.

As she walked toward the elevators, the back of her neck burned. Kirby hadn't moved. He was still staring at her.

When the elevator arrived, she stepped into it and pressed the button for the first floor without looking back at him.

She needed to warn Sam.

* * *

The next morning, sprawled on a chair at his kitchen table, sunlight striping the walls, Sam touched the <u>Chicago Herald</u> icon on his tablet as he sipped his coffee. The first article under the 'Top Stories' section made him sit up straight.

'Developer's son arrested on assault charges. Victim on life support.'

The story detailed the charges, which included assault and battery on two police officers. Sam grinned as he took another sip of coffee. *You go, Jules.*

His smile faded as he continued reading. Kirby had been released on a half-million dollar bond -- a lot less than the two million Julia had said she'd ask the SA to request. One of the reasons was no prior offenses.

Sam stared out the window at his garden, just bursting into bloom. Huh. He would have bet serious money that Kirby had gotten into trouble before. According to Jules, he was arrogant, entitled and had a quick, vicious temper. And Sam had watched him deliver a brutal punch to a guy who was no threat to him. A guy who hadn't even touched him.

No record? Hard to believe.

Continuing to read, Sam saw that a witness had caught the whole incident on camera. No names, though. Thank God.

Kirby's lawyer had argued that it should be thrown out, since it was blurry and could have been altered. The detective in charge had argued it was perfectly clear, and had been shown to a police officer within minutes of the incident.

The judge, after watching the video, had agreed and entered it into evidence.

Kirby had walked out of the courtroom with his attorney, free until the trial.

Julia had been right on all counts. That didn't stop Sam's rush of resentment for the rich kid who was so clearly guilty, but had been able to walk out of the courtroom because he had a slick attorney and bags of money.

Sam wondered if Julia was silently fuming this morning, as well.

He turned on his phone to call her, then hesitated. It was still early. If she wasn't at work, maybe she was still asleep.

He compromised by texting her. 'So he's back on the street?"

Instead of texting him back, his phone rang. "Julia?" he asked as he answered it.

"Yes. I've been trying to get hold of you since last night. Are you all right?"

"Of course I'm all right," he answered, surprised at the

question. "Why wouldn't I be?"

"No one's called you? No reporters?"

"Nope." He tapped on the table. "I turn this phone off at night. I have another one that's always on in case of an emergency. Only my family knows the number."

"I'll need that number, too." She hesitated. "Have you been on-line this morning?"

She sounded… strange. Upset. Maybe because Kirby wasn't still in jail.

"Yeah, I was just reading the story in the <u>Herald</u>. You called it exactly. Must have been tough to watch that little prick walk out of the courtroom."

"Yeah, I wasn't happy, but I wasn't surprised." She cleared her throat. "Derek's father stopped me in the hall afterward. He wanted your name."

"You didn't give it to him, did you?"

"Of course not." There was a long pause. "Someone got hold of your name, though. I take it you haven't seen the <u>Windy City Post</u>?"

"That blog site? No. I don't usually have time to read that." With his other hand he found the icon for the blog, opened it and scrolled down until he saw the headline. 'Bearcats third baseman Sam Marini identified as witness in Nick Angelo beating.' "What the hell?"

"Yes. Someone posted an anonymous blog on the site in the middle of the night. I was sure your phone was going nuts this morning."

Sam clicked on the voicemail icon. His stomach twisted. "I have fifty-three voicemails."

"Delete them. A bunch are from me -- I was worried when I couldn't get hold of you -- but I didn't call you fifty-three times. Look in front of your house. There are probably reporters waiting out there for you."

He stood up and walked toward the front windows. "Damn it, Julia. How did this happen?"

"I don't know, but I'll find out. I promise you."

"There can't be that many people who know," Sam said,

trying to think of everyone who'd been at the scene last night.

"More than you'd think." Julia sounded exhausted. "The paramedics. All those people who saw it happen." A long pause. "The other cops."

"You don't suspect the other cops, do you?"

"I suspect everyone. And I'll be questioning all of them."

Sam walked to his window and raised the blind. A huge news van was double-parked in front of his house. At least ten people stood on the sidewalk. A woman he recognized as the news anchor for one of the local television stations was rattling his gate, trying to unlock it.

"Holy crap," he said, dropping the blind back into place before anyone spotted him.

"Is it a zoo out there?"

"Yeah, it is. I have a game this afternoon. I have to leave in less than an hour."

"Do you want me to send over a uniform to clear them out?"

"No, I'll drive to the park today." He didn't want to drive. "I like my routine of walking to the stadium and back home afterward. I guess that's out of the question now."

"It would probably be smarter to drive for a while." Julia's voice softened, and he heard her unspoken sympathy.

"Yeah. Probably." He edged over to look through the side of the blind again. More lookie-loos had gathered. "Did the reporter call you before he ran the story?"

"Yep. He wanted me to confirm that you were a witness."

"Did you confirm it?" Sam held his breath.

"I told him to go to hell." Julia's voice was a knife slashing through the space between them. Sharp. Hard.

He exhaled. "Thank you."

"You know… you know this changes things," Julia said, her voice subdued. Almost defeated. "You're going to be hounded mercilessly. Those reporters will be outside your house for the foreseeable future. They'll be at the ball park. There will be stories in the papers every day -- newspapers love a celebrity angle to a case like this. Wherever you go, strangers will confront you." Julia was quiet for a long moment. Finally she said, "If you want to back off, back out, of this case, I understand."

He gripped the phone more tightly. "What happens if I back out?" he asked, a possible escape the light at the end of a tunnel.

"You tell the reporters that the anonymous source was wrong. You tell everyone who comes up to you that the paper was wrong. I can get a subpoena to compel you to testify in court, but," she sighed. "I won't do that." Her swallow was audible over the phone. "They'll eventually leave you alone. If you want to refuse to testify, I understand."

"But if I don't testify," he said slowly, "what happens to the video?"

Julia said nothing for a long moment. "We won't be able to introduce it into evidence," she finally said. "Not without the person who recorded it."

"So you wouldn't have a case."

"We could make a case without you." Her answer was immediate. Certain. "I have the names of all Kirby's teammates who watched him punch Nick D'Angelo. They'll step up and confirm that Kirby was the guy who hit Nick. And if they lie on the stand, they'll be charged with perjury."

"Not if they stick together and all deny it."

"One of them will break," Julia said calmly. "I'll find something."

"But it would be easier if I testified."

There was a long pause. Julia's exhale whooshed through the phone. Finally she said, "I won't lie to you, Sam -- yes, we'd have a much stronger case if we could use the video. But I never meant to turn your life upside down."

"Wasn't you," he said immediately. "It was whoever

told the <u>Herald</u> I was the witness."

"I'll be working on that, too," she said, her voice hardening. "I'll haul Kirby senior into an interview room. Then I'll go after anyone else who might have seen you -- the cops at the scene, the paramedics, the witnesses we were able to corral. I won't stop until I find out."

"Thank you."

"No thanks necessary. It's my job." She paused. "You need to make a decision, Sam. Figure out what you're going to do." Was her voice cooler? "The SA will need to know how to prepare the case."

"I'll think about it. Let you know."

The phone was silent for three beats, and Sam felt like a quitter. The kind of guy who walked away when the going got tough.

He'd never been a quitter in his life.

What was Julia thinking? It shouldn't matter so much, but somehow, it did.

Before he could ask, she said, "If you have trouble with anyone, call 911. Immediately."

"I can take care of myself."

"Yeah, that's exactly what I'm afraid of. Call 911. Don't try to be a hero."

The phone went dead, and the word 'coward' whispered through Sam's head as he darkened the screen.

He didn't make snap decisions. He thought about things from all sides. Pondered the pluses and minuses. And if he went public, it would affect a lot more people than just him.

His teammates. Team management. The companies that gave him endorsement deals.

If he denied that he was the witness, declined to testify, his life would go on as usual. Nothing would change.

Except that he'd have to face himself in the mirror every morning.

He took a deep breath. Stabbed Julia's contact icon on his phone.

"Sam? What's wrong?"

"Nothing." He closed his eyes, dreading the shit storm but knowing he had no choice. "I'm in."

CHAPTER 7

Julia walked into the station early the next morning, thinking about all she had to do that day. First on her list was talking to the seven guys who'd been with Kirby the night he'd punched Nick D'Angelo.

Her mind mulling strategies to get them to talk, she walked into the bullpen and spotted Dwyer at her desk. He leaned back in her chair, his feet parked next to her computer, talking to another cop from the night shift.

"Get your ass out of my chair, Dwyer," she said, striding over to her desk. "And you better not have changed the settings on it."

"Chill out, Carleton," he said, sliding his feet off her desk, knocking her pens to the floor in the process. "I was just taking a load off while I talked to Maxwell."

Julia scanned her desk. He'd moved her mouse -- probably kicked it when he dropped his feet next to it. Two or three pieces of paper were wadded into balls on her desk. Her computer monitor had been moved, too. Probably by his feet again.

"Beat it, Dwyer," she said, staring at the smirking officer. "I have work to do."

Dwyer pushed out of her chair, grabbed his wadded up

papers from her desk and lumbered off with a wave of his hand to her. His middle finger lingered longer than the other fingers.

Staring after him, Julia muttered, "You should have retired with your partner Vannetti." When Dwyer turned into the break room, Julia sat down. Landed too hard on her chair. Damn it. "Next time you fiddle with my chair, I'll kick your ass," she yelled at Dwyer as she raised the chair to the correct height.

After Dwyer exited the break room and disappeared down the stairs, she got herself a cup of tea, told Mia Donovan what had happened with Kirby at bond court, then returned to her desk.

She laid seven driver's license photos in two rows and studied each of them until she'd memorized the faces. Seven men. Some looked solemn. A few looked startled, as if they hadn't been ready when the picture was snapped.

Two of them smirked.

These were the teammates who'd been with Kirby at that bar. The seven men who had run away without even looking at Nick D'Angelo, lying in the street.

It would be a pleasure to interrogate them.

She'd save the smirkers for last, instinctively knowing they'd be harder to crack.

Choosing Jason Short at random, she powered up her computer and did a detailed search. When she found his name listed as an employee of Kirby's company, she closed her eyes and rubbed at the headache forming over her left eye. Short wasn't going to be helpful.

At least she could pick him up at work. Use a little public humiliation to soften him up.

Spotting a uniform with his feet up on a desk, drinking coffee, Julia walked over to him. Handed him a picture of Jason Short and his work address. "Hey, Zebretti. This guy is a witness in the Nick D'Angelo case. Could you go pick him up for me?"

Frank dropped his feet to the floor and set the coffee

mug on the desk. "It would be my pleasure."

"He works with Kirby," Julia told him. "Make sure his co-workers see you escorting him out of the office."

Zebretti nodded, his eyes gleaming. "I'll make sure it's *very* public."

After Frank left, Julia fidgeted with the settings for the recording system in the first interrogation room. She intended to document every word that came out of Jason Short's mouth -- she'd need it if he was anything like his buddy Derek Kirby. She'd do the same for the other six guys.

Zebretti returned a half-hour later with Short, who looked way too confident. Bordering on cocky. Julia let him stew in the interrogation room for twenty minutes, then she walked in, closed the door and sat down across the table from Short. He watched her calmly, but she saw the smirk he tried to disguise.

An hour later, she drummed her fingers on the table as Short walked out of the room. He hadn't seen a thing. He'd been talking to Chet Holmes as they left the Seventh Inning Stretch bar. When Derek had yelled goodbye, Jason had taken off. His girlfriend was waiting for him at home.

No matter how many questions Julia asked, or how she phrased them, Short's answers were always the same. He'd been coached well. Probably by Derek Kirby.

Time for the next one on her list. Zebretti went to fetch him as Julia saved the recording of Short and reset the machine.

An hour and a half later, she watched Chet Holmes walk away from the precinct. He, too, worked for Kirby Development. His answers to her questions were identical to Short's. Almost word for word.

Neither had looked particularly concerned when she mentioned they'd have to testify at Kirby's trial. Did these jerks know the meaning of perjury?

Sliding into her desk chair, Julia pulled up the video Sam had taken on her computer. Played it again. Holmes and

Short were on opposite sides of the group. No way had they been talking. She'd get them back in. Play the video while she watched their reactions. Remind them about the penalties for perjury. She'd see if they were as smooth and cocky when confronted with their lies.

She made a few notes in her notebook, then slammed it shut and shoved it into a drawer. Reached for the file she'd started on the case, looking for the next guy's address. Alec Jacobsen. He lived and worked in Lakeview. Not too far. She could pick him up and have him in the box in...

She glanced at the clock. Almost nine-thirty. She closed her eyes, rubbed at the ache in her forehead.

Go home, she ordered herself. She'd gotten about three hours of sleep last night, and hadn't had anything to eat since a late breakfast of yogurt and blueberries. She always got a headache when she forgot to eat -- she was surprised this one wasn't worse.

Her stomach growling, Julia stood up as Mia Donovan and Frank Zebretti rushed past her. Mia glanced over her shoulder and slowed. "Hey, Carleton," she called. "We're going to Bearcats Stadium. Got a call from security. They're holding an unruly customer making a scene. D and D. His name is Derek Kirby. Want in on the fun?"

"Hell, yes," Julia said, ignoring both her hunger and her headache as she trotted to catch up with them. "Wouldn't miss it."

When they got to the ball park, they could hear the roars from the street. Julia and Mia had answered similar drunk and disorderly calls when they were uniforms. Zebretti had handled his share of them, too. Flashing their badges, they headed straight for the security office. The familiar scents of grilling hot dogs, spilled beer and popcorn followed them down the corridor.

Derek Kirby was sprawled on a chair, scrolling through his phone. Pete and George, two security guards Julia recognized, stood close by, their arms crossed over their chests.

"Officers," Pete said with relief when Julia led the way into the room. "Got one for you."

Derek looked up from his phone. When he spotted Julia, his expression hardened. His eyes narrowed. Then he straightened.

"What are you doing here?" he asked.

"We got a call from security that you were making a scene," Mia said.

Kirby's gaze drifted to Mia, and his mouth thinned when he recognized her, as well. "I paid for my ticket. I can express my opinion."

"He threw a beer at Sam Marini," George, the other guard, said.

"Did it hit him?" Julia asked.

"Beer didn't." Pete stared hard at Kirby. "Splashed onto the roof of the dugout. Cup might have glanced off Marini's arm. I don't think he noticed."

"Then why call us instead of just tossing him out?" Julia asked.

"He refused to leave. Pete and I are too old to drag his ass that far. We thought you could escort him out."

"Did you read the fine print on the ticket, Kirby?" Someone was pounding nails into Julia's head. "It says the team reserves the right to toss out losers like you. So let's go."

She gestured for him to stand up, but he didn't move.

Julia clenched her teeth against the pain in her temple and nodded at Mia and Frank Zebretti. "Be my guest, guys."

Mia and Frank each took one arm and tugged Kirby toward the door. Julia half-smiled when she heard Mia murmur to Kirby, "I'm thinking you must have a thing for Tasers. Wanna take ours for a test run?"

"Get him out of here, then you can take off," she called to the two cops. "I'm going to ask Pete and George a couple of questions."

When the two officers and Kirby were gone, Julia turned

back to the security guards. "Someone in the stands complain about that jerk?"

"A whole bunch of people." The older guy, George, shook his head. "Cussing up a storm, calling Marini all kinds of names. There were kids right behind him, but the asshole didn't care. Idiot threw the beer as we were escorting him out of his seat."

Pete grinned. "We got a big cheer when we hauled him away."

"Thanks, guys." Julia managed to smile back at them. "You get a lot like him?"

"Oh, yeah. Always someone who drinks too much and gets obnoxious. Usually they get quiet when we show up. Not that guy, though. He just got worse."

She wasn't surprised. "Kirby clearly doesn't have much impulse control."

A muffled roar came from above her, and the room vibrated with the sound of feet stamping on concrete. The noise went on and on, and the guards grinned. "Sounds like a win."

"You can tell from the sound of the cheering?" Julia asked.

"Yep. They stamp their feet like that when the game is over and we won," the first guard explained.

Julia rubbed at her temple again. She needed to talk to Sam. To see if he wanted to press charges about the beer cup. "I need to talk to Sam Marini," she said. "Can you get him?"

"I'll call the clubhouse," George said, reaching for a phone on the wall.

Pete gestured toward the chair where Kirby had been sitting. "Have a seat, Officer."

She didn't have enough energy to explain that she was a detective. Too tired and hungry to care about titles. And she didn't want to sit down. She might fall asleep on the chair. "Thanks, but I'll stand."

"... Marini," the first guard said. "Great." He hung up

72

the phone and said, "Sam will be here in a couple."

"Thank you." The noise from above them was subsiding, but the room still vibrated.

"You look like you could use a coffee." The second guard lifted a pot from a coffeemaker. "Want a cup?"

Julia shuddered inside as she got a look at the black sludge in the carafe. "Thanks, but I'm good."

A few minutes of awkward conversation later, the door opened and Sam stuck his head in. His hair was flattened and wet, with a line from his cap circling his head. His uniform, damp with sweat, was streaked with brownish red dirt on his chest and legs. The cleats from his shoes clicked on the floor when he shuffled his feet. "Pete? George? What's up?"

"Officer wants to talk to you," George said, gesturing to Julia.

Sam's face lit up when he saw her. "Jul... Detective Carleton. This is a surprise. What can I do for you?"

That smile of his was doing plenty. Places deep inside her quivered.

Only because she was too tired to control herself. "Mr. Marini." She cleared her throat. "I need to ask you if you want to press charges against Derek Kirby. The man who threw the beer at you."

"That was Kirby?" He raised one eyebrow. "Wow. Was he the one shouting, too?" When she nodded, he said, "What an ass. Is that supposed to scare me?"

"Intimidate you, I think." She wanted to add, 'keep you from testifying,' but she didn't want to get into his business in front of the two security guys. "Did the beer cup hit you in the arm? Pete and George weren't sure."

"If it did, I didn't notice. It's just that soft plastic, anyway. Wasn't going to hurt me."

"Not the point. He threw something at you. If he hit you, that's battery."

"I have no idea if it hit me or not. So I guess the answer is no."

"Good enough. Sorry to disturb your... your after-game routine."

He grinned, and Julia quivered again. Damn it!

"Not a problem. I was just heading into the party room when I got the call."

"I'll leave you to it, then," Julia said, pushing away from the wall. She hesitated before turning for the door. "Watch your six, Marini. If Kirby came here to harass you, God knows what else he might do."

"Why, Detective." Sam leaned closer, and the smell of clean sweat, grass and dirt swept over her. For a moment she swayed toward him. Then she pulled away sharply. His eyes twinkling, Sam murmured, "Are you worried about me?"

"I'm worried about the paperwork I'll have to file if he kicks your ass," she retorted.

Pete and George stood to the side, their heads swinging back and forth as if they were watching a tennis match. Finally George asked, "You two know each other?"

Before Sam could answer, Julia said, "We met on a case."

"Ah." Pete's drawn-out syllable made Julia squirm. It sounded far too knowing. As if she and Sam had been...

No. They had *not* been... whatever.

"Go back to your party, Marini. I'll let you know when I have more information on the case." She headed for the door, eager to get away.

To her surprise, Sam followed her out the door. "Take care, guys," he said to the two security guards as he closed the door.

Then he hurried to catch up with her. "Are you going back to work?" When she nodded, he said, "For God's sake, Jules! It's past nine-thirty."

"I know what time it is." Her voice was sharper than necessary, and she rubbed her head again. "Sorry," she muttered. "Long day."

"Yeah." She heard the rough rasp of whiskers as he rubbed his hand over his face.

Her voice softened. "For you, too, I guess."

"You find out who leaked my name to that blogger?"

She didn't have a thing. "No, but I'm working on it."

As they approached the gate, he pulled her into the shadow of a closed Bearcats gear store. "Hold on a minute," he said quietly, nodding at the people streaming toward the exit. "Let's wait until the crowd thins. I'd rather not show my face out there."

"Why? Did you strike out too many times today?" As soon as the words were out of her mouth, she wanted to snatch them back. Hunger and a headache made her dangerously cranky.

"Not exactly."

"Then, what?" Her gaze drifted to the television mounted above the concourse. They were replaying the end of the game. She watched as Sam hit a home run, driving in two men on base. As he reached the dugout, his teammates mobbed him, all of them jumping up and down.

"What does that mean?" she asked, nodding at the television.

"Ah, that's just the guys being all happy and shit 'cause we won."

"You won because you hit a home run?"

"You were telling the truth, weren't you?" He slung an arm over her shoulder and drew her deeper into the shadows. "You don't know squat about baseball."

"Nope."

"That's..." His arm dropped and he cleared his throat. "That's called a walk-off. It's when a player hits in a run in the bottom of the ninth inning to win the game. The fans love walk-offs."

She turned to study him. Red crept up his neck and he wouldn't meet her gaze. "So that's why you don't want the fans to see you. They'd mob you."

He shrugged one shoulder.

"And all that foot-stomping -- it wasn't just because you won."

"'Course it was. They do that every time we win."

She was just tired enough that she was enjoying standing in the shadows with Sam. Teasing him. It reminded her of the gardens at the wedding, creating a private cocoon where they could hide from the world.

Where they'd shared the hottest kisses she'd ever experienced.

She tried to step around him. "I have to go, Sam. We need to talk about Kirby and discuss the possibility of charging him with assault and battery. But we can do that tomorrow -- you need to get back to your party."

"I have a better idea. Why don't you let me drive you home? I have to shower and change my clothes, but that'll take me fifteen minutes. Then you won't have to fight through the crowd on the street."

She was so tempted. The cheers and the yelling outside the park were making her head throb. She'd been on duty near the stadium after Bearcats' wins in the past and knew what it was like. She'd be jostled by happy, celebrating people. They'd step on her feet. The yells and whistles would drive knives into her brain.

If Sam drove her home, she'd avoid all that. But letting Sam drive her home was the first step on a slippery slope.

"Nah, but thanks. I'm not that far."

"It's almost four blocks to your station," he said, studying her.

Four and a half. "I'll be fine. I don't want to make you leave early."

"I don't mind." He stared at the almost empty concourse. "I need an excuse to get out of here," he said after a long moment. "They'll expect me at the post-game press-conference, and half the questions will probably be about Kirby and that damn video. I'm not ready to answer them."

She hadn't thought about that, but he was probably right. What was she supposed to say? *No, go face the press ghouls because I don't want to get into a car with you? Because my defenses are down and I don't want to do something I'll regret?*

After a long moment, she sighed. "Fine, I'll be your excuse to duck out of the press thing. But if you tell anyone it's because I'm too tired to walk back to work, I will hurt you."

"I'd never say that, Jules." He grabbed her hand and tugged her to the door that led toward the security room. "I'll tell everyone there's a hot woman waiting for me. Believe me, the guys will understand."

"Your manager might not."

"I'll tell *him* the truth."

She stared at the back of Sam's head as he led her down a narrow corridor. He surprised her every time she talked to him. He wasn't the entitled, man-child baseball player she'd expected when she learned what he did for a living. He was a thoughtful, considerate man. An honest one.

As they walked down a long corridor, she heard the bass beat of loud music coming from the door in front of them. She slowed, hating the thought of facing all his teammates. Dreading that loud music and how it would make her headache a thousand times worse

But he swerved around a corner and opened a door to a room filled with comfortable-looking couches and chairs, a beverage dispenser and coffee pot. An empty tray sat on the counter. It had clearly held sandwiches -- a few wrappers littered the blue tray with the Bearcat logo.

"This is where we make the press wait until we're ready to talk to them. They're all in the post-game press room now, so no one will bother you. I'll be right back."

Sam squeezed her hand and disappeared out the door. Julia sank into a sofa and let her head tilt back against the cushion. If Sam didn't hurry up, she was going to fall asleep.

That wouldn't look good on a first date.

It wasn't a date.

The tiny devil on her shoulder laughed at her. "Shut up," she muttered as her eyes drifted closed.

CHAPTER 8

Sam walked into the press room fifteen minutes later and found Julia sound asleep, her head tilted back into the cushion, her lips parted. As he studied her, he remembered how she'd tasted at his sister's wedding, seven months earlier.

Like honey and chocolate. Passion and sex. Better than anything he'd tasted in his life.

The way their mouths had spoken to each other had been a revelation. He'd kissed his share of women, but none of them had affected him like Julia. He'd gone from interested to desperate in about ten seconds.

He wanted to crawl onto the couch and press his mouth to hers again. Find out if that long-ago kiss had merely been a combination of wedding happiness, the enveloping lush greenery and her sweet-tart, orange-y scent.

He was pretty sure the setting had had nothing to do with it. Pretty sure it had been all Julia.

When he found himself leaning closer to her, he jerked away. Backed up until he bumped into the counter. Julia had made it clear that dating him was off-limits right now. And he was going to kiss her while she was asleep? What the hell was wrong with him?

Clearing his throat, standing a safe five feet away, he said, "Hey, sleepyhead. Time to go."

She jerked awake, the fluorescent light turning her eyes mossy green as she stared at him. "Sam."

Was that how she always sounded when she woke up? Throaty, a little raspy and completely sexy?

Clearing his throat as he shifted uncomfortably, thankful for the camouflaging suit coat, he said, "You ready to leave? Or do you want to continue your nap on that smelly, lumpy couch?"

"I wasn't asleep," she said, struggling to her feet. He reached out to help her, but she narrowed her eyes and straightened. "Just resting."

"Whatever you say." She had *so* been sleeping. "I have food. In case you're hungry."

The way her gaze shifted to the bag in his hand, as if he'd offered her a handful of diamonds, had him struggling to keep a straight face. "Where did you get food?"

"The team sets up a buffet for us after every game. Different restaurants cater it." He shook the bag. "This is from Francesca's."

"Francesca's? Really?" She stared at the bag as if she'd just won the lottery. "One of my favorites."

"Great. Let's go before it gets cold."

He reached for her hand, surprised and happy when her fingers curled around his as he opened the door. As soon as they stepped into the corridor, though, they came face to face with one of his teammates. Gonzo was shirtless, his uniform pants soaked with what smelled like celebratory beer.

"Hey, man, everyone's looking for you for the beer toast." His gaze fixed on Julia, Gonzo swayed on his feet. Clearly, not all the beer had ended up on his clothes.

Julia dropped Sam's hand and side-stepped down the corridor toward the exit. Cursing to himself, Sam clapped Gonzo's shoulder a little too hard. "Got some business to take care of," he said easily. "You take care of the toast for me. Make sure you spray Javvy real good for setting it up. Gotta go."

Turning away, he hurried to catch up to Julia. "Hey," he called. "Wait up."

"You have things to do," she said. "I shouldn't have come down here."

He caught her hand and tugged her to a stop. "I wouldn't have offered to drive you home if I had obligations here," he said, a little offended that she thought he was the kind of guy who would duck out of work without a second thought. "My job is important to me, and I wouldn't blow it off."

Julia slowed and glanced over at him. Studied him for a long moment and then sighed. "I know you take your job seriously. But your friend…"

"Gonzo will spend the next three hours in the party room," he interrupted. "He wants company, and that's fine. But I don't have to be there."

He hesitated, then continued. "I talked to my manager and explained why I don't want to face the press right now. Ken agreed. Told me to get out of here."

Julia's gaze lingered on him, as if she could see deep inside him. "What if he'd said you had to talk to the reporters?"

"I wouldn't have been happy, but I would have done it." He shrugged. "It's part of the deal."

He grabbed her hand again, holding it tight as he started to walk toward the player's parking area. "But instead of answering inane, clichéd questions in the post-game room, I'm taking you home to eat dinner." He held up the bag, smiling as her hungry gaze dropped to look at it. "I even grabbed a bottle of red wine from the bar."

Her eyes narrowed. "Are you sure that's okay?"

"Of course it is." He swung her arm back and forth as they headed toward his car. "Even after the trainers and clubhouse guys eat, there's always a ton of food left over. A lot of the guys take stuff home for their families."

He clicked on his key fob to unlock his car, a late model Toyota SUV, and opened the driver's side for Julia. As she slid onto the leather seat, he stowed the food on the floor in the back.

"This isn't exactly the kind of car I pictured you driving," she said as he slid onto the seat next to her.

"Yeah?" He turned to look at her before putting it in gear. "Why not?"

"I figured you'd drive something like that." She pointed to a low-slung red sports car that cost well over six figures.

"What do you think Cilla would say if I drove up in one of those?"

"She'd laugh her head off. Then tease you for the rest of your life."

"Exactly right. My family keeps my head from getting too big to walk through the door." He smiled as he drove toward the exit. "I got this car when I was a minor league player. I like it. So I kept it when I got promoted."

He put the car in Park at the gate, where the usual handful of fans stood. He'd begun stopping to talk to them when he first came up from the minors, and now it was a habit.

"Hey, how's it going, guys?" he asked, sticking his hand out the window.

"You were amazing, Sam," one kid gushed as he handed him a ball and pen.

"Everyone did great tonight," Sam answered as he signed his name on the ball and handed it back. "Did you see that play Javvy made?"

One by one, every person waiting said something to Sam and handed him a ball, a shirt or a photo to sign. Sam chatted briefly with each of them, signed their souvenirs and handed them back.

When he'd finished, he raised his hand and smiled. "Catch you later, guys." He closed the window, hesitated at the street and looked at Julia, who watched him with an odd expression. He couldn't read it -- was it surprise? Respect?

Impatience? Not the last, he hoped, but it didn't matter. This was who he was. "Which way?"

* * *

"Hey, Jules." Sam's voice, low and sexy. Close. Right next to her. Was he in her bed? She rolled toward him, her mouth curling into a smile.

"We're home," he said, his breath caressing her cheek. "Wake up, babe."

Her eyes flew open. Sam hovered over her, his blue eyes gleaming with amusement in the faint light from the street lamp. "Do I need to carry you up to bed?" he asked, his smile matching his teasing expression.

"Of course not," she managed to say, straightening in the seat. Edging farther away from him. "Sorry I fell asleep on you."

"A man can hope," he said with a tiny grin as he leaned close again. "Unfortunately, it was just the headrest of your seat. Next time, though..."

"In your dreams, Marini," she said, grabbing for the door.

"I think those were *your* dreams, Jules," he said, snickering as she tried to get out of the car and was jerked back by the forgotten seat belt.

He reached across her and unbuckled her seat belt. His knuckles skimmed her belly, sending sparks along her nerves. "Based on the way you were smiling when I woke you up."

She stumbled out of the car, mortified and embarrassed that he was right. She *had* been dreaming about him. And it was definitely R-rated.

Julia slammed her door shut with a little more force than necessary and stepped onto the parkway. Sam's car beeped as he set its security system, then he joined her on the sidewalk, holding out his hand.

"Don't push your luck," she muttered, fishing in her bag

for her keys. She tightened her fingers around them to remind herself that taking his hand would be a huge mistake.

"You always wake up this cranky?" He pushed open the outer door to her building and held it as she unlocked the inner door.

"How I wake up is none of your business, Marini." *Especially* when she woke up dreaming about him.

She twisted the key in the lock and shoved the door open too hard. It bumped into the wall, leaving a tiny dent in the plaster. Closing her eyes, she took a deep breath and started up the stairs. She could do this. She could invite him into her apartment, share some food with him, then wish him a pleasant goodnight as she ushered him out of her space.

Taking him back to her place meant nothing. It was a convenience. She was hungry and tired, and her head hurt too much to face the crowds on the street.

She touched her forehead, which wasn't totally throbbing. He had a quiet car, she told herself. She'd calmed down.

Unlocking the door to her apartment, she walked inside and dropped her keys into the deep blue Steuben bowl on the table against the wall. Flicked on a switch, and soft light filled the living room. Sam stepped in behind her, closed the door, and turned slowly, studying her living space.

Her chest tightened. This was a mistake. She'd been too tired and too hungry to think through the implications of letting Sam into her personal space. He'd see too much.

Tugging at the bag in his hand, she said, "Let's go into the kitchen. I'm starving."

"In a minute." He glanced at her. "I like your place."

"It's just a place to live."

"It's more than that. It's beautiful." He glanced down at the antique Persian Serapi rug that covered the golden hardwood floor. "That carpet is gorgeous. It... it almost glows."

"Thank you." She wasn't about to tell him that the rug had come from her parents' house. That it and the Steuben near the door were among the few things she'd taken when her mother had sold the family home. She wouldn't tell him that she and her sister had played Barbies on that rug. Lain on it while they watched television.

It covered the floor beneath a navy blue Ikea sofa and a white Ikea coffee table. White Ikea bookshelves lined the wall. The same furniture any twenty-nine-year-old woman on a limited budget would have.

Dropping the bag of food beside the door, Sam wandered over to the bookshelves. Ran his finger over the spines of her books, studying all of them. There were thrillers and romances, biographies and histories. A mixture of pop culture and classics, shelved together in no particular order. A number of them were first editions she'd received as gifts over the years. To a casual observer, though, they'd just look like old books. The kind you'd find in a used book store.

Sam paused in front of a misshapen lump of orange-painted clay. He picked up it, drawing his finger down one of the many cracks. She had painstakingly glued it back together after...

Pressing her lips together, she strode over to him, snatched the pumpkin out of his hand and set it carefully back on the shelf. "I'm starving," she announced again. "I need food. You can explore to your heart's content, but I'm going to eat."

"Cranky when you're hungry, too," he murmured. "Okay, I'll feed you."

"I can feed myself." She scowled at him, off-balance and uncomfortable about his careful perusal of her home. "I was just warning you, in case you wanted something before it was all gone."

Grinning, he followed her into the kitchen. "I love a woman who knows exactly what she wants."

Heat flooded her face at the innuendo in his suddenly sexy voice, and she elbowed him in the gut. Was stunned when it felt as if she'd connected with rock. "You're getting the idea. Don't get between me and my dinner."

"So noted."

She stepped into the pantry for plates and silver, setting the table quickly. Poured glasses of water, then opened the refrigerator. Hesitated. "Do you want a beer?"

He opened a foil container, and the glorious smell of cheese, tomatoes and garlic wafted out. Glancing at her as he opened another container, he said, "I'd love a beer. I brought that wine, too."

"I'll have the wine," she said, bringing a bottle of Goose Island Honkers Ale to the table as he searched her drawers for a corkscrew.

It all felt way too domestic. Comfortable.

Ignoring her nerves, she got a wine glass, held up her hand after he'd poured half a glass, and sat down. She helped herself to the pasta with eggplant, a piece of chicken, and Caesar salad. Then began to eat.

She closed her eyes as the spicy, cheesy flavors of the pasta and eggplant exploded in her mouth. Muffled a groan as she took a taste of the chicken, another of her favorite dishes from Francesca's. Across the table, Sam hummed his appreciation as he ate.

Sharing the food, not talking as they ate, felt… comfortable. Relaxing. No pressure to carry on a witty conversation. None of the nerves of a first date, figuring out what to say, how to connect with a stranger.

This wasn't a date.

Sam was being kind. Grabbing food from the clubhouse and driving her home. That's all it was.

Her appetite gone, she pushed away her plate and drank the last swallow of wine in her glass. Time to get back to business. "Are you sure you don't want me to pick up Kirby and charge him with assault and battery?"

Sam shrugged while he swallowed a bite of food. Took a drink of beer. "What good would it do?"

"He was harassing you. You can harass him right back."

He paused with his fork half-way to his mouth. Smiled

slowly at her. "That's cold. I like it."

"So is that a yes?"

"I think... not," he said after a moment. "Let's see what he does next. You think he's trying to intimidate me?"

Julia nodded, pouring another mouthful of wine into the glass. "Most likely." She put both elbows on the table and studied him, the glass dangling from her hand. The fruity aroma of the wine drifted over her. "He was at your place of work. I'm guessing he's trying to throw you off your game. His ultimate goal is probably to get you to bow out of the case."

Sam snorted as he pushed his plate away. "If he's trying to intimidate me, he's a rank amateur. Throwing a beer at me?" He made a scoffing noise. "High school stuff. I get more than one lousy cup of beer on my uniform in the clubhouse. We dump the stuff on each other whenever we win a game."

"What if he escalates?" Julia worried at her lip. Sam needed to take this more seriously.

"Then you can haul his ass back into your station. Arrest him again."

"Okay," she said slowly. "I don't like it, but I can't force you to press charges. Kirby strikes me as the type who will see your restraint as weakness. It'll embolden him."

Sam shrugged one shoulder. "We're leaving on a road trip tomorrow. That'll give him time to settle down."

The thought of Sam being gone made her feel... hollow. And that was a huge red flag. She jumped up from the table and carried both plates to the sink.

"That was delicious," she said, her voice too bright. "Thanks so much for getting the food. And for driving me home."

Sam stood up, too. "I think that's my signal to get out of here and leave you alone."

Julia pressed her fingers into the edges of the plates. Huh. The thought of Sam being gone really *had* upset her. That was alarming. But it was no excuse for being rude.

He'd been really thoughtful. Driven her home. Gotten her food. Dropping the plates in the sink, she turned to face him. "I'm sorry, Sam. It was a long day, and I'm really beat. I know that was rude. I'm... I'm not in the mood for company."

"Not a problem, Julia," he said easily. "It's been a long day for me, too. I have a day game tomorrow before we leave. So I need to get out of here."

"How long... how long will you be gone?" She'd sounded... bereft. *Damn it.*

Sam raised one eyebrow, his lips twitching in a barely concealed smile, and Julia remembered why he got on her last nerve. "In case I need you for the case," she said, hoping she sounded dismissive instead of pitiful.

"Six days. But you can call me whenever you need to talk to me." He paused, his eyes twinkling, and she gritted her teeth. "About the case," he added, his voice too innocent. "What did you think I meant?"

"Good night, Sam," she said, opening her front door.

"'Night, Jules." He leaned toward her and brushed his mouth over hers. Before she could react, he'd straightened and stepped into the hall. "I'll be in touch."

As Julia closed the door, she touched her mouth with one hand. If she was a fanciful woman, she'd say her mouth tingled.

Dropping her hand, she muttered, "Spicy tomato sauce, idiot."

But she found herself at the window, watching Sam's car pull away.

CHAPTER 9

Three days later, Julia watched as Tim Busey walked out of the interrogation room. Busey was the last of the seven guys who'd been with Derek Kirby at the Seventh Inning Stretch the night he'd punched Nick D'Angelo. All seven of them had the same story -- they hadn't seen Derek punch the kid, they hadn't heard anything, they were all simply heading home.

Julia had memorized their spiel and could barely control her eye-roll as Busey had repeated it.

Her gaze now tracked Busey as he trotted down the stairs and out of sight. He'd been the only one of the seven who'd acted uncomfortable. As if the lies bothered him. Maybe he was the weak link she'd been looking for.

She'd wanted to press him, but decided to let him leave. She'd let him stew for a while. Let all of them think they'd outsmarted her.

Julia would go over the tapes of their interrogations and make notes. She'd dig more deeply into their lives. Find out who they were. What mattered to them. She'd ferret out their secrets. Then, when she'd worked out her strategy, she'd get them in the box, one at a time.

Expose their lies and destroy their excuses.

In the meantime, she'd head over to the hospital. The interviews with Kirby's friends, the way they'd all lied, had left her frustrated and angry. She needed to see Nick again. See his mother Sandy, who hadn't left his bedside. Fix the images firmly in her head before she talked to Kirby's buddies again.

Pushing away from her desk, she stuck her head in her captain's office. "I'm heading over to the hospital to see how the D'Angelo kid is doing. His mother is there, and I want to fill her in on what I've done."

Captain Francisco nodded. "Thanks for letting me know." He hesitated. "I'm glad you caught this one, Carleton. You're a bulldog with a bone on a case like this, and I don't want this one dropped. Kirby needs to pay for what he did."

"I'll do my best," Julia promised.

"Yeah. I know you will."

As the captain bent over his paperwork again, it looked as if his short dark hair bristled with indignation about Kirby. Relaxing her shoulders, letting go of the tension, Julia ran down the stairs to her unmarked squad car. Her captain would back her up.

She had two other cases she was juggling. Maybe she didn't need to visit Nick's hospital room -- it wouldn't change anything about how she handled his case.

But Kirby's seven buddies had left her steaming. Their lies, and their casual dismissal of what had happened to Nick, had lit her fuse. She wasn't going to stop until Kirby was behind bars. Seeing Nick in his hospital bed would fuel her determination. And Sandy needed to know Julia would never give up.

Half an hour later, she stepped off the elevator and walked toward the ICU. Sounds were muted, unlike regular hospital floors. The quiet hush of voices, a doctor and nurse huddling with a patient's family in one corner, blended with the mechanical beeps and pings coming from the cubicles.

The nurse's station sat in the center of a large circle, with the individual rooms fanning out like the spokes of a bike. The ugly tan walls and the white linoleum were bare bones. Practical. Easy to clean. Institutional.

The ICU wasn't carefully decorated. There were no homey touches, like pictures on the wall or flowers on the nurses' desk. It was business-like. Practical. All about saving lives. Fancy decorations would be obscene in this place of terror, anxiety and wrenching sorrow.

She'd visited Nick once before, so she knew which cubicle was his. As she walked toward it, she saw the bellows on the ventilators in other rooms inflate and fall. Numbers flashed in bright red and green on various machines. EKG monitors beeped steadily.

The same machines she'd seen in Nick's room the last time she was here.

She slowed as she reached Nick's room. His mother was sprawled over him on the bed, clutching him to her chest, her shoulders shaking. The ventilator was gone. The machines beside Nick's bed were silent and dark.

She stared into the room for a moment, bewildered. Then it hit her.

Nick had died. Shoving her fist into her mouth, Julia backed away. But she couldn't wrench her gaze away from Nick's still form. The sight of his bereft mother, sobbing over her son's body, would be forever etched into Julia's memory.

Grief was a living, breathing shadow, hovering over Sandy D'Angelo.

As Julia backed away, she stumbled into someone behind her. Turning, she saw a nurse in pink scrubs. "You're the detective on Nick's case, aren't you?" the woman asked quietly.

"Yes. Are you…" She swallowed. "You were his nurse?"

"One of them." The nurse clenched and unclenched her hands as she studied Nick and his mother. Then she transferred her gaze to Julia. "You're going to make sure the person who did this to Nick pays, aren't you?"

"Yes. I'm not going to let Kir... the man who punched Nick get away with it. That's why I came here today -- to remind myself what that man did to Nick. To his mother and all Nick's friends. And to assure his mother I'm completely committed to this case."

The nurse touched her on the arm. "I'll let Sandy know you were here. And what you said. She'll appreciate it."

Julia glanced once more at the devastated woman holding her son and felt the weight of her agony. The heavy, suffocating anguish that had overwhelmed Julia after her father died was now a scar that only occasionally ached. But she remembered the deep, searing pain of it. The shock at his sudden death.

She hoped Sandy D'Angelo had plenty of support to get her through the next days and weeks and months. "I don't think Sandy will appreciate anything for a long time."

By the time Julia made it back to her car, her weeping had subsided to only a few tears. Swiping the moisture from her face, she inserted the key into the ignition, but didn't turn on the car. Instead, she turned the key just far enough to roll down the windows.

It was a beautiful spring day. The lilac bushes clustered in front of the apartment building across the street had burst into fragrant lavender blooms. The sun warmed the air and carried the scents of those blossoms into the car, softening the smells of a squad car. The vinyl seats, forever carrying the stench of fear. The disinfectant that couldn't quite banish the stink of urine and vomit. The faint, lingering scent of the late shift guys' burritos that lingered in the small space.

The contrast between the trees and plants, bursting with life, and the emptiness death had left behind in the ICU, sent a few more tears trickling down Julia's cheek.

Taking out her phone, Julia dialed the SA assigned to Nick's case. "Teresa. This is Julia Carleton."

"Hey, Julia," the woman said. "What's up?"

"I'm at the hospital. Nick D'Angelo passed away."

There was a beat of silence. Then Theresa said quietly, "Damn it."

"Yeah. I know his prognosis wasn't good, but still…"

"We hope," Teresa finished.

"Yeah. We hope." Julia swallowed the lump of tears. "Will you upgrade the charges?"

"Damn straight I will. It'll be second degree murder, because his blood test came back this morning. Positive for steroids. His doctor didn't prescribe them, so they're illegal." Theresa sighed. "I wish I could go to first degree, but there was no pre-meditation."

Julia hadn't yet seen the paperwork on the blood test, but she was pleased with the results. It meant the judge could tack a few more years onto his sentence. "Any chance of revoking Kirby's bail?" She wanted Kirby off the street before he could hurt anyone else. Another drunk, stupid kid like Nick.

Or Sam. *Oh, God.* What if Kirby went beyond throwing glasses of beer at him?

"I wish. But I don't think so."

"Okay. I'll try to find enough evidence to make your case a slam dunk."

"Not going to be a slam dunk, Julia," Teresa warned. "He's got a good attorney. One who knows all the tricks. We need airtight evidence."

"Which we have, in the form of that video," Julia pointed out.

Teresa sighed. "You would think. But you know how juries are. Nothing's a slam dunk. And you can bet the asshole's attorney will want a jury trial."

Julia closed her eyes and tilted her head back. Teresa was right. "You might want to call Nick's mom in a few days and tell her you're upgrading the charges against Kirby. It won't bring Nick back, but it's something."

"Yeah, I'll do that." Teresa sighed. "I'll talk to you soon, Julia."

"Yeah. Take care," Julia said as she ended the call.

Forty-five minutes later, Julia's phone chimed as she walked into the bullpen. Pulling it out of her pocket, she saw Sam's name. Her finger hovered over the 'refuse call' icon. She didn't want to tell him Nick had died.

But she'd have to tell him eventually. Might as well do it now. Besides, he'd called about this time every day since he'd left on his road trip. It would be odd if she didn't answer today. He might worry. It could affect his game tonight. So she cleared her throat and pressed the call button. "Hi, Sam."

"Jules." She heard the smile in his voice. Pictured his twinkling eyes. "How's my favorite detective? Are you managing to feed yourself without me there to supervise?"

"Uh, yeah. I'm… I'm eating."

"Jules. What's wrong?" All hint of teasing was gone from his voice. Serious Sam was on the other end of the line. The guy who'd agreed to testify about the video he took, even though he knew it would bring the press down on him. "Tell me."

"Why… why do you think something's wrong?" she finally asked.

"I can tell by your voice. What is it?"

"Hold on a minute." She hurried down the corridor and stepped into the women's room. Locked the door behind her. She didn't want anyone walking in on this conversation. "I just got back from the hospital." Her throat tightened again. She drew a deep breath. "They took Nick off life support today, and he passed away."

"Oh, God," Sam murmured. "That's awful. Jules, I'm so sorry. Especially that I'm not there and you have to deal with it alone."

That's why she'd taken his call, she realized. Because he'd understand. Stand with her.

"I… I didn't know. I went to the hospital without calling. And… and Nick and his mom were still in the room. I left, but it brought back so much… it was so hard."

There was a long pause. "What did it bring back, Jules?" he murmured.

Damn it. She hadn't realized she'd let that slip. She finally said, "We've all lost people. That's all I meant."

"Yes. My dad passed away a few years before I made it to the majors." Sam's voice was subdued. "Saw me play in the minor leagues, but it's not the same. I think about him before every game."

"That has to be hard." She swallowed. "Sorry I brought up those memories."

"Don't be," he said immediately. "Losing my dad left a void, and I'll always miss him. But it's not like Nick's mom, losing her son to senseless violence." Sam cleared his throat. "I don't know how you do your job, Jules. You see this almost every day."

Julia stared at the tiny hexagonal tiles on the restroom floor. The beehive pattern was somehow soothing. If she focused on the tiles, she wasn't picturing Nick and his mom. "I do," she said slowly. "I see a lot of death. But some are a lot harder than others. Nick is one of the hard ones."

"I'll be home in three days," Sam said. "But I'll be thinking about Nick and his mom. And you." There was a pause. "Call me tonight?"

"Yes. I will," she said.

"Okay. Take care of yourself, Jules."

"You, too, Sam."

The phone went dead, and Julia slipped it back into her pocket.

Tears prickled in her eyes. He'd called her every afternoon, between batting practice and his game. She called him late every evening, with updates on the case. Before today, their conversations had been about the fight and the video -- Sam asking questions, her telling him any progress she'd made in the case. But beneath the business had run a current of something definitely un-business-like. Flirting. Teasing. Subtle innuendo.

And she liked it. Her conversations with Sam were the

highlight of her day.

It was okay because it was long distance, she'd told herself. The flirting was safe. Nothing could happen when they were hundreds of miles apart.

When he got back to Chicago, she could change the tone of their interactions. No sexy subtext would color their conversations.

When they were face to face, she'd shut down the flirting. Shut down the connection she felt to him.

Their conversation today blew those lies out of the water.

They hadn't flirted today. Instead, they'd comforted each other. He'd shared something deep and intimate with her. She'd barely stopped herself from blurting out the truth about *her* father's death.

She was kidding herself if she thought they could go back to casual when he returned to Chicago.

Sam was growing on her. She'd been leaning on him today.

That had to stop.

And it would. As soon as Sam got home.

CHAPTER 10

As the team bus rolled down Addison, Sam stared out the window at the night-time city, all bright lights and hidden shadows. The bars and restaurants were lit up, with smiling, laughing people visible through the windows. Couples strolled down the sidewalks, arms wrapped around each other, heads bent close together.

Groups flowed over the sidewalks, as well, splitting to go around the couples, then re-forming. Happy people, enjoying a night on the town.

Sam wanted to be one of those couples. Wanted to be out walking on this beautiful night, his arm wrapped around Julia, her arm tight around his waist.

Dream on, buddy.

Sam and his teammates were mostly quiet after a bruising loss and a short, very bumpy flight. It was late, almost one AM, and the people on the street were probably heading home for the night. Exactly where Sam wanted to be. In his own place. By himself.

Or with Julia.

He closed his eyes and leaned his head on the seat. Julia wouldn't be *there*, either. Not anytime soon.

They'd spent a lot of time talking while he was gone.

The day Nick died, though, their conversations had changed. Become deeper, like the kinds of conversations close friends would have.

But beneath all the phone calls, all the innocuous conversations, awareness hummed like a live wire, snapping and crackling in the charged space between them.

Sam opened his eyes and huffed a laugh as he stared at the mostly dark houses they were passing. That awareness was nothing new. It had been there since the moment they'd spotted each other at his sister's wedding.

It had only intensified since the night they'd met again -- the night Kirby punched Nick. Deepened since their conversation the day Nick died.

Julia wouldn't act on it. And as much as Sam wanted to, he knew he couldn't push her. This case was too important. If they got together and were caught, that expensive lawyer of Kirby's would push to get Sam disqualified as a witness.

The bus turned into the ballpark and rolled into the parking lot. Grabbing his bag, Sam climbed off, said goodnight to his teammates and headed for his car. No one stuck around after a road trip. The guys who were married or had girlfriends were eager to get home. The rest of them just wanted to sleep in their own beds.

Instead of turning left out of the parking lot, though, Sam automatically turned right. Toward Julia's place. He didn't realize it until he was already driving toward her apartment.

Telling himself to turn around, he kept going until he reached her street. Drove slowly past her apartment. No lights. She was in bed.

He slowed to a stop and stared up at her windows. She'd tried to call, but he'd been on the plane, his phone turned off. Too late now to call her back.

"What are you, some kind of creepy stalker?" he muttered to himself.

He pressed the accelerator too hard and his car leapt forward. When he took one last glance in the rear-view mirror, close headlights, bright enough to blind, burned into his vision. Shifting his gaze back to the street in front of him, he turned the corner and headed for home.

At his apartment, the stale, unlived-in air of a home unoccupied for several days greeted him when he walked in the back door. Dropping his bag on his bed, he walked through all the rooms, as he did every time he returned from a road trip. He'd had a break-in a few years ago, when he was in the minor leagues, and checking had become a habit.

When he reached the living room, he opened the blinds. He liked walking out of the bedroom in the morning to sunlight streaming into the room. The street was quiet, as it usually was this late at night. An unfamiliar SUV, large and black, was parked right in front of Sam's house. Someone on the block had company tonight.

Images of Julia scrolled through his mind, and he turned away. Too bad it wasn't him.

The next morning, gripping a cup holder containing a cup of coffee and one of tea, he pulled open the door to Julia's station. The same desk sergeant was at the desk. When the older man looked up and recognized him, his face lit up.

"Hey, Marini. Tough game last night," he said.

Sam rolled his shoulders -- he hated losing. "Yeah. Their pitcher was really on. Can't win them all."

"You here to see Carleton?"

Sam held up the cardboard holder. "Thought I could bribe her with her favorite hot beverage to get some updates on the D'Angelo case."

"You bringing coffee to a cop house?" The sergeant snickered. "Like bringing beer to a ball park."

Sam leaned closer, as if he was divulging a secret. "This is *good* coffee, Sarge. I'll bring one for you next time so you know the difference."

Snorting, the sergeant nodded at the stairs. "You know where to find her."

Sam wanted to take the stairs two at a time. He felt the

sergeant's gaze on his back, though, so he walked up calmly. Like it hadn't been a week since he'd seen Julia.

She'd warned Sam that cops were the biggest gossips he'd ever meet. And if word got around that he was in a hurry to see her, Sam knew she'd be teased unmercifully.

Finally at the top of the stairs and out of sight of the sergeant, he spotted Julia at her desk. A curl from her braid was already loose, and she bent over a stack of papers, frowning.

"Hey," he said as he got close. "Thought you could use some tea."

Her head shot up and her gaze softened as she spotted him striding toward her desk. "Sam," she said, her voice low and soft, a smile lighting her face. "What are you doing here?"

He set the tea next to her hand and settled into her visitor's chair. "Wanted to find out what's new on the case. Since we didn't talk last night." He leaned toward her and lowered his voice. "You called while I was on the plane. I didn't want to talk on the bus, with all the guys around, and once I got home, I didn't want to wake you up."

"I was probably still awake," she said, tucking the curl behind her ear. "You could have called."

She'd missed talking to him. The disappointment in her expression gave her away. Sam sat back in his chair, trying to contain his grin. "That's why I stopped in. To make up for not calling you. Anything new?"

Julia's expression hardened. "Not a thing. I've gotten three of Kirby's pals back in for a second interrogation. When I show them your video, then play back their statements, they just shrug. Say they must have been mistaken who they were talking to. A big group, a long night, a few beers -- you know how it goes."

"What are you going to do?"

"I'm saving one guy for last. Tim Busey. He was the uncomfortable one the first time around. I'll let him hear from all his buddies about their second round with me before I talk to him again.

"I dug into his background," she continued with a 'gotcha' smile. "He's going to law school at night. That might be the perfect wedge to pry him away from Kirby. If he goes under oath and lies, then gets convicted of perjury, he'll never be admitted to the bar." Her eyes gleamed with satisfaction. "If I can get him to crack, some of the others might fall into line. And the ones who don't?" She leaned toward him, her eyes green as sea glass. "I'll have Teresa put them on the stand and dare them to perjure themselves."

"Good job," Sam murmured. He wanted to reach for her hand, touch her, but he curled his hands around the coffee cup instead. "Anything else new?"

"Not a lot." She closed her eyes and took a deep breath. "Nick's funeral is tomorrow."

"Are you going?"

"Yes." When he opened his mouth, she held up her hand. "And I know what you're going to say -- you want to go, too. Right?"

"Of course." He wanted to be there to support her. He knew how hard she'd taken Nick's death. "I want to go with you."

"No. You can't go with me." Regret flickered across her expression, then vanished. Before Sam could figure out if he'd imagined it, Julia continued, "The last thing we need is the appearance of being a couple. And that's exactly what it would look like if we went together.

"I can't stop you from going to that funeral," she added, "but think about it for a moment. The press will be there. With cameras. You're a celebrity. They'll zero in on you." She slid her fingers toward him, as if she wanted to touch him, too. Drew away at the last moment. "You got lucky. Not many people read that blog that named you as the witness. I'm guessing you didn't get any questions about it on your trip?"

"Not one," he said.

Julia nodded, looking satisfied. "That leak didn't work out like they hoped it would. Kirby senior knows, but you haven't had reporters hounding you. Trust me, if you go to Nick's funeral, they'll be on you like a pack of dogs on a bone."

Sam shrugged. "I don't give a damn about reporters. I talk to them every day."

"About your job," Julia pointed out. "That's a lot different than being a witness in a murder case."

This time, she let her fingers drift over his arm. "Think about it, Sam. I know you want to go, but it might not be a smart move."

As she drew her hand away, he stared at her fingers, long and slender and tipped with polished, dark blue nails. A silver ring topped by a flat, black stone adorned her middle finger. He wanted to see her hands on his chest. His face. Feel those delicate fingers on his...

Not here. He grabbed his coffee and took a too-big gulp. It scalded the roof of his mouth and had him sucking in air through pursed lips.

Julia laughed and sat back in her chair. Nodded at his suit. "I assume you're on your way to work?"

"Yeah. Day game. Tough after a road trip, but that's the job." He tilted his head and studied her. "You want me to bring dinner again? Meet you at your place?"

He saw the 'no' in her expression and added quickly, "So you can fill me in on what happened this past week?"

She hesitated, and like an infield pop-up, he knew he had her. So he pounced. "I hear it's going to be barbeque tonight. From Smoque."

She groaned. "You fight dirty, Sam. Okay, fine. Give me a call a half-hour or so before you leave so I can get home."

"Will do," he said, fighting a triumphant smile. He had no idea which restaurant was supplying the food after the game today, but he knew Julia liked Smoque. He'd spotted a bag from the barbeque restaurant in her kitchen pantry.

* * *

It was almost seven that evening when Sam turned the corner onto his street. He'd change his clothes, call Julia, then head over to Smoque to pick up some food.

As he walked toward his house, he spotted the same black SUV that had been there last night. Maybe someone on his block had gotten a new car. Although why they weren't keeping it in their garage was a mystery.

He'd turned onto his sidewalk and was running up his steps when a car door slammed behind him. "Hold on, Marini," a man called.

Sam turned and saw a tall, stocky man with gray hair walking around the front of the black SUV. He remembered the bright lights in his rear view mirror last night, when he was on Julia's street. Had this guy been following him? *Stalking* him?

"Who are you?" Sam asked, tucking his keys between his fingers. They were the only weapon he had if this guy was dangerous.

"I'm Ronald Kirby. Derek's father."

Sam let the keys fall free of his fingers, but held onto them. "You've been following me."

Kirby stared at Sam, his eyes cold. Hard. "I can drive wherever I want."

"You were parked in front of my house last night, too."

Kirby shrugged, as if invading Sam's privacy was his right. "Needed to see which house was yours. I waited for it to light up. Took off after I saw you open the blinds."

"What do you want?" Sam stared down at the man from two steps above him. From the way Kirby's mouth tightened, he didn't like having to look up to Sam.

"Come down here where I can talk to you," he demanded.

"I can hear you just fine where I am. And you've got about five seconds to tell me why you're stalking me."

"I'm not a stalker," Kirby said immediately.

"You just admitted that you'd followed me home. Parked in front of my house twice. I think that constitutes stalking. I should probably call the police."

Sam pulled his phone out of his pocket, his finger poised over the call icon. Kirby reached out, as if he would knock the phone out of Sam's hand. When Sam tightened his fist around the phone, Kirby's fingers curled into his palm. When Sam didn't back down, Kirby slowly lowered his arm.

"You need to refuse to testify at Derek's trial," he said abruptly.

"Why would I do that?"

"Derek made a mistake, but he doesn't deserve to have his whole life ruined. He's just starting out. He has a bright future ahead of him."

Anger coiling in his gut, Sam said, "Nick D'Angelo had a bright future, too. Did you know he was a brilliant computer engineer? That he'd started his own company and got patents for several programs? He was poised to earn a lot of money and make a difference in the world."

Kirby waved his hand, as if dismissing everything Nick was. "An accident."

"It was *not* an accident," Sam said, drawing himself up and sliding the keys between his fingers again as he watched Kirby clench and unclench his fists. "Nick never touched your son. He was half Derek's size. Not a *mistake*, either. Derek punched Nick so hard that he killed him."

"D'Angelo hit Derek first."

"He didn't," Sam said immediately. "I saw the whole thing. Made a video. Nick didn't touch him."

"That video was altered, and I can prove it," Kirby said, climbing the first step. As his jacket flapped open, the gold threads in Kirby's Brioni suit glittered in the lights beside Sam's front door.

He was closer to Sam, but Sam still towered over him.

"It wasn't altered, but go ahead and try." Sam's fist tightened around the keys as he looked down at Kirby. At the rage in his expression. "It won't change a thing. The jury will see that video. They'll see Derek hit Nick, a kid half Derek's size. They'll hear about how he died."

A vein at Kirby's temple pulsed. His face reddened. "I know the owner of your team. I can have you busted back to the minor leagues."

Sam shook his head. "That all you got? You don't know much about baseball, do you?"

"You better not show up in court, Marini."

"Or what, Kirby? You'll make sure I'm fired? Not going to happen. Now get off my property before I call the police."

Kirby stared at Sam for a long moment. Sam stared back. Kirby was bulkier than Sam was, but Sam was quicker. Pretty sure he could take the guy, whose muscles had gone to fat. When Kirby didn't move, Sam lifted his phone. Pressed 911, then let his finger hover over the call icon.

"Last chance, Kirby."

"You have no idea who you're dealing with." Kirby's low voice rumbled with threat. After staring at Sam for a few more seconds, Kirby spun around. He almost lost his balance but managed to recover and stumbled down the step onto the sidewalk.

He stalked to his SUV, slammed the door after he got in, and gunned the engine as he pulled away.

Sam memorized the license plate as he watched the SUV roar down the street, going way too fast.

This had gotten scary very quickly. He'd tell Julia about Kirby's visit when he saw her later.

Julia. The headlights behind Sam when he'd driven to Julia's last night and stopped in front of her building had been Kirby's. Sam had led the bastard right to Julia's home.

Sam hit the call button beside Julia's name as he ran through the gangway toward the garage and his car.

CHAPTER 11

Julia's phone buzzed, and she bit her lip to hide her smile when Sam's name appeared on her phone. Glancing around the bullpen, making sure no one was close enough to overhear her, she pressed the icon.

"Hey, Sam. Are you getting ready to leave the ballpark?"

"Julia." It sounded as if he was running. "Where are you?"

"I'm still at work," she said, her smile slipping. "Is something wrong?" Gripping her phone tight, she shoved away from her desk. Fumbled in her drawer for her purse, ready to run down the stairs and out to her car if he needed help.

"Thank God. Stay there." Sam sounded breathless, and Julia heard a garage door rumbling in the background. "Don't leave before I get there."

Drawing her hand out of the drawer, she asked, "Sam, what's going on?" Her voice was too sharp. Too loud, because Mia Donovan glanced at her from the other side of the room. Mouthed, "Need help?"

"Not sure," Julia mouthed back. Turning her back, she pressed the phone into her ear, hard enough to make the cartilage ache.

"Kirby was just at my house." Sam's hoarse, panting voice had her rising again. "Daddy Kirby. And I think he knows where you live. You shouldn't go home alone."

"He was at your house?" Her heart jump-started. Began to pound. "Are you all right? Did he hurt you?"

"I'm fine. I'm worried about you…" Something crashed, and Sam yelled, "Damn it all to hell."

"What's that?" she demanded, flinching at the noise. "What just happened?"

"I knocked over my garbage can. Gotta clean up the mess. Stay put until I get there."

The phone went dead, and Julia pulled it away from her ear. Stared at it, as if it could magically show her that Sam was all right.

"Hey, Carleton." Mia Donovan stepped in front of her and grabbed her arm. "You okay? You don't look good."

Julia slid her phone into her pocket. "That was Sam Marini. Kirby senior was at his place. I don't know what Kirby said or did, but Sam's… agitated. He hung up before I could get any details."

He'd said he was fine, but he'd knocked over his garbage can. Sam wasn't clumsy. Had Kirby been chasing him? Did the bastard have a gun?

Sam was a smart man. If Kirby had threatened him, he would have called 911.

Wouldn't he?

Smoothing her hands down her jacket, she took a step toward the stairs. Then realized she didn't know Sam's address. It was in the file of information on the D'Angelo case, but she hadn't memorized it.

Sighing, she flipped her braid over her shoulder and headed for her desk again. "Sam said he was on his way to the station," she told Mia. Could she wait that long to make sure he was all right? If she left now, she would probably pass him going the other way.

She strode to the window behind her desk and looked out, as if she could somehow see Sam arriving.

106

Damn it. What had happened to her coolness under fire? Her analytical mind that sorted through the facts before jumping to conclusions?

It all flew out the window when the victim was someone you knew. Someone you... cared about.

Slapping her hand on the window frame, she spun around to find Mia in Julia's desk chair, her hands poised over Julia's keyboard.

"What's your password?" Mia glanced up at her. "I'm gonna look Kirby up. Find out where he lives so we can haul the bastard in here. Charge him with harassment."

Julia nudged Mia out of her chair and took her place in front of the computer. Closed her eyes for a moment to let herself settle. Then her fingers flew, looking for Kirby's address and make of car. "Getting a little ahead of ourselves, Donovan," she said as she searched for Ronald Kirby. "We need to talk to Sam first."

She nodded in satisfaction as Kirby's driver's license popped up on the screen. Scribbling down his address -- another high rise in the loop -- she wanted to agree with Mia. Go pick Kirby up and harass *him* a little.

Spinning her chair away from the computer, she took a deep breath. Closed her eyes and took another. She needed to think like a cop, not a... a smitten woman, damn it. "We don't even know what happened -- only that Kirby showed up at Sam's house," she finally said to Mia. "We need more information."

Mia dropped onto the corner of her desk. "You're no fun, Carleton. Can't you picture us arresting Kirby senior?" She bit her lip around a smile, her eyes twinkling. "I can. Good times. I'd pay to be in on that."

In spite of the worry gnawing at her, Julia smiled briefly at Mia's enthusiasm. "Yeah, I want to drag him in here. Throw him in an interrogation room and let him stew for an hour or two. And maybe we will, after Sam gets here."

"Donovan. My office." Captain Francisco stuck his head out the door and motioned to Mia. His dark hair looked wrong. As if he'd run his fingers through it too many times.

She slid off Julia's desk and glanced over her shoulder. "Don't you go after Kirby without me."

"You're first on the list," Julia assured her, then watched, her gaze switching from Mia to the captain. Something was up.

Mia waved over her shoulder as she walked into the captain's office. After a moment, the door closed, and Julia frowned. Mia wasn't in trouble, was she?

That was hard to believe, because Mia, who'd passed her detectives exam six months ago, was already one of the best detectives in the district. Julia was glad she'd stayed at the twenty-third after she got her detective's shield.

She glanced at Mia's brother Connor, who was also watching the captain's office. "Hey, Con," she called in a low voice, "everything okay with Mia?"

"Far as I know," Connor said, still staring at the office door.

Julia realized she still had her phone clutched in her hand. She glanced at it, but there was nothing from Sam. Nerves jumped beneath her skin as she noticed the time. Sam had called fifteen minutes ago.

She stood, calculating in her head. Sam had been walking home from the ball park the night of the fight, so he had to live close by. The station was close to the baseball stadium, so it shouldn't take him long to get here.

Had he damaged his car when he knocked over his garbage can?

Run into traffic from the baseball game?

Had Kirby come back?

Damn it! She shoved her hand through her hair and began to pace. She should have told him to stay put. That she'd come to him. He wasn't supposed to rush over here to protect her. Protecting people was *her* job.

She wasn't used to people trying to protect her. She liked being in charge. Liked being the one with a gun. Sam going all protective should irritate her.

It hadn't, though. Knowing Sam had her back felt... good. It was nice to have someone to lean on once in a while.

Snatching her purse from her desk drawer, she slung it over her shoulder and pushed the call button next to Sam's name as she hurried toward the stairs. The sound of a phone ringing drifted up the stairwell, and footsteps pounded up the stairs. Sam burst into view, running toward her desk.

"Julia!" He skidded to a stop and wrapped his arms around her. Pulled her close and buried his face in her hair. "You're here. Thank God."

For the space of a heartbeat, Julia was so relieved to see him that she sagged into him. Let herself cling to him. After a few moments, though she tore herself away from Sam, her face flaming. Put two feet of space between them. "Stop it," she groaned, even though every cell in her body screamed at her to move back into his embrace. Touch him everywhere. Reassure herself that he was okay. Make sure Kirby hadn't hurt him.

Instead, she shoved him farther away, then glanced around the room to see if anyone had noticed. Connor Donovan raised an eyebrow at her and smirked. Then fluttered his eyelashes and made kissing noises.

She was going to kill Sam. "Stuff it, Donovan," she yelled, cringing at the way the sound echoed off the walls.

Then she grabbed Sam's arm and steered him toward her desk. Pushed him into her guest chair. "What the hell were you thinking?" she hissed at him. "Hugging me where everyone could see?"

Sam leaned closer. "I was thinking how damn glad I was that you were still here. I was afraid you'd ignored me and gone home. Found Kirby waiting for you." He rubbed his hand over his face, and Julia heard the faint rasp of his whiskers. "I was so relieved to see you." He closed his eyes. "I didn't stop to think. Just reacted."

Julia stared at Sam, his fingers now pressed into his eyes. Her anger faded away, replaced with what felt like... pleasure. She was gooey inside, like a marshmallow that's crispy on the outside and soft sweetness in the middle. *Damn it, Sam*. When had he turned her into a sap?

"Don't touch me like that here," she muttered. Her face was still hot, and she pressed her palms against her cheeks. "Do you have any idea how much crap I'll get for that?"

"No one's here besides Donovan." Sam shot a glance at Connor, who was bent over his desk. "He's not going to say anything."

"Not the point, Sam. You're a witness in one of my cases. And you get all huggy in front of other cops? What were you thinking?"

"I already told you. I wasn't thinking," he said with a sigh. "Do you have any idea how terrified I was that you wouldn't take me seriously?"

"I take you very seriously, Sam," she said, realizing it was true. She'd counted down the hours for his phone calls every day. Like a teenager with her first crush.

A disorienting mixture of fear and excitement bubbled through her veins. She blew out a breath, trying to calm down. To regain control.

Sam leaned closer, his breath warm on the sensitive skin beneath her ear. "I take you pretty seriously, too, Jules. And not just because of this case."

There it was. The line she'd drawn in the sand was obliterated. And she was as much at fault as Sam.

Okay. She'd work at figuring this out later. Right now, it was time to do her job. "You want to tell me what happened with Kirby?"

She let her gaze drift over his body. No marks on his face. His suit wasn't wrinkled. His shoes weren't scuffed. She picked up his right hand -- no scrapes or swollen knuckles. "It doesn't look like he attacked you physically. Right? You're not hurt?"

Sam's eyes darkened as he watched her study him. As

she touched his knuckles, trailed her fingers over his palm, his skin heated beneath her touch. When she let him go, he reached for her. Gripped her hand for a moment, calluses on his palm rough against her skin.

"I'm fine, Jules." His voice was low, meant only for her. "He didn't touch me. Just blustered and threatened." He shook his head. "Like he thought I was going to fold as soon as he showed up at my house."

"How did he find out where you live?" Julia's heart was racing. But it wasn't because she was worried about Sam. It was because...

Because she was touching him.

Clearing her throat, she extracted her hand from his. Resisted the impulse to touch the places he'd touched. Instead, she curled her hands together on her desk, a reminder not to touch Sam again.

A muscle in Sam's jaw clenched and unclenched, and he drummed his fingers on her desk. "He followed me home last night," he finally said, and she heard his irritation. "There are usually a few fans at the park when we get back from a road trip. He probably stood with them, waited until I pulled out of the parking lot, then got into his car and followed me. Easy enough, especially when the person you're following has no clue what's up. I didn't even look for a tail."

"Why would you?" she asked, drawing a deep breath. This was what she needed to do. Focus on business. Not on the way Sam's hand felt in hers. "It's not like you were expecting Kirby to come after you."

"I should have thought about a fan following me." His shifted in the chair, suddenly uncomfortable. "Some of them can be pretty aggressive."

Julia wondered if he'd been followed home before. Wondered if it had been a female fan. When she realized her fingers had curled into claws, she pressed her palms on the desk and took a deep breath.

"I'm going to fill out a report." She opened her

computer program to the right page as she spoke. "Based on what you tell me, I'll make a decision about arresting him for stalking and assault." She took a deep breath. This was good. She needed to focus on her job.

"He didn't touch me."

"Doesn't matter. Did he threaten you? If he did, that's assault."

Sam shrugged one shoulder. "He didn't threaten me physically." Some of the tension in his shoulders eased. "He said I had no idea who I was dealing with. Right after he said he was gonna get me busted back to the minors."

"Arrogant jerk," she said. Then she tilted her head. "He couldn't do that, could he?"

Sam's expression eased into what could almost be called a smile. "Not a chance in hell."

"Okay. Good." Anger at Kirby simmered, and she nurtured it. It was good to be reminded who the Kirbys were, both father and son. Swaggering, entitled bullies.

It kept her focused on how important it was that they be held liable. That she succeed.

"You said you think he might know where I live," she said in a low voice.

Sam glanced around the bullpen. "Not here," he said. "I'll tell you later. Can you leave?"

"After I fill out a report about this," she said, clicking on the correct form.

"Are you going to arrest him?" Sam asked, leaning over to look at the form.

"Depends on what actually happened. Start at the beginning."

Forty-five minutes later, Julia saved the report and closed it. Swiveled in her chair to face Sam. "We can't make an assault charge stick -- 'I'll have you fired' was the worst of it -- and you sounded pretty positive he can't back it up. I *am* going to arrest him for witness intimidation, though. His expensive lawyer will get him out on bail, just like he did for Kirby junior, but it's important to send a message."

Fury churned inside Julia. She wanted to rush to Kirby's place now and haul him in. She took a deep breath. Let it out slowly.

"I'm going to make sure he understands that witness intimidation is a crime. If he does it again, there will be consequences. Even his fancy lawyer won't be able to get him bailed out the next time he comes near you."

"Finally, I'm going to ask for an order of protection against him. He won't be allowed to come within a hundred feet of you."

"No." Sam shook his head immediately. "I don't want you to do that. Orders of protection make the news, especially if a celebrity is involved." He rolled his shoulders. "Not that I consider myself a celebrity," he added hastily. "But if you get that order of protection, people will find out. And it won't take long before they make the connection to Nick's case and Derek Kirby and his father. They'll know I was the witness who saw Kirby punch Nick.

"No reporters asked me about it on the trip. Not even the Chicago beat guys, and I have no idea why. That blog *did* name me." He scrunched his forehead, as if he was puzzled.

Julia was, too. She'd expected that to be big news, and she'd wondered why it hadn't been. Something else big must have broken in the news that day. "Okay. No order of protection." She sat back in her chair, bouncing a pen against the desk. Deciding how much to tell Sam. "I want him to be publicly humiliated," she finally admitted.

"Then don't go after him tonight," Sam said immediately. "Arrest him at his office tomorrow morning. Take him out of the building in handcuffs."

One side of Julia's mouth curled into a smile. "That's cold. And brilliant." She turned to see if Mia was still here, to make sure she was working the morning shift, but didn't spot her. "Not nearly as much drama if we arrest Kirby at his home."

"We done here, then?" Sam asked.

"Give me a minute, then we can go."

She pushed away from her desk and hurried over to Connor, who was studying some autopsy photos. Thank goodness Julia had left Sam at her desk. "Hey, Con, is Mia still around?"

Connor frowned. "No. She took off right after talking to Francisco. She's on an undercover op. No idea how long."

"Damn. She wanted to help me to arrest Kirby senior. I'm gonna do it tomorrow morning."

"Get him at work?" Connor smiled. "Great idea. I'll be here, and I'd love to be your backup." He looked over her shoulder and shuffled the graphic photos beneath some other papers. "Hey, Marini," he said as Sam came up behind her. "What did Carleton arrest you for?"

"For kicking your ass at your mother's Sunday dinner a couple of weeks ago," Sam said immediately. "You suck at softball, man."

"Not exactly a level playing field," Connor shot back. "Let's shoot some hoops, funny guy, and then we'll see who sucks."

Julia looked from Sam to Connor, surprised they seemed to know each other well. And oddly pleased that they clearly liked each other. "Sounds like it could be an interesting basketball game."

"You in, Carleton?" Connor said immediately. "If I get Mia, too? I know the two of you play in a winter league."

"I could be convinced," she said.

"You're on my team," Sam said.

"No way, Baseball Boy." Connor shook his head. "She's on the cop team."

"We'll negotiate," Sam said.

"Whew!" Julia interrupted, fanning the air in front of her. "I've got to get out of here. You two go ahead and bump chests, but I'll get testosterone poisoning if I breathe this air much longer." She headed back to her desk, saying over her shoulder, "So long, Sam. Take it easy, Con. Tell

114

Mia I'll miss her tomorrow."

Julia smiled to herself as she heard Sam's footsteps behind her, hurrying to catch up. He followed her down the stairs and out the door into the parking lot.

"Trying to get away from me, Jules?" Sam's voice rasped against her ear.

"No, just ready to eat dinner." She stopped beside her vehicle, a small hybrid, and looked over her shoulder. "I was told Smoque was on the menu at the ballpark today."

Sam cleared his throat. "Yeah. About that. I wasn't entirely truthful."

Julia frowned, happy to be teasing Sam instead of taking his statement about Kirby. Maybe lightening the mood was something they both needed. "You lied to me? About food?"

"Not exactly. There would have been food from Smoque, if Kirby hadn't shown up at my house."

Julia leaned against her car, her cheerful mood dissipating. "What's that supposed to mean?"

"I saw a bag from Smoque in your pantry the last time I was there." Sam's ears reddened. "I was going to go to the restaurant and pick up some food."

In spite of herself, Julia was charmed. And touched. He would have gone out of his way to get a meal he thought she liked. "That's sweet, Sam," she said, her voice too soft.

He shrugged. "I'll do it next time. You have a favorite carry-out place near you?"

Next time. That sounded as if Sam thought they'd be eating together regularly. Ignoring the burst of happiness glowing inside her, she tried to focus on business. She needed to hear the rest of his story. Why he thought Kirby might know where she lived.

"There's a good Chinese place a few blocks away. I'll stop there and meet you at my place," she said as she slipped into the car. Just business, she told herself.

Really? When butterflies were dancing in her stomach? When had she gotten into the habit of lying to herself?

CHAPTER 12

Sam watched Julia drive away in her little blue hybrid -- who knew the tough detective would drive such a whimsical vehicle -- then climbed into his SUV and headed toward her apartment.

He found a spot at the curb a few buildings down from hers and stepped out of the car. Locked it, but kept the keys in his hand.

Kirby didn't strike him as a stupid man. He wouldn't have gotten far in business if he didn't think before he acted. But the man who'd driven away from Sam's house a couple of hours ago had been livid. Completely incensed. So maybe he wasn't thinking clearly. Maybe he'd stormed over here, not even thinking about the repercussions of showing up at a cop's house, spoiling for a fight.

Her street was deserted. No one walked down the sidewalk. No cars driving on the street. As he approached Julia's house, he stopped and listened.

The rumble of cars on Lake Shore Drive, a few blocks east, was faint but steady. A helicopter flew overhead, probably checking traffic on the Drive. Somewhere to the west, a car horn blared.

But here on Julia's block, all was quiet.

Sam didn't like the quiet. Or the dimming light. Dusk was creeping over the neighborhood, turning the trees into long, twisted shadows against the buildings. The purpling of the sky cast the bushes in front of the three-flats into darkness.

He wanted to see people on the sidewalk, commuters coming home from work. He wanted other cars to be looking for parking spots. He wanted to see a bunch of high school kids, laughing and talking, coming home from an early evening soccer game.

Something to make the moment feel normal.

Walking up the sidewalk toward Julia's building, he saw a flicker of movement on the gangway between her house and the one next door. There just for a moment, then gone.

Without thinking, Sam trotted down the narrow cement path toward Julia's back yard. As he got closer, he spotted the white garage behind the three-flat. Did Julia park there at night?

Had someone been waiting for her?

Sam wrenched open the gate and stepped into the alley. A man dressed in dark clothes and wearing a dark ski hat slid through an open gate three houses down. The gate clicked shut behind the guy, and the six-foot-tall wooden fence didn't allow Sam a view into the yard.

Sam stared at the fence, waiting for the man to reappear. Listened for the sound of a door opening into a house. Or another gate opening.

Nothing. It was as if the man had been a ghost, gliding into the shadows, then disappearing.

Not Kirby, though. Shadow-man had been too slender. He'd moved too quickly, too fluidly, to be the bulky older man. So maybe it was just someone taking a short-cut home.

Or maybe not. Who wore a ski hat on a mild day in May?

Sam was damn glad he'd accompanied Julia home.

Five minutes later, the garage door springs groaned as

the heavy door rumbled up. Julia drove into the garage, killed the engine and got out of the car, holding her purse and a brown paper bag, stapled shut at the top.

"All good here?" she asked, walking out of the garage and pressing a button to close the door.

"I'm not sure," Sam said slowly.

Julia spun around to face him. "What does that mean?"

"Let's go inside." He took the paper bag and followed her up the poorly-lit back stairs. The light by her kitchen door was off, and the locks were silvery circles in the gathering darkness.

As Julia started to insert the key into the deadbolt, Sam snatched her hand away. "Have you looked at the lock? Made sure no one tampered with it?"

Julia glanced at him over her shoulder. "You *are* jumpy tonight."

But she crouched in front of the door, pulled a flashlight from her purse and shone it on the metal. Stared at it for what felt like hours.

Finally she stood. "There are marks on the lock," she said, her voice flat. "Like someone tried to get in."

She turned to face him. "I've never looked at the lock closely. Those marks could have been here for a long time. But they're shiny. Like they're fresh."

She stared at him for a long moment, and Sam's heart raced at the uneasiness in her expression. Then she unlocked the door, used her coat to open the knob, and walked inside.

Once the door was shut and the deadbolt engaged, she flipped on the lights. "I'll get the evidence techs out here tomorrow to dust for prints." She shrugged out of her jacket, leaving her in a pale blue shirt with her black pants. Clutching the jacket, she stared at the back door. "Those scratches could have been there for a long time."

"Or maybe not," Sam said quietly. He set the bag of food on the table, opened her fridge and helped himself to a beer. "You mind?" he asked, glancing at her over his shoulder, belatedly realizing he should have asked before he raided her refrigerator.

"Of course not. In fact, grab one for me."

Julia didn't seem to mind that he'd made himself at home. He suddenly felt much more cheerful.

Sam pulled out two bottles of New Glarus Spotted Cow and stared at them. "Where did you get this stuff?" He knew it was only sold in Wisconsin.

"A friend was up there last weekend, and I asked him to bring some back for me."

Julia walked toward the living room, flicking on lights as she went. Sam wanted to ask her who her friend was. A fellow cop? Someone closer to her?

When she returned moments later, he was still staring at the beer. "Is there a problem?" she asked. "Don't you like Spotted Cow?"

"No, I love the stuff. Just surprised you had it." The question burned on his tongue, but he refused to ask. Not his business. He had no claim on Julia. No matter how much he wanted to stake one.

Julia sighed and sank into one of the kitchen chairs. Studied him. "Just ask, Sam. I know you want to."

"Ask what?" He frowned, trying to look completely bewildered.

Rolling her eyes, Julia said, "Quinn Donovan. He and Tessa went to Wisconsin to visit his cousins. I asked him to pick up the Spotted Cow while he was up there. Okay?"

"I wasn't going to ask," Sam muttered.

"You were *so* going to ask. You wouldn't have been able to stand it."

She was right. Sometime during the evening, he would have blurted out the question. Clearing his throat, he said, "Moving on. I asked you to check the lock because I think there was someone in your back yard when I got here."

Julia's tiny smirk disappeared as she shot upright. "Are you sure?"

"Not positive," he admitted. "But I think so. I saw

something against the bricks on the side of your building when I walked toward your front door. I ran down the gangway into your back yard, but no one was there. So I went into the alley. A guy wearing all black, including a black ski hat, was going into a yard a few houses down. I didn't get a look at his face. But I stood there and listened until your garage door opened. Didn't hear a thing. Like he was waiting behind that fence for me to go away."

"Do you think it was Kirby?" Julia's fingers were pressed into the table, darkening her nails.

"I'm sure it wasn't." Sam paced around Julia's tiny kitchen. "He was shorter, thinner and faster than either of the Kirbys." He sat down and reached for Julia's hand. "Kirby has plenty of money," he said. "He can hire people to do all kinds of things."

"But why would he send someone to my house?" Julia asked slowly. "It's *you* he's trying to influence. I'm just the detective who arrested his kid."

She hadn't taken her hand away, and Sam tightened his hold on her. Ran his thumb across the back of her hand. Touched the calluses on her palm with his fingers and wondered how she'd gotten them. "Maybe he wants you to stop doing your job, at least where his kid is concerned. Scare you into backing off. Or maybe he wants you to get me to forget about testifying."

Julia tightened her grip on his hand. "He doesn't know me very well if he thinks I'm backing down. Or that I'd ask you to step away."

"No, he doesn't." Sam grinned. "I'll bet you a thousand bucks he's going to be shocked when you arrest him tomorrow."

"I wouldn't take that bet, even if I had a thousand dollars." A shadow crossed her face, disappearing so quickly he wasn't sure he'd seen it. Sam leaned closer. He wanted to know where that shadow had come from.

Before he could ask, Julia let go of his hand and reached for the bag of food sitting on the table. "I'm starving. Let's eat before the food gets cold."

Sam motioned for her to stay seated. He got plates from the pantry and silverware from the drawer he'd seen Julia open last time they ate together. Maybe Julia had forgotten that he'd said Kirby might know where she lived. He hoped so -- he didn't want to confess that he'd driven by her place last night.

By the time he set everything on the table, she'd opened the containers of food. "I didn't know what you liked," she said. "So I got a bunch of things."

The sharp, tangy aroma of garlic and ginger drifted out of the cartons. Sam leaned closer and smiled when he saw moo goo gai pan. "You must have read my mind. This is one of my favorites."

"Mine, too." She lifted a pancake out of the carton, then pushed the box toward him. As she smeared sauce on the pancake and piled on meat and vegetables, she said, "Tell me why you think Kirby knows where I live."

Sam's hand faltered, and a splash of the sauce dropped onto his pancake. He should have known Julia wouldn't forget. "I think he might have followed me over here last night. When he followed me home."

He didn't look at her, focusing instead on constructing the moo goo gai pan. He didn't want to see her expression. She'd be angry. He could deal with her anger. But he didn't want to see exasperation, as if he were a fly she wanted to swat.

And he didn't want Julia to see his embarrassment. He'd never meant for her to find out that he'd driven past her apartment like a callow, love-sick teenager.

Her fingers brushed his arm, and he jumped. Dropped his filled pancake onto his plate and looked at her.

"Sam. Why did you drive by my place last night?" She didn't look exasperated or angry. Only confused.

Wiping his hands on a napkin, he dropped it onto the table and stood up. Paced the confines of her tiny kitchen. "I missed you, Jules," he said, knowing he was treading on forbidden ground. "I missed you a lot. Talking every day was great, but I wanted to see you."

Shaking his head, he dropped back into his chair. "It was stupid. I was looking for a light in your apartment. I'm not even sure what I would have done if I'd seen one. And when your apartment was dark, I realized how late it was. So I went home."

"And you think Kirby followed you to my place, then followed you all the way home," she said slowly.

"Yes. There were bright headlights in my rear-view mirror when I stopped in front of your building. And I didn't pay any attention after I drove away. But since he didn't deny that he'd followed me home from the ball park, I think it's a safe bet he suspected you lived here. Easy enough to pay an online site to confirm it."

Julia didn't say anything as she took another bite of her rolled-up pancake. Finally, after she'd washed it down with a drink of beer, she reached for Sam's hand.

"Don't worry about it, Sam. If he wanted it badly enough, he would gotten my address. You said it yourself - - he's got the money to pay for what he wants. Don't beat yourself up. You're not a cop. Why would you have thought of that?"

"It was stupid," he muttered. "*I* was stupid. Wasn't thinking."

Her hand tightened on his. "It wasn't stupid, Sam," she said softly. "I missed you, too. More than I thought I would. And that's a problem."

She tried to draw her hand away, but Sam held it tightly. "I know it is. You don't want to do anything to endanger the case against Kirby. I get that. But would it really be that bad if we were dating?"

"I think so," she said, tugging her hand away from him. "If someone saw us in public and Kirby found out we were dating, his attorney could claim we were conspiring to incriminate Derek. He couldn't prove it, but the jury would hear it. Worse, he might be able to get you taken off the witness list."

"But we weren't dating when Nick was killed. I didn't even know where to find you." And he'd looked. But his sister Cilla had refused to tell him where Julia worked. All she would say was that Julia didn't date guys who were in the public eye. The Donovans had all kept their mouths shut, too.

"Doesn't matter," Julia said, pushing the remains of her pancake through the dark brown sauce on her plate. "What matters is the way his lawyer will frame it for the jury. So, no, we can't take a chance on being seen together in public."

She took a deep breath. "Which is why we won't work. I can't date anyone who's high profile. Anyone who's in the public eye."

"Why is that?" he asked, frowning.

Julia shook her head, avoiding his gaze. "I just can't."

"Mia Donovan is a detective," he pointed out, "and she's engaged to a damn movie star. Finn O'Rourke is a lot more high-profile than I am."

Julia pushed away from the table. "It's not about the job. It's personal. I don't want to be in the spotlight."

Tiny lines bracketed her mouth. She was biting the inside of her lip. Her hands were clenched tightly at her sides. It was easy to read the stress in her tight, tense expression.

"We won't go out in public, then." Sam reached for her hand again, disappointed but not surprised when she moved out of his reach. "If you're telling me this can't get serious, that's okay. I get it." He was actually relieved that he didn't have to have the 'I'm not looking for anything serious at this point in my life' conversation with Julia. He didn't want to settle into a relationship until he was firmly fixed in his career. When he didn't have to devote all his energy to his job.

Ignoring the sense of loss, the hollowed-out feeling of turning his back on something precious, he said, "We can get carry out for meals, and instead of going to movies, we'll watch Netflix. Nightclubs?" He shuddered. "Not crazy about that scene, anyway. Too many fans." He curled his pinky finger around hers, ridiculously thrilled when she didn't pull away. "We'll do what we've *been* doing. Talk. Hang out. At your place, or at mine. We don't need to go out in public to have fun together."

"Sneak around, in other words." She looked over at him, her tense shoulders relaxing as she popped the last bite of her pancake into her mouth. A tiny spot of shiny sauce lingered in the corner of her mouth, and he reached up and wiped it away.

Her lip was soft beneath his thumb. Smooth as silk. He dragged it over her plump bottom lip, then licked his finger while holding her gaze.

Her eyes darkened, and he reached for his moo goo gai pan again, smiling. "You have no idea how much fun sneaking around can be."

He locked his gaze on hers as he stared across the kitchen table. Leaned closer. "Wanna give it a try?"

CHAPTER 13

Julia's lip burned where Sam had caressed it. She wanted to ignore it. Wanted to take another helping of food and pretend his touch hadn't affected her. But she couldn't resist running her tongue over her lower lip.

Sam's eyes darkened as he watched her. He froze, his fork clattering to his plate, still as a hawk who'd spotted his prey. She could almost hear his heart rate speed up as he calculated the best time to pounce.

Julia stared back, helpless to look away. Helpless to break the tension that quivered between them in the too-small space of the kitchen. The walls pressed closer, nudging her toward Sam.

The air heated. Pulsed with the sharp, clean scent of him.

Blended with the scent of her own arousal.

She moved. Away from him? Toward him? She wasn't sure, because Sam swooped at the same time. His hand curled around the back of her head, his fingers tunneling through her braid. The pressure of his fingertips on her scalp had her eyes fluttering closed. A tiny whimper escaped, and Sam swallowed the sound with his mouth.

She expected him to plunder. To devour her mouth, to

plunge inside, to *take*. To do everything she'd dreamed of him doing. Everything she yearned to do to him.

Instead, his mouth gentled on hers. He touched her lip with his tongue, making her shudder with need. Licked at the traces of plum sauce he'd smeared over her lower lip, humming with pleasure. Took tiny, teasing nips that had her opening to him. Welcoming him.

But instead of invading her mouth, instead of deepening the kiss, he trailed his tongue along the sensitive flesh on the inner side of her lip. Lazily, as if he had all night to explore. As if he wanted to savor every part of her mouth, catalog every flavor he found.

Not enough. She wanted more. Needed more. Without taking her mouth away from his, she shoved away from the table, pushed him back into his chair and swung one leg over his thighs. Settled on his lap, the heat of his body burning into her. Through her thighs. Her hands, which cupped his face. Her chest, flattening against his.

Between her legs, where the hot, heavy weight of him pressed against the juncture of her thighs.

"Jules," he groaned, sliding his tongue against hers. Caressing it. Heating her blood to boiling. She opened her mouth wider, wanting more. Wanting all of him.

As their tongues danced, Sam eased his chest away from hers. Her aching, swollen breasts missed the contact immediately, and she fumbled for the lapels of his jacket, trying to pull him close again.

He smiled against her mouth. "I knew it would be this way," he murmured as he brushed her hands to the side. Moments later, she felt an eddy of cool air against her chest. Then his hands, covering her bare breasts.

She arched into him as his fingers traveled over her skin. He tested her weight in his palms, one finger stroking the undersides of her breasts. He drew circles around her areolae, coming closer and closer but not touching her tight, throbbing nipples. Squirming on his lap, she reached for his hands, trying to direct him where she wanted him.

He resisted her easily as he drew away from their kiss. "I'm playing here," he said as he trailed his mouth down her neck. "My rules."

She squirmed against him, pressing him more tightly against her, and he froze as his cock surged against her. Through the barriers of her clothes and his, he was growing even larger, and his heat burned into her.

"I want to play, too," she said, nipping on his earlobe, then sucking it into her mouth. As she pulsed it against the roof of her mouth, he slid his mouth down to the valley between her breasts. Kissed his way to her right nipple, finally swirling his tongue around it.

Julia gasped, letting his earlobe pop free. Rocking into him, she nipped desperately at his neck as he sucked gently on her nipple. His lips curved at the sounds he drew from her, and he switched his attention to her other nipple. His fingers replaced his mouth on the one he'd abandoned.

"Saaam." Her moan stretched out his name as her climax gathered, tightened in her belly. "Don't stop," she managed to say. "Please don't stop."

He let her go long enough to lift her, repositioning her so her breasts were closer to his mouth. So her clitoris was closer to his cock. When his mouth and hands returned to her breasts, she rocked faster against him, desperate for the release that was right there.

When he slid one hand to the seam of her pants, pressing hard, she exploded, her cries bouncing off the kitchen walls. She collapsed against his chest, her orgasm going on and on and on, and he stroked his hands down her back, holding her tightly. Gentling her.

Finally, after her breathing slowed and her body cooled, she eased away from him. Lifted to his mouth and kissed him again, gently this time. "Sam. That was... that was amazing." She did what she'd wanted to do for days -- let her fingers tangle in his hair. It was softer and thicker than she'd imagined, and she dragged her short nails over his scalp. Kissed him again, letting herself taste him this time.

The ginger and sesame lent an exotic overtone to the taste of the beer. Lost in the flavors of his mouth, she lingered until he gently eased away.

"Sam." She rocked against him, thrilled when he arched into her. "I want you. Want *my* chance to play. I want to watch *you* come apart when I…"

He clamped his hands on her hips, holding her still, gripping her so hard that she felt his desperation. How much he wanted to continue. When she stopped trying to move, he loosened his grip and touched his mouth to hers. "I want that, too, Jules. But not tonight. I wasn't expecting this to happen, and I'm pretty sure you weren't, either. I don't have protection. Unless you do?"

He raised one eyebrow, his expression desperately hopeful.

She shook her head, wrapping her arms around him and burrowing close. "No," she murmured into his neck, aching with regret. She didn't keep condoms in her nightstand drawer. She wasn't into one night stands, and it had been a long time since she'd been in a relationship. "But we wouldn't need condoms if I…"

"No. Not that, either. I want to be inside you, Jules, and I don't want to make a mistake in the… in the heat of the moment."

He wrapped his arms around her and pulled her against him. "Let's put this food away, then I'm going home. The longer I'm here, the more I'm tempted. And I don't want to take any chances with you." He rubbed his cheek against her hair, the rasp of his stubble making her shiver. "I'll be more prepared the next time. And when we're naked in bed, we'll talk about how we'll stay below the radar."

Julia felt a pang of sorrow. She'd told Sam that it couldn't be serious, and she knew that whatever was between them would have to end eventually. If she and Sam went public, sooner or later, someone would recognize her. The whole sordid, ugly mess that was her father's life and death would be resurrected, and Sam would be tarred with the brush of that scandal.

She wouldn't do that to him. Couldn't. Since he'd walked back into her life, she'd devoured every story about him in the Chicago newspapers. The articles made clear he was one of the most popular players on the Bearcats, a young star destined for greatness. She wasn't going to drag him into the mud. Tar him with the stain of her father's crimes. Because even if he could weather the storm, he would always have the shadow of her past in his life.

So she and Sam would enjoy each other privately and keep their distance in public. Eventually, they'd go their separate ways. It made her heart ache, but she'd let him go, for the sake of his career and his life.

And her own.

She'd had to prove herself, time and again, as a police officer and then as a detective. If everyone knew about her past, she'd be on the defensive for the rest of her career as a police officer. Savvy criminals would use it as a weapon when she arrested them. Some of her fellow officers, or their parents, had no doubt lost money because they trusted her father. Julius Landon's victims had included both the wealthy and small investors -- he hadn't cared who he stole from.

She'd gone to great lengths to hide her relationship to Julius Landon -- even taken her mother's maiden name at the height of the scandal.

For both her sake and Sam's, this could never be more than casual.

She slid off his lap, the loss of contact with his body an aching loss. Instead of looking at him, she focused on buttoning her shirt. If her hands trembled, he'd think it was because of the way he'd made her come undone.

He wouldn't know it was the thought of eventually saying goodbye to him.

At the front door, she wrapped her arms around him and held him tightly. Closed her eyes and breathed in his fresh-air scent. Sam smoothed his hand down her back, and she felt the hardness of his erection against her belly. Next time, she vowed, it would be his turn.

"I have a night game tomorrow," he murmured into her hair. "I won't get out of the ballpark until after eleven, and that's if it doesn't go into overtime. I know you probably have to work the next day. I'll call you tomorrow, though. See if we can find a way to get together."

"Okay." She wanted to tell him to come over anyway. That it wouldn't be too late. She'd welcome him whenever he was done working.

"I'll see you soon, Jules," he murmured, leaning away to look down at her. She met his gaze, saw the desire in his eyes, the determination in his expression. "Next time we get together, we'll figure out a place to meet, somewhere we don't have to worry about Kirby seeing us."

Pressing one last kiss to his mouth, she murmured, "Yes, Sam. Soon. Please."

This time, as she watched his car pull away from the curve, she pressed her palm to the glass, not caring if he saw her. She stayed at the window until his taillights disappeared around the corner, two blocks down.

She couldn't fall for Sam. Couldn't allow this to become serious. She knew that.

But the ache in her chest tightened until she could barely breathe. How the hell was she supposed to hold herself back from Sam?

* * *

The following morning, Julia took a deep breath as she reached for the door to the downtown Kirby Building. She glanced at Quinn Donovan, nodding to Connor's twin. He'd taken Connor's place when Con caught a case. Quinn nodded back. They were ready.

She'd done her homework. Ronald Kirby's office was on the top floor, and required a key for access. Fortunately, the police and fire departments had elevator keys for all the

130

buildings in Chicago, so she and Quinn didn't have to wait for someone to unlock it.

Striding to the reception desk, she held up her badge. "I'm Detective Carleton. Detective Donovan and I have business in the building. Just a courtesy notice that we're here."

Instead of waiting for a response, she headed for the elevators, with Quinn beside her. They stepped inside as the receptionist called, "Wait a minute!"

Inserting her key into the lock, she pressed the button for the forty-first floor and the doors slid shut. The elevator rose swiftly and silently, and in moments the door opened with a muted ding. She and Quinn stepped into a lavish reception area. Dark red wood paneling covered the walls, matching the hardwood floors. The reception desk was a slab of dark granite veined in bright blue -- the most expensive granite option.

Julia knew because the same granite had made up the counters in the kitchen of her childhood home.

A stunningly beautiful young blond woman sat behind the massive desk, typing on a computer. She looked up as Julia and Quinn walked toward her, her eyes puzzled. Her forehead didn't move, however, and Julia had seen botoxed faces too many times not to recognize its effects.

"May I help you?" the blond asked, her gaze evaluating both of them. They clearly didn't pass muster, because her eyes frowned again. "Do you have an appointment?"

Julia pulled her badge off her belt. "I'm Detective Carleton and this is Detective Donovan, Chicago PD. We need to see Ronald Kirby."

"I'm sorry," the blond said. "Mr. Kirby isn't available right now. Perhaps you'd like to make an appointment?"

"Is he in his office?" Julia nodded at the door behind the blond.

"I'm afraid I can't answer that…"

Before she could finish, Julia strode toward the door, Quinn right behind her. "We'll check for ourselves," she tossed over her shoulder. She loved to burst the I'm-so-important bubbles of rich assholes like Kirby. It was petty, but putting them on the defensive often made the arrests go more smoothly. And in Kirby's case, she'd enjoy every second of it.

The blond sprang up from her chair, tugging her skin-tight dress down so it covered her ass. "You can't go in there," she cried.

Julia paused for a moment and smiled to herself. She couldn't wait to tell Sam about this arrest, starting with the blond bimbo and the extravagant office. He'd...

No. She couldn't think about Sam now. She had to do her job.

Putting Sam firmly out of her mind, Julia opened the door and stepped into an office that was almost as big as her whole apartment. The dark red wood paneling and flooring from the reception area continued in here, with the central area covered by an Oriental rug she recognized. She knew that particular rug cost at least $50,000.

"What the hell?" Kirby yelled, surging to his feet.

"Ronald Kirby, you're under arrest for witness intimidation and assault." Julia recited the Miranda warning as she removed her handcuffs from her belt. "Turn around," she said, reaching for him.

Instead of turning, he backed away. "You can't arrest me."

"I can and I will." She pulled the warrant from the inside pocket of her jacket and held it up. "Here's the warrant. Signed, sealed and delivered. Are you going to cooperate, or do Detective Donovan and I have to take further restraint measures?" She rested her hand atop the Taser on her belt.

"I'm calling my lawyer," Kirby blustered as he reached for the phone on his desk.

"You'll get your phone call after you're booked." Julia grabbed his wrist and slapped one of the cuffs around it. Quinn seized Kirby's other wrist and pulled it behind his back. In moments, the cuffs were secured. Julia took one arm, Quinn took the other and they began walking Kirby toward the door.

"You're going to regret this." Kirby's guttural voice was cold. Threatening. Julia had no doubt he'd intimidated a lot of people with that voice and that threat.

Instead of feeling threatened, though, she was pleased at Kirby's response. Pleased that they'd managed to shake him up. This was when she was most herself -- when she was finding justice for victims of crimes.

She bit back her satisfaction as she and Quinn opened the office door and walked him through. Two building security guards stood in the waiting area, along with several other people who were probably employees.

"What's going on?" one of the guards asked.

Julia pulled out her badge once more. "Detectives Carleton and Donovan, Chicago PD, making an arrest," she said. "Will you call the elevator, please?"

Julia kept her face expressionless as she surveyed the gathering crowd, but inside she smiled. Word of Kirby's arrest would spread like wildfire through his company. Someone would call a newspaper. Employees would post it on their Facebook pages. Instagram photos of the boss in handcuffs would pop up. A few might post it on their blogs.

The news of his arrest would be public knowledge before they made it to the station with Kirby.

She preferred to make arrests at suspect's homes. People had a right to privacy, and she didn't want to publicly shame any suspect. Everyone had a right to be considered innocent until proven guilty.

For Kirby, though, she'd made an exception. He'd overstepped the boundaries with her and Sam, trying to intimidate both of them. He was clearly not used to hearing the word 'no', and even more clearly wasn't willing to accept it.

Julia hoped that being forced to take the walk of shame out of his own office building would unnerve him. Knock some of the arrogance out of him.

Keep him away from Sam.

The elevator dinged its arrival, and she and Quinn escorted Kirby inside. As the doors closed, Kirby tried to shake off their hands. "Let go of me," he snarled.

"Sorry, Mr. Kirby," Julia said. "Arrest protocol is to have hands on the subject until he or she is in the squad car."

Kirby's face reddened and a vein throbbed in his forehead. "I'll have your badge, Carleton." He glanced at Quinn. "Yours, too, Donovan. The mayor will be calling your captain."

"Captain Francisco always enjoys chatting with the mayor," Julia said calmly. "And can't you come up with something better than 'I'll have you fired'? It makes you sound like some old, clichéd movie villain."

Julia hadn't thought it possible for Kirby's face to get any redder. But he looked like a tomato. He shoved his face close to hers, close enough for her to smell the coffee he'd been drinking. And catch a hint of bourbon. Had he added it to his coffee this morning? Or was it left over from the night before?

"You are going to regret this, Carleton," he growled, his eyes flat. Malignant.

"I doubt it," she said as the elevator opened into the lobby. She focused her attention on Kirby, on steering him safely to the car, but she was aware of the people staring at them. A low gasp from one of the bystanders made Kirby stiffen beneath her hand.

Outside the building, as Julia pressed down on Kirby's head to ease him into the back seat of the squad car, he turned his cold, reptilian gaze on her. "I always do my homework on an opponent, Carleton, and I've had you checked out. Does your captain know who your father was? Do your co-workers? Your friends?"

Inside, Julia reeled as if Kirby had slapped her. Her ears rung and panic fluttered in her chest. On the outside, though, she managed to keep her face expressionless. "My captain knows all about me, Kirby."

No one else did, though. If Kirby followed through on her threat, all the men and women she worked with would know her sordid story.

And Sam would, too.

CHAPTER 14

As Sam stepped to the plate in the eighth inning of the game, the crowd began to roar. Clap. Out of the corner of his eye, he saw the Wave moving through the park and grinned. Best. Fans. Ever.

There were men on first and second, and the 'Cats were two down. A base hit could tie it up. So Sam took his stance, crouched, and focused on the pitcher. The crowd quieted, but he knew, from the tense silence that spread through the park, that the fans were holding their breath.

As the pitcher hurled the ball, someone shouted, "Marini, you suck!"

Sam's hands twitched on the bat, and the umpire called, "Strike."

Sam touched the tip of the bat to home base, then turned to see where the shout had come from. Spotted him immediately.

Derek Kirby, in the first row, right above the 'Cats' dugout. The asshole smirked as he yelled, "Loser!"

Sam turned and faced the pitcher again. Took his stance. Blocked out everything but the pitcher's expression. Nothing but the ball spinning toward him. High and wide. Ball one.

He took another strike. Fouled off a third. Dimly, in the background, he knew Kirby was still yelling at every pitch. But Sam called on all his control and focused only on the ball as it left the pitcher's hand.

In the second or two it took for the ball to reach him, he'd assessed the pitch. Knew it was good. Swung as hard as he could.

The impact of the bat hitting the ball vibrated through his hands and shuddered up his arms. He began to run full out as he watched the ball soar through the air. Land five or six rows up in the bleachers for a home run.

As he rounded third base and trotted toward home, he resisted glancing at Kirby. But he allowed himself a tiny smirk of his own.

At the post-game press conference, his first question was from the Herald's beat reporter, asking about the heckler and the game-winning home run. Sam shrugged. He'd known the question was coming. Had thought about how he'd answer it. "When I'm at the plate," he began, "my job is to hit the ball. When I'm in the field, it's to catch the ball and get the runner out. I'm not paid to listen to hecklers. So I don't." He shrugged. "People buy a ticket, they can express their opinion. Doesn't mean we have to pay attention to them."

He answered a few more questions. When another reporter asked about Kirby again, Sam said, "Thanks, guys. I'll give one of the other players a chance to talk to you."

As he headed back toward the clubhouse, Pete, one of the security guards, was waiting for him. "Hey, Marini," he said, falling in place and walking beside him. "The guy in the first row over the dugout is the same one we had to remove from the park a couple weeks ago. We were on our way to pick him up again when you hit that homer. You want us to keep an eye open and pull him out of his seat if he shows up again?"

Sam stopped at the door to the clubhouse and turned to face Pete. "Don't do a thing. Let him yell all he wants."

Sam smiled at Pete and bumped shoulders with the guard. He'd always liked Pete, and was grateful the guy wanted to have his back. "After we won today, I'm going to think of that asshole as my good luck charm. Maybe I'll do better if he's yelling at me."

Pete grinned. "Oh, yeah," he said. "I like it. That'll make the little prick furious."

"I hope so," Sam said. He nodded toward the clubhouse door. "You coming in to get some food?"

"Later. After I write up a report on the guy. Just in case he comes back. We need to document this stuff."

"That's good thinking, Pete." A sudden thought made Sam frown. "Did the people around him complain?"

"Not after you hit that long ball. They were all taunting the guy. Making fun of him. He looked pretty damn angry."

Sam smiled happily. "Music to my ears, Pete." He clapped the guard on the shoulder and hurried into the room, eager to grab some food and take it home to Julia.

Home. He stilled. He wasn't going home to Julia. Hell, he wasn't even going to *her* home. They weren't getting together tonight. When he'd talked to Julia earlier, she said she had to take a pass tonight.

It was probably smart. He shouldn't go to her place again, in case Kirby had someone watching. He and Julia had to figure out a safe place to meet, where Kirby or one of his minions wouldn't spot them.

He opened his locker, his gaze settling on the box of condoms he'd picked up on his way to the park. Wouldn't need them tonight.

They'd talked for fifteen or twenty minutes after she'd broken the news. Julia had been distracted -- she'd been about to leave to arrest Kirby.

He'd been waiting to take batting practice.

He'd call her again as soon as he got home. He wanted to know how the arrest had gone. How the rest of her day had gone.

He wanted to tell her about Derek Kirby at the ball park.

About the home run Sam had hit when Kirby was yelling at him.

He wanted to hear the sound of her voice.

God! He slammed his locker shut and headed for the buffet set up in the big room. If anyone heard his thoughts, they'd assume he and Julia were a real couple. The kind who talked about their day as they ate dinner, watched a little television, then fell into bed together.

They weren't a real couple. Sure, they'd share some meals. They'd talk about Kirby and the case against him. They'd even have fun and games in the bedroom. But there was an asterisk beside the word 'couple'.

This relationship came with an expiration date.

So instead of rushing through his shower and grabbing food to take with him, he ate a meal with his teammates, teasing and talking smack like always. Then he showered and headed home.

Restless, on edge, he passed the popular bars on Clark and turned onto a side street he seldom took. Two blocks from his house, he spotted a small neighborhood bar. Chi-town Tap. It was dark inside, but full of people, judging by the noise drifting out of the open door.

He didn't want to go home and think about Julia. About not being with Julia. So he opened the door to Chi-town Tap and stepped inside.

Froze after two steps. A cop bar. A lot of uniforms mingled with people dressed in street clothes who nevertheless screamed 'cop'. Not everyone in the bar was a police officer, but Sam began to back out the door.

Wrong place to stop. He didn't need the reminders of Julia. Didn't want the knowledge that he wanted her badly, and she wanted him just as much, but that's all they'd share. As he turned toward the door, someone called, "Hey, Marini!"

Damn it! Not only a cop bar, but someone had recognized him. So he pasted on his fan smile and turned to find the guy. He'd autograph a bar coaster, talk about the

139

game for a moment, then escape.

Instead of an anonymous fan, one of the Donovan twins was winding his way through the crowd, a smile on his face. "What are you doing in this dive, Marini?" Quinn clapped him on the shoulder. "I thought you drank at classier establishments."

"Nah. Not me. I was looking for something real tonight." The words were out before he thought about them, but he realized they were exactly right. He'd been thinking about Julia. He wanted real.

"This is as real as it gets." Quinn jerked his head toward the back of the bar. "We got a table. Join us."

Sam relaxed as he followed Q toward a corner of the bar. Having a beer or two with the Donovans was a good way to spend an hour. Shooting the shit with them, talking about the next dinner at their mom's house, would take his mind off Julia.

His steps slowed as he reached the table. As if his thoughts had conjured her, Julia sat on a bench next to Q's twin Connor. She had a beer bottle half-lifted to her mouth as she said something to Con. He was laughing his ass off. Sam couldn't tear his gaze away. Relaxed, in her element with her friends, Julia stunned him.

He managed to greet the rest of the people at the table, other cops he recognized from the precinct. Then he zeroed in on Julia again.

"Look who's slumming tonight," Q said as they reached the table.

Connor turned and grinned at him. "Hey, Baseball Boy," he said happily. His grin widened as he followed Sam's gaze to Julia. Then he scooted over on the bench, making room between himself and Julia. "Have a seat."

Sam nodded to Connor, but focused on Julia like a laser. She stared back, slowly lowering her beer bottle to the table. "Sam," she said, the bottle rocking for a moment as she set it on the table. Her hand was shaky, and Sam hid a smile.

"Hey, Carleton," he said, slipping onto the bench beside

her.

Connor hadn't left him much room. Sam's thigh squashed against Julia's, and when she lifted her beer to her mouth, her shoulder grazed his. Julia stilled at the contact.

Sam swallowed.

She took another sip of her beer, and her whole body canted against his as she said something to Connor on his other side. Sam had no idea what she'd said. Every atom in his body was focused on the feel of Julia beside him. The heat from her arm bled through his suit jacket. The jut of her hip poked into his. Her thigh was plastered against him, all the way to his knee. It conjured memories of the weight of Julia on his lap the night before, the way she'd rocked against his cock.

The way she'd moaned his name, telling him not to stop.

The sounds she'd made as her orgasm crashed over her.

Sam closed his eyes and inhaled slowly, trying to get his libido under control. They were surrounded by Julia's co-workers. In public.

That should have been a reality check.

Why wasn't it?

Quinn leaned across the table. "Carleton tell you about picking Kirby up today?" he asked, his mouth twitching with a barely-suppressed smile. "Fun times."

"No," Sam said, pathetically grateful for the distraction. He turned to Julia, clenching his fist and putting it on his thigh when he realized he was reaching for her hand. "Tell me about it."

She told him about the bimbo secretary, about Kirby's rage, about his threats of having her and Quinn fired.

He loved watching her talk about her job. Her passion, her commitment to justice, had him reaching for her again. He pulled back before he took her hand, but he *had* to touch her.

Beneath the table, he whispered his fingers over Julia's thigh. Froze when his hand settled on warm skin instead of fabric. She was wearing a skirt.

He went from idling to pedal to the floor in about a second.

Her leg twitched. Her breath hitched twice, then she cleared her throat. "When we got him back to the precinct..." She swallowed as Sam drew his index finger along the edge of the skirt. Slid it beneath the heavy fabric, trailing his finger over silky soft skin. She shifted her leg away from him until he had to let her go.

Gulping in a breath, she continued, "We weren't even inside when he demanded his lawyer. By the time we booked him, printed him, took his mug shot, he was purple with anger. He didn't say a thing, waited for his attorney -- the same one little Kirby used -- and bonded out. The judge warned him his bail would be revoked if he came near you again, or tried to retaliate against you in any way."

"Anything I forgot, Q?" Julia leaned toward Quinn again, and Sam missed the sensation of her body against his.

"Nope," Quinn said. "You hit all the high notes."

Sam wanted to hit some high notes, too. He burrowed beneath her skirt and headed north. Heat poured from her skin. She stiffened beside him, her fingers white around her beer bottle.

Sam trailed his fingers over her skin, dipping toward the inside of her thigh. Her muscles trembled. He felt her try to still them, so he crept higher.

"Sorry I missed the fun," he said, trying to look sufficiently serious.

He was having lots of fun now.

As Sam crept closer to where he wanted to be, Julia sucked in a breath. Quinn started talking about another case, and Sam pretended to be listening as he drew tiny circles on the soft skin on the inside of her thigh. Her muscles tensed and he wanted to lean closer and press his mouth to hers. Drink in the tiny sounds he knew she was swallowing.

Every one of his senses was tuned to Julia. Her tangy orange scent made his heart beat faster. She shifted a fraction on the hard bench, and her breast pressed against his side. He imagined he could feel her heart beating too quickly where their bodies crowded together.

Suddenly a warm foot slid up the leg of his pants. His hand holding the beer bottle jerked, and beer splashed onto the wooden table. Julia bit her lower lip to hold back a smile.

He understood immediately. This was payback for distracting her when she was trying to talk. Payback for his fingers dancing along her thigh. For teasing her. Making it difficult for her to focus while telling him about Kirby.

As her toes crept up his leg, she said something to Quinn about the case. It sounded like an alien language to Sam. All he could think about was how much he wanted to devour her. How her mouth would taste if he pressed his lips to hers and showed her exactly what he wanted to do with her.

Julia continued to talk, and Sam took a long gulp of his beer. It was too damn hot in here. He struggled out of his suit coat and flung it toward a hook on the wall. Rolled up his sleeves. Julia leaned into his side a little harder, and the weight of her breast flattening against his chest made him bite the inside of his cheek to keep from groaning.

He shouldn't have touched her. Hell, he should've sat at the other end of the table. As far away from Julia as possible. Sitting this close to her, not able to take her hand or touch her the way he wanted to, was torture.

He had to get out of here before he embarrassed himself. Embarrassed Julia. But he wasn't going anywhere until he got his cock under control.

So he forced himself to think about the game today, replaying every pitch from each of his at-bats. When he was certain he could stand up and walk away without embarrassing himself, he eased away from the heat of Julia's body and slid off the bench. "Thanks for the company," he said, smiling around the table. "I'll catch you all later."

Julia looked up at him. "You walking home like you

usually do?"

"Yeah."

She slid off the bench, as well. "In case Kirby decided he wants another shot at you, let me give you a lift."

"You already have," he muttered, shifting on the bench.

He didn't think she'd heard him over the noise in the bar, but Julia stilled. A flush rose up her chest and onto her neck. Her throat rippled as she swallowed.

The moment stretched out too long. They stared at one another, and he saw desire bloom in Julia's eyes.

He forced himself to look away. Stood slowly. "You don't have to leave," he managed to say. "I'm good."

"I insist." She reached down to adjust her skirt, and when she looked up again, the sexy, aroused woman was gone. In contrast to the heat and sex and *want* coursing through him, she was all business. "Kirby was pissed off today. So far, he hasn't exhibited very good impulse control. So I'm driving you home."

"Fine." He turned to Connor and Quinn. "See you at your mom's in a week?"

"Absolutely," Connor said. He nodded at Julia. "Bring Carleton with you."

"*What?*" He barely got the word out as he stared at Connor. He knew what the Donovan's meant when they told a guy to bring a woman to their mom's for dinner. It meant he and the woman were a couple. Together. Had Connor figured out he and Julia were... something? "Not a chance."

"See you both next week," Connor replied, his eyes twinkling.

Sam tossed enough money on the table to cover everyone's bar tab, taking advantage of the flutter of bills to give Con the finger. Then he grabbed his jacket and murmured his goodbyes. He heard Julia behind him, talking to the other cops, but instead of waiting for her, he began to weave his way through the patrons. He needed air. Space. A moment to calm down.

Julia's shift from leg-caressing lover to cop had been disconcerting. Annoying. He understood she was concerned about his safety, but her abrupt shift made his head spin.

Connor Donovan assuming they were a couple had shaken him.

"You need to wait for me, Sam." Julia stepped up beside him and sent him a questioning look, as if asking why he'd rushed ahead. "In case Kirby's out there."

"Pretty sure he's not going to jump me in here."

"I need to walk out that door first," she said, squeezing past him. Her ass brushed against his thigh, and her confident steps faltered. Half a breath later she moved forward, but her knuckles swept over his hand as she passed him.

Was it an accident? On purpose? The bar was so crowded that it could have been either. Her body brushed his several more times as they juked and dodged the patrons standing in the open space between the bar and the tables.

Every tiny contact made his heart lurch in his chest. Made his pulse race faster.

Made his cock harder.

Even in the space crowded with dozens of people, Julia's sweet-tart scent surrounded him. His fingers twitched to take her hand, but he shoved them into his pocket.

This wasn't the way he'd imagined their next meeting -- Julia acting as his bodyguard. In his fantasies, there had been far fewer clothes involved and a lot more touching.

God help him. Even when he was irritated with her, she turned him on.

As they reached the door, Julia put her hand on his chest, stopping him, and stepped onto the sidewalk. All cop, she scanned the street. After a long moment, she fumbled for his hand and tugged him through the door.

"I don't see him," she said, letting him go as her head swiveled from side to side. Watching. Assessing. "Don't see anyone sitting in a car. But anyone could have followed you from the ball park. Easy to blend in with all the pedestrians on Clark Street. Assume someone's got eyes on us right now."

"There's a libido killer," he muttered.

"Unless you like to have someone watching." She shot him an impish look, and it took all his resolve to keep his hands to himself.

"Jesus, Julia." He ached to reach for her, but forced himself to stay two steps away. He was irritated with her bodyguard role, he reminded himself. "You're gonna kill me."

"Good. Because *you* killed *me* when you walked into the Tap tonight." Julia grabbed his hand and drew him closer as she crossed the street. As if she intended to put herself between him and any possible danger.

His irritation blossomed into pissed-off as they began down a dark cross street that was mostly residential.

"Is that right?" He angled himself so that he was in front of her as they walked, tightening his grip on her hand.

"Yeah, it is." She frowned. "And what the hell are you doing?" She shoved him to the side, making herself a target again.

"You think I don't see what you're doing?" he said, building up a head of steam. "Making yourself the target instead of me?"

"Of course I am." She stopped walking and turned to face him, frowning. "That's my job. *I'm* the cop, Sam. I'm the one with a weapon. Not you."

Sam took a deep breath. Another. She was right. But he hated that she was putting herself in possible danger for him. "Yeah, I know. I don't have to like it, though."

Her expression softened. "I get it. And I lo... like that you're protective." She swallowed. "Not many people in my life have tried to protect me." She started walking again. "Doesn't change the facts. Protecting you is my job."

He blew out a breath. "Not sure why we're arguing. Kirby is probably sitting in his fancy penthouse, drinking his fancy whiskey. Not skulking on the street, waiting for me to walk by."

"You're probably right," she said as she resumed walking. "But I... we can't afford to take any chances."

They walked in silence, Julia constantly scanning the area, when she asked, "What were you doing in the Tap, Sam?"

He shrugged. "Impulse. I was walking home. Decided to go inside."

"Why that bar?"

"Unlike the joints on Clark, it looked real. The kind of place ordinary people hang out. I wasn't in the mood for fawning fans tonight."

"Did you know I was going to be there?"

He stopped dead. She took another step, then stopped when he didn't budge.

"How would I have known that?"

She shrugged one shoulder. "Maybe you talked to Connor. He seemed pretty interested in whatever's going on with us."

Her words were like a bucket of cold water drenching his heated skin. "Why would you ask me that, Julia? What time did you decide to come here?"

"A couple of hours ago," she said, still not looking at him as she walked purposely down the sidewalk.

"A couple of hours ago, I was playing baseball. Not gossiping on the phone with Connor." He caught up with her and swung her around to face him. "What's going on? You were playing footsie with me in the bar fifteen minutes ago. Now you're trying to pick a fight."

She stared at him for several seconds, then closed her eyes. "I didn't mean to. I don't want to fight with you, Sam."

Here on the street, without the cover of the other people in the bar, he finally saw the misery in her expression. The strain in her shoulders. It had been there since he sat down beside her in the bar, but he'd been too busy fighting his libido to notice. "What's wrong, Jules?"

A breath shuddered out of her and her shoulders slumped. Rather than meet his eyes, she let her gaze travel over the cars and vans parked on the street. "There's something I need to tell you. Maybe I was trying to avoid it."

"You can tell me anything." He tried to draw her close, but her shoulders were stiff and her body rigid. "Let's get in your car. We can go back to my place and talk."

She finally swung her head around. Stared at him. "Don't you get it? I don't want to talk. I want to continue what we started last night. But… but we can't, until I come clean."

CHAPTER 15

*S*he had to come clean?

Yeah, maybe that had been a little melodramatic.

Julia swallowed the lump in her throat. It wasn't fear. No. She'd gotten past that weak emotion a long time ago.

Anxiety, maybe. Shame, certainly.

She glanced at Sam as they neared her car. He was staring at her with a slight frown, as if trying to decipher her cryptic announcement.

She didn't blame him. She'd just dropped a bomb, and the fallout had completely silenced him.

But a day spent staring at paperwork without actually seeing it, drinking tea until she was wired, had made her realize she had to tell Sam everything.

It was the last thing she wanted to do.

Her father's crimes made her feel ashamed. Tainted by sharing his genes. Dirty, as if a speeding car had splashed through a puddle and showered her with mud. She didn't think Sam would blame her for what her father had done -- Sam was a rational man. Intelligent. Fair.

But she didn't want his pity.

She was so tired of seeing it in the expressions of everyone who found out her father was Julius Landon.

Even worse was the voyeuristic nosiness. As if she should be delighted to share the ugly details of her family's ruin with the world.

Watching pity replace desire in Sam's eyes would be painful. Worse, though, would be Sam finding out the truth from someone else.

He'd be hurt that she hadn't shared that important part of herself. Sad that she hadn't trusted him.

So they'd reached the point when she had no choice -- she couldn't get any more involved with him until she told him. It was the only honorable thing to do.

Out of habit, she'd parked beneath a streetlight, and her light blue car stood out like a beacon. Squaring her shoulders, determined to see this through, she pressed the unlock button on her fob and the door chirped at her. Blinked its lights once.

"Hop in," she said, opening the driver's door.

Sam carefully folded his long legs into the limited room. When he pulled the door shut, it looked as if his knees hovered beneath his chin.

"Sorry for the tight fit," she muttered as she turned on the ignition. There was no sound, but the D in the dashboard told her the car was ready. Taking one last look around the street, spotting no one sitting in a parked car, she pulled out of the spot. "What's your address?"

"You mean you haven't looked me up? Run a background check on me?"

She jerked her head to stare at him. Did he really think she'd do that?

"Joking, Jules." He put his hand on her knee and squeezed. "You look pretty tense over there. I was trying to lighten things up."

There would be no lightening up until she'd told him her secret. "Right. No. I haven't done a background check on you."

He rattled off his address, then said, "If you pull into the alley, you can park your car in my garage. That way it's not sitting on the street for Kirby to see."

"Thanks," she said, feeling like an idiot. She'd insisted on driving him home, but was so distracted she hadn't even thought about leaving her car parked on his street.

Five minutes later, after she'd watched the rear view mirror the whole way and hadn't spotted a tail, they were bumping down a dark, shadowy alley. "Stop here," Sam said, and swung his legs out of the car as she braked.

He hurried to a garage and pressed the keypad on the frame next to the door. It rumbled open, and he stood to the side to let her drive in.

As soon as her car had cleared the door, he stepped into the garage and closed the door again.

The overhead light threw shadows from his car onto her tiny one, and barely illuminated the tools stored on the walls of the garage. Dreading the coming conversation, Julia exited the car slowly. Stood up like she was a ninety-year-old woman, stiff and tight.

Waiting by the side door, Sam reached for her hand and tugged her into his back yard. In the faint light from the crescent moon, a sweet fragrance hovered over dark bushes lining the garage and sidewalk. Lighter blotches indicated flowers, but she couldn't tell what they were. She'd need to see them in daylight.

Would she? Probably not. She'd decreed that her relationship with Sam was one of darkness and secrecy. A pang of regret shivered through her as Sam led her along a narrow sidewalk, up two steps and unlocked a door.

They entered through a mudroom the size of her kitchen. She began to take off her shoes, but Sam shook his head at her. "Don't worry about it."

His kitchen wasn't huge, but it looked carefully planned. A nook with a small table nestled beneath a window, and a Wolf stove and Sub-Zero refrigerator formed a perfect triangle with the sink. Green granite counters, empty of clutter, gleamed beneath the soft lights.

"Nice kitchen," she said.

"It's wasted on me. I hardly ever cook. Too busy. Gone too much."

"That's a shame." Julia drank in her surroundings. If she had a kitchen like this, cooking would be a pleasure instead of a chore.

He glanced over his shoulder as he opened the refrigerator. "You want a beer?"

"No. I had one at the Tap, and I have to drive home."

He started to say something. Stopped. Nodded. "Okay," he said, shutting the door without taking one himself. "Why don't we sit in the living room?"

Julia followed him through a dining room with a long table that looked as if it had never been used, and a buffet that held a dried-flower arrangement. She'd bet a hundred bucks a woman had given it to him -- she couldn't picture Sam putting together the delicate vase and flowers that complemented the soft grey walls. Or even thinking about buying it.

A tiny spurt of jealousy erupted in her gut, but she ignored it. This wasn't high school. She had no right to be jealous.

Although a secret corner of her heart wished she did.

In the living room, a huge flat-screen television covered one wall, positioned to face the leather sectional that curled into one corner. Two large matching armchairs filled the rest of the space. Kids' drawings covered the remaining walls, each of the pictures outlined by brightly colored frames in green, yellow, blue, orange or red. A different child's name was on each of them, carefully printed with crayons.

"These are nice," she said, running her finger down the frame of a picture of a family. Stick figures of parents and three children. Two dogs and a cat.

"Thanks." Sam glanced over his shoulders as he moved to the windows and closed the blinds. "Teammates' kids drew them. One of the guys thought my walls were sadly blank. As a joke, he got some of the guys' kids to draw

152

pictures for me. So I framed them." He grinned. "I like them better than a lot of the art I've looked at."

Julia went all gooey inside. How many single men would hang kids' drawings on the walls of their living room?

If she wasn't determined to stick to their agreement, that this was casual, she could fall hard for Sam. But that was off the table. She and Sam were on the same page about that.

When all the blinds were shut, he turned on the lights, took Julia's hand and drew her to the sectional. She tried to tug her hand away, but Sam twined their fingers together and held on. He sat too close, as well. Close enough that his heat washed over her, along with his familiar fresh-air scent.

"Okay, Jules, what's your big confession?"

He drew circles on the back of her hand with his thumb as he waited expectantly, but his touch distracted her. She couldn't concentrate on what she had to tell him when he was sending delicious sparks up her arm and all through her body.

She tried to pull away and stand up, but he drew her hand into his lap. "Nope," he said. "Not letting you go. You want to pace around and put space between us. I don't want space from you, babe."

"Babe?" She raised one eyebrow and stared at him. *"Really?"* He didn't get to fluster her by calling her 'babe' when she was struggling to get her story out.

He shrugged. "Slipped out. You like sweetie better? Pookie? How about snookums?"

"How about you're an idiot?"

He frowned, but his twinkling eyes gave him away. "I'd never call you an idiot, Jules. You're one of the smartest women I know. Right up there with my mother and my sisters."

"I'm trying to tell you something serious, Sam." She swallowed, wishing he wasn't so damn *nice*. "It's not a joke."

He let go of her hand, wrapped his arm around her

shoulder and drew her against him. "I know it isn't," he murmured, making her shiver when he pressed a kiss to the sensitive spot beneath her ear. "It's serious, and you're upset. I was trying to get you to relax a little."

Without letting her go, he shifted to face her. "You can tell me anything. I'm not going to be scared away by what you say." He brushed a kiss over her mouth, lingering long enough that the desire that had been simmering all night ignited into a flame.

Horrified, she pulled away. He was distracting her, and she was falling right into his trap. "Do you know who Julius Landon is, Sam?"

His arm tightened around her shoulders. "Of course I do. Everyone in Chicago knows who he was. Are you trying to tell me he stole money from you, too?"

"Yeah, you could say that." She was pretty sure she'd failed to keep the bitterness out of her voice. "He was my father."

"What?" Sam reared back, making it easy to read the shock in his face. "Landon was your *father?*"

"Yes. I changed my name after... after the stories came out. After he died. Carleton is my mother's maiden name."

She took a deep breath and untangled herself from Sam's arms. Stood up, smoothed down her skirt and paced the open area in his living room. "I was named after him. Julia Landon and Julius Landon? Everywhere I went, people jumped on me. I understood why -- a lot of families lost money to my father. He ruined so many lives. People have a right to their anger."

Instead of watching her face, Sam was looking at her hand. She followed his gaze. She was turning the ring and hadn't realized it. It was a bad habit -- she did it when she was nervous. A tell for anyone who knew her.

"It was my father's," she said, her voice soft. "I adored him. My relationship with my mother was... is... complicated. But my dad was always there for me."

Swallowing, staring at the black onyx that had so

fascinated her as a child. "It was passed down in his family from father to son for a few generations. Dad didn't have any sons, so he left it to me. In his will."

Since it was a family heirloom, they hadn't had to sell it. One more thing her sister resented.

"Because I was so close to my dad, it was even harder when people acted as though he was the devil. I know he stole a lot of money. I know he ruined a lot of lives. But he was my *dad*.

"And even though I knew those furious people had a right to be angry, those confrontations were scary for a college kid who'd never been exposed to the real world. I had to drop out of the expensive private college I was attending -- our money was gone. I changed my name to Carleton. Finished college at the last place anyone would expect to find Julius Landon's kid -- a small state school. Changed my major from finance to criminal justice. Got hired by the Chicago Police Department."

She cleared her throat and looked away from him. "Justice had become important to me. And hiding in the anonymity of the uniform while I pursued it for victims of crimes felt... right."

"That's why I can't get involved with anyone who's in the public eye. Especially not someone like you. I can't bear to think of you being smeared by associating with me." The stain of her father's crimes would cling to her for the rest of her life. No one close to her would escape contamination.

"Julia." Sam stood up from the couch. Wrapped his arms around her and pulled her close. "*You* didn't do anything wrong. So why would I not want to be associated with you?"

She tried to pull away from him, but he only held her more tightly. "Do you want the newspapers to run stories about how Sam Marini is dating Julius Landon's daughter?" Without conscious thought, she found herself cupping his face. The bristles of his five o'clock shadow tickled her palm, and she relished the sensation. It was real. Just like Sam was real.

Too real for the complications she would bring to his life.

"My father hurt a lot of people, Sam, and they have long memories. I don't want the stigma to attach itself to you. Or your career."

He rocked her back and forth as he nuzzled her neck. "There's no guilt by association here, Jules. Not for either of us. You were a teen-ager when it happened. It wasn't your fault, and you have no blame. So how could any blame rub off on me?"

He eased away from her to study her face. "It must have been horrible to go through that." He skimmed his hand over her hair, and she wanted to weep at his tenderness. "I can't imagine losing your father, the life you knew and your last name. Losing friends."

He cupped her head in his hands, and she felt comforted. Consoled. "Especially losing your father that way."

He pressed her face into his neck again, and she burrowed in. Some other time, she'd tell him about hearing the gunshot. Finding her father. About rescuing the pumpkin now on her living room mantle. Gluing it together after the bullet had shattered the sculpture she'd made when she was five.

Sam's lips brushed her hair, and she melted into him. "What brought on this urge to share with me?"

She sighed into his skin. Couldn't resist pressing one tiny kiss to the soft skin of his neck. "Somehow Kirby found out who I am. He threatened to tell reporters, my co-workers, basically the whole world. That's why I said we couldn't get together tonight. I needed to figure out a way to tell you about my father."

"I'm glad you did," he murmured into her hair. "Glad you shared it with me."

He rubbed his hand down her back, and she relaxed

against him. Let the tension drain from her body. "But it doesn't change anything, Jules. Not what I think of you, and certainly not what I feel for you."

Julia allowed herself to absorb Sam for a long moment. The feel of his body against hers. The security of his arms, banding tight around her. The scent of... of *goodness* that surrounded him.

She couldn't ruin all that.

She eased away, clinging to his hand as she increased the distance between them. Finally, only their fingertips were touching, and she took one final step back. Separated from him.

Sam's eyes narrowed. "What are you doing, Jules?"

"I'm going home. Giving you time to absorb all this."

He took two strides and grabbed her hands. Held them tightly. "I don't need time to absorb anything. Didn't you hear what I said? Nothing has changed for me."

He moved closer and stared down into her face. "You think you're tainted because of something your father did. You want to know how much of a screw-up I was when I was a teenager?"

"You don't have to tell me anything, Sam." She put two fingers over his mouth.

He tilted his head as he studied her. Finally, he said, "Yeah, I think I do. Because if you think my feelings about you would change once I knew about your father, I'm worried that you'll run far and fast once I tell you what I was like back then.

"I coasted my way through high school on a smile and a three-base hit. I knew I was talented, and I thought that made me special. Thought the rules didn't apply to me.

"I was a player in high school. Had any girl I wanted. Then I got to college."

He rolled his shoulders. "I was a star there, too. Until my junior year. I tore my Achilles tendon during a practice because I thought I didn't have to stretch. Thought I was just that good. I spent a couple months in a cast, couldn't play at all that year.

"Suddenly, I wasn't special anymore. When I couldn't hit the game-winning home run or make the flashy play at third base, I was just another benchwarmer. Just another guy who had some talent, but wasn't good enough to actually help the team."

"I can't believe you were ever a jerk like you're describing." She searched his expression and saw nothing but truth. Regret. "Based on the man you are now, it's almost impossible to imagine."

He snorted. "Believe it. It was a painful lesson, but one I had to learn." He snorted. "Even when I was in the minors, I'd call Cilla to get me out of jams. Until she pointed out that I was still acting like an arrogant asshole."

His grip on her hands tightened. "We all have pasts, Jules, and yours is no worse than anyone else's. Especially when you did nothing wrong. No one blames children for the sins of their fathers."

"They do when the fathers stole money from them."

Sam took a deep breath as he studied her. Opened his mouth. Then closed it again. "I'm not letting you go," he finally said.

"That's not what you started to say."

He shrugged. "Doesn't matter. The only thing that matters is that I don't give a damn who your father was. You're not Julius Landon. You didn't do anything. End of discussion."

"No. Tell me what you started to say, or I'm leaving right now."

"You are one tough woman, Julia Landon Carleton." He took a deep breath. "My parents lost some money to Landon. Not a lot…"

Horrified, shamed, Julia reared back. Put her hand over her mouth. "Oh, my God."

"Jules." He grabbed her hands. Held them tightly. "Listen to me. Because they lost that money, they made a lot more."

Julia tried to tug her hands away from him, but Sam was strong. He held on. "My mother told all three of us what had happened. And what they did afterward, so we all learned about persistence. When they lost that money, they decided to expand instead of retreat. The one shop they had was always booked weeks in advance. So they borrowed some money and opened a second location. Then a third and fourth. They told us they never would have taken a chance and done that if Landon hadn't stolen their money. So it worked out well for them."

Thank God. At least Sam's family had been able to recover. "Not everyone was so lucky."

"I know that. But no Marini is going to hold your father's identity against you. That lost money is ancient history. The start of bigger things for them."

Didn't Sam understand she was trying to protect him? "People will find out," she said, desperate to make him see. "They'll…"

"I. Don't. Care." He brushed a kiss over her mouth. "What other people think doesn't matter." Kissed her again, making her shiver.

"But even if I did care, no one's going to find out. We're not going anywhere in public because of Kirby. So no one will see us together."

She should walk away. Getting involved with Sam was dangerous on every level. But she wanted to spend time with him. Wanted to explore the attraction that burned so hot between them. "We can't come here, and we can't go to my place. So where are we going to spend time together?"

"Already got that figured out," he said, bouncing on his toes. His excitement was contagious, and more of her tension eased. "There's a boutique hotel a few blocks from the ball park. The Houston is small and very discreet. I'm going to get a suite there. Tell them I'm having work done on my place. We'll meet there whenever we can." He grabbed her and pressed his mouth to hers. "It'll be perfect."

Julia thought about it for a moment, then nodded slowly. "You're right. That's a good idea." She stepped closer and brushed a kiss to his lips. "Let me know when you've got it set up. I can't wait."

She tried to ease away, but Sam wrapped his arms around her. "You think I'm letting you go home? After all the trouble we went through to make sure no one followed us? No way, Carleton. I have plans tonight, and they definitely include you."

CHAPTER 16

Leaving now would be the smart thing to do. It had been an emotional day for her. For Sam, too. He said nothing had changed, but maybe both of them should take a step back. Think about what they really wanted.

As she watched desire darken Sam's eyes, though, Julia knew what *she* wanted. Knew what Sam wanted, as well. And it wasn't as if they were making a life-long commitment here.

That realization brought a pang of regret. She couldn't be in a relationship with someone in the public eye. Sam wasn't ready to settle down. They knew where each other stood. Even if sometimes, in the dark of the night when her bed was a lonely place, she wished things were different.

But she wasn't alone now, and it was impossible to be rational when the heat of Sam's body wrapped around her, urging her closer. A glancing brush against his chest made her breasts ache with need. She wanted to tear off his shirt and hers, feel the delicious slide of Sam's bare skin on hers. The mere thought had heat rising inside her, painting a flush over her body.

Sam's cock swelled against her abdomen, telling her his yearning matched hers. A low level of arousal had been simmering beneath her skin all day, fed by the memories of what they'd shared last night. The moment she'd seen him in the Tap tonight, it roared back to life. His teasing, wandering hands as they sat at the table had only sharpened her desire.

So she put her mouth against his. Nibbled on his lip until he opened to her with a tiny sound. She stroked his tongue with hers, then drifted over his cheek to his ear. Tugged on his lobe. "You left something out of your house tour, Sam. The most important room in the place."

"I showed you the kitchen," he said, nipping at her neck. "Lots of counter space there. Good for preparing... appetizers."

"Not in the mood for appetizers." She kicked off her shoes and slid her toes up his pants leg. Stroked over his calf until he shivered, and she burned. "Already had some of those. They fueled my appetite..." she sucked on his lower lip, released it with a pop, "for a full meal."

"I love a woman with an appetite," Sam said, tugging on her hair. Her braid relaxed, and she realized Sam had removed the tie. He combed his fingers through her waves, pulling it into a curtain that draped over her shoulders and down to her breast. He tangled his hands in the heavy strands, brushing her nipples as he let the curly mass slip through his fingers. "I already know what the main course is going to be."

He let her go so abruptly that she stumbled, but his hands steadied her as he dropped to his knees in front of her. "I've been wondering how you taste for months, Jules," he said, his voice a low slide of velvet over her skin. "Tonight I'm going to find out."

"Tonight was supposed to be my turn," she said, stroking his cheek. "I want to play, too."

"You can have as many turns as you want. But I have to taste you. I spent last night and most of the day thinking about making you come again."

He slid his hands up her thighs, inch by excruciating

inch. The calluses on his palms caught against her skin, sending bursts of sparks straight to her core. "Why'd you wear a skirt today?" he whispered, and his breath against her thigh made her shudder. "Did you know you were going to see me? Was your plan to drive me crazy?"

She clutched fistfuls of his hair to hold herself upright. "I wore it because I was thinking about you. Wondering if you'd like it. *Hoping* it would drive you crazy."

"Yes and yes," he murmured into her skin. His hands had stopped when she spoke, but now he moved again. Higher. Her legs trembled and she swayed into him. If he went farther, her legs would turn to jelly. She'd end up sprawled on the floor in front of him.

"Let me show you how much," he said. His breath against her ear made her quiver. Raised goosebumps up and down her arms.

He nudged her toward the couch as his hands crept higher still. High enough that she felt their heat at the juncture of her thighs. High enough that she squirmed against his hands, trying to get them where she needed them.

"Impatient?" She could feel his smile against her skin. "I am, too."

He slid both hands beneath her boy shorts, cupping her ass with his warm fingers. She drew a stuttering breath as he dragged a finger down her cleft, stopping when she stilled against him.

"How's your appetite doing?" he asked as he dragged the shorts down her legs.

He left them at her knees, and she shifted restlessly. "I'm starving," she whispered, wriggling her hips. She needed that underwear off *now*.

Sam lowered her to the couch and knelt in front of her. Trailed his fingers down the outside of her thighs. Even through the heavy material of her skirt, his touch burned.

When he reached the hem, he bunched the material in his hands and dragged it up inch by inch. He paused to kiss the insides of her thighs after every minuscule adjustment.

She shifted on the couch, trying to get the boy shorts past her knees. Trying to kick them off. Trying to get the skirt higher.

Ignoring her attempts, Sam kept moving. Slowly. By the time he was close enough that she could feel his breath between her legs, she was panting and frantic.

"Are you trying to make me crazy?"

"Hmm," he hummed against her skin. "Is it working?"

"Sam," she whimpered.

"God, Jules!" His fingers tightened on her thighs, then he swept the boy shorts down her legs and threw them to the side. Bunched her skirt above her waist. He spread her thighs and groaned as he stared at her. "Can't wait. Not a second longer."

He pressed his mouth against her, tasting and licking. Circled her clitoris before taking the swollen, sensitized nub into his mouth and sucking gently.

She was so ready that she shattered with a cry, bucking against his mouth. Sam pressed the flat of his tongue against her, and she screamed again as her climax went on and on.

He finally let her go and sat back on his heels with a self-satisfied grin. "Sounds like you enjoyed your meal."

"Not a meal," she said, her voice deep and raspy. "Just the first course." She bunched his shirt in her fists as she drew him closer. "I want this off."

Her hands shook as she tried to force buttons through tiny holes. Finally, he eased her hands away and did it himself. Shrugged it off his shoulders, revealing wide shoulders and lean, ropy muscles in his arms. A flat abdomen with defined six-pack-abs. A dusting of hair on his belly that arrowed down to the waistband of his pants. She reached for his belt.

"I want to see this, too." She sat up and pressed her palm against the bulge behind his zipper. Ran her finger down his length and back to the tip, feeling his heat through the fine wool of his suit pants.

He fumbled with his belt, but she moved his hands away. "My turn. I'm going to make you as crazy as you made me."

He dropped his hands to the couch obediently. Braced himself against the leather as she opened the belt buckle. Undid the button. Drew the zipper down tooth by tooth.

"Jules," he warned with a gasp as she freed him from his navy blue silk shorts and bent her head toward him. "I know what you want, but don't. Please." He edged away from her mouth. "I want this to last longer than five seconds."

"Really, Sam? Five seconds?" She trailed one finger up his long, thick length, delighted when he twitched against her hand. "I thought you had better self-control."

"I thought I did, too," he said, standing and pulling her to her feet. She wobbled on unsteady legs, and he curled one arm around her. "When it comes to you, apparently I don't."

He led her into a darkened bedroom. The blinds on the window were slanted to allow minimal light into the room. Moonlight striped the dark cover of an enormous bed and dappled the walls.

Sam let her go long enough to tear off the quilt and upper sheet. They puddled onto the floor at the foot of the bed, and he unfastened her skirt. Unbuttoned her blouse. In moments, she was bare in front of him.

"You're beautiful," he murmured as he swept his hands over her skin. Lingered at her breasts as she sucked in a breath. Finally, she reached for his silk boxers and tugged them down his legs. He kicked free of them, and they stood naked in front of each other.

He drew both hands down her sides to grip her hips. Drew her against him. "I've been waiting so long for this."

"It's only been three weeks," she said against his chest. Without her heels, her head only reached his shoulder.

"Three weeks?" He lifted her, lowered her onto the bed and followed her down. "It's been seven months. Ever since Cilla's wedding. No one would tell me where to find you -- not Cilla, not Brendan, not any of the other Donovans. I was getting impatient enough to bribe Rose to find out for me."

"Rose?" Julia lifted onto one arm and studied him, trying to beat down the jealousy. "Who's Rose?"

"The Donovan's mom. Sneaky enough to be able to worm it out of her kids. But I was never alone with her." He scowled, as if he'd just realized something. "Those bastards knew I'd get Rose on my side."

"That's sweet, Sam."

"Not sweet. Desperate."

"I'm desperate too, Sam," she said, reaching for him. "I've been thinking about you this whole time, as well." She pressed her mouth to his, opened when he touched her lips with his tongue. "I want you just as much," she sighed.

Sam bent over, reached for his pants and pulled out a box of condoms. "Got them today on the way to the park. Wishful thinking. Thank God I was optimistic."

She brushed his hand away as he opened the box, pulled out a foil packet and opened it. Rolled the condom over his penis. "I'm so glad you're an optimist."

"You and me both."

She expected him to get right to the main event. But Sam surprised her again. He kissed her for what seemed like hours, exploring her mouth until she shifted restlessly beneath him. Their tongues danced together, showing each other what they wanted. Then he trailed his mouth down her throat, between her collar bones and focused on her breasts. He made her whimper. Moan his name. Drew her hips off the bed.

Finally, aching with need, desperate to join with him, she raised up on her elbows. "Now, Sam. Please. I can't wait any longer. I need you."

Holding her gaze, he rose above her. Slid into her slowly, inch by inch, until she shuddered with want. When he began to move, she wrapped her legs around him. Cupped his face between her palms and gazed into his eyes.

"Jules," he said as he moved, his voice almost reverent. His eyes fluttered closed and he moved faster. Her own climax hovered just out of reach, and he seemed to sense it.

He adjusted his angle and she tightened her legs on him. Fastened her mouth to his when he reached between them, as if he already knew everything about her body.

She shattered with a keening cry, and Sam followed her over the edge. When he finally collapsed on top of her, all she could do was wrap her arms around him and hang on.

"Jules," he said after a long time. "That was... you were amazing. *We* were amazing."

She'd never experienced anything like their lovemaking. But she couldn't tell him that. Couldn't let him think she was staking a claim. So instead, she said, "I can't feel my legs. Or anything else, for that matter."

"Give me a minute," he said, nuzzling her neck beneath her ear. "I'll make sure you feel everything, now that I know what you like."

She tightened her arms and tried to draw him closer. Stroked one hand down his back, tangled the other in his hair. For just a moment, she wanted to pretend they were two lovers without a care in the world. Nothing to worry about except what happened in this dark, quiet room.

She drew a deep, shuddering breath, barely registering when he flipped them over so she lay on top of him. His hands, warm and strong, stroked her back. Her ass. She buried her face in Sam's neck and drank in his scent.

* * *

Sam's heart continued to race as Julia melted into him. She pressed tiny kisses into his neck, and her fingers combed through his hair. He wondered if she realized what she was doing.

When she shifted on top of him, his cock noticed. Decided it wanted to come out and play again. He shifted Julia to her side and slid down so they were face to face.

"Hey, babe," he whispered.

Her eyes fluttered open, soft and sated and smiling at him. "Sam."

He needed to taste her breasts again. Drink in the sexy sounds she made when he played with them. He slid a little lower. Teased one nipple with his tongue. "I think it's time for dessert."

"Yeah," she said, her voice throaty and deep. She reached down and cupped him as she said, "I'm hungry again, too."

Hours later, Sam jolted awake to the weak light of early morning and an insistent ringing. His phone.

He patted the night table next to the bed, but didn't find it. Rolled over and bumped into a warm, soft body. *Julia*.

He'd half expected her to be gone when he woke up, but she hadn't run away. His mouth curled up as he watched her sleep. Maybe she'd intended to leave, but they'd worn each other out last night. Hadn't gotten much sleep.

The ringing phone was distracting him from Julia. He slapped the night table, trying to make it stop. Couldn't find it. Sweeping his hand over the table, he realized the phone wasn't there. Moments later, the noise stopped.

As he curled his arms around Julia, the phone shrilled again. What the hell?

He squinted at the clock. Six-ten AM. Who the hell called at that hour?

He wanted to nestle into Julia. Kiss her awake. See if she was interested in round four. Or was it five?

He'd lost track.

But the phone kept buzzing.

Now he was irritated enough to identify that the noise came from the floor.

Reaching down, he snagged his pants and fumbled out the phone. Frowned when he saw Cilla's name.

Sitting up, he punched the icon to answer the call. "Cill. What's wrong? Are you in labor?"

"I wish," she groaned. "I have another two weeks." She

covered the phone and murmured something Sam couldn't hear. Cleared her throat. "Mom didn't want me to call you. She didn't want to make you lose your focus or some shit like that. But you need to know. There's a problem at the Irving Park shop. City inspectors were here two days ago, and they found a leaking drum of used diesel oil next to the dumpster."

Sam glanced at Julia, who was awake now. Watching him. He combed his fingers through her hair, felt her shiver where her body pressed into his. Smiled.

"Sam?" Cilla said sharply. "Are you listening to me? Is someone else there?"

He hastily untangled his fingers from Julia's hair. "Of course I'm listening to you, Cill. Don would never pollute like that. Neither would Mom."

"Of course they wouldn't. Someone put it there. Coincidentally, right before an inspector showed up. Now the shop is being fined. Inspectors are going over the rest of the shops with a fine-toothed comb. God knows what was planted at the other ones."

"Are you at the Irving Park shop?" he asked, rolling out of bed and reaching for his clothes.

"Yeah. I'm getting ready to head over to the one in Edison Park."

"Stay put," he said, sliding his legs out of the bed. "I'll be right over."

"Another thing you should know," Cilla said, her voice low. The door banged, and wind whistled through the phone. She'd moved outside. "Mia Donovan is here. She's been undercover for the past week. Play along."

CHAPTER 17

"Play along? I know what undercover means." Sam reached for a pair of jeans and a tee shirt. "Do you think I'm an idiot?"

"I don't know, Sam. You tell me," Cilla shot back. "You're giving grief to a woman who's nine months pregnant. This kid is using my bladder as a trampoline, I can't bend over without falling over, and now something shady's going on with our mother's business. I'm here at the butt crack of dawn to help *our mother*, even though I'm supposed to be on desk duty. So keep your smart cracks to yourself and get your ass over here."

"Sorry, Cill," he said immediately as he held the phone to his ear with his shoulder and pulled on a sock. "You're right. I'm a complete idiot. I'll be right there."

He turned off the phone and heard Julia behind him. "What happened?" she asked as she searched for her clothes.

He explained as he finished dressing, then called over his shoulder as he went into the living room to retrieve Julia's red polka-dot boy shorts. "On top of that, Cilla's got a bug up her ass."

He heard a snort of laughter from his bedroom. "You better not let Cilla hear you say that." He could hear the smile in Julia's voice. "Pregnant women are not to be messed with."

"Yeah, I know that," he said, swiping her silky underwear from the floor. "I'm just in a bad mood."

"Really?" she said, tugging on her skirt at the end of the bed. "After the way we spent the night, you're in a bad mood?"

"Only because I wanted to pick up this morning where we left off when we fell asleep." He drew her close, her underwear still gripped in his fist. "Sorry, babe," he said, wrapping his arms around her and breathing in her scent. It would have to hold him until tonight. "I was thinking about more interesting ways to wake up than a phone call from my sister."

"After last night, I'll let the 'babe' go," she murmured into his neck.

At her words, his cock sprang to life. Pressing kisses to her neck, he gripped her ass in both hands, his mother and sister forgotten. "You want to shower here?"

"I know what you mean by 'shower'," she said, pressing her hand against his erection. "Neither of us have time for that." She eased away from him, but caught his hand and pressed a kiss into his palm. The sweep of her lips made him shudder. Ache to draw her into the shower. But Julia backed away before he could.

"Trust me, you don't want to piss Cilla off anymore than you already did this morning."

She grabbed him again and brushed a kiss over his mouth. Let him go before he could pull her in for more. "I'm going to shower at home," she said, fingers flying as she wove her hair into an elaborate braid. "Where I'll do some actual showering. Call me as soon as you know what's going on."

Snatching her red polka-dotted boy shorts from his hand, she wriggled them on, lifting her skirt to settle them in place. "I'm gonna run," she said.

"You make me watch you twitch your way into that underwear, and then you leave?" Sam reached for Julia, burying his face in her hair, wishing Cilla hadn't called him quite so early. He really didn't want to let Julia go.

"Of course I'm leaving." Julia eased away from him, letting her fingers trail down his arm. "I'm not going to risk the wrath of a pregnant woman." She pretended to shudder as she brushed a strand of hair off his forehead.

As much as he wanted to stay, wanted Julia to stay, she was right. He had to get to his mother's shop. Had to help his family.

"Want me to make you some tea before you leave?"

"Nah. You need to get going, too. I'll have tea when I get home." She touched his face once more, and he shoved his hand into his pocket when he began to reach for her. He had to get going. And so did Julia.

"I'll be waiting for your call about your mom's shop." She hesitated as she studied him. "I hope Kirby's not involved in this," she finally said.

Sam frowned. "Kirby? You think he might be? I figured it was an inspector looking for a bribe."

"I hope it is. But we have to consider that it might be him. Maybe he thinks destroying your mother's business will make you back off."

He was getting damn tired of the Kirby family. "I'm sure you heard Cilla say that Mia Donovan is undercover at my mom's office," he said slowly. "Maybe your captain was worried that Kirby would go after her."

"I'll ask him." She pressed a kiss to his lips again, lingering too long for someone who was in a hurry. "Talk to you soon."

"You will." He caught her hand when she had his back door half-open. "I have a charity gig tonight after the game -- I'm the guest MC at a concert in one of the small venues in Lakeview. Want to come?" He wiggled his eyebrows. "I might need protection from the band's groupies."

"Sounds like you need to have a cop there," she murmured, her eyes darkening. "Can't have a bunch of groupies feeling you up."

"You got that right. The only one I want feeling me up is you." Sam leaned closer to steal a kiss, then pulled back. If they started, he'd never get to his mom's shop. And he had to be at the park early for the afternoon game. "So you gonna be there?"

"Yeah, I'll meet you there," she said. "Text me the time and place."

"I'll put your name on the VIP list."

"Ooh, I feel so special," she said with a grin, and Sam's heart clenched. She *was* special.

"I'll get that suite at the Houston today, too," he added. "We can go there after the event."

Her eyes darkened as she nodded slowly. "I'm looking forward to it, Sam."

He moved to the window and watched the sway of her hips as she walked down the narrow sidewalk to his garage. Heard the door rumble open, then saw a flash of light blue as her car moved down the alley. He pressed the remote for the garage that he kept in the house, then headed for the shower. Although he didn't really want to wash Julia's scent away.

He froze, hand on the faucet. *He didn't want to wash Julia's scent away?*

This was supposed to be a fling. Fun and games for both of them until they moved on. Instead, he'd turned into a total softy.

Not smart, Marini.

But before he replaced Julia's scent with that of his soap, he inhaled deeply one more time.

* * *

Fifteen minutes later, Julia unlocked her back door and stepped inside. Froze. Her apartment smelled… wrong. A

173

faint hint of onion-y body odor. Stale cigarette smoke, the kind of stink that clung to a smoker's clothes.

Fumbling at her waist for her gun, she swore silently. She'd left it locked in her car's glove box. She listened for a long moment, but heard nothing. No floorboards creaking. No disturbances of the air. No sharply drawn breaths.

The intruder was probably gone, but she wasn't going to take a chance without a weapon.

She backed out of the door slowly. Closed it and locked it again. Then pressed 911. "This is Detective Julia Carleton out of the Twenty-Third," she said, watching for movement through the window on the door. "An intruder was in my apartment." She spoke her address slowly, knowing that rattled victims often said their address too fast and had to repeat it. "Not sure if he's still there. I didn't go past the door because I left my gun in my car."

Damn, she was off her game. She should have remembered to take her gun out of the glove box.

She knew why she hadn't. She'd been thinking about Sam. About their night together, when she should have been focusing on the Kirbys.

Sam was distracting her. Making her sloppy.

And she'd been caught without a gun.

"I'm sending a patrol car now." The nasal voice from dispatch interrupted her thoughts. "Should be less than two minutes. Stay on the line."

"Thank you," Julia said. She lowered the phone from her ear, but kept it in her hand. Stared hard into her apartment, watching for signs of life. Motion.

Bracing for an intruder to fly at the door, trying to escape.

The seconds dragged out until the whine of approaching sirens grew louder. Abruptly cut out. Moments later, car doors closed quietly. Footsteps pounded down the gangway between her building and the one next door, and a patrol officer sprinted up the steps. She had a gun in her hand when she reached Julia's porch.

"Hey, Sobieski," Julia said. "Thanks for getting here so fast."

"Not a problem, Carleton. Jonas has the front door." She nodded toward the door. "Anything going on inside?"

"Haven't seen or heard a thing." Julia rolled her shoulders, embarrassed about being caught without her weapon when she'd called in the intruder. "Walked in the door, caught unfamiliar smells, backed out and called it in."

"You want to get your gun and back me up?" Sobieski asked, staring into the kitchen.

"Absolutely. Wanted to keep eyes on the place until you got here." She dashed down the stairs, hurried to her car and extracted her gun and holster. Strapped it on, then rejoined Sobieski.

"You ready?" Julia asked the officer.

"I'm good." Sobieski waited while Julia unlocked the door, then shouldered in first, Julia close behind.

They didn't take long clearing the apartment. As far as Julia could tell, nothing had been taken. The few pricey items she had, like the blue Steuben bowl, were still there. The laptop she'd left on the living room coffee table didn't look disturbed. But she lifted the lid and turned it on anyway.

The little light for the camera on the top of the screen glowed at her, and she froze.

She never turned that camera on.

Someone obviously had, though.

Had her intruder installed spyware on her laptop?

Turning the computer off again, she slid it beneath her arm as she and Sobieski returned to the kitchen. When Sobieski opened her mouth, Julia slashed her hand across her throat and jerked her head toward the back porch.

Once they were outside, with the door closed, Sobieski radioed Henry Jonas, told him the apartment was clear and thanked him. He radioed back that he'd gotten another call and was taking off.

"I figured you two rode together," Julia said.

"I ride alone." Sobieski's voice was flat. Final. No discussion.

Julia nodded. She got it. Katya had transferred into their station about a year ago. Right around the time that Cilla and Brendan Donovan had exposed a group of dirty cops in her previous district, the Twenty-Second. One of them had been Katya's partner, Derek Johnstone, who'd tampered with a DNA sample from a serial rapist.

Johnstone had been fired and prosecuted, along with the other dirty cops, and Sobieski had transferred out. Julia was glad she'd landed in the Twenty-Third. She was a good cop, and she'd be a great addition to the detective squad after she passed the exam.

"Here's the deal, Katya." Julia spoke quietly even though there was no one around to overhear. "I'm working on the Kirby case, and that dirtbag's father has gotten aggressive. I wouldn't put it past him to plant a bug in my apartment. He wants an out for his kid, and he might think I'll say something on the phone or to a visitor that'll help his case."

She nodded at the laptop tucked beneath her arm. "Camera light is on. I never use that camera. I'm afraid whoever was in my place installed spyware. I'm taking it into the station to have the geeks look at it."

She paced the porch as she talked, angry and determined to outwit that bastard. "I need the techs to do a sweep of my place. But tell them not to remove anything they find. And not to talk about searching for a bug. I want that asshole to think he's outsmarted me."

Sobieski nodded, her mouth twitching into a tiny smile. "I love it when jerks like Kirby think they're smarter than we are. I'll take care of it. I'll let you know later today if we find anything."

"Thanks, Katya." Julia bumped shoulders with the other woman. "I know you'll handle it. You always do." She opened her back door, then said over her shoulder, "You'll make a good detective. If you need another rec, let me know."

Sobieski's face softened. "I'll do that. Thanks, Carleton."

"You're welcome."

With Sobieski waiting in her kitchen, Julia turned on the shower, then wondered if someone had a camera focused on her. Revulsion rippled through her, and she wrenched the water valve off. Her skin crawled as she threw a few changes of clothing into a duffel bag, as if she was going to the gym. Was someone watching? Hoping she would give them a show?

She'd shower at the station.

Stuffing her laptop into the duffel, she returned to the kitchen.

"Thanks," she mouthed to Sobieski as she unlocked the back door. "I'll get the keys later," she said in a barely-there whisper.

Thank God she was meeting Sam at the Houston Hotel tonight. Even if the tech team didn't find any bugs, her home had been violated. The wall she'd erected between herself and the rest of the world had been breached. She needed twenty-four hours away from her place.

Damn those Kirbys. Derek was already awaiting trial, but now she wanted to nail Ronald's ass, too. She wanted to make him pay for the way he'd harassed Sam. For the way she suspected the jerk was harassing Sam's mom.

She wanted him to pay for the way he'd made her feel unsettled in her own home.

By the time she reached the station, she'd gathered her composure. She'd need it while she talked to Captain Francisco.

Twenty minutes later, showered and dressed in clean clothes and a mug of tea in her hand, she knocked on his door. When the captain saw her, he motioned her in. "Carleton. What can I do for you?"

"A couple things, sir." She wrapped her cold hands

177

around the warm mug. "First of all, Sam Marini. Our witness in the Kirby case."

She cleared her throat. "I ran into him last night. I was at the Chi-town Tap with a group from the station and he came in. He knows the Donovans, and apparently sees them socially," she said carefully. "So we have mutual friends. It's possible we could be seen together outside of work."

Francisco studied her for a long moment. "I see," he finally said. Julia wasn't sure, but his eyes might have been twinkling. "I trust you to behave professionally, Carleton, but when you *run into* each other, make sure neither of you do anything *in public* that would jeopardize this case." He took a drink of coffee from his mug. "Are we clear?"

"Crystal, sir." He was sending her a message, and she was pretty sure it was 'what you do on your own time is your business, but don't get caught.' "Thank you."

She inhaled slowly, then said, "One more thing. I had a break-in at my apartment last night. Nothing taken, as far as I could tell, but I think someone messed with my laptop. The camera light was on when I opened it this morning."

Francisco froze, then his face turned red. "Someone broke into one of my detectives' places? And might have messed with her computer?"

"The geeks are looking at it now." She hesitated for a long moment. "And I'm having the techs sweep my place for bugs and cameras. Sobieski was there, and she won't let the techs remove anything they find. If there are bugs or cameras, maybe we can use them."

"You think this is related to the Kirby case?" Francisco asked.

She shrugged. "If there are bugs, it seems likely. Daddy Kirby is angry. He's a guy who's used to getting his own way."

"Make sure the techs keep me in the loop," the captain said, scowling. "I don't like this one damn bit."

She didn't either. "One more thing, Captain. Is Mia

178

Donovan's undercover job related to the Kirbys?"

Francisco's eyebrows snapped together. "Why would you ask that?"

"I got a message from Sam Marini this morning that his mother's auto repair shop has a problem." The captain didn't have to know the message was delivered in person. "An inspector found a leaking drum of diesel oil in the back of the lot. Sam said his mother would never leave a leaking barrel where it could contaminate the soil or water, and that his sister Cilla told him Mia was working there. Do you think the Kirbys are going after Sam through his mother?"

The captain stared at her, his eyes unreadable. Then he jerked his head toward the door. "Close that."

As soon as the door clicked shut, Francisco leaned forward. "Ronald Kirby is the world's biggest asshat. Ever since you arrested his kid, he's been hounding the mayor to have you fired.

"I know how the guy works," the captain continued, pressing two fingers to the bridge of his nose. "I've dealt with Kirby and his demon spawn before. So I was expecting him to escalate." He smiled grimly. "Sam Marini's high profile. Ronald Kirby can't do much to him. But Marini has a mother who runs a chain of auto repair shops. Based on my experience with the old man, I figured he'd target her -- she's a small businesswoman. Older. He'd see her as vulnerable. That's why I put Mia undercover in her shop. To keep an eye on things."

"Did Mia find anything?"

"Hasn't been there long enough. But she called me early this morning and filled me in. Said that everyone who works for Joanie Marini swears they never saw that oil drum before. And that the inspector who found it wasn't the regular guy. So Donovan is on it."

"Thanks for letting me know, sir. I'll let Mia handle that end of the case, then." She hesitated. "Can I ask what kinds of problems you've had with Derek Kirby and his father?"

Francisco pursed his lips, acknowledging where she was

headed. "Nothing you can use in court, unfortunately. But Nick D'Angelo isn't the first person Derek has assaulted. Hasn't killed anyone else, but Derek likes to party in the bars around the ballpark, and he's gotten into a lot of fights. Usually unprovoked. Up until now, every single one of the people he's assaulted has declined to press charges. Or refused to testify if charges had already been filed. I'm positive his father either pays them off or threatens them. Probably both."

"I suspected as much," Julia said. "Based on Ronald Kirby's recent stunts."

"You keep on this case," the captain said. "Because if Derek doesn't go down for murdering Nick D'Angelo, he's gonna kill someone else."

"Believe me, sir, I know." Julia pushed away from the desk and stood up. "Thanks for filling me in."

"Probably should have told you earlier. And one more thing, Carleton? The next time you... run into Marini, tell him to be careful. Kirby doesn't like to be thwarted."

Julia clenched her teeth. If Francisco was worried about Sam, this case was getting out of control. "I'll tell him, sir."

"Get some corroborating evidence, too."

"Working on that, sir." One of Derek's buddies would crack. She'd lean harder on them. Find their vulnerabilities, places she could apply pressure.

Clutching her now-lukewarm mug of tea, Julia hurried to her desk. Glanced at her watch as she pulled out her phone. Almost eight o'clock. Sam might still be with his mother and Cilla.

The break-in at her apartment was the least of her worries. Julia was far more concerned with the damage Kirby could wreak on Sam. His mother. Cilla, his pregnant sister.

Julia had a gun. She could protect herself. But, short of locking up both Kirbys, how could she prevent collateral damage to the innocent?

The only way was by wrapping up this case as soon as

possible.

She slid her fingers over the edge of her phone. She wanted to talk to Sam. Badly. To fill him in on what had happened at her apartment. To get the story about his mother's auto repair shop.

Even more urgently, she needed to reassure herself that he was okay. That the rest of his family was safe, as well.

She dropped the phone on her desk as she ran her hand over her braid. Yeah, he needed to know about the break-in at her apartment. And she needed to know what was going on with his mother's shops.

But those were secondary concerns right now.

After finding out that someone had broken into her apartment, she needed to hear his voice. Almost as much as she needed to draw her next breath.

She was in *so* much trouble.

CHAPTER 18

Julia's finger hovered over Sam's contact number as she set her tea down on her desk. But before she could sink into her chair, she changed her mind. She didn't want the rest of the department listening to her conversation with Sam.

Ducking into a little-used back stairwell, she pressed the icon next to Sam's name and listened to his phone ring.

After two beeps, he picked up. "Jules? Everything okay?"

Now that she'd heard his voice, it was. "I'll get to my news," she said, her shoulders relaxing. "How are things at your mom's shop?"

"Fucked up." The wind whistled through Sam's phone -- he was outside. "I was just gonna call you. There's an inspector here, trying to shut the shop down. He's got a fistful of citations and fines. My mom is in shock. Her partner Don is locked in the office with Mia after he threatened to kick the guy's ass. And I want to punch the smirk off the asshole inspector's face."

"Don't hit him, Sam." Julia clenched the phone so tightly her hand ached. "That's exactly what Kirby wants you to do."

"I know that," Sam said impatiently. "Why do you think

I'm outside right now?"

"What's Mia doing?"

"She's working the phone. She called a testing service to check the oil in the drum, and she's hoping to have the results by tomorrow. Don said that it's most likely from a facility that works on semi cabs. If it is, it's proof the drum was planted.

"She also contacted our sister Livvy, who's an assistant state's attorney. Livvy's checking into this inspector. Now Mia has the cops checking surveillance cameras in the area, looking for someone leaving the oil drum at the shop. Slow going, but maybe they'll get lucky and see something.

"Cilla also has a lawyer filing injunctions to prevent the inspector from closing the shops. I feel like a fifth wheel. Nothing for me to do but hold my mom's hand. And it looks like Don has that covered."

She could hear Sam's scowl over the phone. "Sounds as if there's a story."

"Yeah, one that none of us saw coming."

"Sometimes those are the best kind," Julia said, thinking about the previous night with Sam.

"Yeah," he said, his voice softening. "Sometimes they are."

Warmth flooded her, and for a moment, Julia allowed herself to dwell on memories of the night before. Then she stood straighter and drew a deep breath. Neither of them had time for memory lane right now.

"I have some news, too," she said, trying to keep her voice even. Steady.

"Yeah? What's up?"

She cleared her throat. "When I got back to my apartment, I realized someone had broken in. Nothing was taken, as far as I could tell, but there had definitely been an intruder. I could smell him. Onions, B.O. and cigarette smoke."

"What the hell?"

Sam was so loud that Julia had to hold the phone away

from her ear. "The guy was gone, Sam. But it pissed me off." She took a deep breath. "Creeped me out, too," she confessed. She hesitated, but he needed to know. "I think the intruder put spyware on my laptop. The geeks are checking it out. And the techs are scanning the place for bugs and cameras."

"I'm on my way." She heard him running, the jangle of his keys in time with his steps. "I can be there in fifteen, twenty minutes."

"Sam. Stop. Stop!" she yelled into the phone when she heard a car door slam. "Listen to me."

"What?" he said over the roar of a car engine cranking too hard.

"You need to stay there. With your mother and Cilla. Help them however you can. I'm all right." She sank down onto the top step of the staircase and pressed the phone hard to her ear. "I just needed to hear your voice. Know you were okay."

The words slipped out before she could stop them. Damn it! How had she let that confession escape? "I mean, I was concerned about your mom and her shop," she said hurriedly, hoping to distract Sam. "And Cilla shouldn't be on her feet -- she's supposed to be on desk duty. So it's good to know that Livvy's wading into the battle. I've got my break-in covered. You take care of your mom and Cilla."

* * *

Instead of pulling out of the parking lot of his mom's shop, Sam held the phone away from his ear. Stared at it. Had Jules really said that? Admitted that she'd called because she'd needed to hear his voice?

"Jules? Are you really okay? Is there something you're not telling me?" he asked, his voice rising. "Are you in the hospital?" A hundred scenarios raced through his head, each one worse than the next. "You're not hurt, are you?"

There was dead silence on the phone for a heartbeat. Then Julia said, "Wow. You went from A to Z at the speed of light. With an imagination like that, if the baseball thing doesn't work out, you could write screenplays like Brendan. No, I'm not in the hospital, you goofball. I'm at the station."

Hearing the laughter in her voice, Sam took a deep breath. Let it out. Allowed himself to relax. "Okay," he said, trying to tamp down the relief. "I'll relax, as long as you say it again."

"You're a goofball."

She'd had a bad morning, and he'd gotten her to smile. This was the first light moment since he'd arrived as his mom's auto repair shop. Trying to suppress the tiny grin, he pressed the phone to his ear. As if that would bring him closer to Julia. "No. Tell me again that you called because you needed to hear my voice."

Dead silence. Finally she said, "I might have let something along those lines slip. Only because I wasn't thinking clearly. I was blinded by my total pissed-off-ness at Kirby."

"You think he's responsible?"

"Who else besides Kirby would want to tap into my computer? Put mics and cameras into my apartment? I'm not that interesting, Sam."

"Oh, you're plenty interesting, Jules," he said, his body remembering all the ways she'd aroused his interest the night before. "But I'll add you to my list."

"What list is that?" she asked, clearly bewildered.

"My list of places to send my security guy. He's installing a system at Mom's shops. I'm gonna have him put some cameras and alarms at her house, too." He frowned. "Don's too, I suppose, since apparently she spends time there."

"So Don is more than your dad's old partner?"

Sam pursed his lips. He wanted to bleach his eyes to erase the image of the lip-lock his mom had shared with

Don that morning. "News to us, but apparently so. After Dad died, Mom inherited the business, so she started working at the original shop on Irving Park Road. Cilla and Livvy and I thought it was a great idea -- give her something to focus on, you know?

"She and Don fought about everything, down to what kind of coffee filters and toilet paper to buy. Cilla and Livvy and I thought it was hilarious." He blew out a breath. "They're not fighting so much anymore."

"That's sweet," Julia said, her voice softening. "And installing a good security system at the shops is a great idea. But don't worry about my place. I'll take care of it."

"Hell, no, Jules. I'm getting a group rate. And when do you have time to deal with this? The work will be done by tomorrow. All I need is a key to your place."

"I don't want cameras in my apartment, Sam." He could practically hear her shudder over the phone.

"'Course not. There'll be cameras at the doors and the garage. All outside. I just want Mark to be able to go inside, look around, see if you need anything else."

"You're not responsible for my apartment's security," she said. "I'll contact my landlord. Make him put something in."

"And when would he get to that? In a month? Two? You need protection right now." He hesitated, knowing that if he pushed too hard, she'd dig in her heels. "I'm on road trips about half the time," he finally said. "I won't be able to focus if I'm worrying about what that bastard Kirby is doing. Worrying whether you're safe. So this is for me as much as it is for you, Jules."

"Now you're playing dirty," she said, her scowl coming through the phone loud and clear.

"Not playing dirty if it's true," he retorted. And it was. Kirby was off the rails. Julia was an obvious target. On his next road trip, Sam would spend his time wondering if she was all right instead of concentrating on how to hit that sneaky bastard Tennyson's curve ball.

"I'm a cop," she said. "I can protect myself."

"I know that. But someone got into your apartment last night," he pointed out. "If you'd had cameras at the door, you could have seen who it was."

He heard her blow out a breath, and he knew she was frustrated that he had answers for all her objections. "Fine," she said grudgingly after a long pause. "Go ahead and have your guy install the security system. But I'm paying for it."

"Of course." No way was Julia paying for it. "Okay if I send Mark over to pick up your keys? I want security in place at your apartment and my mom's shops today."

"I suppose so," she said. "I'll be here for a while. Just have him call in case I get a case and have to leave."

"Will do," Sam said, pleased with the win. "I'll see you tonight at the event, right?"

"I'll be there, Sam." Her voice lowered. Softened. As if she'd been thinking about last night as much as he had. "Take care of your mom and Cilla in the meantime."

"On it," he said.

Before he could add an endearment, she said. "Later, babe," and disconnected.

Babe. He lowered his phone and grinned at the screen. Had she realized she'd called him that? He'd guess not. Especially if she was at the station.

He shoved his phone into his pocket and got out of his car. Headed back into the auto shop, feeling lighter. He'd already called Mark, the guy who'd installed the security in his house. The guy would be here soon, and he'd send him over to the station to pick up Julia's keys.

* * *

"Gotcha, Busey," Julia said, pushing away from her desk with a triumphant fist pump. "I own your ass."

She leaned back in her desk chair, studying the screen of her computer. Tim Busey, one of the guys with Derek Kirby on the night Nick was killed, was going to law school at night. He was in his third year, taking a class or two each semester. On track to graduate next year. So close he could taste it.

She'd marked him as the weak link the first time she interviewed him, and now she knew why. Ronald Kirby would have made it clear Busey was expected to lie about what had happened that night. Testify at the trial, if necessary.

That was the last thing a guy in law school would want to do. He knew the consequences of lying under oath. But Kirby was paying his salary. Possibly paying for his education, too. That was a perk at a lot of big firms.

The kid probably hoped he could fade into the woodwork and avoid testifying.

Not going to happen. Julia would be shining a big spotlight on aspiring attorney Busey.

She stood up, scanning the room for a uniform to pick him up, just as her phone rang.

"Carleton," she said impatiently.

"This is Beechwood in the tech lab," came a low drawl. "I'm finished with your laptop."

"Did you find anything?" Julia asked, her heart suddenly pounding.

"Come on down and pick it up," Beechwood replied. "We'll talk then."

The line went dead, and Julia set the phone carefully back in its cradle. Beechwood would have said no if he hadn't found anything. Wouldn't he?

Frank Zebretti strolled into the bullpen, and Julia flagged him down. "I've got another one of Kirby's buddies I need to talk to. Could you pick him up for me? I'm headed down to the lab."

"Sure," Zebretti said. "Give me the deets."

It was a Saturday, thank goodness. Scribbling his name and home address on a piece of paper, she handed it to Zebretti. "We're not waiting until Monday to do the walk of shame at work with this one," she said. "I want to keep him in my back pocket for now."

"Got it. On my way."

"Thanks, Zebretti," Julia called after him. She turned in the opposite direction and ran down the stairs to the lab.

Ozzie Beechwood had been a tech at the station since Julia landed there after the Academy. His mocha skin was lined and his hair was gray. The kids called him Gramps, but Beechwood had forgotten more than most of the kids knew.

He smiled when he spotted her, and he waved her over. "Whoever did this was a little sloppy," he began. "Thank him when you catch him. He made my job a lot easier."

"What's on it?" Julia asked, staring at her computer.

"What *was* on it, you should be asking." Ozzie patted the computer, as if comforting a sick child. "The camera would have been recording you whenever you opened the machine. Sending audio and video out to a web address. Haven't found the ISP yet, but I will."

Julia stared at her computer. "Anything else?" she asked faintly.

"Keystroke capture," Ozzie said, offhandedly. "Anything you typed would go directly to the asshole's computer. In other words, a complete digital trail."

"That's... that's disturbing." Julia glanced at the computer out of the corner of her eye, but focused on Beechwood. "So he or she would know what I was doing every time I used this thing."

"Yeah," Ozzie said. He tilted his head. "You use it for work?"

"Occasionally," Julia said, her stomach churning at the thought that whoever did this could have accessed sensitive material. "Won't anymore."

"The spyware and keystroke capture is gone," Ozzie assured her. "After I got rid of the malware, I ran a complete scan, and you're clean." He studied her for a moment. "You're working on that Kirby case, right?"

She nodded.

"You might want to leave your laptop here when you're not at home," he said. "Police station is secure. Your place isn't." He patted the computer lid. "You need to keep this baby safe."

"I'm having a security system installed," she said.

"Good idea. Still, bring the computer. Pain in the ass, but safer that way."

"Okay," she said, drawing a deep breath. "I will."

Ozzie handed her the computer, then jerked his head toward the next room. "The techs found stuff in your place, too. Go talk to them."

"I will. Thanks, Ozzie."

"My pleasure." He shook his head. "That Kirby sounds like a piece of work."

"You're a lot more polite than I would be," Julia said, forcing a smile. "But yeah, he is."

Fifteen minutes later, she climbed the stairs to the bullpen, her head spinning. The techs hadn't found any cameras, thank God, but they'd found plenty of tiny microphones. At least one in every room.

When she reached her floor, she headed for Captain Francisco's office. He spotted her through the window and waved her in.

"Just got the tech's report," he said. "Microphones in your apartment? Spyware on your personal computer?" He frowned. "Does Marini ever go to your place?"

Julia took a deep breath. *Oh, God.* "He's been there twice. Unplanned. We had takeout and talked about the case because I didn't want to discuss it in public. That's it."

"Anyone see him go in with you?"

"Not that I know of," she said slowly. But she hadn't looked in every car on her block. Hadn't checked to see if someone was watching from an apartment across the street. Dozens of spiders crawled over her skin. "But I guess it's possible someone was watching."

"Wouldn't put it past Kirby." Francisco scowled. "It was smart to leave them in place. We might be able to use them. Watch what you say, though, Carleton. And I'd assume someone is following you. Probably Marini, too."

"I'll keep my eyes open, sir."

"You do that. I want to nail Derek Kirby," the captain said. "But I don't want any of my officers getting hurt. Or the Bearcats' prize third base man. Pay attention out there."

"Yes, sir."

"Now go get this case put to bed." He leaned toward her over the desk. "If you find that Ronald Kirby is involved in this, you'll make me a very happy man. I will personally put the cuffs on him."

Julia forced a smile. "I'll back you up, sir."

"Good. Now get back to work."

As she was leaving Francisco's office, her cell phone rang. Hoping it was Sam, she wrenched it out of her pocket. It was a number she didn't recognize.

"Hello?" she said cautiously.

"Ms. Carleton? This is Mark Esperanza. Sam Marini gave me your number. I'm supposed to install a security system at your place, and I need a key."

"Right. Can I meet you somewhere?"

"I'm in front of your station. Panel truck that says 'Esperanza Security' on the side. You want me to come in?"

"No, I'll be right down. Pull into the parking lot up ahead on your right."

Ten minutes later, Julia watched Mark pull out of the parking lot and head in the direction of her apartment. He'd been pleasant and seemed competent. He'd described in excruciating detail what he was going to install at her apartment. The cameras above the doors would be very small, recessed into the wood, but with extremely high resolution. "You'll be able to count the person's freckles," Mark had assured her. He'd come back after the installation to install a program on her laptop and an app on her phone.

She'd asked, "You'll send me the bill, right?"

"Mr. Marini has given me instructions about the billing," he assured her as he swung into his truck.

Julia watched with narrowed eyes until he was out of sight, then unlocked the door to the station and walked up the stairs to her desk. Mr. Marini's instructions had better include her billing address.

She sighed as she climbed the stairs. More complications from the Kirby case. It should have been finished a few days after Kirby punched Nick. But Ronald Kirby was throwing more and more stones into the pond, resulting in larger and larger ripples spreading out from the center. Ripples could grow into waves.

She hoped no one would get swamped.

Or drown.

CHAPTER 19

Julia stared through the observation window at Tim Busey, sitting in an interrogation room. He'd been there for a half-hour. She'd let him fidget for another ten minutes or so. Long enough to make him uneasy. To let his imagination loose.

He wasn't smirking, like the rest of his buddies had done. He was staring at the mirror, which he had to know was a one-way window. She hoped he was wondering who was watching. Wondering why, after the other guys' second interviews, she'd waited so long to bring *him* back in.

Time to enlighten Mr. Busey. And complicate his life.

"Mr. Busey," she said a few minutes later as she walked in the room. The door closed behind her with a solid thump, and Busey twitched.

Julia suppressed a smile. *Good.* She wanted him nervous.

"Why am I here?" he asked. "I answered all your questions last time."

It was the exact reaction she'd hoped to elicit.

Julia set her leather folder and her laptop onto the table between them. Watched the kid's eyes drop to it as she slid into her chair. "You're being aggressive," she said, folding her hands on the table. "Trying to put me on the defensive.

Just like they teach you in law school, right?"

The kid's Adams's apple bobbed. "No, I... how do you know about law school? I didn't tell you."

Julia opened her eyes wide. "Wow. You don't know that the police can find out everything about you? Are you sure law is the right choice for you?"

Busey flushed a deep red. "No, I... I knew. Just didn't think it was important."

Julia leaned closer. "Oh, it's very important, Tim. *So* important for this case." She studied him for a moment. "Have you studied the laws on perjury, Tim?"

"Of course." He straightened in his seat. "What does that have to do with what happened to Derek?"

What happened to Derek? A flash of anger swept through her. "What, exactly, happened to Kirby?"

"He was arrested on a bogus charge. That kid attacked him first."

"Have you seen the video, Tim?"

He frowned. "That video doesn't show shit."

Julia cocked her head. "Really? That's what Kirby said?"

He shrugged. "He said it was all blurry. Couldn't really see anything on it, so it didn't matter."

"Sounds exactly like what a high-priced attorney would say publicly. The guy is trying to influence potential jurors. Why don't you take a look at it and make your own judgment?"

She opened her laptop, found the video she'd loaded forty-five minutes ago, and turned the computer toward Busey. Clicked the 'play' button.

Watched as Busey's face went sheet white. She'd turned off the sound, so there was nothing to distract from the video. It was very clear that Nick D'Angelo had never touched Kirby. Never even came close.

The video ended, but Busey kept staring at the screen. As if trying to convince himself this was all a nightmare. That he'd wake up in a moment and everything would be fine. Normal.

Julia closed the computer and set it to the side. Placed her palms on the table. "That's what the jury is going to see, Tim. That video. They'll see Derek Kirby hit a man half his size. A man who never even came close to touching him."

She leaned toward Busey. "You'll be the first witness called afterward. Are you going to repeat what Ronald Kirby told you to say? That Nick D'Angelo hit Derek first? That the video is blurry and hard to make out? That no one could tell what had happened?"

He stared at her, ashen, but didn't say a word.

"You can't sit in the witness chair and stare at the prosecutor," she said sharply. "You're compelled to answer him. So what are you going to say?"

His throat bobbed again, and he opened his mouth. Closed it.

Satisfied with Busey's reaction, she settled back in the chair. "If you answer the way Ronald tells you to answer, tell the jury that Kirby never hit Nick, you'll be facing perjury charges. And with that video, the jury will need about ten seconds to convict you. That's a felony conviction. Maybe you won't get jail time, although you probably will. But you will never practice law. I guarantee it. You won't even be allowed to sit for the bar exam."

The kid bit his lip. His gaze darted from side to side. He didn't speak.

"No one's going to save you, Tim," she said in a softer voice. Part of her felt sorry for him. Busey might be a basically good kid, but he'd been targeted by an unscrupulous, amoral man. Now he was trapped. "You have two choices. You can answer the prosecutor the way Ronald Kirby tells you to answer, or you can finish law school and practice law. You can't do both."

"I... I think I want my attorney," he finally said.

"Okay. Who do you want me to call?"

He named the same guy who was representing Derek Kirby.

"Really?" Julia tilted her head. "That's who you want looking out for you? The guy who's trying to get Derek off the hook? You want him preparing *your* defense?" She held his gaze, forcing him to look at her. "Who do you think he's going to throw under the bus, Tim? Derek? Or you?"

"That's who Mr. Kirby told me to ask for."

"Of course it is." She wanted to add 'you idiot', but that wouldn't encourage the guy to cooperate. "You are *nothing* to Ronald Kirby. Your only use to him is helping Derek escape punishment for murder. Ronald doesn't care that being prosecuted for perjury will destroy your law career before it even starts. Your employer is telling you to lie on the witness stand. You need to think long and hard about what you're willing to do to keep a job."

She stood up. "It's been a pleasure talking to you, Tim. And I'd advise you not to waste your money enrolling in law school for the summer session. You'd just be throwing it away. You're free to go."

Julia picked up the folder and computer and headed for the door. Before she could step out, Tim Busey said, "Wait, Detective."

* * *

Sam stood at the podium in the press room, gripping the lectern with both hands, and forced himself not to look at his watch. He smiled as he answered the questions, but his mind was three miles away. At Chicago Wine Bar.

He wasn't nervous about the event. He'd done celebrity MC gigs for other charity events, and he always had fun. This would be his second with the PBJ band, and he was looking forward to it. They were good guys. Great musicians.

He'd texted Julia that he'd be there at 8:30 PM. It was already 8:15, so he knew he'd be late. He jerked his head at the <u>Herald's</u> beat reporter. "Last question, guys."

Julia wouldn't get bent out of shape because he was late.

196

Hell, she probably wouldn't even notice. She'd be in cop mode, checking the security at the venue. Scoping everyone out.

The band wouldn't get their shorts in a knot, either. He'd texted them, told them he'd be late but would arrive before they started.

Five minutes later, he hurried out of the room, smoothing down his suit coat as he called a Lyft driver to pick him up. He was covered. Everyone who mattered knew he'd be there in time. So why was he rushing to get to the event?

He wanted to see Julia. He'd missed her today.

He wanted to tell her the rest of the story from his mom's shop. Hear what she'd done during the day.

Just like a couple would do.

He faltered. They weren't a couple. They'd agreed to a no-strings affair, fun and games, yada yada yada.

But this need to see her, to share his day with her, listen to her tell him about her day, went deeper than fun and games.

They'd have plenty of fun and games tonight. But sex wasn't all he wanted from Julia.

The thought shocked him. He hadn't planned on getting in deep with anyone at this point in his life. He needed to concentrate on baseball, on becoming the best player he could be. The kind of player that made a difference on his team. He didn't want any distractions.

Why couldn't he do that and be with Julia, too?

His steps slowed as he frowned. Thought about it. They'd reconnected because he was involved in one of her cases. He'd been distracted by that. By Julia herself, too. And he was hitting the best he had all year.

Derek Kirby's antics from his seat behind the dugout hadn't distracted him, either.

He turned the corner and walked faster. He couldn't wait to tell Julia about today's game. How he'd hit for the cycle, with Kirby's ranting and shouting getting louder as he had a double, then a triple, then a single, then a home run.

The people in the seats around Kirby had taunted him more with each hit. Yeah, Sam had done okay by being distracted.

The Lyft driver slowed as he reached the corner of Clark and Addison, and Sam checked his phone for the license plate to make sure it was the right car. Sliding onto the seat, Sam said, "Hey, thanks for picking me up."

The driver, a guy with dark hair, olive skin and an easy smile, said, "No problem. City Wine Bar, right?"

"You got it."

There was a line out the door of the venue when the driver pulled up. Sam clicked a generous tip on his phone, turned off the screen and slid the phone into his pocket. "Thanks a lot, Omar." The guy had talked baseball non-stop. "Nice talking to you."

"You, too, man," the driver said. "Keep hitting like you have been, okay?"

"I'll try," Sam said with a laugh as he closed the door.

He went to the head of the line, feeling like a jerk but knowing he didn't have time to wait in the line. He showed the bouncer his driver's license and said, "I'm the MC tonight."

The bouncer waved him through without looking at his license. "Go on in, Mr. Marini. They're waiting for you."

Inside the wine bar, the tables in the raised area at the back of the big room were full, and the area in front of the stage was filling up fast. Paul, Bobby, Johnny and Jeff, the musicians, were setting up on the stage, but Sam didn't see Julia. *Damn.* He'd wanted to talk to her before he got caught up in his official duties.

Sam wove his way through the crowd, reaching the stage and taking the three steps up in a bound. "Hey, guys, sorry I'm late. Game went long."

All four musicians came over to shake his hand. They talked about what he'd do tonight, which consisted mostly of introducing the musicians, offering requests for twenty bucks a pop, and working the crowd for donations. All the proceeds would go to a woman's shelter in the area, and Sam would talk about the shelter for a few minutes.

He'd done similar gigs before -- most of the players had. They were part of his job, and Sam was happy to lend his celebrity for a worthy cause.

As he chatted with the musicians, he caught sight of Julia out of the corner of his eye. He had no idea how he'd spotted her in the crowd, but he turned to look and she was there. Leaning against the stage a dozen feet away.

His heart leaped. "Got it, guys," he said hastily to the band. "Give me a signal when you're ready to start."

He jumped lightly down from the stage and hurried over to Julia. "Hey." He wanted to pull her into a kiss, but he stuck his hands into his pockets instead. "Glad you made it."

He mentally rolled his eyes at himself. Lamest line ever. But Julia's stern cop expression softened into a smile.

"Told you I would." She glanced around the room. "What exactly is your role here?"

"I'm the celebrity who cajoles everyone into giving more money than they intended to the evening's cause. Tonight it's a women's shelter on the north side."

"Good cause," she said. "The place is really crowded. Hope you raise a ton of money." She scanned the crowd. "But are you sure it's a good idea to go wading into all these people?" she asked quietly. "Never know who's in here."

"It's fine, Jules. There are several bouncers, in case anyone gets out of hand."

"A lot can happen before a bouncer gets to you," Julia said. Her head never stopped moving. She was constantly scanning the room.

"I've taken care of it," Sam said. She wasn't going to let this whole 'protective cop thing' go. "You want to go backstage?" Sam asked. "You can probably get a better perspective on the crowd from there."

"No way." She shook her head as she nodded toward

the band. "Those stage lights would blind me. And I'm not standing backstage while you're letting every Jim, Jane and Jack get close to you."

"This wasn't supposed to be about you protecting me," he said impatiently. "This is supposed to be fun. Hear a good band, watch me make a fool of myself."

Finally she relaxed. "I didn't have to come here to watch you make a fool of yourself," she teased. "I could take you to the Chi-Town Tap for that." A couple bumped into her, pushing her against Sam. She took advantage of the cover to slide her hand around his hip and squeeze his ass.

It felt as if she'd touched a live wire to his skin. He turned to face her, trying to tug her closer. "Better watch yourself, Carleton. We have an audience. Don't want to give them a show, do you?"

"Hmm," she said, resisting being pulled into him, but sliding her leg between his. "Lots of people here. Pretty dark room. The way everyone's packed together, I bet I could grab your ass all night and no one would notice."

"I'll take that bet." He swallowed hard. He'd missed her so much today. He needed to touch *her*. Right now. "In fact, let's take that bet backstage."

Julia laughed and stepped away from him. "You have work to do. And so do I. What should I worry about more? Kirby showing up? Or all the women who are eyeing you like dessert?"

"Somehow I don't think Derek Kirby is much for philanthropy," he said. "Or supporting women's shelters."

Her smile disappeared. "No, I doubt he is. So I'll worry about the women."

"You're the only woman I'm interested in, Detective." He leaned closer and caught a hint of oranges. Her scent. "You don't need to worry about that. You can take watching my back off your work list."

"You think watching your back is work?" Her sultry smile and bedroom eyes went straight to his groin. He closed his eyes for a moment, trying to get himself under control. He shifted his feet, trying to get more comfortable.

"Watching your back means I get to watch your ass," she murmured. "Always fun, but especially now. When I know what it looks like."

"You're an evil woman," he said in a low voice. "Talking that way when I can't do anything about it."

"Give you something to think about tonight," she said. Nudging him with her elbow, she said, "Go collect some money for the shelter. Clean out everyone's pockets."

"Where are you going to be?"

"Very close to you."

"Exactly where I want you." Sam froze for a moment, but it was true. He wanted her close by. *With him.*

Julia nodded toward the stage. "Get me one of those donation boxes. I'll collect with you."

Her gaze never stopped scanning the room. She was hyperalert. Tense. "You're in cop mode," he finally said.

She lifted one shoulder. "Yeah, I guess I am. After what happened at your mom's shop, it feels as if the Kirbys are escalating. I'm not about to stand in the wings and watch you wade through a crowd." Her gaze scanned the room again, then came back to him. "Collecting donations gives me a reason to stay close to you."

"Not your job, Carleton. I told you I have this covered."

"More eyes on you are never a bad thing." She nodded toward the stage. "One of the musicians wants you."

Sam glanced behind him. Bobby was motioning him closer. Leaving Julia behind, he wove his way over to where Bobby was crouching on the stage. "Johnny reminded me about Stump the Band," he said. "If someone requests a song we don't know, we match their donation. So keep track of how much we'll owe you at the end of the night."

"Are you out of your mind?" Sam shook his head. "You're donating your fee for this gig. Any Stump the Band money will come out of my pocket. I'll keep track of every penny."

Bobby tilted his head. "Thanks, man. That's generous

of you."

"Least I can do," Sam told him. "You're donating your time when you could be making money playing another gig."

The band strummed the chord they'd told him was the signal to begin, so Sam jumped on the stage and took the mic from Johnny. "I'm Sam Marini, and I want to welcome everyone to City Wine Bar," he said. "Give it up for Paul, Bobby, Johnny and Jeff."

The crowd roared, waving their arms in the air. Jumping up and down. Sam relaxed. This was like playing ball in front of a full house. Instead of making him nervous, he fed off the excitement. "Not only are they great musicians, they're generous ones. PBJ has donated their fee for playing tonight to the North Side Women's Shelter. Let's all be just as generous in supporting this needed shelter. I'm going to match all donations, so see how much of my bank account you can drain tonight, okay?"

A room-shaking roar went up from the crowd, the musicians hooted, then they started in on their first song. It was a rollicking tune that Johnny and Paul had written, and it got the crowd revved up. Sam took two donation boxes off the stage and handed one to Julia, who was waiting at the stairs. He smiled as he edged his way into the crowed. Hands waving bills reached out to him, and people stuffed them in the collection box as Sam swung from side to side, trying to get every offered donation.

The crowd pressed closer, surrounding Sam. Hands patted at his back, his chest, his hands. He glanced over at Julia, a few feet away. Maybe she was right. With Kirby on the loose, wading into the crowd wasn't such a great idea, even though he had a plan.

Someone grabbed his ass.

He swung around and caught a short, busty blond woman swaying on very high heels. "Hey, Sam," she said. "Wanna come play with me?"

"Sorry," he said, forcing a smile. "I'm working tonight."

He held out the collection box. "How about a donation to the women's shelter?"

The woman frowned, but then her eyes lit and she pulled a tiny wallet out of her tiny purse. Scribbled something on a twenty, then shoved it into the slot in the top of the box. "That one's just for you," she cooed. "I wrote my number on it."

"I'm sure the shelter will be happy to get it. They'll be calling on you for another donation," he said, before turning away from the woman.

The band had launched into another tune, the crowd shifted and Sam was squeezed even more tightly. He caught a whiff Julia's scent before he saw her. But he felt her body plastered against him. The crowd was so thick that he couldn't move for a moment. Neither could Julia.

"You're playing nice with the customers," she cooed into his ear. "That's good. But I'll play nicer with you later."

He wanted to respond, but he choked on his tongue. "God, Jules," he managed to get out. "Way to make me lose my focus."

"Good. That'll keep you away from the handsy blond barracuda." Under cover of the people crowding around them, she slid her hand down his ass, then backed up. "I've got my eyes on you, Marini."

"I want more than my eyes on you, Carleton."

"Later," she whispered in his ear. A guy lurched into her, pressing her against him more tightly, and she took advantage of the cover to tug his earlobe into her mouth. She curled her tongue around it for a moment before letting it go.

He was sure his eyes rolled back in his head. This sexy playfulness wasn't what he had in mind when he'd invited Julia to the benefit. But he liked how the evening was shaping up.

Behind him, he felt Julia turn to someone. Heard her murmur something that included the word 'donation'. Bills crinkled as they were shoved into the box.

Sam was so attuned to Julia that he knew the moment she stiffened. Went into cop mode.

She tucked her arm through his as though they were strolling the floor together. But she tugged his arm to bring his ear closer to his mouth.

"Derek Kirby just walked in. Working his way toward you. Maybe you should get on the stage for a while."

Sam turned and glanced at the musicians. Paul nodded at him. They'd arranged this, too.

"Okay," he said. "I'm heading up there. Follow me so I know you're safe."

"I'm gonna stay here and keep an eye on Kirby," she murmured. "The little prick is staring at you. And I'm pretty sure it's not because he wants to make a donation."

She handed Sam her collection box and nudged Sam toward the stage. "Get up there," she said. "I've got this."

CHAPTER 20

*T*hank God she was still wearing her gun.

Although it wouldn't do her any good. No way could she use it in this crowded room.

At least she had it this time, though, unlike when she'd returned to her apartment that morning.

Julia began moving toward Kirby, her gaze sweeping the crowded room. Had Kirby brought along a friend? Someone to back him up?

As far as she could tell, no one else was moving toward the stage. Didn't mean there wasn't someone else there. But she focused on Kirby, vowing to stop him before he reached Sam.

She elbowed and shouldered her way through the crowd, certain Kirby hadn't noticed her yet. Determined to keep it that way until she was closer. Kirby was fixated on Sam, up on the stage with the musicians. One of them said into his mic, "As a little bonus for everyone, Sam is going to join us on our next song. Show your appreciation by donating to the North Side Women's Shelter."

The musician shoved a mic into Sam's hands. As Sam joked with the guy, Julia tried to move faster. Ignored the squeal as she stepped on someone's toes. If Kirby reached the stage, this wouldn't end well.

Sam acted as though he hadn't noticed Kirby. He was talking with the musicians. Interacting with the people at the front of the crowd. Smiling. He even signed a couple of autographs.

He was cool under pressure. From what she'd seen while watching games on television, he was just as cool when he was playing baseball.

Finally, one of the guitar players strummed some chords, and Sam began singing the Bob Seger classic <u>Night Moves</u>.

As she switched her gaze between Sam and Kirby, a tiny part of her brain noticed that he had a good voice. Throaty. Deep. And he could definitely carry a tune.

Moving slowly in Kirby's direction, Julia flew forward a couple of steps when someone bumped into her back. Just as Kirby yelled, "Marini, you suck," at a momentary pause in the song.

Sam faltered momentarily. She could tell the moment he zeroed in on Derek in the crowd. His jaw clenched, then he began to sing more loudly. The band amped up their sound too, as Derek continued to yell.

Patrons close to Kirby tried to shush him. A few tried to stand in his way. Kirby brushed them aside as if they were ants as he moved closer to the stage. Closer to Sam.

Julia tried to slide between and around people in the crowd, but it was like swimming in molasses. Way too much effort for little forward movement. Sam was too far away. Too many people were between them. Kirby would get to the stage before she did.

Before she could stop him.

Her gun was useless in here.

Her heart pounding, sweat pouring down her sides, down her back, she tried to move faster. She shoved people aside. Stepped on their toes. Ignored their yells of outrage as she tried to get to Kirby.

Just as he reached the stage, three burly bouncers stepped out of the wings and jumped into the crowd. One of them cleared the way. The other two gripped Kirby's arms. Kirby was a big guy with freakish muscles. But the bouncers made Kirby look like a wimp. They muscled him through the separating crowd as if he weighed no more than a marshmallow man, all air and no substance.

Sam had been right. He *had* been prepared.

More than she had been.

Julia followed in their wake as they dragged Kirby to the door. His mouth was open. Clearly shouting something. But the people jeering and yelling, the music pouring from the speakers, made it impossible to know what he was saying.

The bouncers and their prey reached the back of the room before Julia did. The two men holding his arms dragged Kirby toward the door. The third guy had his phone to his ear. Calling the cops, she hoped.

Julia hung back as they waited near the door. She heard the approaching siren a moment before the bouncers did. By the time they had the door open and had wrestled Kirby through it, she was right behind them.

A squad car pulled up to the curb. The driver's door opened and a cop slid out. Opened the back door. Clapped Kirby on the back, as if reassuring him, guided him onto the seat, then slammed the door.

Huh. The cop hadn't cuffed Kirby. She wondered why.

Then the uniform turned to the bouncers. Smiled and shook their hands.

It was Dwyer.

Julia narrowed her eyes as she watched. Dwyer got back into the car. Turned and said something to Kirby. Then straightened and began to drive away.

Not before she'd seen the smile on Kirby's face.

* * *

Unsettled, wondering about Dwyer and the smile he'd elicited from Derek Kirby, Julia stayed in the raised area at the back of the room. She squeezed into a spot by the railing, where she could see the whole crowd.

No one else appeared to be a threat. Everyone was watching the band, singing along, stuffing money into the boxes Sam and several others carried through the room. Several times, women leaned close and whispered something in his ear. Sam whispered something back, smiled and held out the collection box. Whatever he said, the women lit up. Deposited money in the collection box. And then they backed away.

Julia gradually relaxed, but she didn't leave her spot at the railing, and she didn't let down her guard. One of the bouncers stood a few feet away from her, and she knew he'd be able to get to trouble more quickly than she would.

The band was winding down, calling Sam to the stage for one last song, and there had been no more incidents during the concert. Unless you counted the fan who tossed a pair of underwear onto the stage as Sam and the band finished the show with another Bob Seger song.

If Sam noticed the red lace thong, he didn't react. Instead, his gaze found her at the back of the room. His slow, sexy smile held all kinds of promises, and Julia's heart thundered.

Later tonight, Sam wouldn't have to sing to make *her* lose her underwear. All he'd have to do was kiss her and it would magically disappear.

She really hoped he'd booked that room at the Houston Hotel.

Forty-five minutes later, the venue had cleared out. Sam had received a grateful hug from the director of the women's shelter, he'd shaken hands with the manager of the City Wine Bar, and exchanged handshakes and back slaps with the band, along with promises to 'do this again soon.'

Julia had stayed in the background, watching as Sam charmed everyone in the vicinity. And she knew he wasn't putting on a show. Sam was the real thing -- a kind, generous man who was genuinely happy to lend his name to a good cause.

Finally, he turned around, searching the room. He smiled when he spotted her, sitting at one of the high-top tables. "Ready to go, Carleton?"

"I am," she said, sliding off the stool.

"This is Julia Carleton," he said, introducing her to the band and the manager. "We're working together, and she wanted to catch the show tonight," he said easily.

Smooth. Thank God he hadn't introduced her as a police officer. A business associate was boring. Being accompanied by a police officer, or worse, a girlfriend, was gossip. "Sam said you guys were great, and he was right," she said to the band members. "Do you have a website with your schedule?"

Johnny pulled out a business card and handed it to her. "Or you could just ask Sam. He has my phone number," he said.

"If we're still working together, I'll do that," she said easily. "Thanks."

Only she saw Sam's frown at her words. She tilted her head toward the door. "Ready to go, Marini?"

"Absolutely." He opened the door and escorted her into the fresh air. As they turned onto the side street next to the venue, clouds hovered low in the sky, and the air was as heavy as wet wool. Clouds obscured the moon, and the side street where she'd parked her car was shadowed and gloomy. The air quivered with tension, waiting for the storm that threatened.

It was late enough that most of the homes were dark. Streetlights dotted the corners, but their lights cast a golden circle for only ten feet or so. They left the rest of the street a dark midnight blue.

"I'm a few blocks down," she said as they headed down the silent side street.

"That's okay." Sam wrapped his arm around her shoulders and snugged her against his side. "That will give me time to tell you all the things I'm going to do to you tonight. All the things I want you to do to me."

Julia had been watching the street, but at Sam's words, she shifted to look at him. Desire, never far from the surface when she was with Sam, roared to life. "Is that right?"

"Oh, yeah." His hand slid down her shoulder, and the backs of his fingers brushed the side of her breast. "I've been making plans all day."

"Really?" She nudged him with her elbow, loving his solid muscles. "I thought you were playing baseball today."

"Yeah, not during the game. Or before the game. But the whole time I was at my mom's shop, I wished you were there with me. And after the game? While I was doing the press conference thing, I just wanted to get to the Wine Bar and see you."

"Hmm," she said, unwilling to confess that she'd been anxious to see him, as well. "Sounds like I'm distracting you from your business."

"If you are, you need to keep doing it. I hit for the cycle today."

She frowned. She'd been reading the stories about the Bearcats in the newspaper, but she'd never heard of a cycle. "What does that mean?"

"It means I got a single, a double, a triple and a home run, all in the same game. It's pretty rare." He cleared his throat. "Some people think it's a big deal."

She'd been trying to learn about baseball, and she knew Sam was right. Even though she hadn't yet read about 'the cycle', she knew getting all those hits in one game *was* a big deal.

"Congratulations." She dragged him behind a huge oak tree, where they blended into the shadows, then stretched up and pressed a kiss to his mouth. "That's very cool."

He hugged her against him, lifted her and deepened the kiss. "Yeah, it was. But that's not what I was thinking about this evening."

His eyes gleamed, and heat swept up her chest and into

her face. She was afraid she'd ignite on the spot. "What were you thinking about?"

"I was wondering what color your underwear was. And how fast I could get it off you once we get into my suite at the Houston."

"I'm guessing… not very long," she murmured into his throat.

Sam slid his hand beneath her jacket and dipped one finger into her waistband next to her spine. "Care to place a bet?" he whispered, his voice raspy against her ear.

"Isn't this cozy," a male voice said. Too close.

Julia sprang away from Sam, shocked. She'd been careless *again*. Let this guy sneak up on them. She stepped in front of him as she reached for her gun.

"Don't make a move for the gun, Detective." The wiry man who stood five feet in front of them, dressed in black, wore a ski mask. His voice sounded vaguely familiar, but Julia couldn't place it. "I don't want to hurt anyone. I'm just delivering a warning."

Her hand twitched, but she kept it at her side as the masked man's gaze shifted from her to Sam. "Although the visuals were a nice bonus."

"Just putting on a show for the woman who followed Sam out the door," Julia said, knowing it was weak but unable to come up with anything better.

The guy smirked at her. "You're good actors, then," he said. "Oscar quality." His mouth tightened. "Drop the Kirby case while you can."

"Derek Kirby killed Nick D'Angelo," Julia said, her voice calmer than she felt. "You don't honestly think the state's attorney will drop that case, do you?"

"If there are no witnesses, she will." The man's gaze shifted from her to Sam. "No one has to get hurt here. Videos get lost. Get accidentally erased. And maybe you develop a sudden case of amnesia, Mr. Marini. From being hit by a pitch? Be creative. But get it done."

The man backed away, his hand hovering inside his

jacket. He was warning them he had a gun. He watched them as he crossed the street, then disappeared into the shadows. Julia drew her gun and ran after him. But he'd gotten a head start, and he was gone.

She hurried back to Sam. "Let's go. I'm still two blocks down."

"Aren't you going to call this in?" Sam asked, staring at where the guy had vanished.

"I'm going to call Francisco. My captain," she explained. "Ask him what to do. The guy didn't draw a weapon, although he had one, but he definitely threatened you. If I call this in, the area will be swarming with cops in a few minutes. Mr. 'Lose the Video' will be long gone, but everyone will see us together. A police station is the world's worst gossip mill."

"Isn't it a little late for that? Kirby's man saw us kissing."

"Maybe. But he can't prove anything. It's our word against his. If ten cops see us together? It's not a secret anymore."

The sound of a car engine turning over in the distance rumbled like thunder. It accelerated and faded quickly. Far too quickly for it to be anyone but their guy.

After a moment, all she heard was the usual traffic in a city neighborhood.

"He's already gone," she said. "If I'd called immediately, I'd still be on the phone with the call-center."

They had walked while they talked, and they were close enough that she could see her light blue car, parked directly beneath a street light. "You want to drive?" she asked Sam. "While I call my captain?"

"Sure." He struggled to get behind the wheel of her car, finally finding the lever that moved the seat back. But he needed to spread his knees once he was seated.

"Sorry," Julia said, shaking her head. "You okay to drive?"

"I'm fine. Not that far away. Our next cross-country trip, though? We're taking my car."

"Got it," Julia said. He was teasing her. It didn't mean a thing. But her stupid heart *yearned* at the thought of taking a cross-country trip with Sam. That implied… long term. A relationship. Vacations spent together.

Everything they weren't doing.

Clearing her throat, she punched her captain's contact in her phone.

"Francisco," he said. "What's up, Carleton?"

Thank God he sounded alert. Awake. "I was just at a benefit with Sam Marini. To keep an eye on the crowd. Kirby showed up, made a scene, but the bouncers handled it. Called it in. Dwyer showed up and took him in, I assume.

"Just now, we were walking toward my car when a masked man stopped us. Warned us to drop the D'Angelo case. He said, and I quote, 'No one has to get hurt'. Definitely a threat."

"You call it in?" Francisco asked sharply.

"No, sir, I didn't." Her heart pounded, hoping she'd made the right decision. "I knew he'd be gone by the time a squad could arrive. Sam and I would be sitting in my car on the street. Vulnerable while we waited." She cleared her throat. "And the other issue is precinct gossip. Since I was driving Sam home, I didn't want a lot of cops to see us together."

The silence on the line made her ears burn. Finally, Francisco said, "Good call, Detective. No point stirring things up. Kirby's man saw you together, though. How are you gonna handle that?"

"I told the guy a woman had followed Sam out of the venue. That we were putting on a show for her."

"I told you to keep it private, Carleton. Be more careful next time."

"I will, sir," she said, her face on fire.

"We'll talk in the morning."

"Yes, sir." She pushed the button to end the call and slapped the phone against her thigh.

Waiting at a stoplight, Sam glanced over at her. "Are

you in trouble?"

"I... I don't think so. Francisco sounded more resigned than angry. I'm embarrassed, though. I let myself forget where we were. Because of you, Sam."

She punched his shoulder, a little harder than she should have. She was more upset with herself than with Sam. She hadn't been able to keep her hands off Sam, even though they'd been in public.

"Sorry, babe. I shouldn't have been kissing you like that."

Julia slammed her head back against the headrest. "It wasn't your fault. I wasn't thinking."

She hadn't been thinking because she'd been too busy *feeling*. Anticipating the night she'd been desperately looking forward to.

She was the one who was supposed to keep her head. Not get distracted by sex. But she'd been ready to jump him in public. This whole evening had been building toward that moment beneath the tree.

The way he'd brushed against her when they were collecting donations together.

All those smoldering glances while he'd been singing.

The way his fingers had barely touched her breast, but set off tiny explosions deep inside her.

Everything about Sam made her lose control.

Never in her adult life had she been out of control. Not even with her former fiancé. She glanced over at Sam's profile as the street lights flickered over his face. This *fling* of theirs was morphing into something much more dangerous.

Sam slid his hand over her knee. Squeezed.

She knew it was supposed to be comforting. Reassuring. He was afraid he'd caused trouble with her captain.

But with the grip of his fingers, the pressure of his hand, everything inside Julia clenched. Fire raced through her veins, settling deep in her chest. She burned for Sam.

Kirby could have hurt him tonight. Killed him. The

bastard had almost reached the stairs to the stage when the bouncers intercepted him.

She wouldn't have been able to do a damn thing about it. She'd been too far away. There had been too many people to use her weapon.

She might have lost him tonight.

Giving in to this... this need for Sam that filled her to bursting wouldn't change a damn thing about the Kirby case. It wouldn't make Sam's testimony any different. It wouldn't change one frame of the video he'd taken.

It wouldn't make Nick D'Angelo any less dead.

Ever since her father died, she'd been careful. Guarded. Thought about the consequences of everything she did. She never acted spontaneously.

It had gotten her a job she loved. Honors and citations in her personnel file.

Nothing more.

Tonight she was going to be selfish. She'd forget about the case. Forget Kirby. Forget what her captain would say tomorrow.

Tonight, she'd take what she wanted. What she yearned for.

And she wanted Sam.

She'd worry about the consequences tomorrow.

CHAPTER 21

Her small car crowded them close enough that Sam's warm hand easily blanketed her knee. It was solid. Comforting, just as he intended. But she didn't want comfort tonight. Julia trailed her fingers over the backs of his fingers. Slipped beneath his wrist to stroke his pulse point.

He tightened his grip on her knee. Stroked one long finger over the sensitive skin behind it. Smiled when she shivered.

His smile fell away when she trailed her fingers up the inside of his thigh, stopping only inches from the sudden bulge behind his zipper.

"Jules?" He stopped too abruptly at a red light, and her car rocked for a moment.

"Yes, Sam?"

"What... I thought... we were..."

"You think I'm going to let that tool of Kirby's ruin this evening? I've been thinking about you, about *this*, all day." She leaned over and pressed her mouth to his neck. Licked his skin, tasting the salt from his sweat. "I can't wait to get you alone. Where no one else will surprise us."

A horn blared behind them, loud and insistent. Sam

stomped on the accelerator and Julia fell back hard against her seat as her tiny car shot forward. She pressed her fingers into Sam's thigh, eliciting a tiny groan.

Sam plucked her hand from his thigh and deposited it in her lap. Swallowed. "God, I never thought I'd say this, but you need to stop touching me. I'm on a knife's edge here, Jules. You put your hands on me again, and I'm gonna get into an accident. And I don't want to spend my evening explaining to a cop why I ran off the road."

"Okay. No more touching." She let her legs fall apart. Trailed her hand up her own thigh. "Maybe I'll touch myself instead."

Sam sucked in a breath. "God *damn* it, Jules!" He glanced at her out of the corner of his eye. Groaned. "You are *killing* me here."

"I don't want you to die, Sam. I have plans for you tonight." A rush of power sent heat boiling through her. She'd never felt like this before. Never felt as if she could bring a man to his knees.

No man before Sam had even come close to bringing her to *her* knees.

"Jules. Hands on your knees. Keep them there. *Don't move.*" He took a corner a little too fast, and the tires squealed.

Up ahead, she saw the small, discreet sign for the Houston Hotel. Thank God. She wasn't sure who was going to combust first, her or Sam.

Sam's hand shook as he tried to pull a key card out of his wallet. "I got this earlier today. So we could park and go straight up to our suite. No one'll see us."

Julia took the wallet out of his hands and pulled out the card. Handed it to Sam, who turned into the driveway leading to the underground garage. It took three tries, but he finally got the card into the reader.

Snatched it out as soon as the gate began to rise. He tossed the card on the dash, and Julia retrieved it. Her own hand shook as she inserted it back into his wallet.

The dimly lit garage was half-full of vehicles, but otherwise deserted. The only noise was the low hum of her tires on the concrete. It felt as if they were sneaking up on the Houston, moving silently through the underground space. As if they were entering a protective bubble that would insulate them from the rest of the world.

Exactly what she wanted. Tonight only two people existed. Her and Sam.

By the time she got her door open, Sam had grabbed her bag from the back of her car. He helped her out, then wrapped an arm around her shoulder. His muscles were hard as steel. His hand trembled where he gripped her shoulder. She wanted to pull him into the shadows and devour him. But when she tried to tug him toward a darkened corner, he tightened his grip.

"Not here." His voice was tight with tension. "Security cameras."

The only noise in the cavernous garage was the click of their shoes on the concrete pavement. Neither of them spoke as they pressed the elevator call button. Her skin was on fire where Sam's fingers pressed into her upper arm. Sparks flew to her chest, her belly, her legs, until all she felt was Sam. All she wanted was Sam.

Finally the elevator door opened, excruciatingly slowly. Once inside, she pushed Sam into the wall. Tried to kiss him. But he tightened his arm around her. Kept her snugged to his side. "Not here, either," he said, his voice a low, dark rasp of want.

Julia drew a deep, shaky breath. He was right. Elevators had cameras, too. What was she thinking?

She *wasn't* thinking. Never before had she been so desperate to touch. To *be* touched. Thank God Sam could still think. She didn't want to be the featured video in the security room tonight.

The elevator was barely moving. The floor numbers flashed at too-long intervals. Finally, when they were at the eleventh floor, one from the top, the doors crept open.

Sam let his arm drop and laced their fingers together. She wanted to move quickly, rush to their room, but he held her back. Kept her at his side with an ease that shocked her. She'd never realized how strong he was. Never appreciated those powerful muscles.

Muscles that could lift her easily. Hold her as she wrapped her legs around him. Steady her as she unraveled against him.

The knowledge only turned her on more. She'd appreciate the hell out of them tonight. Sam had turned her into a mass of need and want. He barely touched her and she *quivered*, for God's sake. Vibrated like a tuning fork that responded only to his frequency.

It was an eternity before Sam stopped in front of a door. Another one before he removed the key card and inserted it. The light turned green and she reached for the handle, but Sam tightened his grip on her hand. Opened the door, then stood back for her to enter.

Couldn't he feel the heat pounding through her like a drum beat? Smell the scent of need that must be swirling around her?

He waited silently for her to enter the room. When she'd crossed the threshold, he stepped in behind her. Hung the 'Do Not Disturb' tag on the outside. Double locked the door.

Finally, *finally*, he swooped her into his embrace. Pressed her against the wall next to the door. When she gripped his arms, his biceps were hard. Steady. Strong enough to hold her in place.

Sam fastened his mouth to hers like a starving man falling on a feast.

Her bag dropped to the floor with a muffled thump as she shoved her fingers into his hair. Cupped his head in her palms as she opened to him, savoring his taste. Coffee, with a hint of cream. Something Italian with tomatoes and oregano.

Need that matched her own.

"Jules," he groaned into her mouth. "I've been thinking about you all day. About how you taste. How you feel against me. The scent of your skin." He tugged on the band at the end of her braid, tossing it aside as he combed his fingers through her waves. "I want your hair on me."

He cupped her ass in both hands. Lifted her. She wrapped her legs around his waist and pressed as close as she could get.

"You're not the only one," she said into his mouth, reluctant to break the kiss. "All day I've waited for this. For tonight." She arched against him, crying out when the hardness of his erection pressed against the vee of her legs. "I need you, Sam." She fumbled with his belt. Unbuckled it with one hand. Whipped it out of the loops of his pants and dropped it onto the floor. "Right now. Right here."

"I wanted to seduce you, Jules," he murmured, his mouth wandering across her cheek. Down her neck. He nipped at a tendon, making her shudder. "Touch you slowly. Tease you for hours, until you've forgotten your name. Forgotten everything but what I'm doing to you. What you're doing to me."

"That's for later." She shoved the button on his waistband through the hole and slid her hand inside. Palmed his heavy, hot weight. "Right here, Sam. Right now."

She swirled one finger over his tip, and he swore as his hips jerked. Held her with one hand while he shoved his pants down his legs. Then ripped open her pants and swept them away. Fumbled open a condom and sheathed himself. Slid inside her.

She bit on his neck to smother her scream. Tightened her legs around his waist as they moved together. She was already so close. And Sam was, too, based on the wild way his hips jerked against her.

Arching against him, she felt her orgasm gathering. She tried to slow it. Tried to prolong the pleasure, but it burst through her like the sun exploding. Sam covered her mouth to swallow her screams and shuddered against her.

He held her tightly, his mouth plundering hers as they rode out their climax together. Slowed together.

Finally he sank to the floor, with Julia still in his arms. She burrowed into his neck, inhaling his fresh-air scent, tasting the sweat on his skin. Held onto him like their bodies were sealed together. Joined at every place they touched. She drew one last shuddering breath, then kissed him slowly. Tasting. Testing.

Now they had all night for everything she wanted.

* * *

Sam roused to find them sprawled on the floor, holding each other tightly, their clothes askew. God! He hadn't bothered to get Julia's clothes off. Or his own. Her pants were tangled around one leg, the dark material trailing over the carpet. His shoes were hidden in the dark wool of his suit.

He hadn't been able to wait a moment longer. After the way she'd teased him on the way to the hotel, the burning glances she'd given him, the way she'd touched him, he'd been more desperate to have her than he'd ever been before. He'd never wanted another woman the way he wanted Jules.

And this wild, out of control lovemaking against the wall hadn't even begun to satisfy him. His skin had barely cooled and he wanted her all over again. Wanted to strip off her clothes and worship every inch of her body. Find every spot that made her groan. Every place that made her shudder. He wanted to find out exactly how she liked to be touched. Kissed. Stroked.

They had all night, and he was going to use every second of it.

"Hey, Jules," he whispered as he tugged at her earlobe. "You're way overdressed for this party."

She opened her eyes, forest green in the dimly lit room, and smiled as she nuzzled his neck. He tightened his arms around her. Breathed in the sharp orange scent of her hair. He'd had no idea his tough cop was a post-lovemaking snuggler.

The last time, there hadn't been any snuggling. They'd been too intent on each other. On taking. Giving. Discovering. They'd gotten very little sleep that night.

"Sam." She breathed out his name as if it was the only word she knew. As if he was the only thing she wanted in this life.

He tightened his arms around her and kissed her, lingering this time. Letting the passion pulse beneath the surface. It would burst into life again soon enough. This was Julia, after all. But for now, he wanted to go slow.

He needed to taste her. Touch her. Study her. Catalogue the tiny sounds she made as they kissed. The louder sounds she made when she came. The small, satisfied sighs she made as she snuggled in.

"I've got an idea," she said, sitting up so they were face to face. She rubbed her nose against his. "You wanna try to hit for the cycle twice in the same day?" She rocked against him. Smiled when she felt him respond. "I'd like to hit for the cycle, too."

"God, I love…" *No.* Not going there. He sucked in a breath. "I love your ideas. Four bases," he murmured, sliding his hand beneath her still-buttoned shirt, finding a lacy bra. Her nipple pebbled when he pressed against it. "Four ways to make you come."

"Four ways to make you come, too," she said, sliding up his rock-hard erection. Then back down. She grinned as she pressed her mouth to his. "I like this game already."

She clung to him as he lifted her off the floor and carried her to the bed, tossing her clothes aside as he walked. Stripping back the comforter, he laid her on the sheets and followed her down. "Let the games begin."

* * *

Sam had no idea what time it was when sunlight warmed his face. Struggling to open his eyes, he realized he wasn't in his own place. And he wasn't alone.

Julia sprawled against him. One of her legs was between his. Her arm curled around his chest. Her face mashed into his neck.

His arms held her tightly against him.

They were at the Houston, he realized as he scanned the room. In the suite he'd reserved.

They'd been so focused on each other, so oblivious to the rest of the world, that they hadn't even closed the drapes. Fat drops of rain coated the window that faced a brick wall, and he wondered if there'd been a storm. He hadn't noticed anything but Julia last night.

Closing his eyes, Sam stroked his hand down Julia's back, feeling the bump of each bone in her spine. Every inch of satin-smooth skin. Her firm ass, taut muscles beneath soft skin. He squeezed lightly, knowing he'd never get tired of touching her ass. Or watching it.

As he continued to caress her, Julia began to stir. She raised her head, shoved her tangled hair out of her eyes and smiled up at him. "Hey."

"Hey, yourself." He stroked down her back again. "You sleep okay?"

"Sleep?" She pushed up to prop herself on one elbow. "That thing we did for about ten minutes when we couldn't move?" She pressed her mouth against his, nipping at his lower lip. "I slept just fine. You?"

He pulled her on top of himself. "Never better. Because you were here with me."

She tensed for a moment, then sighed. Laid her head on his chest. "I like sleeping with you, too, Sam." She made it sound like a confession.

"How about some breakfast?"

She raised her head and shifted against him, pressing his erection against the ridge of her pubic bone. "Doesn't feel like you're thinking about a meal."

"I'm not." He mentally kicked himself as he shifted her to the side. Away from temptation. "But we blew through all my condoms last night. I need more."

"You didn't bring enough condoms?" She sat up and stared down at him. "What the hell were you thinking?"

"I was thinking that five would be more than enough," he said, lifting up to sit beside her. "That I wouldn't need more than that, because if I did, I'd be dead." He rubbed his face, hearing the rasp of whiskers against his palm. "I'll get more from the gift shop downstairs."

"But that means you'll have to put your clothes back on," Julia pointed out.

He scooped her up and settled her in his lap. "Which means you can have the fun of taking them off me again."

"There is that." She nipped on his lower lip, pressed her mouth to his and rolled out of bed. "I'm going to take a shower." She headed for the bathroom. "Want to join me? It's an enormous space. With a bench. Want to see how creative we can be without condoms?"

He rolled out of bed, and his cock twitched as Julia let her gaze drift over him. "I'm in."

"Not this time, you're not," she said as she disappeared into the adjoining bath. "But I'm not anticipating any complaints."

CHAPTER 22

Forty-five minutes later, Sam stretched his feet beneath the small table in the suite's living room, capturing Julia's legs between his as he chewed a piece of bacon. He wanted to reach across the table and tug open the gap in Julia's thick, white terrycloth robe.

Julia caught his eye and smiled slowly as she ate a juicy red strawberry. Licked the juice off her mouth. Leaning across the table toward him, she said, "Really? You're thinking about that after what we did in the shower?"

"You can read my mind now?" he asked, reaching for another strip of bacon.

She plopped back in her chair. "Not too tough when our minds are on the same track."

How could he want her again? But he was already pushing away from the table. He'd throw on his clothes and run down to the small gift shop. Come back with a big box of condoms.

Before he could move, his phone rang. He glanced around the living area of the suite and spotted it on the floor, a foot away from the trail of their discarded clothes.

"It's Connor Donovan," he said after he'd retrieved it.

Julia froze. "You better answer it," she finally said. "It

might be about the Kirby case."

So much for their few remaining hours together. He had to head over to the ball park in the middle of the afternoon for tonight's game. And if he knew Julia, she'd go into work, even though she had the day off.

Sighing, he pushed the icon to answer the call. "Donovan. What's up?"

"Hey, Marini, we're having a war council in an hour," Connor said. "It's about your mother's shops, so you need to be there. And bring Carleton. No one's been able to get hold of her."

"You're assuming I can?" His hand tightened on his phone. Had he been that obvious? Did everyone know what was going on?

Connor snorted. "She's probably with you right now. And if she isn't, she'll answer her phone for *you*." His voice lowered. "Don't worry, I haven't spread any gossip. But she's the lead detective on the Kirby case, so she needs to be there."

"Okay. Your mom's house?"

"We're going to be at Mia and Finn's. They have more room than Mom." He rattled off the address, which was on the Gold Coast. "See you in an hour?"

"We'll be there."

He disconnected and tossed the phone onto the table. Julia was watching him, a tiny frown between her eyes. "What was that about?"

"Donovan and Marini family powwow. To talk about the Kirby case and how it relates to Mom's repair shops."

Julia's frown deepened. "When do you need to leave?"

"*We*. In forty-five minutes."

"*We?*" She shot upright in her chair, clearly horrified. "Why do I need to go? Sure, I know Con and Quinn and Mia and Brendan. But I don't know the Fibbie. Or all the spouses. Or their mom. And there are kids, right? Probably lots of kids."

"Julia Carleton, scared of an FBI agent? And a bunch of

babies?" He grinned at her, delighted to see her less than composed. "Wow. You better keep this close to your vest. Anyone finds out, your bad ass rep is gone." He bit his lip to hide his laugh. "Gone, baby, gone."

"Shut up, Marini." She tossed a strawberry at him. Rolled her eyes when he caught it with his mouth. "This is a family gathering. I'm not part of the family."

His smile disappeared and he reached for her hand. Instead of pulling away, Jules tightened her grip on him. Wow. She really *was* freaked out. "You know, the first time Cilla dragged me to the Donovan's family dinner, I thought it was weird. Why would I want to hang around with these people I don't even know?"

He brought Julia's fingers to his mouth, kissed her palm. Then curled his hand around hers. "But they acted as though it was perfectly normal for a stranger to show up for a family meal. By the time I'd been there for half an hour, it felt like I'd known all of them for years," he said slowly, trying to explain. "They do this once a month at their Mom's house. All five of the sibs, plus their mom's sister Helen and her family. My sister Livvy and her fiancé Ryan were dragged there by Cilla, too, and now *they're* regulars. That's how I got to know Con and Quinn and Mia and Brendan."

He shrugged. "And right now, you're with me. So you're invited, too."

She frowned. Opened her mouth. He knew what she was going to say -- that they were having a fling. That she probably wouldn't be around next month.

This wasn't a fling for him anymore. And after last night? With the connection they'd shared? He didn't want to listen to her reduce what they had to mere sex. So before she could say anything, he added, "You're the lead detective on Nick D'Angelo's case. So you're the one who's dealing with the Kirbys. They need your input."

He glanced around the room. Spotted the paper and pen hotels always supplied. Stood up to grab it. "I'll make you a family tree. A cheat sheet on the Donovans."

He scribbled for a few minutes, then pushed a piece of paper toward her.

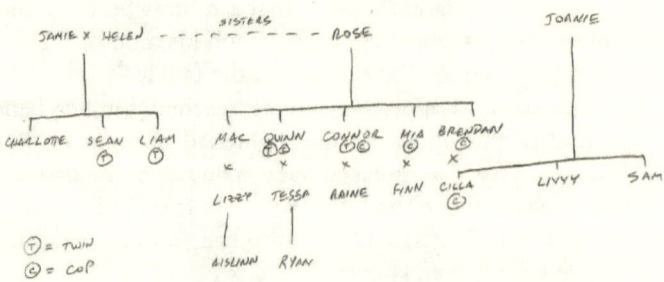

Tightening her grip on his hand, as if he was her anchor, she studied the crude drawing for a couple of minutes. As though she was memorizing it. Finally she pushed away from the table. "I guess I better get dressed."

* * *

An hour later, as Sam angled his car into a parking spot, Julia stared at the huge, intimidating house in front of them. *Full of intimidating people.*

Sure, most of them were cops, just like her. But they had actual *lives*. Wives and husbands. Children. A mother who made family dinners once a month.

Julia's stomach twisted. The Donovans were a happy family. They loved each other. Wanted to spend time together.

People who were nothing like her fractured, wrecked family.

And they all thought she and Sam were together.

She'd heard Connor at the Chi-Town Tap, telling Sam to bring her to dinner at his mom's place. She hadn't missed Sam's panicked reaction, either.

And yet, here she was. Getting ready to meet the rest of the Donovan family.

As Sam's… what? Significant other? Girlfriend?

Sam's fling. That's what she was.

No matter how much a secret part of her wanted it to be *girlfriend*, that didn't make it true. She was here as a cop. The woman who was dealing with the Kirbys. The woman who needed to come up with some ideas about how to stop Ronald Kirby from ruining Sam's mother's business.

She didn't realize Sam had gotten out of the car until he opened her door. Reached in to take her hand and help her out.

"You already know more than half the people here," he reminded her as he closed the door and beeped the lock. "The rest of them are just like the Donovans. Good people. Lots of fun. And my mom is great."

She grabbed his arm and pulled until he stopped. "Your *mom* will be here?"

"Of course she will. It's her shop that Kirby's trying to destroy. Because of *me*." He slid her arm through his and put his hand on hers. To keep her from running?

Julia swallowed. As a cop, she'd faced down stone-cold killers with guns. And in her personal life, she'd faced down people who'd lost money to her father. People who'd told her they were glad he'd killed himself. Told her that *she* should kill herself.

Surely she could face the mother of the man she was… having sex with.

Squaring her shoulders, she took a deep breath. Touched the back pocket of her jeans, where she'd stashed Sam's family tree. She'd studied. Memorized her homework. She'd be fine.

Lacing her fingers with Sam's, she started up the steps. "You're right. I've got this."

"Then let's go join the crowd."

As the front door opened, Julia's first impression was noise. The sound of multiple voices, all talking at once, with a high note of children squealing. Then Mia stood there, smiling, reaching for her and pulling her into a hug. "Julia. I'm so glad you could make it."

She nudged Julia farther inside, where the fragrant scent of cheese and tomato sauce filled the air. Mia hugged Sam. "Sammy. Got time for a little baseball today?"

"Season started last month, remember?" he said, wrapping his arms around her and dropping a kiss on her head. "Baseball isn't just fun on a Sunday afternoon anymore." He nudged her and grinned. "But I'll make time in my schedule soon to kick your ass, Mimi."

Mia narrowed her eyes. "Which one of them told you about Mimi? I will *kill* him." She poked him in the chest. "After I school you on the baseball diamond."

Julia was familiar with that particular smile of Mia's, and she bit her lip to keep from grinning. Poor Sam.

"Bring it, Donovan," Sam said. "We'll see who comes out on top."

"Don't get cocky, Baseball Boy," said a familiar voice. "Calling her Mimi *and* saying you're gonna kick her ass? You obviously like living dangerously."

The voice belonged to Finn O'Rourke. *Movie star* Finn O'Rourke. Sure, Julia knew Mia was engaged to the guy. She'd met him when he threw a party for Mia after she was promoted to detective. But seeing his familiar face, familiar smile, up close and personal, was a little weird.

"Hi, Julia." Finn reached for her hand. "You probably don't remember, but we met at Mia's party. I'm Finn."

"I remember," she said, her shoulders relaxing. "Nice to see you again, Finn." She shook his hand. Gave him a genuine smile. He was sincere, she realized. He honestly wasn't sure she'd remember him.

Finn gestured toward a large living room on her right. "Come in and meet everyone else. We're almost ready to start."

The room was full of people. A girl who was about two years old was busy in one corner, taking toys into a large teepee then removing them. Four babies who all looked around the same age scooted across the hardwood floors in different directions. Julia recognized Ryan, Quinn's son, because his wife Tessa was chasing the boy. She touched her back pocket again, wishing she could pull out the sheet of hotel paper hidden there and remind herself who the other three belonged to.

A hugely pregnant Cilla was sprawled in a deep, wide chair, watching the babies, as her husband Brendan perched on the arm. Cilla smiled dreamily as she rubbed her enormous belly.

Okay. Julia took a deep breath. Relaxed a little. She knew Cilla and Brendan. Had worked with both of them. Maybe this wouldn't be so hard, after all.

Or maybe it would be.

"Mom," Sam said, dragging Julia her toward a woman who looked like an older version of Cilla and Livvy, with the same wavy, caramel-colored hair. She stood next to an older man with short gray hair.

Sam's mother smiled at her son as Sam engulfed the older woman in a hug. She clung to him for a long moment, then pushed away. "Thank you for getting that security system in so fast, Sammy. Don and I slept better last night, knowing the shops were protected."

"Yeah, thanks, Sammy," the older man said, punching him in the arm. "Good to know those cameras will catch anyone who's snooping around."

"That's the plan, Don." Sam tugged Julia forward. "Mom, Don, this is Julia Carleton. She's in charge of the case against the Kirbys. I met her at Cilla's wedding, and we reconnected after I shot the video of the mugging."

Sam's mother studied Julia for a moment, then smiled and pulled her into a hug. "Nice to meet you, Julia. Sam said you're doing a great job on this case."

"Thank you, Mrs. Marini, but it's obviously not good enough." She rubbed a sweaty palm down her thigh. "I'm sorry that ass... Kirby targeted your shops. We'll get him, but I wish you didn't have to deal with the fallout until we do."

"It's Joanie. And it's not your fault. Asshole was the right word for that loser. I know you're going to get to the bottom of this. I look forward to seeing Kirby taken down. Legally," she added, nodding toward her son. "Make sure he doesn't do anything stupid."

Joanie looked so fierce, so determined, that Julia smiled. Joanie reminded her of Sam, with the focused way he'd pursued her, even when she'd kept him firmly at arm's length. The fierceness with which he'd gone after justice for Nick D'Angelo.

"Trust me, Joanie, I'll make sure Sam doesn't get in trouble. He's going out of town for some road games in a few days. That will help." She'd gotten a Bearcats' schedule so she'd know when he'd be gone and where he was. Which was kind of pathetic, since this was supposed to be casual.

Right. There was nothing casual about what had happened between her and Sam last night.

And now Sam's mother was smiling at her like she and Sam were going to live happily ever after. Julia rubbed her sweaty palm down her thigh again.

Joanie held her gaze for a long moment, then nodded. They understood each other. Julia would keep safe the man they both cared about.

Connor wandered in, his wife Raine holding his hand. "Can we lower it to a dull roar?" he said, raising his hand. "We need to get started so Sammy can go to work."

The babies were chasing each other around the floor, and she'd forgotten who they all belonged to. All the names on Sam's list blurred together in her brain. Finding Mia in the crowd, Julia murmured, "Rest room?"

Mia pointed her toward a door off the hall. Once inside, Julia pulled out her cheat sheet. "Aislinn. The girl belongs to Mac and Lizzie. Ryan, the boy, is Quinn's." She took a deep breath. Looked again. The twin boys belong to Helen and Jamie. Okay. She could do this.

An hour later, they'd discussed all the aspects of what had happened at Joanie Marini's auto repair shops. Sam had talked about the security systems he'd had installed. The cameras that would catch any intruders. The alarms that would go off at the closest police station.

The attorney Livvy had hired had gotten injunctions to keep the shops open while the dumping was investigated. Joanie and Don's insurance had paid to have the leaky drum removed from their property. They were still waiting for the test results from the oil drums. And techs from the twenty-fifth district were looking at surveillance tapes, trying to spot someone approaching the repair shop with the leaky drum.

Finally, Connor nodded at Julia. "Carleton, what about you? Any good news?"

"Yes, actually." She glanced at Sam, sitting next to her, an apology in her eyes. She'd meant to tell him, but they'd both been... distracted. She promised with her glance that she'd tell him about Tim Busey as soon as they left.

Giving her a tiny smile, he nudged her knee with his, forgiving her. It was getting scary how in sync they were.

"This goes no further than this room, but another witness has come forward." She kept her knee pressed to Sam's. "More witnesses are always good, and this new witness will strengthen the case against Derek Kirby. I'm cautiously optimistic."

"I've already talked to the State's Attorney." Livvy shifted forward to the edge of her chair. "I asked her to move the trial forward. Kirby is causing problems for our mom. He's harassing witnesses. It needs to stop, and getting an early trial date will help."

"Kirby's got a big-money lawyer." Julia shook her head. "He'll try to delay this as long as he can."

Livvy's gaze burned into Julia. "My boss is a pretty good attorney, too. If we can prove that Kirby was behind the shady business at Mom's shop, the judge won't have a choice. We can argue it's a public safety issue."

"I'll update Mia every day," Julia said. "She can keep Joanie and Don in the loop."

"Just one last thing," Connor said. "We need to start a lottery. For who gets to go with Carleton to arrest Ronald Kirby, when we nail him for what he did to Joanie."

"Sorry, Con," Julia said with a laugh. "Captain Francisco already called shotgun on that collar."

A woman with dark hair shot with grey stuck her head around the corner. "Perfect timing. Brunch is ready."

"That's Rose," Sam murmured to her.

Julia nodded. Her kids all looked just like her.

Over the next hour, as they sat around a huge dining room table, Julia chatted with Mac, the FBI agent, and his wife Lizzie. Their seven-month-old daughter Aislinn had her father's bright blue eyes, her mother's curly blond hair and an adorable smile.

She also spent some time with Rose's sister Helen, her husband Jamie and their three children. Charlotte gave her a shy smile, but hid her head in her father's neck when Julia said, "Hi, Charlotte."

Sam had been right. Everyone was welcoming. Friendly. Interested in her, and not just because she was pursuing the man who'd damaged Joanie and Don's business. Julia wanted to relax and enjoy these people. Get to know them. Hold their kids, make them giggle and inhale their sweet baby scent.

But they were making assumptions about her and Sam. Believing they'd be together forever. That she'd be a part of this family someday. Knowing that made Rose Donovan's lasagna sit in her stomach like a rock.

None of that was going to happen. She and Sam had an expiration date. There would be no happily ever after for them. She couldn't be with Sam. He distracted her from her job. Cops needed to be focused on what they were doing, not worried about how it was going to affect the person they loved.

If she got into an actual relationship with Sam, someone

was going to get hurt, and she'd never forgive herself.

If it was Sam, she'd never get over it.

By the time Sam needed to leave, her head was pounding. She made the rounds, saying goodbye to everyone. Promised Joanie Marini again she'd let Mia know about any new information on Kirby.

Only Charlotte, Helen and Jamie's oldest, made her relax. The adorable child with wavy dark hair and blue eyes made no assumptions about her and Sam. All she was interested in was playing peek-a-boo with Julia from her father Jamie's shoulder.

Julia sucked in a deep breath once they were on the sidewalk. Her ears were ringing from the volume inside Mia's house. And her head was still spinning from all the introductions.

All the assumptions.

Sam squeezed her hand before letting her go to open the car door. "How're you doing?" he asked as he helped her into the car.

"Overwhelmed," she said with a deep, steadying breath.

"Yeah, that's pretty normal after a Sunday with the Donovans. Don't worry, you'll get used to it."

He closed her door and hurried around to the other side of the car.

Used to it? As in, she'd be doing this again?

"Hell no." She murmured the words into the quiet of the car.

But the part of her that *wanted* whispered, "Yes, please."

CHAPTER 23

On Monday afternoon, Julia's phone rang as she was studying the murder scene at a pricey Southport Corridor home. She ignored the demanding shrill as she scribbled down what she knew about the case.

A woman had been shot in her living room. Single GSW to the chest. Based on the photos over the fireplace and the purse found in the kitchen, the victim was the home owner. There were no signs of forced entry. No signs of a struggle. No gun.

Husband missing.

He hadn't shown up for work today. He wasn't answering his phone. There was only one car in the garage, and it looked like it belonged to the woman. A Volkswagen Bug with a bright pink daisy in the vase near the steering wheel. A pink water bottle with vines painted on the cylinder in the front seat cupholder. Small red leather gloves on the passenger seat.

It didn't take mad detecting skills to surmise it was a woman's car.

She'd just finished her notes when Quinn Donovan clattered down the hardwood stairs to her left. He'd been searching the second floor for anything that might give a

236

clue to where the husband might have gone. "You call in an APB on the husband yet?" he asked.

"Fifteen minutes ago," she answered. She glanced at the medical examiner, who was taking pictures of the victim.

Quinn stepped up next to her. "Looks like it won't be a tough one to solve."

"Yeah. The murderer's not a criminal genius," she said.

"Oxymoron," he said, nudging her.

It was an old cop joke, but Julia smiled, appreciating Quinn's efforts to lighten things up. Julia's phone rang again, and she pulled it out of her pocket. 312 area code. The loop. *Kirby?*

"Detective Carleton." She made her voice confident. Authoritative.

"Detective, this is Tim Busey. I need to talk to you." His voice was shaky. Whispering, as if trying not to be overheard.

"Sure," she said, softening her tone. "Do you want to meet me somewhere?" She didn't think the kid would want to be seen talking to a cop at his office.

"I'll come to the police station." Busey swallowed. "Where we talked the other day."

"Maybe not the station." The fewer people who saw Busey, the better. She needed to keep his identity under wraps. "There's a coffee shop down the street. I'll meet you there. What time?"

"In an hour?"

"I'll be there," Julia said.

"See you then." Busey's voice quivered. What was wrong? She punched the icon and ended the call. Sighed, closing her eyes.

"Trouble?" Quinn asked.

"That was my new witness in the case we discussed yesterday. He needs to talk to me."

"You think he's backing out of testifying?"

"I hope not, but I wouldn't be surprised." She shoved the phone back into her pocket. "He sounded upset."

Busey had to know how vindictive Kirby was. She stared down at the woman who was most likely a victim of domestic violence, seeing instead Nick D'Angelo, lying in the gutter. "A lot of witnesses get cold feet." Especially when the suspect was paying his salary.

"Go," Quinn said, waving her toward the door. "I got this."

"Thanks, but we're meeting in an hour. Let's see how much we can nail down here before I have to go."

Putting Tim Busey out of her head for now, Julia squatted next to the current victim. Linda Sherrold. Fifty-three years old. Her husband, fifty-seven-year-old Rick Sherrold, worked for an investment banking company in the Loop. With any luck, the police would spot his flashy red Porsche Boxster and bring him in. Maybe she and Quinn could get this case wrapped up today.

It was so easy to murder someone. A gun. The element of surprise. A willingness to pull the trigger.

Far more difficult to avoid being caught, but if you had enough money to hire a good lawyer, there were possibilities.

Would Kirby try to hurt Sam? Kill him, even?

Her heart pounding, she stared at Linda Sherrold. Pictured Sam's body in her place. Ronald Kirby was arrogant enough. Entitled enough. And blind enough to think he could get away with it.

Oh, God. Would Kirby go after Sam? Eliminate the most vital witness against his son?

She needed this case to be over. She had to focus on Ronald and Derek Kirby. On what they might do.

Find a reason to lock them up.

Unless the wealthy Rick Sherrold took a page out of Kirby's playbook. Threatened witnesses. Threatened cops. Denied the evidence. If he did, she'd have to divide her attention.

A headache forming behind her eyes, Julia took a deep breath and sent up a silent prayer. Please, not another Kirby type. She had to focus on Sam. On getting Kirby off the street.

An hour later, after leaving Quinn to finish up at the Sherrold house, Julia walked into the small, mostly empty coffeehouse. Busey sat at a booth in the back, his hands cupped around a white mug.

After ordering tea, Julia slid into the booth opposite Busey. "Hey, Tim," Julia said quietly. "Good to see you."

Busey slid one hand onto his leather messenger bag on his lap. Glanced at her with desperate eyes. "Detective Carleton," he said, his voice unsteady.

Oh, God. What had happened? "What's wrong, Tim?" she asked.

"Mr. Kirby fired me today." His voice wavered a little, but he loosened his grip on the leather bag. "He said I didn't fit in with the rest of the group. That I wasn't performing up to expectations. But that's total bullshit." His voice rose. "I bring in almost twice as much business as the next best guy in my department."

"Did Kirby have you escorted out of the office?" she asked.

The flicker of his eyes told her that he understood her unspoken question -- had he had time to take some proof of that? Letting out a breath, he nodded. "He did, but not immediately. I had time to get my stuff together." His hand tightened on the bag, as if someone might snatch it away. "Kirby went to talk to some of the other guys in our department." He swallowed again. "The other guys who'd been with Derek that night."

So instead of getting Tim out of the office immediately, Kirby had taken time to gloat. And to remind the other witnesses what would happen to them if they stepped up to testify. Julia leaned toward Tim. "This is why you're going to win. Ronald Kirby should have shown you the door immediately. Instead, his arrogance gave you time to gather the evidence you need."

The question was, how had the bastard found out that

Tim would testify against Derek? Because she was certain he had. Otherwise, he wouldn't have fired Tim and warned the others.

She'd told no one but Francisco.

But she'd written the report on her work computer.

Her hand gripped the mug hard. Someone must have hacked into that computer. It was the only way they could have found out about Tim.

Tucking the thought away to deal with later, she nodded at the bag on his lap. "Did you take what you needed for a lawsuit?"

He glanced down at the bag. Rested his hands on the top of it. "I hope so. I pulled out all the statistical sheets Mr. Kirby gave me during my reviews, going back to when I started with the company. They compare my results with everyone else in the department. Also, letters I got from clients, thanking me for the job I'd done. I've won a couple of awards, too." Busey took a deep breath. "I think I have a case that I was fired because he knew I was going to testify against Derek. I'm going to see a lawyer after we're done."

Julia nodded. "That's a good idea. It sounds like a retaliatory firing."

He leaned toward her. "You promised me no one else would find out about our deal. But he must have found out somehow."

"I agree, Tim. To fire you for what sounds like bogus reasons? Right after you talked to me? He must have found out."

She clenched her teeth. *Damn it.* Was it her work computer? Her cell phone? She reached into her pocket, turned it off.

She leaned closer to Tim and lowered her voice. "I didn't tell anyone but my captain, and I trust him implicitly. He wants to nail the Kirbys as much as I do. I'll get to the bottom of this," she promised. "I'll find out who ratted you out to Kirby."

Another thought had her sucking in a breath. Was Tim

in danger now? Would Kirby try to harm him, to prevent him from testifying?

She reached into her bag and pulled out a business card. Scribbled a name and phone number on it. "This is the woman at the state's attorney's office who's going to prosecute Derek. You need to talk to her. Tell her what happened. See if she has any suggestions." She turned the card over, circled a phone number. "This is my personal cell number. Call me immediately if anything doesn't feel right.

"And Tim, this might be a good time to get away from Chicago. Where does your family live?"

He frowned at her. "In Milwaukee."

"Maybe you should go visit them."

He stared at her for a long moment. "Are you worried that Mr. Kirby might try to *kill* me?"

"Probably not, Tim." Although Ronald Kirby was completely off the rails. "But he's been harassing other witnesses. Threatening them. Talk to the State's Attorney, then make yourself scarce for a while."

"I need that job, Detective." Busey stared at the white rectangle on the table, his hands tightening on the leather bag. "For rent. Groceries. School." He drew in a deep, shuddering breath. "The company pays my tuition -- it's one of the perks -- but I have to pay for everything else. I'm already stretched thin."

"Talk to the prosecutor." She pushed the card toward Busey. He picked it up. Studied it. Placed it carefully into an inside pocket of the bag.

"I'm meeting a few of the guys in my group for drinks later tonight," he said. "If they say anything about what Kirby said to them, I'll let you know."

"Thank you, Tim. Just don't mention that you're testifying against Derek. The fewer people who know that, the better." She leaned closer. "I'm sorry this happened to you, but you must get some kind of severance pay, right?"

"Two weeks." He swallowed again. "Not much."

She had to get this case wrapped up in less than two weeks. Get Tim re-instated at Kirby's company. Get Derek off the street. Along with his dangerous father Ronald.

"I'm going to check a few things. Please keep in touch. Let me know what the other guys have to say tonight. And think about visiting your folks tomorrow."

"This isn't what I signed up for, Detective." He swallowed. "Getting fired? Having to worry that Mr. Kirby might *hurt* me?"

"I know, Tim. You're doing a very brave thing. A crucial thing. Derek needs to be locked up, and so does his father, so they can't hurt anyone else." She leaned across the table. "Do you want police protection?"

"Jesus. I shouldn't need that."

"No. You shouldn't. But when someone thinks he's above the law, when he has a hair-trigger temper like both of the Kirbys, I worry about my witnesses. I don't want anything to happen to you."

He drew a deep, shuddering breath. "I'll go to Milwaukee tonight. After I meet with the other guys. They'd think it was odd if I didn't show up."

"I think that's a good idea. Keep in touch. And call 911 *immediately* if something seems off. Trust your instincts. Pay attention to your gut."

"You're scaring the crap out of me, Detective."

"Good. People who are scared are more careful. Please call me when you get to Milwaukee, Tim."

"Okay. I will."

Hot, fierce anger swirled inside her as she watched Tim walk out the door. Tim had stepped up to do the right thing, and as a result, he'd lost his job. Was forced to flee to his parent's home in another state.

Slapping her hands on the table, she put the two mugs in a black buss container, then hurried back to the station. Instead of going to her desk, she detoured into the basement lab area and found the tech division.

Opening the door, she scanned the five people working

at benches. *There.* That's who she wanted.

"Hey, Tonya," she said to the tech who was taking apart a cell phone. "I need my desktop computer scanned for some kind of bug," she said in a low voice. "Don't want to write up a form. Don't want to broadcast it. Can you come upstairs and take a look?"

"Definitely, Carleton." Tonya's eyes lit up, as if Julia had offered her a gift. "Let's check it out."

Ten minutes later, Julia paced the bullpen, her cold hands wrapped around a mug of hot tea. Tonya sat in her chair, her hands flying across the keyboard, absently brushing a shocking pink dreadlock behind one ear.

Finally she nodded. Gave a feral smile. Caught Julia's eye and jerked her head toward their break room.

Carefully closing and locking the door behind her, Tonya grabbed a Diet Coke from the refrigerator, hesitated and glanced at Julia. "This going to piss someone off?"

Julia's mouth twitched. The Diet Coke belonged to Dwyer. "Probably. But don't worry about it." Dwyer would leave a nasty note on the bulletin board. Other cops would add rude comments, mostly directed toward him.

"Okay." Tonya twisted the cap off and took a long drink.

"What did you find, Tonya?" Julia asked, adding more hot water to her cup.

"Someone installed a keystroke capture program on your computer. It's sending everything you type to their computer." She shook her head, sending her pink dreads flying. "Whoever did it is a stupid fuck. Left a trail of bread crumbs that a ten-year-old kid could follow."

"So you'll be able to figure out who did it?"

"Yep. Might take a little while, but we'll nail him. Or her." The tech set the half-empty Diet Coke bottle on the counter. "Have to wait until he turns on the computer to check what you've written today."

Julia's hand tightened on the mug. She hated knowing that someone had been standing over her shoulder, reading everything she'd written, but maybe this was the break they needed. "By 'a while', are you talking hours? Days? Weeks?"

Tonya shrugged. "Depends on when the guy checks in. I installed a bug that will ping me. It'll send me his IP address, then I'll look up who that address belongs to. Bingo. Stick a fork in him, 'cause he's done."

The tech took another drink of Coke and studied Julia. "You know it's gotta be someone who works in this building."

"Yeah. I know." Someone she worked with had betrayed their oath. Or one of the civilians in the building -- a janitor, secretary or clerk -- had taken money from Kirby. The realization made her stomach churn.

She pushed away from the counter. "What about my cell phone?" Julia's voice was almost a whisper. "Do I need to worry about that?"

Tonya frowned. "You have it with you most of the time?"

"All the time. I don't have a land line."

"Then it's probably safe. You want to leave it with me and let me check it?"

She had to get to Sam. She needed to see him. Warn him about Kirby. "Not tonight. I have some things I have to do."

"Then leave it off for now. Turn it on at the hour, so I can get in touch. And so you can check your voice mail. Come down to the lab first thing tomorrow and I'll run a few checks on it."

"Thanks, Tonya. You're the best."

"Any time, Carleton." She drained the Coke and tossed it at the wastebasket, ten feet away. Nothing but net. "I'll let you know as soon as I figure out who tapped your computer."

"Any time. Day or night," Julia said.

Tonya tilted her head. "You must want this guy bad."

"You have no idea."

The tech smiled, a nasty glitter in her eyes. "You have any reports you need to finish? Paperwork you've been putting off? Might be a good time to catch up. Someone sees you typing your fingers to the bone? They're gonna be all over that computer later today."

"You're a devious woman, Tonya. I like that."

The tech sauntered out of the room with a wave, and Julia pushed away from the counter. Headed toward her desk until her captain beckoned her into his office.

"Why was Tonya Simmons checking your computer?" he asked. "Is there a problem I should know about?"

Julia closed the door. "Yes, sir. There is."

Francisco stared at her as she explained, his eyes hard. Ice cold. When she finished, he said, "Someone in this district is dirty. Maybe even a cop." His voice was flat, but his eyes had gone from cold to blazing hot.

"Yes, sir. I told Tonya to call me as soon as she knows."

"And you'll call me immediately," Francisco said.

"Yes, sir. I will."

"Anyone you suspect, Carleton?"

Julia twisted her fingers together in her lap. "I don't know, Captain," she said slowly. "I told you about Derek Kirby showing up at Sam Marino's celebrity MC gig last night. Dwyer was the cop who picked him up. I didn't find an arrest report about the incident, although maybe Dwyer got busy and hasn't filed it yet."

There had been something... off about the way he'd acted when he picked Derek Kirby up at the Chicago Wine Bar last night. And, in retrospect, something off about his behavior at the D'Angelo crime scene, as well.

And the morning she'd found him sitting at her desk.

Was Dwyer really involved? Or was she focusing on him because she didn't like him? Because she didn't think he was a good cop? Dwyer took shortcuts. He was always looking for the easy way.

She lifted one shoulder. "Kirby has money. Maybe he found someone who needed money badly."

Francisco nodded once, and his eyes burned into her as she left his office. She almost pitied the man or woman working for Kirby. Francisco would show no mercy.

She liked that about her boss.

When the clock turned over to six o'clock, Julia left her computer on, as Tonya had instructed, gathered her belongings and walked out of the station. She'd checked in with Quinn before she talked to Tonya, and found out they'd grabbed Linda Sherrold's husband. His flashy car, the one that screamed 'I'm hot and I have money', had been spotted by a patrol cop who'd seen the APB. Sherrold had been stopped on the Dan Ryan just before he reached Indiana. And unlike Kirby, the guy had confessed almost as soon as Quinn walked into the interrogation room.

Quinn had promised to do the paperwork, leaving her free to concentrate on the D'Angelo case.

Which she would do as soon as she found out who had hacked into her computer.

Tonight she was going home to pick up fresh clothes, then meeting Sam in their suite at the Houston. She froze for a moment, then resumed walking. *His* suite, she reminded herself. *Their* suite sounded as if they had an actual relationship. As if they were going steady, for God's sake.

Brunch at Mia and Finn's yesterday had shaken her. She'd told herself it was part of the job, but it had felt like more than that. Like she was somehow committed to Sam.

She was committed to what they'd do together in that suite tonight. Committed to having great sex for as long as their fling lasted. That was it.

A tiny voice whispered that she was fooling herself. That she had gone far past a fling with Sam.

Julia inhaled a shuddering breath as she reached her car. *No.* They'd agreed to casual. She'd talk to Sam. Make sure he understood this was nothing more than sex.

They'd have that talk tonight. The sooner the better, before their lives became even more tangled together.

Satisfied that she had a plan, she texted Sam that she was leaving the station, then spent the drive back to her place planning on what she'd gather to take to the hotel. No way was she staying in her apartment until this case was over and the bugs were removed. The thought of someone listening to every word she said? Every sound she made? Revulsion crawled over her skin.

After parking in her garage, she hurried through her tiny back yard toward the stairs. She'd almost reached them when movement in the shadows made her reach for her gun. Loosen the strap and wrap her hand around the grip.

"Who's there?" she called. "Make yourself known."

Ronald Kirby stepped out of the shadows.

CHAPTER 24

Julia tightened her fingers around the Glock. Drew it out of its holster. Her grip was steady, thank God, as she held it at her side. If he moved at all, she'd aim at Kirby's chest. Center mass, like she'd been taught. This guy had threatened too many people. No way would he get the jump on her.

"This is private property, Mr. Kirby. You're trespassing. Leave now, or I'll arrest you. Won't look good in front of the judge, after your previous arrest for harassing a witness."

"I'm not armed, Detective." He held his hands up as if surrendering, but the gleam in his eyes told her he was doing no such thing. "I'm just here to deliver a message. You need to get Sam Marini to bow out of the case against Derek. If he doesn't, I'll be forced to go to the press. Point out that your pursuit of my son is fueled by your hatred for wealthy people. After all, they hounded your father until he killed himself. How can you be unbiased against my son?"

Shock, then dread swirled through her, the sticky strings snarling together with anger to lodge in her stomach and cinch tight around her chest. Kirby's threat to reveal the pain and anguish she thought she'd put behind her was like a blow to her gut.

"That's a ridiculous argument, Ronald," she managed to say. "I didn't arrest Derek because he's rich. I arrested him because the evidence indicated he killed Nick D'Angelo." Her finger inched toward the trigger before she realized what she was doing. She froze. Slid the gun back into her holster. *Keep your shit together.*

"That will be for the judge to decide," Kirby said casually. As if he wasn't worried at all. "And the jury. Lots of people lost their life savings because of your father. When your face is splashed all over the front pages of the newspapers, they're all going to know you're his daughter.

"And how about your fellow police officers? I bet some of them lost money to Julius Landon. Maybe some of their parents, as well."

The public *had* blamed her after her father was gone, because she'd become the public face of the family. The one forced to face the press. Make the funeral arrangements. The one whose picture was splashed across all the newspapers.

Her mother and sister had refused to deal with any of the mess. It had all fallen on Julia's shoulders.

"You've given me so much ammunition, Detective," Kirby continued with a nasty smirk. "Not only are you a Landon, but you're screwing a witness in an open case. An important case, because it involves a Kirby. My attorney will have all sorts of information for potential jury members."

"Bring it on, Kirby," she said, anger helping to steady her. "Go ahead and tell the world who I am. I'm not responsible for my father's crimes," she said, keeping her voice calm. Even. The therapist she'd seen after her father's suicide had helped her understand that. "And you have no proof I'm dating a witness. Marini needs protection from you and Derek. I'm providing it."

Ronald scowled for a moment, as if he'd hoped to see her pain. Her fear. Then he smiled, his expression gloating. "Maybe you *don't* care if your past is dragged out again for

MARGARET WATSON

public consumption. It was a long time ago, although I'm betting more than a few people remember Julius Landon. But even if you don't care about having your past in the headlines again, I bet you care about your reputation in the police department. Screwing a witness? I bet that's frowned upon."

"Go ahead and take out a big ad in the <u>Herald</u>," she said with a shrug. "Pay some unscrupulous reporter to write a story about my father. It won't change a thing. The case against Derek isn't going away. Sam Marini isn't going to back down. I won't ask him to. Even if I did, why would he listen to me?"

"Men think with their dicks, Detective. You're fucking him." His gaze flicked over her. Dismissed her. "You could convince him to drop this."

"You're pathetic, Ronald." His lips tightened, and Julia stood straighter. When he took a step toward her, Julia grabbed her Taser from the back of her belt. "Get off of my property. And don't come back." She turned on the small, black rectangle, and its vibrating hum filled the air between them. She wanted badly to use it. And she would, if he took another step toward her. "Next time, you won't like what happens."

He stared at her for a long moment, hatred thinning his mouth and flaring in his eyes. Kirby wasn't used to taking orders from a woman, and he resented it. "If you don't do what I'm telling you to do, you might not like what happens, either, Detective."

"Are you threatening me, Ronald?"

He raised one eyebrow. "I have the utmost respect for the police, Detective Carleton."

"Take your respect and get off my property." Her finger tightened on the Taser trigger. "Three seconds, Kirby. Then you're down. One. Two."

Before she could say three, he spun around. Disappeared into the shadowed catwalk between her building and the next one. Sliding the Taser onto its clip, she followed him.

As she reached the front of the building, a Cadillac SUV roared to life directly in front of her. Pulling out her phone, she snapped pictures of the vehicle, Kirby visible in the front passenger seat, angling the camera to include her building. Her address. The street sign at the intersection three doors down. She tried to get a picture of the driver as they pulled away from the curb, but saw nothing but a dark ski hat.

As the Escalade accelerated away from her, she continued snapping photos, making sure she got a clear view of the license plate in case she needed to prove Kirby had been at her place. After it turned the corner and disappeared, Julia slumped against the side of her building. Shut down the camera on her phone and gripped it with shaking hands.

She should call it in. Have Kirby picked up for threatening a police officer. For threatening a witness again, after he'd been already been warned.

But he hadn't threatened Sam. Not directly. Kirby had threatened *her*.

What would he do if she had him arrested? She was very certain the lead story in tomorrow's Herald would be about her. Not only about her father, but about dating Sam. Exactly as he'd threatened. Questioning her judgment. Her motives. Tainting the jury pool.

Should she call? Not call?

Wait?

Maybe she had a window. Kirby might assume she'd talk to Sam. Get him to back down. Maybe Kirby would hold off on his big reveal.

Tapping her finger against the screen of her phone in a tense, jittery rhythm, she finally turned it off completely and slid it into her pocket. The whole business about her computer being hacked had freaked her out. She wasn't sure how anyone could have gotten to her phone, since it was always with her, but she'd do as Tonya had instructed, keep it off except for every hour on the hour.

Maybe tonight Tonya would find the person who'd bugged her computer. They'd arrest the person or persons responsible, and the hacker would give up Ronald Kirby.

Kirby would be arrested. Jailed, after the warning the judge had given Ronald when he'd confronted Sam. Ronald Kirby would have more to worry about than outing her in public.

Drawing another deep, shaky breath, Julia unlocked her front door and opened her mailbox. Grabbed the envelopes that stuffed it and trudged up to her apartment. She'd give it twenty-four hours, she decided. See if Tonya found the hacker.

If Tonya ferreted him out, and Julia arrested Kirby, she wouldn't have to face the public firestorm. The clamor of the press hounding her. She could stay safely in the shadow of her job. The life she'd made. The anonymity she'd finally found.

Shame crawled up her throat. She was taking the coward's way out.

But maybe the judge wouldn't see Kirby's words as threats. Maybe he'd throw out the case, and Kirby would get even more vindictive. More dangerous.

She had the pictures. She could prove Kirby had been to her apartment. Twenty-four hours wouldn't change anything.

As she threw a few changes of clothing into a suitcase, she knew she should at least call Captain Francisco. Tell him what had happened.

But she wasn't going to do it.

She was going to meet Sam at the Houston. Warn him that Kirby was escalating once again. Tel him to be more alert. To expect trouble. Protecting Sam was her first priority.

And protecting yourself is your second.

Julia froze for a moment, then shook her head. She couldn't think about that right now. She needed to get to

Sam. Make sure Kirby hadn't paid *him* a visit today. That was all that mattered.

* * *

Sam paced the living area of the suite at the Houston, staring at his phone. Julia should have been here half an hour ago. How long did it take to go home, throw some stuff in a suitcase and drive here?

He'd called her fifteen minutes ago, but she hadn't answered.

If she'd gotten called back to work, she would have let him know. If she'd had an accident on her way home, she would have called him.

He tightened his fingers around the phone. Unless she *couldn't* call.

He punched the icon for her number, and once again, it went straight to voicemail.

No! Damn it, he wasn't going to get all bent out of shape because Julia was later than he'd expected her to be. There was an explanation. A perfectly logical one. And she'd tell him as soon as she got here.

He glanced at his phone again. Forty minutes late. "Jules, where the hell are you?" His voice was too loud in the still silence of the suite. He knew he sounded panicked. Scared.

Which was ridiculous. Julia was a police officer, for God's sake. She had a gun. She could protect herself.

So why wasn't she answering her phone?

He dropped onto the couch and stared at the phone, as if it held the answers. "Damn it, Jules! Call me!"

His words were muffled by the thick Oriental carpet. He jumped up again. He couldn't sit still. He had to move. *Do* something.

A key card slid into the reader on the door, and the next moment it clicked open. Julia walked in, trailing a wheeled suitcase behind her.

"Jules!" He dropped the phone on the coffee table, ignoring the loud crack it made, and hurried to her. Grabbed her and engulfed her in a desperate hug. Burying his face in her hair, he inhaled her sweet-tart orange scent and felt himself settling. She was here. She wasn't hurt.

"What the hell happened?" he said into her head. "I was worried. Your phone was turned off."

She gripped the back of his shirt with both hands. Pressed her face into his neck. "You're okay," she said against his skin. "Thank God you're okay." She lifted to kiss him, sliding her mouth against his, her tongue sweeping over his lips. Demanding entrance.

He went from worried to needy in two seconds. Yanking her shirt out of her waistband, he ran his hands over her back. Felt her shudder all the way to his toes. His cock hardened instantly.

Before he could lift her against him, she boosted herself into his arms, wrapping her legs around his waist. Fisting her hands in his tee shirt, she ripped it over his head. Dropped it on the floor. Sucked on a tendon in his neck until he was afraid he'd lose every last scrap of self-control.

Or they'd lose control together. Julia was as desperate as he was. Just as needy.

He carried her into the bedroom and dropped her on the bed. As she bounced, he toed off his shoes and unbuckled his belt. His hands trembled as he shoved his jeans and boxers down his legs. He fell onto the bed next to her, already reaching for her. He tore her pants down her legs, hearing fabric rip. Ignoring it. Now. He needed Julia now. And from the way she was running her hands over him, she needed him just as much.

He brushed open the shirt she'd managed to unbutton. Popped open her bra. Shoved it aside, only far enough to find her.

Took one breast into his mouth. Sucked hard as she bucked into him.

"Now, Sam. *Please*. Now," she moaned, her fingers

scrabbling over his back. Digging into his muscles. Gripping his ass so hard she'd leave bruises. Urging him toward her.

Without releasing her, he fumbled in the nightstand drawer for the box of condoms he'd left there. Managed to get a packet open and sheath himself.

Finally releasing her nipple with a tiny pop, he spread her legs and slid into her.

She grabbed his hands and twined their fingers together. Wrapped her legs around his waist, digging her heels into his ass. They moved together, perfectly in sync despite the frantic desperation.

Jules buried her face in his neck and cried out her release, and he followed her moments later. They both continued moving until the last of the aftershocks eased, then Sam collapsed on top of her. Rolled so she was on top. Jules was a strong woman, but he was a hell of a lot heavier.

After his body cooled and his breathing evened out, he lifted his head from her neck. Tucked a strand of dark red hair behind her ear. Cupped her cheek. "What happened? Why was your phone turned off?"

She stared at him for a long moment, and he wondered if she was going to answer. Finally, she slid off him and fastened her bra. Pulled her shirt together and began to button it with hands that shook.

"I was afraid someone was using it to track me," she said. "Tim Busey was fired today. And the only way Kirby could have known Tim was going to testify against Derek was through my computer. One of the techs found a keystroke capture program on it. She's set up a program to find out who it was. I was afraid that my phone was bugged, too. So I turned it off. I'll turn it on for five minutes every hour."

She took a deep breath. "When I got home, Kirby was waiting for me."

"What the *hell*?" Sam pushed himself up beside her, anger rushing through him. "Did he hurt you?"

Julia shook her head. "Didn't touch me. Threatened

me, though."

She told him what Kirby had said. How she'd responded. When she got to the part about Sam's dick controlling him, that he would do what Julia told him to do because they were having sex, Sam shook his head. "Kirby's a stupid fuck. You would never ask me to do that just because we're making... having sex."

Her face softened as she gazed at Sam. What was she thinking? He'd almost used the word 'love'. Love wasn't supposed to be on the table, but it had almost slipped out. Finally she said quietly, "No, Sam. I wouldn't."

He exhaled. She wasn't calling him on it. "You had him arrested, right?"

She looked away from him. Fiddled with one of her buttons. "No." Her voice was barely above a whisper. "I'm going to wait to see if Tonya calls me. See if we can catch this hacker tonight and have him roll on Kirby. If I can arrest Kirby, it makes everything go away."

Sam picked up Julia's hand. "You're afraid he's going to out you?" he asked, twining their fingers together. "No one's going to blame you for what your father did. You think any cop is going to respect you less because of *that*? Kirby was trying to mess with you."

"Maybe." As Sam watched, she twisted one of the buttons on her shirt, over and over, until if finally ripped free of the shirt. Landed on the sheet, white against white. She stared at it as if it fascinated her. "But why take the chance?" she asked quietly.

"Derek and his dad are escalating," Sam said, trying to keep the anger out of his voice. "This, tonight? Derek coming to the benefit last night? That guy who confronted us on the sidewalk afterward? You need to get both of the Kirbys under lock and key. Make sure they can't hurt anyone else."

"I know." She scanned the bed. "Is my jacket on the floor? I need to turn my phone back on. Get those photos onto my computer, before the techs start messing with my phone."

"Forget the photos," he said impatiently. "Call your captain. Tell him what happened and have him send someone to arrest Ronald. Did you find out what happened to Derek last night? Did they arrest him?"

"A cop picked him up." She drew a breath. Blew it out. "Dwyer. Remember him? The first cop on the scene the night of Nick's… Nick's assault?"

"Yeah, I remember him." Sam's mouth tightened. "I didn't like him. He was acting as if *I* was the suspect."

"I remember. Dwyer doesn't like it when people don't ask 'how high' when he tells them to jump. You were defying him, and he was reacting the way I expected, so I didn't think anything of it."

Julia frowned, and Sam's stomach twisted. "But there was no record of Dwyer picking up Derek last night. Maybe he just hasn't written up the report yet, but after the way he acted with Derek? Like they were old buddies? I don't think he arrested him. It's as if it never happened."

Sam frowned. "He should have been charged with disorderly conduct, at least."

"Maybe more than that. He was harassing a witness in a case against him."

Sam reached for her hand. "We're not talking about Derek, though. We're talking about Ronald. Don't pay attention to his threats. You can't count on your tech person finding the hacker tonight or tomorrow or the next day. All you can control is Kirby. The guy has a God complex, and you need to get him off the street. Probably solves two problems. If Derek's daddy's in jail, I'm guessing he'll be toothless. He's counting on Daddy's money to keep him out of trouble."

Julia looked up at him, her eyes anguished. Terrified. Then she stared down at her hands. "I'm scared, Sam. Scared of what will happen if Kirby goes to the newspapers."

"What are you scared of, Jules?" He tried to keep his

voice level. Calm. "Do you think the people you work with will turn on you? Don't you trust them?"

"Yes. I do. It's more than that." She swallowed. "I can't bear the spotlight that would shine on me. You don't know what it was like after my father was indicted. Reporters were camped out in front of our house. No one would talk to the reporters, so I had to. I didn't think my father had done anything wrong. I *trusted* him. Defended him. Said there had been some mistake."

She closed her eyes. "Then he killed himself. Left a note apologizing for what he'd done. Leaving me alone to deal with everything. There were stories in the newspaper every single day, talking about how this elderly widow had lost everything. How that family with a disabled child had all their retirement money stolen. And I was the one who had to answer the questions."

She closed her eyes, and Sam wanted to gather her close. Hold her tight, so she'd know she wasn't alone. But he could tell by the expression on her face that any softness from him would destroy her right now.

"My mother and sister couldn't deal with any of it," she said quietly. "They just pretended like nothing had happened. I was the face of my family after Dad died." She shifted to face him. "I've avoided the spotlight ever since. And Kirby's threat brought that all back.

"After the funeral, the estate sale, after we moved out of the house, I escaped. Changed my name and went to a different school. My mother and sister never forgave me for 'abandoning the family'." She swiped vicious air quotes in front of her.

"And I never told you about my fiancé." He recoiled at the word, but Julia was lost in her memory and didn't see it. "Three years ago, I was supposed to get married. I should have told him about my family, about who I was before it got to that point, but I convinced myself it wouldn't matter to him.

"The guilt ate at me, so a week before the ceremony, the

day we went for the marriage license, I told him everything. That I was Julius Landon's daughter."

A tear rolled down her face. He wanted to wipe it away, but he curled his fingers into his palms instead. He didn't want to distract her from the story.

She swiped the tear away impatiently. As if ashamed of her emotions.

"Turned out his parents had lost money to my father. Not everything. Not by a long shot -- they were a wealthy family. But he broke it off. A week before the wedding. Said he could never trust me, since I'd been lying to him the whole time. And he was right. I had been. I begged him to forgive me, but he walked away. He said I would be a painful reminder to his parents, every time they saw me.

"On top of all that ancient history, Kirby knows we're dating. He threatened to reveal that, as well. I knew I shouldn't get involved with you, but..." She swallowed. Stared down at her laced-together fingers. "I wasn't strong enough to resist my attraction to you.

"So, yes, Sam. I'm worried about what people will think. I'm worried that knowing I'm Julius Landon's daughter could influence the jury pool. I'm worried what will happen if Internal Affairs finds out we're dating." She drew in a shuddering breath. "I don't think I'd be fired. But... it would affect my career." She'd been a coward. "I should have called Francisco. But I didn't."

"You told me about your father. It didn't change how I feel about you. Do you really thing other people are going to judge you?"

"I don't know. But I know I don't want to face a crowd of reporters again and rehash the most private, painful part of my life," she said fiercely. "And I don't want the people I work with to look at me with pity. I've had as much pity as I can take."

"I don't think you're giving your coworkers and friends enough credit," Sam said slowly. "It happened eight years ago. You were nineteen. No way are you to blame."

"I know that. But blame doesn't always matter when people are hurt. Angry. Bitter. They lash out at the most convenient target."

"I think you're wrong, Jules. I think people will surprise you."

"I hope so." She wiped the tears off her face and sat up. Smiled at him. It was wobbly, but it looked real. "Thank you for being the logical one. The calm one. That's supposed to be my job."

"I have hidden talents," he said, pulling her into his lap. She curled into him, wrapping one arm around his neck. Using the other to hold onto his upper arm.

"You should call your captain and have Kirby arrested," he repeated into the top of her head.

Julia sighed. "You're right. I need to suck it up and call Captain Francisco. Tell him what happened, and let him make the call."

Sam pressed a kiss to the crown of her head. Inhaled the citrusy tang of her. "You're the bravest woman I know, Julia Landon Carleton."

"Not so brave," she murmured into his shirt. "*Brave* would have called Francisco immediately."

She eased off his lap as if it physically hurt to release him. "I'm going to find my phone and call him right now."

He tangled his fingers with hers, held onto her hand. "I'll be right beside you."

She looked up at him. Smiled. It was strained, but genuine. "Thank you, Sam."

As she searched for her jacket, Sam's phone rang. His mom. Smiling, he touched the icon. "Hey, Mom. How did today go?"

"Sammy." His mother's voice trembled. "Don is... Don is hurt. I am, too. A man came into the shop right before we closed. Wearing a ski mask. Carrying a tire iron." She sucked in a deep, shaky breath. "I called 911 for an ambulance. I think Don needs to go to the hospital." She took a shuddering breath. "Can you come to the shop?"

"Irving Park shop?" Sam asked, reaching for his clothes.

"Yes."

"Hang on, Mom. We'll be right there."

CHAPTER 25

Sam stared out the windshield, clutching the steering wheel too tightly. He was driving on autopilot. Barely noticing the streets flashing past. Gripping and releasing the steering wheel, over and over.

"Your mom called you," Julia murmured. Her left hand covered his knee, one finger smoothing over his kneecap. "That's good, right? If it was really bad, she wouldn't have called. She'd be taking care of Don."

She was trying to reassure him. Make sure he realized that his mom wasn't critically injured.

Critical injury or a broken fingernail, didn't matter. That *asshole* had hurt his mother. Hurt Don, too.

Because he was testifying against Derek Kirby.

"I'm going to kill Ronald Kirby," he said, glaring at the dawdling car in front of him. Clenching his teeth, he pressed the accelerator to zoom around the guy who thought it was okay to go twenty-five in a thirty-mile-per-hour zone.

"Hey," Julia murmured, tightening her grip on his knee. "You won't be any help to your mom if you get into an accident." She rubbed a finger over his patella. "And we don't know for sure it was Kirby. If it was, I'll take care of him. He won't be hurting anyone else, anytime soon."

Maybe if Julia had called it in after Kirby threatened her tonight, he wouldn't have been able to hurt his mom.

No. It wasn't Julia's fault. This was no one's fault except whoever had hurt his mom and Don.

Still. She should have called it in.

The stoplight up ahead turned yellow. His foot hovered over the gas pedal as he prepared to speed through. Julia's fingers pressed into his leg.

He jammed on the brake instead, and his head bounced against the headrest. She was right. He needed to calm down. Get his head straight. Drive more carefully.

He covered her hand with his, knowing she would feel his hand trembling. "Thanks, babe. You're right. I'm just… I need to get to her. Right now."

"Do you want me to call your sisters?" Julia asked. Her voice was tight, as if she was having trouble holding it together, too. "Let them know what happened?"

"Call Livvy," he said immediately. "Not Cilla." Would his massively pregnant sister go into labor if she got upset? He didn't know, but why take the chance? "Livvy can figure out if she should call Cilla."

Julia reached between his thighs to grab his phone, her fingers brushing his groin. Any other time, he would have teased her about it. Made a sexy suggestion. Probably several of them.

Not tonight.

Tonight, all he could think about was getting to his mom.

And that Julia should have called her captain immediately to arrest that son of a bitch Kirby.

Moments later, Julia was talking to Livvy in a steady voice. Telling her what happened. Where Mom and Don were. Asking her to call Cilla if Liv thought it was okay.

By the time they pulled into the parking lot at Marini's Auto Repair, the indigo sky was darkening to purple and red lights flashed in the street. There were two ambulances. A fire truck. Three squad cars.

Throwing his car into Park, Sam ripped the keys out of the ignition and leaped out of the car. Ran into the shop.

* * *

Julia got out of the car more slowly, her stomach twisted into a knot. She had a bad feeling about this. The attack had come an hour after her confrontation with Kirby. Almost as if Kirby had been so angry with her that he'd driven around, getting more and more furious, then impulsively headed to Sam's mom's shop.

As she pushed through the door of the auto repair shop, the smell of oil and the sharp ozone of electricity permeated the air. But no blood, thank God.

Don lay on a gurney, still and pale. A soft cast covered his left arm from wrist to shoulder, and a paramedic bent over him with a stethoscope, listening to his chest.

Another paramedic was examining Joanie as she sat on another gurney. Checking her eyes with a small flashlight. Taking her blood pressure. Murmuring a series of questions to her.

Sam stood beside his mother, holding her hand. "Mom, what happened? Are you hurt?" His voice was soft. Quiet. But Julia heard the tremble.

His mom curled her fingers around Sam's. "I'm fine, Sammy. Just a bruised back." She must have heard the fear in Sam's tone, because her voice was strong. Steady.

Her gaze drifted to Don, so quiet on the other gurney. "I'm worried about Don."

Then she turned back to Sam, and it looked as if her shoulders relaxed. As if the cavalry had arrived.

God! If this was Kirby's doing, Julia would never forgive herself. If she'd called Francisco as soon as Kirby left her apartment, maybe this wouldn't have happened.

As if Sam could hear her thoughts, he glanced over at her just then. Beneath the concern for his mother and Don,

Julia saw a hint of reserve. As if he was thinking the same thing Julia was -- this was *her* fault.

Joanie looked back at Sam. "The shop was closing in five minutes, but we hadn't locked the door. One of our customers was running late. He said it might be a few minutes after seven when he got here.

"A car pulled into the lot, and we assumed it was our customer, so I was taking the invoice out of the folder. When the door opened, I looked up, and instead of the man we expected, a masked man was rushing toward me.

"He tried to hit me with a tire iron. Don pushed me to the side." She swallowed, and tears filled her eyes. Julia suspected it was the first time that Joanie had cried since the guy burst into the shop. Now it was safe to break down -- help was here. So was her son.

"I fell over a chair," Joanie continued. "Hit the floor. The masked man swung the tire iron at Don's head. Don put up his arm to block it. There was a horrible cracking noise, and Don dropped to the floor."

A few more tears leaked out of Joanie's eyes. "I'm sure his arm is broken. The guy bent over to hit him again, but I reached up and pulled off his mask. He jumped back, kicked Don in the side, then ran out the door."

Julia moved closer to Sam, although her proximity made her face burn with shame. If her fears were right, she was responsible for Don's injuries. For Joanie's fear and pain. "Did you get a good look at his face, Joanie?" she asked his mother, swallowing the lump in her throat.

"I did." She tried to smile at Julia, but managed only a grimace. "And maybe that fancy security system of Sammy's got a picture of him."

"We'll check it, Mom. Right now, I'm getting you and Don to the hospital."

Joanie shook her head. "I'm going to the hospital, but only so I can be with Don. I'm sore and bruised, but nothing that a few aspirin and a good soak in a tub won't fix." She squeezed Sam's hand. "You and your Julia stay here and look at those security tapes. See if you can identify that man."

The door flew open and a man and a woman rushed in. Sam's sister Livvy and her fiancé Ryan. "Mom!" Livvy grabbed her mom's hand, using the other to touch her mother's arms. Legs. Face. "Where are you hurt?"

"I'm fine, Livvy." Joanie patted her daughter's cheek as she went through the whole explanation again. "I'm going to the hospital with Don. Sammy and Julia are staying here to look at the security tape." She pursed her lip as she studied her older daughter, and a tiny grin curved her lips. "You and Ryan go on home. Finish what you started. I don't need you hovering over me."

Julia looked more closely at Sam's sister and Ryan. Livvy's shirt wasn't tucked in and was buttoned crookedly. Ryan wore his tee shirt inside out. His belt hung off his pants, threaded through the loops but unbuckled.

"Nice look, Liv. Ryan," Sam said, smirking.

Julia clenched her teeth as she looked from Liv to Ryan. She'd done one thing right, at least. She and Sam had managed to get dressed before running out the door.

Livvy punched her brother in the shoulder as she stepped in front of Ryan, her face flaming red. Behind Sam, Julia mouthed an apology to Livvy over Sam's shoulder.

Sam's mother was actually smiling.

Amazingly, some of the tension had dissipated from the room.

"Cilla's on her way," Livvy muttered.

Sam leaned close to her sister. "You and Ryan better go get straightened out, or Cilla will never let you live this down."

"Thanks for the tip, Sammy." Cilla scowled at him as she dragged Ryan around the corner. Toward the restroom.

"Don't take too long," Sam called after them. "Or we'll all know what you're…"

Julia slapped a hand over his mouth. "What is *wrong* with you?" she hissed. "Your mom is hurt. Don is on a gurney.

And you're needling your sister about *that*?" She leaned closer, nipping his earlobe a little harder than necessary. "You want me to tell your mom what *we* were doing right before she called?"

"You're supposed to be on my side," he muttered.

"Not when you're being an ass."

"It's all right, Julia." His mom patted Julia's arm. "Seeing my children acting like their usual goofy selves makes me feel better. Like some things are still normal in my life." She slid off the gurney, clearly stiff and sore, and walked slowly to the other gurney holding Don. Took his hand. Leaned over and whispered something in his ear.

Don opened his eyes and gave her a weak smile. "We'll get the bastard," Julia heard Don say. "Sammy's girl will make sure of it."

"I will," Julia said, curling her hands into fists. If Kirby had done this, it was her fault. She'd make damn sure she made it right. If they could prove Kirby was behind the attack, she'd personally drag his ass to Cook County Jail.

Sam glanced at her, the first time since he'd run into the shop. She knew her face was sheet white. Knew her jaw was clenched, her mouth a thin line. He frowned, his eyes clouded.

"Jules," he began, but she held up a hand to stop him. She couldn't bear to talk to Sam about this right now.

"Stay with your mom. I'm going to talk to the cops who are going through the security tape," she said. "See if I can get a look at the guy's face."

Careful not to touch him, in case he felt the shudders that wracked her body, she walked over to the desk where a uniformed officer sat in front of a computer. Julia reached for another chair and sat beside him.

The kid glanced at her, frowning, and she reached to shake his hand. "Detective Julia Carleton from the twenty-third." She opened her jacket to display her badge. "I think this might be related to one of my cases. I'd like to get a look at the assailant, if you don't mind me staring over your shoulder."

"'Course not, Detective," the kid said, scooting over a little so she had a better view of the monitor. "I'm Sean Lacey." He nodded at the screen. "Car hasn't pulled into the lot yet. I thought I should start from the beginning."

"Good."

Behind her, she heard the paramedic announce they were going to load Don into the ambulance. That Joanie could ride with Don, but anyone else going to the hospital would have to meet them there.

She'd make sure Sam followed his mom to the hospital. Julia needed time and space to watch these tapes. To identify the assailant.

She needed a little distance from Sam, too. Looking at him was a painful reminder that this was probably her fault.

Blocking out everything else, Julia focused only on the tape, watching each frame intently. When Sam put his hand on her shoulder, she jumped.

"Sorry, Jules. I needed to get my mom settled with Don."

Julia turned to face him. "You're going to the hospital, aren't you?"

He frowned. "If I do, you'll be stranded here. And I have no idea how long it will take with Don."

"Don't worry about it," Julia said. She tried to sound calm and unworried, hoping he'd just go. "Your mom needs you. Sean here can have someone drop me off at the station when we're done."

"Or the hotel," Sam said, concern edging into his expression.

"Or the hotel," she agreed. No way would she be going to the hotel. Her gut told her Kirby was involved in this attack. And she'd stay up all night, if she had to, in order to make a case for arresting him.

"Okay, Jules," Sam said. "I'll keep in touch." He squeezed her shoulder. "Would you turn your phone on, please?" he asked in a low voice. "So I can call you?"

She wanted to hear from Sam, too. She wanted to know how Don was doing. How badly he was injured. So she could make out her arrest warrant accordingly.

And what did it matter now if Kirby was tracking her phone? If he'd been involved in this assault, he'd already know where she was.

"Can you pause the feed for a moment, Sean?" she asked, pulling her phone out of her pocket. She powered it up and waited impatiently for it to go through its starting ritual. Finally, when her screen flashed, she hit her phone log to see if Tonya had called her.

Not yet. No texts, either.

"I'll leave it on," she promised Sam.

"Thanks, Jules," he said. Instead of bending to kiss her, he squeezed her shoulder again.

His gaze held hers for a moment, then slid away. "I'll call as soon as I know anything," he said. He nodded toward the screen. "You do the same."

"As soon as I call Captain Francisco," she promised, a sick feeling in her stomach. Sam was second-guessing her decision not to call Francisco immediately. And she couldn't blame him.

Of course it would change the way he felt about her. Her negligence had gotten his mom and Don hurt.

Sam squeezed her shoulder once more, then walked out the door and climbed into his car. In seconds, he'd zoomed out of the parking lot and disappeared.

The next time she saw Sam, the concern, the caring she always saw in his eyes would be gone. When she told him that Kirby had been behind the attack on Don and Joanie, Sam would put the blame exactly where it belonged. On Julia.

She closed her eyes for a moment as her heart crumbled inside her chest. Then she took a deep breath and blocked out the part of her brain that already mourned his loss, the part of her soul that missed him already. She turned her attention back to the monitor. It might be too late for her and Sam, but Julia would do her job.

On the screen in front of them, a large, dark SUV bumped over the ridge of asphalt into the parking lot and rolled to a stop. Julia's fists clenched in her lap. It looked identical to the SUV at her three-flat.

As she and Sean watched, a man got out of the driver's seat and stood with his back to the cameras. Had he known the new surveillance equipment was there? Or was he just being careful?

Reaching into the front seat, he retrieved a stocking cap and tugged it on. Yanked down the mask.

He knew about the cameras.

When his face was concealed, he opened the door to the passenger compartment and reached toward the floor. Stood up with a tire iron in his hand.

As he walked around the front of the car, the window on the passenger side rolled down. Far enough for her to see a forehead and a pair of eyes, but nothing more. The masked guy turned to look, as if the guy in the car had said something. He nodded, then continued toward the shop.

Sean rewound the feed to where the masked man had exited the car and began writing down the time stamps on a pad of paper that said Marini Auto Repair. When the passenger window rolled down, he scribbled again.

The scene unfolded just as Joanie had described. The masked intruder raised his hand holding the tire iron. Slashed down toward his mother, but Don pushed her away. Took the blow on his arm and crumpled to the floor.

As the intruder bent closer to Don, his mom struggled to sit up. Reached for the guy's mask and yanked it off his head.

The tech stopped the tape. Started it again, more slowly this time. One frame clicked to the next, making the guy's movements jerky and robotic in slow motion.

Finally he straightened and appeared to look directly into a camera. Julia gasped. Signaled for the tech to stop the tape.

She said a prayer of thanks that Sam had spent the money to get the high definition camera. The assailant stared at her, every wrinkle and line on his face visible in harsh detail.

Julia sucked in a breath. "Richie Vannetti," she breathed.

"You know the guy?" Sean asked.

"I do. Ex-cop."

Her hands tightened on the desk as all the pieces fell into place. She needed to call Francisco. Right now. But she needed one more piece of evidence first.

"I need to call my captain," she said. "But before I do that, can you see if the cameras got a clean picture of his license plate?"

"Sure."

Sean scrolled through the tape quickly until the SUV turned around to leave. Going one frame at a time, he finally found a shot where the license plate was illuminated by a street light.

"There," she and Sean said at the same time.

Julia grabbed her phone and scrolled through the pictures of the SUV from her apartment, looking for a clear shot of the license plate. She wrote it on Sean's pad of paper, then peered at the monitor. The plate was a little blurred because the SUV was moving, but judging by the shape of the letters and numbers, she knew it was the same.

The techs could clean up the image so it was solid, but it was enough for Julia.

"Sean, I need to get to the twenty-third district station, ASAP. Can you have someone drive me? And can you make me a copy of this surveillance tape?"

"Can do. You have a flash drive with you?"

Julia dug in her purse, where she always kept a few spare ones. Closed her fingers around the small rectangular stick and handed it to Sean.

As he made the copy, Julia pushed away from the desk and dialed her captain.

"Francisco," he said wearily.

"Captain, this is Julia Carleton. Are you still at the station?"

"Getting ready to head out."

"Please stay, and make sure there's a tech available. I'll be there in twenty or thirty minutes. We have a breakthrough in the Kirby case, and we need to take action tonight."

CHAPTER 26

Julia sat beside Sean Lacey in the front of the patrol car, the car's laptop computer tray crowded into her lap, her fingers curled around the flash drive holding the feed from the security cameras. Sean had turned on the siren and lights as she'd requested, and they flew toward the station. In a few minutes, she'd be back at work. First she and Francisco would confirm that Ronald Kirby had been in the passenger seat of the SUV.

Then they'd decide how to take him down.

Until she could get busy on that, she had only her thoughts for company. And they were unpleasant companions.

She hadn't acted like a cop tonight.

She'd acted like that nineteen-year-old girl who'd been in the next room when her father ate his gun. And she'd reacted the same way. Scared. In denial. Unable to think about anything but what she needed. What she wanted.

Unable to face the harsh truth. Unable to do what needed to be done.

That night, all she'd wanted was her father back. To be enclosed in his loving arms one more time. To be ignorant of his betrayal. To be protected from the ugliness that had swallowed her whole world.

Tonight, after her encounter with Kirby at her apartment, all she'd wanted was Sam. She'd needed to see him. Feel his comforting arms surrounding her. Hear his voice, telling her that everything would be okay.

She'd needed to banish the fears of what newspaper stories would bring. The attention. The intrusive requests for information that should be private. Reporters following her everywhere, badgering her with endless questions.

She'd run to Sam, leaned on him, instead of doing her job.

If she *had* done her job, if she'd called Kirby in immediately for threatening a witness and threatening a cop, maybe Richie Vannetti wouldn't have made it to Don and Joanie's shop. Don wouldn't have been hurt, and neither would Joanie.

But she'd made a bad decision, and two people she liked, two people Sam *loved*, had been injured. All because she'd wanted Sam.

Because she'd wanted to protect herself.

"Detective Carleton?" Sean's voice was puzzled. "Um, we're here. Can I help you with something else?"

Julia shook herself out of her daze and made an effort to smile. "Sorry, Sean. I was thinking of all the things I need to do tonight, trying to prioritize. I apologize for not noticing you'd stopped."

"No problem, Detective." Sean reached for the swing arm on the computer tray to pull it out of her way. "I admire your focus. We should all be so into the job."

"Thanks, Sean," she managed to say, although his words pinched her heart. If only he knew what her 'focus' was about, he wouldn't be so admiring. "I appreciate the lift. Keep me posted on what you find at Marini Auto Repair. And give me a call as soon as you're done with the surveillance feed. I'll come by and pick up the computer with the original."

"That's not necessary. I can bring it to the twenty-third."

He nodded toward the building.

"Absolutely not," Julia said. "You've got other things to worry about. I'll come to the seventeeth and get it." She'd screwed up enough on this case already. She didn't want any questions about control of the chain of evidence from Joanie's shop.

"Okay. I'll give you a call when we're done. Probably be tomorrow."

"I'll see you then." She smiled at him, although her lips felt stiff. Hard to move. "Thanks again, Sean."

She stepped out of the car and onto the sidewalk. It was a beautiful, balmy May night, warm and clear. The blooming lilacs from the building next door to the station almost masked the scent of exhaust from the street. There were even a few stars visible through the Chicago light pollution.

If things were different, maybe she and Sam would be out walking the neighborhood. Trying to decide where to go for dinner. Knowing that afterward, they'd be heading back to the hotel together to spend the night making love.

That wasn't an option tonight.

She wasn't sure it would ever be an option again.

She headed into the building and up the stairs. The light was still on in Captain Francisco's office, and she could see his dark hair over the top of his computer monitor.

She took a deep breath. Let it out slowly. She pushed Sam out of her head and walked to the door.

"Captain. I think I've put the pieces together on the Ronald Kirby case."

Francisco looked up from his computer. "Do we *have* a Ronald Kirby case, Carleton?"

"Yes, sir. I believe we do."

* * *

Sam made another circuit around the emergency room waiting area, counting off each of the forty squares of carpet that made up the perimeter of the room. The main carpet was dark blue, with red, green and yellow squares as the border. Probably supposed to be calming, with a side of cheeriness.

Neither was working for him tonight.

He wanted to be in that tiny cubicle with Don and his mother. Wanted to know what was going on.

He wanted to *do* something. Something more than this endless pacing.

He wanted to hunt Ronald Kirby down and beat the shit out of him. *Hurt* him, the way he'd hurt his mom. Don.

It probably hadn't been Ronald who wielded the crow bar. Kirby was the kind of guy who wouldn't want to wrinkle his expensive suit. The kind of guy who paid other people to do his dirty work. But Sam would bet his next paycheck Ronald had been behind it.

He curled his fingers into his palms until the nails cut into his skin. Making Ronald pay was Julia's job.

And she'd get it done. Julia was nothing if not dedicated to her job. She was a good cop. Worked hard. Struggled to get justice for the victims of crime.

Then why hadn't she had Kirby arrested after he showed up at her apartment?

His footsteps slowed and he jammed his hands into his pockets. If she had, maybe it would have prevented the confrontation at the shop. Maybe Don and his mom would be home right now, having dinner, instead of at the hospital.

Sam knew he wasn't being completely fair. What Kirby had done wasn't Julia's fault. She had no way of knowing he'd attack Sam's mom. He didn't blame her. Not exactly. But the idea she might have been able to prevent it ate at him.

If only she'd called Francisco immediately…

When had the kick-ass woman he knew turned into a coward?

Shoving his fingers through his hair, he paced back the way he'd come. Counted the squares again. He wasn't thinking straight. Julia wasn't a coward. Not at all.

But she should have arrested Kirby, damn it! If he'd been off the street, none of this would have happened.

As he turned once again, he glimpsed Livvy and Ryan huddled together on the uncomfortable chairs, their heads close as they talked. Their hands were twined, and their shoulders and upper arms were touching. As if they had to be in contact with each other. As if the other's physical presence was a necessity, not a choice.

Sam stopped pacing to study Livvy and Ryan. They were joined by more than their hands and shoulders and arms. There was a bond between them forged in pain and danger and struggle.

A bond no one could break.

He and Julia could have had that kind of bond.

Now? He wasn't sure. But how could he want someone who might have been responsible for his mom and Don getting hurt? Julia had screwed up. But did that mean he wanted to walk away from her?

The idea of saying goodbye to Julia was devastating. Even after what had happened tonight.

He was lost. Adrift. Unsure of his direction.

This was scary shit.

He glanced at Liv and Ryan again. They looked... whole. As if they'd both found the person who was the missing piece of themselves.

Could Julia be that to him?

Before he could think it through, the door to the emergency room whooshed open and Cilla waddled in, one arm curving beneath her huge belly as if holding it up. Brendan had his arm wrapped around his wife's shoulder. Before Sam could reach them, the nurse from behind the triage desk grabbed a wheelchair and rushed over.

"Let's get you in the wheelchair, sweetie," she said in a chirpy, overly sweet voice as she tried to guide Cilla into the chair. "You came in the wrong way, and we need to get you up to Labor and Delivery. You can fill out your paperwork there."

Sam bit his lip to keep from laughing as Cilla shook off the nurse's hand. Scowled at her. "I'm not in labor," she said, her voice low but tinged with warning. "And my name is *not* sweetie. My mother is in the emergency room with her partner, Don Young. I need to know how they're both doing."

Whoa! Sam took a step back. He'd never seen Cilla like this. She reminded him of Julia in her 'I'm in control' mode. *Cop* mode.

"Sorry, Ms., ah…"

"Marini. Detective Marini," Cilla answered.

"My, there are a lot of cops in your family," the nurse said brightly.

"Yes. Yes, there are." She gestured to Brendan. "This is my husband, Detective Donovan."

The nurse cut her gaze to Brendan, then hurried toward the entrance to the ER, where she flashed her ID tag in front of a reader. "I'll check on Mr. Young for you," she said over her shoulder.

"Thank you," Cilla called, but the nurse was already through the double doors.

"Way to scare her off, Cill." Sam hurried over to give her a hug. "Is that baby falling out? You look like you're trying to hold it in."

"You're a funny guy, Sam," Cilla said, heading toward Cilla and Ryan with Brendan trailing behind her. "Where's Carleton?"

"Trying to catch the guy who broke Don's arm," he said.

She whipped her head around to stare at him. "Does she know who it is?"

Sam frowned. He hadn't heard from Julia since he left the shop. "I don't know. I'll call her."

Julia's phone rang four times before she picked it up. "Hey, Sam, I was just going to call. We know who the guy with the crowbar was. That security system you put in works great. I could count every wrinkle on the guy's face."

The tension in his shoulders ratcheted higher. "That's one accounted for. What about Kirby?"

"Working on it. We have a partial shot of a face in the passenger seat, and we're going over the tape with a tech." Julia's voice was flat. He couldn't read her at all.

"Okay." He loosened his too-tight grip on the phone. "Will you call me when you have more information? Are you going to arrest crow-bar-guy tonight?"

"I think so. I'll keep you posted." She cleared her throat. "How's Don doing?"

"Still in the ER. We're all stuck in the waiting room. Cilla just got here, and the nurse is checking on him for us."

"Call me when you find out?" Her voice had softened. She sounded sad. Regretful.

"If you're not going to be too busy."

"Not for that. I'll be here for a while, though."

"I figured." He spotted the nurse coming through the double doors. "Here's the nurse. I'll talk to you later."

"Bye, Sam."

He stared at the screen for an extra few seconds. The note of sadness and regret in Julia's voice sounded awfully... final.

Sliding the phone into his pocket, he turned to the nurse. Her cloying sweetness was gone. "They're prepping Mr. Young for surgery," she began. "They have to put a couple of pins in his arm to stabilize the fractures. And he needs a chest tube."

Before she could continue, all five of them began talking at once. Shooting questions at her. The former Ms. Chipper held up her hand, her face suddenly tired. "Let me explain," she said when they were quiet.

"Mr. Young has two broken ribs, and one of them punctured a lung. There's blood in his chest cavity, and he's having trouble breathing. That's why he needs a chest tube. Your mom said she'd be out as soon as they take Mr. Young into surgery."

"Thank you, Ms.," Sam gazed at her nametag, "Ms.

MARGARET WATSON

Dickinson. We all appreciate you checking for us."

"You're welcome," she said, her face relaxing into a smile. "I know how stressful it is when a family member is injured." With a flirtatious smile at Sam, she returned to her post behind the desk.

"Does every woman on the planet look at you like that, Marini?" Brendan asked when they were out of earshot of Ms. Dickinson.

"I have no idea what you're talking about, Donovan."

"Like you're the sun god, and she's looking for a good tan. Does Carleton look at you like that, too?" Brendan's mouth curled into a sly smile.

"Leave Julia out of this," Sam said too sharply. "For God's sake, she'd be here if she wasn't busy trying to get the guy who hurt Don and Mom."

Brendan studied him for a few minutes, then said, "Got it. I'll wait until the next dinner. She and I will talk."

Brendan was assuming that Julia would be at the next Donovan family dinner. But Sam wasn't so sure. She'd acted a little... aloof at the shop this evening. And her voice had held an odd tone just now. *Distant.*

Because she'd been talking to *him*. Oh, God. Julia was a smart woman. Reading people was part of her job. And she'd had no trouble reading him. She'd heard the accusatory tone in Sam's voice.

This was what she'd been talking about. People treating her differently. Second-guessing her judgment. And it hadn't been some stranger on the street. It had been *him*. Instead of standing by her, *he'd* been the one questioning her judgment.

Feeling sick, he reached for his phone to call her back. But before he could dial, his mom emerged from the emergency room. She moved too carefully and her face was pale.

All five of them surrounded her. Sam took her hand and led her to one of the chairs, and they all clustered around. Sam didn't let go of her hand.

"Don's in surgery," she said, her lip quivering. "They said it was routine for the kind of break he has. That he just needs two pins in his arm. They also have to put a tube in his chest to drain the blood. They normally use a local for that. But it's *surgery*. Anesthesia. And bleeding into his chest cavity. My God."

Sam tightened his grip on her hand, and Cilla took her other hand. "Will he be okay after the surgery? Did they find anything else?" Cilla asked.

His mother shook her head. "No, they said he was good, other than the broken arm and broken ribs. That he should be back to normal in six to eight weeks."

"Why don't we all go up to the surgical waiting area?" Livvy said. "The nurse told me where it was. Sam, you want to hunt down food for all of us?"

"On it," Sam said. He stepped away from them and pulled out his phone. Dialed the Italian place they all liked and placed an order as the rest of his family stepped into the elevator and disappeared from sight.

Leaving Sam waiting for the delivery guy, standing in the now-empty room. Alone except for his searing regret for the way he'd treated Julia.

* * *

Julia stood beside Francisco in the tech lab as Tonya displayed the security tape from the shop on a large monitor. She stopped the feed every few seconds to make a note or improve the resolution of the picture.

She stopped longer at the place where the man in the passenger seat rolled down his window. Tonya frowned as she studied it, advancing it frame by frame as Sean had done in the shop. Muttering under her breath, Tonya pulled up a menu that listed all the cameras installed inside and outside Marini Auto Shop.

When the feed switched to a camera inside the shop, Tonya's hands flew over the keyboard. In moments, she'd switched to the outdoor camera again and progressed the feed frame by frame.

The man in the passenger seat lowered the window an inch at a time. He moved from side to side, as if trying to get a better view. Finally the window went all the way down, and it was clear that the man was Ronald Kirby.

"Got you, asshole," Tonya muttered. She inserted several markers for slightly different views of his face, then switched back to the feed from inside the shop.

By the time they reached the point where Joanie snatched the mask off the intruder, Julia was shifting from one foot to the other impatiently. She knew damn well it was Richie Vannetti. She wanted to haul him into the station. Right now.

Francisco turned to study her. "You have someplace you need to be, Carleton?"

"No, sir. Anxious to keep moving on this case." She had business with Sam, but like the coward she was, she wanted to delay it as long as possible. "I want to pick up our suspect." She wasn't going to tell Francisco who it was -- he'd confirm it for himself. And she'd double check. She'd made enough mistakes on this case.

"Keep going with the feed, Tonya," the captain ordered.

Finally they got to the money shot, the one where Vannetti was looking directly into the camera. Francisco reared back. "Richie Vannetti?" he said, incredulous.

"Yes, sir. Dwyer's old partner. As I recall, he retired two years ago instead of facing a board of inquiry about a civilian shooting."

"You're right," Francisco said. His jaw worked and his face reddened as he stared at the monitor. "God *damn* it. Tonya, see if you can get a clear view of the license plate on that SUV."

Tonya advanced the feed until she found the clearest shot of the rear license plate. It took a while, but she managed to manipulate the settings so the license plate jumped into clear focus.

Julia scribbled it down and looked around for a computer.

Tonya nodded to a tiny cubicle against the wall. "Use mine. My password is puppydog."

"Puppydog? Really?" Julia stared at the tech, her mouth curving into a smile. "I had no idea you were such a softie, Tonya. I'm surprised it wasn't pinkunicorns."

The tech held up her middle finger while she continued to study the tape. "I've got the most secure computer in the lab. You think any of the geeks in here would guess my password?" She rolled her eyes. "And pink unicorns? Good idea. Maybe that'll be my next one."

As Francisco and Tonya finished looking at the tape, Julia looked up the license plate. Slapped her palm on the desk when it flashed on the screen. Cadillac Escalade, registered to Ronald Kirby

She copied his home address and hurried back to Francisco and Tonya.

"It's Kirby's," she said. "We have him at the scene, along with his vehicle. More than enough to pick him up. And Vannetti, too."

Francisco nodded. "Call the judge who handled little Kirby's bond hearing. Have him send me arrest warrants for both Ronald Kirby and Vannetti. And I want a search warrant for Vannetti's house and vehicle, Kirby's house and that Escalade. I want that weapon, too."

"Make sure the warrant specifies Kirby's and Vannetti's laptop," Tonya added. "Let's see which of them was monitoring Carleton's work computer. Probably the same person who's tracking the bugs in her apartment."

"Good thinking, Tonya," Francisco said, his eyes glued to the monitor. His jaw clenched as he watched Kirby enjoying Vannetti's assault of Don and Joanie.

"What about Dwyer, Captain?" Julia asked.

"What about him?" Francisco frowned as he studied Julia.

"He acted… off the night of Nick's assault," Julia

answered slowly. She described Dwyer's odd actions that night. How he'd tried to take Sam's phone. How he hadn't called in a request for the taxi drop-off information, even after he'd seen Sam's video of Derek Kirby driving off in an identifiable cab.

"And that's on top of the night of Sam's MC gig at Chicago Wine Bar. It wasn't just that he didn't file an arrest report," she said carefully. "I watched Dwyer load Kirby into the squad car. Dwyer acted like they were buddies. Slapped him on the back. Smiling and laughing with him. If I didn't know Dwyer was a cop, I'd think it was a friend picking him up."

Julia sighed, hating that she had to say it. "Dwyer and Vannetti were tight. They'd been partners for a long time. With Dwyer's odd behavior…" She let her voice trail off, hoping Francisco would connect the dots.

The captain narrowed his eyes. "Yeah. He and Vannetti *were* tight. Dwyer wasn't happy when Richie was forced to retire. And with all these little details, I suppose it's possible Dwyer's involved."

Francisco clenched and unclenched his jaw. Stared at the picture of Vannetti on the monitor. "As much as I hate to think one of my cops is dirty, you're right. I'll order a tail on Dwyer. And I'll ask one of the other detectives to go through Derek Kirby's complaint forms and find out which police officers were involved."

"Good idea, sir. I'd bet a lot of those complaints that didn't result in an arrest were Dwyer's calls."

Francisco nodded once, sharply. "Ronald Kirby and Vannetti? I want them both locked up. Tell the State's Attorney we want no bail, and make real clear why it's necessary."

He pointed at Julia. "Make it happen, Carleton."

CHAPTER 27

Julia slid the key card into the slot on the door of the Houston Hotel suite and crept inside. A single lamp was lit in the living area, and the door to the bedroom she shared with Sam was ajar.

After double-locking the door, she dropped her bag on the couch, then walked silently over the thick Persian carpet and stood in the entrance to the bedroom, watching Sam sleep. He sprawled over the bed, taking up most of the space with his long arms and legs. The pillow she'd used last night was snuggled into his chest, and Julia's heart broke a little more.

She gripped the molding around the door and tried to turn away. Breaking things off with Sam was going to be hard enough without watching him sleep, wrapped around her pillow.

She should wake him up now and get it over with. Rip off the bandage and tell him goodbye, then escape to her own apartment. With Richie Vannetti in custody, she was pretty sure no one was monitoring the bugs in her place. She could live with them until the techs removed them tomorrow.

The judge had wanted more information before issuing

an arrest warrant for Ronald Kirby, since he was an "upstanding citizen" and prominent member of the Chicago business community. Julia had sent him plenty of evidence, including the pictures of him, in his car, at the crime scene at Marini Auto Repair.

Tomorrow, she and Captain Francisco would pick Kirby up.

Tonight, though, she needed to end things with Sam.

She couldn't do it tonight, she suddenly realized. The hard knot in the pit of her stomach eased.

She swallowed. Of course she was relieved. Everyone dreaded painful moments. But she wasn't putting it off for her own sake.

It was almost three PM. Sam hadn't gotten to bed until a couple of hours earlier. He had a game tomorrow afternoon, and he needed to get some rest.

She hadn't had a problem with depriving him of sleep the past two nights. When they'd spent most of their time making love.

Turning away from Sam's room, she walked to the other bedroom. It felt lonely and cold, but she refused to go back into the living area. Back to Sam.

They'd talked twice in the previous hours. Julia had called him around midnight, when Richie Vannetti was safely in custody. She'd explained who Vannetti was, told him they had Dwyer under observation and were still waiting for the Kirby warrant.

Julia had tried to be business-like. Tried to keep all emotion out of the conversation, even though Sam had thanked her profusely for acting so quickly to arrest Don's attacker.

It had been easy to read between the lines. He'd blamed her for not getting Kirby off the street after their confrontation at her apartment. He was trying to make up for it.

That wasn't necessary, since *she* blamed herself, as well.

Sam had called her after Don was out of surgery. Everything had gone well, he'd be in the hospital for at least that night, and none of Joanie's children had been able to convince her to go home and rest. She was staying overnight with Don.

Julia envied Sam his close, loving family. Even though he and his sisters teased each other constantly, it was clear they were close. And all of them adored their mother, who adored her children right back.

Her family had never been like that. From the beginning, it had been her and her father ranged against her sister and her mother. And once her father died, Julia had been completely alone.

Her mother and sister had accused her of grabbing the spotlight afterward, when Julia had been the one to face the press. But neither of them would do it. Neither of them wanted the cameras in their faces or their pictures in the newspapers.

Julia talked to her mother on Mother's Day. Christmas. Her mother's birthday. Her mother made an obligatory call on Julia's birthday. But neither her mother nor her sister had forgiven her for changing her name and starting from scratch after her father died.

The last time she'd talked to her mother, a couple of weeks earlier on Mother's Day, her mother had hesitated when Julia had asked how she was doing. As if she might actually open up and *tell* Julia something about her life. Reach out to her older daughter.

Instead, her mother had eventually said 'fine' in the cold, dismissive voice she always used with Julia. As if their infrequent conversations were an unpleasant duty she wanted to get through as quickly as possible.

Her heart aching, Julia had ended the call after a few more stilted minutes of painfully cold conversation.

Wept afterwards, as she usually did after talking to her mother. She missed her father desperately after those calls. The conversations with her mother were a brutal reminder than she was now an orphan, with no family left.

She'd call again on her mother's birthday in August.

Those infrequent conversations would be even more painful now, after seeing the close, supportive relationships in the Donovan and Marini families.

Julia yearned to know what it would be like to be part of a family like Sam's. Or the Donovans. A family that sustained each other. Was there when a sibling or a child or a mother needed someone to lean on.

A family who loved and enjoyed each other.

She hadn't been thinking about that with Sam. But deep in her heart, she longed for that kind of connection. Tonight, knowing she wouldn't find that with Sam made her chest feel hollow. Empty.

Squaring her shoulders, Julia closed the bedroom door, blocking any glimpses of Sam. Any hints of his scent. If she gave into temptation and slipped into his bed, cuddled beside him, she couldn't do what she needed to do in the morning.

* * *

Sam stretched and yawned without opening his eyes, sweeping his hand across the cool sheet on Julia's side of the bed. Searching for her.

Julia's side of the bed?

After only a few nights together?

Uneasiness at both the thought and the cold sheet had him opening his eyes. The other side of the bed was empty. And Julia hadn't slept there, because he was still clutching her pillow to his chest.

Scrambling out of bed, he tugged on his jeans and went into the living room. Her bag lay on the couch, so she was here. She had to be in the other room.

Breathing a sigh of relief when he spotted the closed door, he headed toward Julia. She probably hadn't wanted to disturb him, knowing he had an early game today. But he wished she had. Her pillow was a lousy substitute for Julia herself.

Knocking softly, he was surprised when she said, "Yeah, come in." As if she was already up and wide awake.

When he pushed open the door, he found her dressed. She was strapping on her gun, like she was ready to head out.

"You're running off?" he said, frowning.

"We're arresting Ronald Kirby this morning. The warrant came through, and Francisco wants to do it early. I need to be at the station in a half-hour."

He reached for her, needing to hold her, but she stepped out of his reach. It felt as if she'd punched him in the chest. "Jules? What's going on?"

"We need to talk, Sam." She didn't meet his gaze. Instead, she brushed past him into the living room.

A ball of ice settled in Sam's stomach at her words. 'We need to talk' was never good news. "What's up?" he asked, stopping a few feet away from her.

"I can't do this anymore," she said, her gaze directed behind his left shoulder. "Your mom and Don were hurt yesterday because I didn't do my job. I've made a lot of mistakes on this case, and because of them, people were hurt. *You* could have been hurt."

She bit her lip, and her eyes glittered with unshed tears. "I made those mistakes because I was distracted. Because I wanted you. I was smitten, and I lost my focus. Made bad choices. That's dangerous for a cop. I need to be focused on my job."

"What the hell?" He took a step closer to her, but stopped when she backed up a step. *She was breaking up with him.* A gaping cavern opened in his chest. "So you're telling me that you'll never have an actual relationship because you're a cop? That's bullshit, Jules. Cops have relationships all the time. They get married. Have kids. So what's really going on?"

"This was always a short-term thing, Sam." She swallowed, and he watched the ripple of her throat, wondering if she was swallowing tears. "We both agreed to that."

"What if I've changed my mind?" He hadn't been sure last night, but Julia walking away crystallized his feelings. Yeah, he was still a little pissed at her. Didn't matter. He didn't want her to go.

Didn't want to lose her.

Julia rubbed a finger down the pleat of her pants, staring at it as if fascinated. "I know you were angry at me last night, and that's fine. I deserved your anger. This isn't about that. You said all you wanted was a fling," she said, finally meeting his eyes. "That's what we had, and now it's over. You might think you've changed your mind, but I haven't." A tear escaped from her eye and she swiped it away roughly.

Sam studied her and found the signs he was looking for. Her hands were wrapped around her waist, and he could see her slight sway from side to side. She sucked in a deep breath -- she was trying to hold back more tears.

"You said you're smitten." It was a sweet word. Tender. "I'm smitten, too. You might be running away, but it's not for the reasons you just gave me. What's really going on, Jules?"

"Exactly what I told you." Another tear slid down her cheek, and she grabbed her bag. Slung it over her shoulder. "Someone from the State's Attorney's office will be in touch about the trials for Ronald and Derek Kirby. For Richie Vannetti, too. Last night he confessed that he was the guy who stopped us after the concert at the Wine Bar. The guy who broke into my place and hacked into my laptop."

Her eyes narrowed, and she was a cop again. In control. Tough. Burying her emotions.

She turned to leave, and Sam hurried over to take her elbow. "Jules." He tried to turn her around, but she resisted. "At least be honest with me. Tell me the real reason you're doing this."

At that she turned around. "I told you the real reason. What else could it be?"

"Maybe you're afraid," he said, knowing he'd hit the mark when she paled. "Maybe you don't want this to be over, either. But I know you, and I know you don't like feeling vulnerable. You don't like feeling out of control. I get that. We can figure this out together. Take it as slow as you want."

"What I want is for this to be over," she said. "I screwed up this case because I was thinking about you rather than the Kirbys. I can't do that anymore." Her face softened. "It was wonderful while it lasted, though."

"I don't even get a kiss goodbye?"

She looked away. "Not a good idea, Sam."

Her hand slid off the door handle. She swiped her palm down her leg, then fumbled with it again. She finally got it open, then slid through the door as soon as the crack was wide enough. The door clicked shut with a finality that echoed in the silence of the suite.

Sam grabbed the door and yanked it open. Julia was just turning the corner toward the elevators. He started out the door to run after her. But the air from a vent blew across his chest, and he realized he was wearing nothing but his jeans.

Stepping back into his room, he shut the door. He wasn't going to let Jules go.

She was right. A little fling, short-term and casual, was exactly what he'd wanted. He'd told her so, more than once. And she'd been straight about wanting the same thing.

So why did he feel broken? As if she'd reached inside his chest and ripped out his heart. Why did this big, luxurious suite suddenly feel completely barren?

He sank down on the couch and stared at the wall, seeing Julia's pale, strained face as she'd walked out of his life.

Wondering if he'd ever feel whole again.

* * *

Julia walked into the station fifteen minutes later and

headed straight for the washroom, managing to slip inside before anyone noticed her. She'd spent the drive from the Houston with tears running down her face, and she needed to regroup. Put on some makeup to hide her red, swollen eyes and blotchy face.

Ten minutes later, after splashing cold water on her face until it felt numb, then applying mascara and foundation, she examined herself in the mirror. Her face was too pale, even under the makeup, and her eyes were still red. If anyone asked, she'd blame it on lack of sleep.

Straightening away from the mirror, she dropped the makeup back into her bag and walked into the bullpen. Francisco spotted her and waved her into his office.

"You ready to roll on this, Carleton?"

"Yes, sir. More than ready."

He narrowed his eyes as he studied her. "You sick? You don't look good."

"Long night last night, sir," she said, shrugged. "Not a lot of sleep." She lifted her chin. "You don't look so hot yourself."

"Point taken," he said. He checked his hip to make sure he had his gun. Touched the back of his belt for his cuffs and Taser. Then nodded to Julia. "We'll take a squad. Make a statement, parked in front of Kirby's building."

For the first time since the previous evening, Julia's lips curved. "Great idea, sir."

"Yeah." His jaw worked for a moment. "With the history Kirby and I have involving his kid, he won't be happy to see me."

"He'll be less happy to see me. He's not a big fan of women in authority."

Francisco smiled. "Then we're the perfect pair to pick him up. Let's go."

Rush hour started early in Chicago. As they crept through heavy traffic on Halsted, Julia told her captain about Kirby's visit to her apartment.

She hadn't told him the night before -- they'd been

focused on what had happened at Marini Auto Repair. And maybe Francisco didn't need to know now. They had Vannetti, and they were picking up Kirby.

But it felt dishonest not to tell him about it.

"Why didn't you call it in?" Francisco demanded.

Julia stared out the windshield, seeing Ronald Kirby's hate-filled, angry face instead of the rush-hour traffic. "Because I didn't want that whole sordid mess about my father to start up again," she finally said. "It was wrong, and I know it. I guess I hoped we'd be able to figure out who had hacked my computer and arrest Kirby before he could do any more damage."

"Two civilians were injured because you didn't call it in," Francisco said.

Julia pressed her fingers into her thighs to hide the tremble, pinching the material of her pants into a pleat. "Yes, sir. I know." *They were people I knew and liked.*

"I might not ever have found out about this if you hadn't told me."

"Maybe not." Julia's stomach churned as she thought about the possible consequences of her omission. Whatever they were, she deserved them. Trying to keep the incident hidden would compound her mistake. "But it's part of this case. Kirby should be charged with threatening a police officer. It can't hurt to add another charge to his already long list."

"You're right. Especially since we're going to ask the judge for no bail."

"Yes," Julia said, watching the streams of people heading for subway and bus stops. Going to school. To meetings. To their jobs.

Could she lose her job over her mistake last night?

Francisco reached up and turned on the siren and lights. "I've had enough of waiting in this traffic. I want to grab Kirby before he has a chance to cause any more trouble."

As cars and buses squeezed toward the curb, she and Francisco sped south on Halsted. In a few minutes, they'd parked in front of the Kirby Building. Francisco left the flashers on, and they strode into the marble foyer and waited for an elevator.

This time, when they walked into Kirby's office, his secretary recognized her. "Detective. I'm sorry, but Mr. Kirby is on a conference call. I'm going to have to ask you to wait."

Francisco stepped to her desk and flashed his badge. "I'm Captain Francisco. We're not waiting."

He headed for Kirby's door, as if he'd been here before. Pushed it open and stepped inside, Julia right on his heels. The secretary trailed behind her, voice raised in protest.

Kirby was on the phone, so at least his secretary hadn't lied. He scowled at them and held up a finger. *You'll have to wait.*

Francisco reached across his desk and depressed the button on his desk phone, ending his call. When Kirby jumped to his feet, Francisco said, "Ronald Kirby, you're under arrest for assault and battery, for threatening a police officer, and for aiding and abetting an assault." He pulled out his handcuffs and spun Kirby around. "You have the right to remain silent. You have the right to…"

Before he could finish getting the cuffs secured, Kirby yanked away from him. "What the hell are you talking about?"

Julia came around on his other side, grabbed his wrist and held it while Francisco finished cuffing him. "Nice show of outrage, Ronnie," Francisco said. "Save it for someone who might believe you. We have you on tape at Joanie Marini's auto shop, watching from the car while Richie Vannetti assaulted Joanie Marini and Don Young. Detective Carleton has pictures of you at her apartment yesterday, and she's reported that you threatened her." Kirby scowled, but Julia saw fear behind his bluster.

Francisco cocked his head. "Maybe we should add being a stupid fuck to the list of charges. You let your ego and your temper control you when you went after Detective

Carleton. When you sent Vannetti into the Marini's auto repair place. And yes, Vannetti is telling us everything. In detail. So your new accommodations will be Cook County Jail." His smile was feral. "Let's go."

Kirby's mouth had flattened as Francisco spoke, but he didn't say a word.

Julia took Kirby's left arm. Francisco took his right. They escorted him out of his office, and instead of taking the closest elevators, they led him across the building to the bank of elevators farthest away. His employees watched as they perp-walked the boss down rows of desks. People in cubicles peered over the tops of the dividers.

A number of them tried to hide smiles.

Julia wished Sam could have been here to witness Kirby's humiliation. He deserved that satisfaction.

She shoved the image of Sam's smiling face away. He'd deserved better for himself and his family, too. And he hadn't gotten it.

Kirby's face got redder as they proceeded. His mouth grew thinner and thinner. He stared hard at each person who seemed happy at his plight.

As if mentally taking names.

Kirby wouldn't be back here to enact revenge for a while. Julia was confident they had a solid case for denying bail. Judges took it seriously when defendants disobeyed their orders. They took it even more seriously when defendants threatened witnesses.

As they rounded a corner and headed toward the elevator bank, Kirby sputtered, "Francisco, my attorney will have your badge for this. You've had a hard-on for me for years."

"You're right. I have. Ever since the first time that kid of yours was arrested as a juvenile and not charged. Funny how that keeps happening. People keep refusing to press charges against him after he assaults them." He turned to stare at Kirby. "You have anything to do with that?"

"I can't control what other people do." The asshole had

the gall to smirk. "No jury would blame a father for standing by his boy."

"*I* can blame you. You turned Derek into an entitled asshole by constantly paying people off so they wouldn't press charges. Nick D'Angelo might be alive today if we'd put Derek in jail before he killed the guy." Francisco jabbed at the elevator call button. "On the bright side for you? Maybe you and your boy can share a cell in Cook County."

"Fuck you, Francisco." Kirby's jaw worked and his red face purpled with rage.

Julia and her boss helped Kirby into the elevator. As the doors closed, Francisco smiled. "Sorry, Ronnie. The only one fucked here today is you."

CHAPTER 28

Julia led Ronald Kirby into a holding cell, then held his angry, menacing gaze as she slid the door closed with a solid clang. The snick of the locks engaging was the most satisfying sound she'd heard since...

Since the last time she and Sam made love.

Spinning away from Kirby's gaze, Julia tried to shove the memory out of her head. She'd tried to avoid thinking of Sam since she walked out of his hotel suite early this morning. At first, it had been easy. She'd been too busy to dwell on her personal unhappiness. Arresting Kirby, all the paperwork involved, summoning his lawyer, the phone calls to the state's attorney about his bond hearing, had taken all of her focus. Consumed all of her attention.

Now, though, with most of the items on her to-do list checked off, her mind was free to wander. And the memories from earlier that morning were filling her head.

Sam, wearing nothing but unbuttoned jeans that rode low on his hips. His chest and abdomen bare, his six-pack abs rippling as he moved.

The way his eyes had lit up when he saw her.

The devastation in his expression when she'd told him they were over.

Damn it! Why couldn't he have merely shrugged? Said it was fun while it lasted, he'd see her around, blah blah blah. The kind of thing a guy who'd wanted only a fling should say and do.

Instead, he'd acted like he really *did* want more than a casual romp in the sack. That he hadn't expected her to walk out the door.

Like he'd wanted a real relationship.

She frowned. Had she over-reacted this morning? Maybe she hadn't had to break it off with Sam. Maybe should have said, *I screwed up because I got too close to you. I have to step away from us for now. Until this case is over.*

Instead, she'd said they were over and walked away. Hadn't even given Sam a chance to persuade her to stay.

She'd hurt Sam, a man she cared about. Shoved him away as if he was nothing. Because she was scared. Terrified by the feelings Sam stirred inside her. She'd known that if she let Sam in, he'd be her weakness. Her vulnerability.

She didn't want to be vulnerable, ever again.

"I'll be getting out this afternoon," Kirby called from behind her. "You're going to be sorry you arrested me. So will your captain."

Julia paused at the elevator. Pushed the button before she glanced over her shoulder at Kirby. "I'm not sorry at all, and neither is Captain Francisco. You crossed a line too many times. You're a danger to our witnesses. None of them are safe as long as you're free to cause trouble."

"You're going to regret this, Carleton."

The elevator doors creaked open, and she stepped inside. Hit the button for the first floor, then stood with her hand blocking the door. "I don't think so, Kirby. Everyone is safer with you locked up."

"Derek won't be happy," he said.

"Do you really think I care if Derek is happy or not?" She shook her head and removed her hand from the door. The heavy panels moved slowly together.

"*I* would be. If I were you."

The doors met in the middle, blocking Kirby's face. His knowing, triumphant expression. Julia's hand hovered over the panel. She wanted to return to the holding area and demand to know what Kirby had meant.

Her hand dropped away. Not only would he refuse to elaborate, he'd be gratified that she'd come back to ask. No, she wasn't going to engage with Ronald Kirby. She'd ignore his boasts, his warnings, his ego-driven threats.

As the doors creaked open on the bullpen level, Julia couldn't get Kirby's vague threats about Derek *not being happy* about his father's arrest out of her mind. Uneasiness stirred in her gut. Derek *was* the Kirby who had actually killed someone. Where was he? She hadn't seen him that morning when they'd arrested his father.

Was he at work, holding down the fort in his father's absence?

Derek didn't strike her as the responsible type, but Julia slid into her chair and called Kirby's office. It took a few minutes, but she was eventually connected to Derek's assistant.

"I'd like to speak to Derek, please," Julia said. "This is Detective Carleton."

"I'm sorry, Detective, but Mr. Kirby isn't in today. He left shortly after his father's, ah, departure. To speak to his lawyers."

"Thank you," Julia said, ending the call. She drummed her fingers on the desk. She hadn't really expected him to be at work.

But the back of her neck itched. She needed to know where Derek was.

He'd be enraged by his father's arrest. He'd need to make someone pay. And the person he'd most likely blame?

Sam.

Heart pounding, Julia glanced at her watch. Three PM. Her shoulders relaxed. Sam was at the ballpark, playing baseball. Derek was usually at the games, harassing Sam and trying to distract him. But at least he couldn't get to Sam. Couldn't hurt him.

There were all those rooftops around the ballpark.

Derek had the money to hire people to do almost anything. Like take out a baseball player with a well-placed shot from a rooftop.

Her hands shaking, Julia punched in the number for the ballpark. Asked to be put through to the security office.

"Pete Kruski," a gravelly voice said.

"Pete, this is Detective Julia Carleton. I've had to come to the park a few times recently because a patron has been harassing Sam Marini. I think he sits on the third-base line. Yells, throws stuff at the dugout, that sort of thing. Derek Kirby. Do you remember the guy?"

"Everyone in security remembers Derek Kirby," Pete assured her. "Annoying little shit."

"Yeah, that sums him up. Do you know if he's there today?"

"You want to hold? I haven't gotten any complaints about him yet, but I can check."

"Thanks, Pete."

Less than five minutes later, Pete came back on the line. "Not here today. The security guard in that section is disappointed. He looks forward to throwing the guy out."

Julia's gut churned and her heart squeezed tight. "Can you put out the word to the guards to keep an eye open for him? Give me a call if he shows up?" She recited her phone number.

"Will do, Detective. I'll tell everyone to watch for the asshole."

"Are there guards near where the players exit the ball park?" Julia asked, hoping that there were.

"Definitely. We've got the guys covered."

"Let those guards know, too," she said, hating the tiny wobble in her voice.

"Don't worry, I'll tell everyone. The good news is that everyone knows what Kirby looks like. So if he's here, or sniffing around the player parking lot, we'll find him."

"What about the rooftops around the park?"

There was a moment of silence on the line. Then Pete said, "They all have security. You want me to notify them to watch for Kirby?"

"Yes, please." She blew out a breath. "I'll email you Kirby's driver's license photo. You can forward it to the security guys at the rooftops."

"Good idea." He recited his email address.

"Thanks, Pete. I appreciate the help."

"Anytime, Detective."

Julia ended the call and set the phone on her desk. Her fingers flew over her keyboard as she pulled up the DMV photo of Derek Kirby and forwarded it to Pete.

Then she slumped in her chair. She'd done all that she could do. Sam should be safe for now. And he'd be safe for a time after the game. She knew the players and manager met after the games to rehash the plays. Sam would be busy with that for a while. Then he'd shower and dress. He'd participate in the press conference. And there was the meal the players shared after that.

Since Sam wouldn't be meeting her after the game, he'd probably stay for that tonight.

Her heart pinched at the idea of not seeing Sam tonight. Of going home to her now-bug-free apartment and eating a lonely dinner by herself.

It had been her choice, she reminded herself. Her decision to back away from Sam before she got even more attached. And right now, staring at a string of lonely, Sam-less nights, it looked like another bad choice in a long series of them.

She didn't have to worry about Sam right now, she told herself as she stood up. He was at the ballpark. Playing in front of thousands of people. Nothing would happen to him there.

She still wanted eyes on Derek Kirby. She had no idea how he'd react to his father being arrested. No idea what he'd do if his father wasn't released on bail.

But her instincts told her that Derek would blame her. And Sam.

No one involved in this case would be safe until Derek was locked up.

She could protect herself. She had a gun. A Taser. The instincts honed from years as a cop.

Sam was smart. Coordinated and quick. Strong.

None of those were worth a hell of a lot against a gun.

She'd check the Bearcats score frequently on the app she'd installed on her phone, so she'd know when Sam's game was over. When it was, she'd give him a call. Tell him to keep an eye out for Derek. Insist on sending a uniformed officer to the ballpark to accompany him home.

It wasn't much. But it was all she could do until they found Derek.

* * *

Sam tapped the bat on home plate, then squared off to face the pitcher. The guy was the fourth starter for their opponents' team. He had okay stuff, but Sam had handled him easily the last time he'd faced the guy.

Not today. Sam had already struck out twice. Grounded out once into a double play. It was the bottom of the ninth, and if he didn't get on base this time, the 'Cats had only one more out before the game was over. A loss.

The pitcher had a complete game going. If Sam got on base, the opposing manager would likely bring in a new pitcher. Give the 'Cats next batter a chance at fresh meat. Maybe Gonzo could kick off a rally.

The first pitch was a ball, high and inside. Sam reared back, then stepped out of the batter's box. Sneaked a look over at the third base seats. Kirby wasn't here today. Maybe that's why Sam was playing so badly. He'd gotten used to the catcalls, the insults, the yelling from the little prick.

He stepped back into the batter's box and clenched his

teeth. Kirby's absence had nothing to do with his lousy game. He knew exactly why his mind was drifting.

Julia.

What had happened that morning was eating at him. Distracting him. Taking his attention away from his job.

Was this what Julia had meant when she said she wasn't able to focus on her job because she was thinking about him? That she was screwing up because she was distracted? Smitten with him?

He was doing the same thing.

He played a game for a living, but Julia had a dangerous job. And as a result of her distraction, his mom and Don had gotten hurt.

And he'd blamed her, even if he hadn't come out and said it to her face.

That hadn't been fair. Or right. Could he fix it?

Instead of touching the tip of the bat to home plate to judge his stance, he smacked it on the base, harder than necessary. The impact vibrated up his hand and into his wrists. He was doing what he'd always sworn he wouldn't do -- letting his personal life interfere with his job.

He faced the pitcher again, forcing himself to focus on the ball. The overcast day made it harder to see the ball's spin, but Sam watched it as it left the pitcher's hand, trying to gauge its rotation.

The crowd noise swelled to a roar as the pitcher wound up. Let the ball fly.

Sam swung and missed.

He made contact with the next pitch, but it was a hard liner right to the third-baseman. He made the catch easily, and Sam was out.

He made his way to the dugout, shoved his bat into its cubicle, and threw himself on the bench. His manager nudged him with his shoulder. "Thank Christ you had a bad game. I was beginning to think you were a robotic android or something."

"Funny, Ken." Sam watched Gonzo square off against

the pitcher. "You do stand-up on the side?"

Ken clapped him on the back. "Don't brood, Marini. With the season you're having, getting your panties in a twist over one bad game is stupid."

He wasn't pissed off because he'd had a bad game. He was pissed off because of the *reason* he'd had a bad game.

His manager stood up and leaned on the fence, watching what was either the last out of the game or the beginning of a rally.

Gonzo flied out to left on the first pitch. Game over. It had been an unusually short game, too. Just over two hours. Mostly because he and the rest of his teammates had played dead against the Blue Jays.

Sam grabbed his equipment and headed into the locker room. Sat through the post-game meeting, showered, put in an appearance in the press room. Gritted his teeth as he answered questions about the game. Acknowledged he'd been 'off'. Shrugged and said it was one of those games. Gave the opposing pitcher credit for throwing a complete game.

Finally it was over and he could step off the podium. He trudged back into the locker room, where the buffet was already set up.

He hadn't eaten with his teammates in a while -- he'd been too eager to see Julia. But Julia wasn't waiting for him tonight. She'd sent him a few texts, letting him know they had Kirby in custody. Updating him on the status of Ronald's bond hearing.

All of the texts were impersonal. Business-like. They made him want to hurl his phone across the room.

He pulled his phone out of his locker. Nothing new.

Shoving it into his pocket, he headed for the buffet. He didn't want to go home to an empty house infused with Julia's presence. So he'd hang around for a while, eat dinner and have a few beers with the guys.

Maybe they'd be able to make him forget his regrets about the game. Forget about Julia. But he doubted it.

* * *

As Sam drove home through the lengthening dusk a couple of hours later, he barely noticed the traffic or the beautiful late spring evening. All he could think about was Julia.

He ran his hands up and down his steering wheel, wondering what she was doing. Hoping that Kirby had been denied bond and was sitting in Cook County Jail. He glanced at the clock on the dashboard and frowned. Julia was supposed to let him know.

Maybe Kirby had gotten bail and she hadn't wanted to tell him.

No. She would have contacted him immediately. Hell, she probably would have sent a cop to the ball park as a precaution. Julia wouldn't leave him vulnerable. She'd make sure he was protected. Her guilt over the attack against his mother and Don was crushing her.

And you didn't help matters, his conscience reminded him.

He tightened his grip on the steering wheel. He'd make that right, as soon as possible. She'd be working late tonight. Tying up the loose ends in the Kirby case, making sure it was airtight. So he'd leave her alone.

Tomorrow, though, he'd make sure he saw Julia. Make sure he apologized for letting her think he blamed her for what had happened to Don and his mom. Make sure she understood that he was interested in far more than a fling.

He needed to get it done tomorrow morning, because the team was leaving on a road trip immediately after their night game. He'd beg, if he had to.

He couldn't lose her.

The streetlights flickered at the entrance to the alley, but their illumination didn't reach the middle of the narrow strip of concrete. That never bothered him. This was a safe neighborhood, and he'd never had any problems. Except for the night Kirby had shown up.

But Ronald Kirby was in jail, and he didn't see a soul in the alley. So he bumped through a couple of potholes, pushing the remote door opener when he was three garages away from his.

He glanced at his phone, sitting on the seat beside him. Four missed calls. Huh.

As he reached for the phone, he glanced at the alley again. A bulky shadow hovered near his garage. Just for a moment. As if someone had ducked beneath the rising door.

He dropped the phone, staring at the spot, wondering if he'd imagined it.

Heard a muffled thump from inside the garage, as if someone had bumped into his tool bench.

No. He hadn't imagined it. Someone had been waiting for him. And now the guy was in Sam's garage.

CHAPTER 29

Julia glanced at her watch. It was five-thirty, probably too early for Sam's game to be over, but she'd check anyway. She tapped the app, eyebrows rising when she saw the game was over. The 'Cats had lost. Sam hadn't gotten any hits.

Guilt tightened her chest. Was it because of the way she'd walked out on him that morning?

She needed to talk to him. Apologize for the way she'd walked out. Tell him she wanted...

What *did* she want? A relationship with Sam? More?

Julia wasn't sure. But she knew she didn't want to say goodbye.

She pressed Sam's contact icon and listened to his phone ring. After seven buzzes, it went to voicemail.

Okay, he was probably in the team meeting or at the press conference. She'd keep checking.

As she slid the phone into her pocket, she spotted Sobieski walking through the bullpen holding Dwyer's arm. The older cop was in handcuffs.

Julia shoved away from her desk and hurried after Sobieski. The room went silent as every cop watched their fellow officer being led through the large space in handcuffs. Sobieski didn't seem to notice as she escorted

Dwyer to an interrogation room and closed the door.

By the time Julia reached the two-way mirror into the room, Dwyer was alone, sitting at the table, staring at his now-uncuffed hands.

"Hey, Katya," Julia said as Sobieski rounded the corner.

Katya stood beside her at the observation window, watching their fellow-cop. Sobieski's hands were clenched into fists at her side. "Do you have any idea how much I hate him right now?" she asked quietly.

"Can't possibly be more than I hate him," Julia answered. *He endangered the man I...* No. She wasn't going there. "What happened?"

"Francisco assigned me to tail him," Sobieski said. She glanced at Francisco's office. "Pissed me off, because he knows why I transferred to this district. He knows my last partner was dirty."

"That's how Francisco operates," Julia said. "He knew you'd be motivated. If you said Dwyer was clean, he'd believe you. But if you found out he was dirty, you'd be all over him like white on rice. He knew you'd get the goods on Dwyer."

She touched her fingers to her phone, knowing she should check on Sam. He hadn't answered a few minutes ago, though. He was busy with something. She slid her hand out of her pocket and nodded at their fellow officer in the interrogation room. "What happened?"

"He was on patrol. Stupid fuck didn't realize I was tailing him. I'm not sure he ever looked into his rear-view mirror." Sobieski snorted. "Lazy, too. A few calls came through, and one was a block away from him. I couldn't take it, because I was supposed to follow him. He was the closest car, but he said he was a mile away."

She shook her head, and the spiky wisps of her blond hair fluttered around her head. "He drove around, aimlessly, I thought, until I realized we'd gone past the same strip mall four times. Finally he pulled in and went into one of those shipping stores that have their own PO boxes."

A muscle in Sobieski's jaw clenched and unclenched. Julia shoved her hands into her pockets, hoping this was going where she suspected it was. Held her breath.

Her fingers brushed her phone. Sam. She pulled it out, texted him. *Call me.*

"I pulled into the lot in time to see him open a box and pull out a blank envelope. No stamp or address on it. As if someone else had used a key to open the box and slide the envelope in. Easy way of making exchanges -- no one caught together in a compromising position."

As if she wanted to get her hands on Dwyer, Katya pressed her fingers to the window as she studied him. "I guess the shitheads exchange information. That's how Johnstone got his cash from the other dirty cops in my old district."

She rubbed her nape, never taking her eyes off Dwyer. "Envelope was thick. Like someone had stuffed more into it than it could hold. Dwyer didn't look inside. He just tucked it into the pocket of his shirt. Beneath his vest, which I thought was interesting. Those things are uncomfortable as it is, without putting a thick envelope between the vest and the uniform shirt."

Sobieski skimmed a hand over the fringe of her hair, as if she was agitated. "When he got back into his squad car, he pulled his keys out of his pocket. Something landed on the ground. It was a passport."

Julia rubbed one finger over the edge of her phone, listening to Katya as she waited for a ping indicating a text from Sam. Her fingers curled around and she pulled it out of her pocket. He was probably still at the press conference. Probably couldn't look at his phone right now.

Sobieski glanced at Julia, her gaze traveling down to where Julia had the phone clenched in her hand. Then she returned her gaze to Dwyer. "The captain had filled me in on the Kirby case, so I knew why I was following Dwyer. With Kirby and Vannetti locked up, I was afraid Dwyer was getting ready to flee. I called the captain, and he told me to arrest him." She glanced at Julia again. "What happened that Francisco wanted me to pick him up?"

"The captain was questioning Vannetti. Dwyer's ex-partner. Richie retired a couple of years ago rather than go in front of a board of inquiry. My guess? Vannetti rolled on Dwyer."

Sobieski nodded, her mouth a thin line. "Thank God there's no honor among thieves." She flicked a gaze at Dwyer, then turned away, as if he wasn't worth her time. "So I cuffed him. Frisked him. Found a switchblade in his pocket. Back-up piece on one ankle and a throw down piece on the other.

"Dirty prick." She shoved her hands into her pockets. "That old dude doesn't like female cops much. Has a mouth on him, too." One side of her own mouth curled up. "Made it more of a pleasure to haul him in here wearing the bracelets."

Her smile disappeared. "The envelope had around ten thousand dollars in it. I asked him who it was from, but he clammed up. Didn't say another word. So I stuffed him in the back of my unmarked and went in to talk to the clerk."

Katya's smile was triumphant. Clearly bad news for Dwyer. Julia glanced at Dwyer as he looked around the room. Shifted his legs. Folded his hands, then unfolded them. Katya continued, "I persuaded the kid to tell me who owned the box. Told him I could get a warrant, but we'd be very grateful for his help. I can be sweet and sugary when I have to be."

Finally Sobieski smiled. "The box is owned by Ronald Kirby."

Julia wanted to hug the other cop. She'd just delivered Dwyer like a present with a tidy bow tied on top. "My God, Katya. That's great work. Thank you."

Sobieski shrugged. "Doing my job."

Captain Francisco appeared from around the corner. He stood beside Sobieski, watching Dwyer. "Thank you," he said to Katya. "Catching the bad guys is even more important when they're one of us. Good work, Sobieski."

"Thank you, sir," she said, stepping away from the window. She closed her eyes and shook her head as if she'd seen enough of Dwyer to last a lifetime. "Now I'm going home to take a long, hot shower to wash away the stink of this arrest."

As Sobieski left, Julia said, "She's a good cop," as she pressed the call button next to Sam's name again. Tension twisted her stomach as it rang and rang. Went to voicemail.

"Yeah," Francisco said. He waited a beat, then asked, "Problem, Carleton?"

"I'm not sure, sir," Julia said, staring at the screen, her heart roaring in her ears with the beginnings of fear. "I'm trying to get hold of Sam Marini, to warn him to watch for Derek Kirby. Sam's game was over a while ago, but he's not picking up his phone."

"Keep trying," Francisco said. "That kid is trouble."

"I know he is," Julia said grimly. Too many scenarios raced through her head, and none of them ended well for Sam.

Francisco continued, "Vannetti is cooperating. He knows a lot about Derek's previous arrests. About the payoffs the Kirbys made to the victims. The way he and Dwyer threatened the victims when they wouldn't accept a payoff. He kept a log, because he didn't trust Kirby. Probably didn't trust Dwyer, either." He clenched his teeth. "Said he showed Dwyer how to install those programs on your desktop computer." He clenched his teeth. "Vannetti knew people would notice if he was here."

Julia barely heard him. "Yes, sir," she muttered as her hand clenched around her phone. She took a deep breath. Tried to focus. "I'll follow up on all those previous victims once we've got Derek Kirby locked down." She glanced at her phone. Nothing. Not even a text. "I have to check on Sam Marini right now, sir. Sorry."

She hurried toward her desk, aware of Francisco's gaze burning into her back. But he didn't stop her.

Not that she would have paid attention if he did.

As soon as she reached her desk, she turned on her computer. While it was booting up, she tried to call him one more time. Straight to voicemail.

Her breathing hitched. Why wasn't he answering her call?

Sam always answered when she called. And he'd known she'd be calling tonight.

"Come on come on," she muttered to the slowest computer in creation.

Finally it opened, and she pinged his phone. He was in his garage.

Although it killed her to wait, she counted off the seconds. After a minute, she pinged him again.

Still in his garage.

Ice filled her veins and compressed her chest. Grabbing her bag and her keys, she spotted Connor Donovan walking into the bullpen as she was running out. "Send a squad over to Sam's house. His garage," she yelled. "Something's wrong."

Without pausing to explain, Julia ran down the stairs.

* * *

Before he took his foot off the brake, Sam called 911. Gave his address, told the dispatcher someone was in his garage, then ended the call before the dispatcher could tell him to stay on the line.

Twisting around, he reached into the back seat for the bat and bag of balls he'd brought home with him. He needed to sign the balls tonight for a charity auction, then turn them in tomorrow to the woman who coordinated their charity events.

He'd brought the bat, as well, thinking he'd sign it and add it to his contribution. Now, he loosened the drawstring on the bag, and several balls rolled onto the seat when he bounced through another pothole. He propped the bat on the floor, the handle near the console between the front seats.

He could sit here in the alley and wait for the cops. They'd come quickly, but the person in his garage, most likely Derek Kirby, would be long gone. He'd go out the door into Sam's backyard, scale the fence and disappear.

Maybe go after Julia.

That wasn't a chance Sam was willing to take.

His heart thundered against his chest as he pulled into his garage. The car rolled to a stop, and Sam scanned the shadows, looking for the intruder.

One corner was darker than the others. He studied it carefully.

There. A darker form crouched beside his workbench moved. Sam turned off the SUV, listened to the engine shut down. Then he took the bat in his left hand. Stuffed two baseballs in his right pocket. Opened the car door and slid out, being careful to keep the barrier of metal and glass between himself and the intruder.

The shadow elongated and separated from the wall and stepped into the dim light. Derek Kirby edged toward him. He held a knife in his hand, and Sam's hand loosened a little on the bat. He'd been afraid whoever was waiting would have a gun. Not much a bat and a ball could do against one of those.

Knives could kill just as efficiently as a gun. But Kirby would have to get closer to use that knife. Give Sam a chance to use the bat. Kirby had done him a favor and evened the odds a little.

"Kirby. Get out of my garage," Sam said, keeping the opened door between him and Kirby for the time being.

"You gonna make me, big man?" Kirby moved closer, his knuckles white on the knife handle. His eyes glittered, and Sam tensed. Was the bastard high? Or just excited about the idea of killing him?

Sam would bet on excitement.

After all, Kirby had already murdered one man. People

said it was easier to kill a second time.

Or a third.

Sam's grip tightened on the bat. Kirby wasn't going to get a shot at Julia. Not as long as Sam was breathing. "Bring it on, asshole."

Kirby grinned, a grotesque tightening of his lips that terrified Sam. "I'm gonna have a good time gutting you, Marini."

"Now why would you want to kill me?" *Keep him talking. Buy some time. Get into the open, where Sam would have a better chance.*

Hope that the cops show up.

"Why do you think, moron? Keep you from testifying." Kirby frowned, as if Sam was hopelessly dense for not seeing that.

Eyes still glittering, Kirby shifted the knife in his hand easily. As if he'd done this before.

He probably had.

Fear nibbled at the edges of Sam's consciousness, and he drew in a deep breath. Pushed the fear away. He needed to focus. Zero in on the threat.

His life depended on it. Julia's too, most likely.

Fortunately, Sam knew how to focus. He faced pitchers every day who threw one-hundred-mile-per-hour baseballs at his head.

"You know they have the video," Sam said, struggling to sound calm as he swung the bat back and forth. "It clearly shows you punching Nick D'Angelo. Also shows he never touched you." Sam braced himself, widening his stance. "Killing me doesn't make the video go away."

"Sure it does." Kirby tracked the movement of the bat as he shifted the knife in his hand. Pointed it directly at Sam. As if positioning it before he launched himself for the fatal blow. "You disappear, the video disappears. They can't admit it if you can't testify about it."

"You're wrong, buddy. They already have my testimony about it. And even if you're right, it won't matter. Because they'll have video of you here in my garage. Killing me."

Kirby scowled. "The hell they will." He took another step closer.

"I have a security system. The best that money can buy. Of course there are cameras in here."

There weren't.

Kirby glanced around, but his gaze came back to Sam before Sam could make a move. Kirby was closer to the car door. Close enough that he could reach out and slam it on Sam. Trap him between the car and the door. Easy pickings for a strong guy with a knife.

Sam backed away from the door. Faced Kirby in the space between the car and the wall, leaving a couple of feet between them.

Kirby shoved the door out of his way and lunged. Sam danced backward. Curled his right hand around one of the baseballs in his pocket.

"Why'd you pick a knife?" Sam asked conversationally. "Why not a gun? A gun's easier than a knife. Less messy. Less personal." He continued to move toward the alley as he talked, trying to get away from the narrow space beside the car. "Let me guess. You couldn't get a gun permit, right? Because you have mental health issues. They don't let crazy people have guns."

Kirby's jaw clenched. His fingers turned white on the knife. "I am *not* crazy."

"Then why the knife?" Sam was at the back of the car now. In a place where he could swing the bat if Kirby charged him. "You'll get blood all over those fancy clothes of yours. And look at those expensive shoes. They'll never be the same."

Kirby glanced down at his shoes, and Sam whipped the ball out of his pocket. Fired at Kirby's hand. Hit it with a dull thud and a cry of pain from Kirby. The knife fell to the cement floor and spun wildly.

When Kirby bent down to retrieve the knife, Sam switched the bat to his right hand. And when Kirby charged, holding the knife in front of him, Sam swung for the fences and connected with Kirby's arm.

The sickening crack of the bone breaking in Kirby's upper arm echoed through the garage a moment before Kirby let out a piercing shriek. He fell to the floor, screaming, clutching his arm to his chest.

"That's for Don, asshole," Sam said.

He walked over to Kirby, kicked the knife beneath the tool bench, then put his foot on Kirby's injured arm. "You lie there, nice and still," Sam ordered. "If you don't move, neither will I. But if you so much as twitch, I'll kick you. And I won't go for your ribs, like your daddy did to my friend Don. No, I'll aim for that break in your arm."

Sam touched the toe of his shoe to Kirby's rapidly swelling upper arm. "Do you understand?"

"Yes," Kirby gasped. "Stop. You're hurting me."

"Not such a big man when you're not the strongest guy in the fight, are you?" Sam stared down at Derek Kirby, repulsed by the now-begging bully. "Be a good boy and you won't get hurt again."

Sam's stomach convulsed as he pulled out his phone. He'd broken a man's arm with his bat. He managed to beat back the nausea, but he'd live with that knowledge for the rest of his life.

Him or you, buddy. It was him or you.

He knew that. *He did.* But he'd used the tools of the game he loved to commit violence. His stomach churned again.

Sam watched the weeping Kirby as he pulled his phone out of his pocket. As he began to dial 911, he heard a car speeding down the alley. Bottoming out in the potholes.

"911 operator," a nasal voice said.

"I called a few minutes ago about an intruder in my garage. He had a knife," Sam said, surprised at how even his voice was when he was shaking so much inside. "We're gonna need an ambulance."

"Are you injured?" the woman asked sharply.

"No. But the intruder is. Broken arm."

"Stay on the line this time," the woman ordered. "The squad car is almost there. I'll call for an ambulance."

"Thank you," Sam said, ending the call. He didn't want to be distracted by the voice on the phone. He needed to focus on Kirby. Make sure the little worm didn't slither away.

The car in the alley was closer, but Sam didn't bother to look. No siren, so it was probably a neighbor, and Sam didn't want to be distracted right now. Instead, he slid over so he blocked the view into his garage. He didn't want to answer questions, either.

The car screeched to a halt and the door opened. "Sam! Are you okay?"

Julia.

He glanced over his shoulder and saw her running full tilt toward him. Then he turned back to Kirby, who was looking around wildly. As if scouting for an escape route.

"What did I tell you, asshole?" Sam said. He hurried toward Kirby, touching the guy's broken arm with the toe of his shoe. No pressure. Nothing like his daddy had done to Don. But Kirby squealed again, a high-pitched sound that hurt Sam's ears.

Julia's body collided with his, shoving him forward a step. She wrapped her arms around his waist and pressed her face into his neck. "Oh, God, Sam! I was so scared." His skin was damp. Then Julia sniffled. Was she *crying*? "Are you all right?"

He wanted to relax into her embrace. Turn around and hold her tight. Instead, he kept his gaze on Kirby.

"I'm fine," he said, putting his left hand over Julia's. He twined their fingers, and she pressed both of their hands into his waist. "The little shit didn't touch me."

"What happened?" Her words were muffled, because her mouth was still against his neck.

"He was waiting for me when I got home." Sam nodded toward the work bench. "Sneaked into the garage when the door opened and hid. He had a knife. It's under there. Thought that if he killed me, the recording wouldn't be admissible in court."

Julia lifted her face. Cocked her head. "Sirens. They're almost here."

She unwrapped her arms from around his waist and stepped away. He wanted to grab her hand and pull her close again. Instead, he drew a deep breath. Glanced over at Julia.

Heavy strands of hair had come loose from her braid, as if she'd jammed her fingers through her hair while driving toward his house. Her face was sheet white, and her eyes were red-rimmed. She drew a deep, shuddery breath, as if it was the first full breath she'd taken in a while.

He wanted to smooth the hair away from her face. Wipe away her tears. Kiss the strain from her face and tell her how glad he was to see her.

He started to move toward her, but heard a rustling behind him. Kirby was trying to slither away again. He was half under Sam's SUV.

Sam let the bat dangle from his hand. "Kirby. Have a little self-respect. Get out from under my car."

Kirby didn't budge. Sam hoped he bumped against the still-hot muffler and burned his sorry ass. "What a chicken shit you turned out to be."

The sirens' wails became closer, and Sam heard a car bouncing through the potholes in the alley. Behind it, a heavier vehicle scraped harshly against the asphalt as it bottomed out in the big pothole.

Two cops swarmed into the garage, their guns drawn. They slowed when they saw Julia. "Carleton?"

"Hey, Jackson. Grimes. I just got here." She pointed to Sam's car. "Our perp has decided to hide beneath the victim's car. See if you can get him out."

The officers looked at each other. Grimes rolled his eyes. Then they squatted next to Sam's car. Reached beneath it. Yanked Kirby out by his ankles as he screamed about his broken arm.

"Here's the bus," Jackson said as the ambulance rolled into view. "They can deal with this jerk."

"He needs to be cuffed to the gurney," Julia told them as they reached for Derek to haul him to his feet. "He's a runner." She glanced at where he lay, half under Sam's car. "Actually, he's a crawler."

One of the cops snorted a laugh as Julia added, "Tell the evidence techs his knife is under the tool bench."

As the EMTs trotted over to Derek and bent to assess him, Julia moved to Sam's side and took his hand. Slid her fingers between his and squeezed.

Sam's brain was still going ninety miles an hour. He blew out a long, shaky breath as the adrenaline roared through his body. Julia was here. Apparently glad to see him.

He had no idea what the hand-holding meant. Was it relief on Julia's part that he was okay? A reaction to the threat being neutralized? Would Julia go back to 'this is over' and 'it was just a fling' when *her* adrenaline burned off and life went back to normal?

He hoped it was more than that. Hoped that Julia had second thoughts about what she'd said that morning.

But he had no way of knowing for sure. So he'd play it cool for now. He didn't want to spook her. He'd wait until they were finished with all the questions and paperwork. Once they were alone, he'd ask his questions.

CHAPTER 30

Julia clung to Sam's hand as they watched the EMTs load Derek Kirby onto the gurney. She needed to feel his fingers against hers. Needed the reminder that he was okay, that Derek hadn't succeeded in hurting him. Or worse.

She couldn't let him go, even though both of the patrol officers were glancing at their intertwined hands.

Suddenly, what her co-workers thought about her relationship with Sam was a trivial thing. Not worth caring about. Sam could have been killed this evening. Derek Kirby could have taken him away from her.

She might never have had the chance to tell him how sorry she was about the way she'd walked away from him.

Julia was still shaking from her frantic drive to Sam's house. Sirens blaring and lights flashing, she'd driven faster than was safe all the way from the station to Sam's alley. At one point, she'd driven over a sidewalk when she needed to turn a corner that was blocked by stopped traffic.

When she'd seen Derek Kirby facing off against Sam with a knife, she'd leaped out of her car. Pulled her gun out of her holster, knowing Sam was between her and Derek. Knowing she wouldn't have a clear shot unless Sam moved. Or Kirby reached him first.

Thank God Sam had that bat in his hand. When Derek went down, Julia had slumped against the side of her car, struggling to re-holster her gun.

It had been fifteen minutes since she sped into the alley, and her heart was still racing. Her hands shook from the adrenaline burn. And all she wanted to do was retreat someplace private and throw herself into Sam's arms. Press her body against his. Put her hand on his heart to feel it beating against her palm. Reassure herself he was safe. Unharmed.

But she didn't have that luxury. Once Kirby was on his way to the hospital, Sam had to give his statement. He'd have to go to the station and answer a lot of questions.

It would be a long time before they were alone and she could say what she needed to say to Sam. So she clung to his hand and hoped he understood.

As she and Sam watched, the EMT's stepped away from Kirby after settling him on the gurney. Jackson grabbed the hand of his unbroken arm and tried to snap a cuff around his wrist. Kirby wrestled his hand away.

The cop sighed and stepped back. Moved around the gurney and reached for his broken arm. "You really want me to cuff this hand, I will. Gonna hurt like a son of a bitch, though, whenever they hit a bump."

Kirby stared at him for a moment. Jackson stared right back. Finally Derek hunched his shoulders and rested his broken arm across his chest. Extended his right hand to be cuffed.

"You sure? Because I'm not asking again," Jackson said. "You give me any shit, I'm cuffing the broken one."

Derek stared at the garage ceiling without speaking. Moments later, he was secured to the gurney. As the EMT's rolled him toward the bus, Jackson called, "Leave him on that gurney until I get to the ER. I don't want that little shit trying to hide under a hospital bed."

Derek flushed red, and the EMTs laughed. "Will do," the driver called as he and the other EMT lifted the gurney into the back of the bus.

The driver hurried around to the cab as the other EMT secured the gurney, then slammed the doors closed. Moments later, the ambulance bumped down the alley and disappeared from view.

Grimes, who'd been crouched on the floor, making notes in a small notebook, stood up. "Can you tell me what happened, Mr. Marini?" he asked.

"Yeah." Sam cleared his throat. "When I got close to my garage and opened the door, I thought I saw a shadow duck into the garage. Wasn't positive, though, because I was, ah, glancing at my phone."

He shot her an apologetic look, and Julia realized he'd been looking for a text from her. Or a missed phone call.

Her pings and phone calls had distracted him when he was getting ready to face off against Derek Kirby. Horrified, she squeezed his hand more tightly. Hoped it conveyed how remorseful she felt.

Sam continued, telling the two cops how he'd called 911 and gotten ready to face whoever was in his garage.

He finished by saying, "He rushed at me with the knife, and I used the bat to stop him." He glanced down at the bat, lying on the floor of the garage with an evidence marker beside it. He swallowed, the muscle in his neck rippling.

Then he stared at the space between his SUV and the garage wall, where the patrol cops had put down more markers for evidence left behind. "Didn't want to hurt him, but he didn't give me any choice."

Julia heard the guilt and regret in his voice and tightened her grip on his hand. Swung around to face him. "You have a right to defend yourself, Sam," she said fiercely. "After dealing with Derek Kirby these last few weeks, I'm convinced he wouldn't have hesitated to kill you."

Sam opened his mouth to answer her, but Jackson interrupted him. "She's right, Marini," he said. "I arrested Kirby a couple of years ago. Same kind of incident as the D'Angelo kid -- an unprovoked attack. Luckily, that kid didn't die. But Kirby was cocky as all hell. Smirking at me, as if he knew nothing would stick. That punk needed a massive wake-up call, which you just supplied. Now he'll have something to think about while he's sitting in jail, waiting for his trial."

Grimes nodded at a van that had just pulled in. "Evidence techs are here. Let's take this back to the station."

"You'll have to ride with me," Julia said to Sam. "The evidence techs have to go over your SUV."

"I need my phone," Sam said, nodding toward the car. "On the front seat."

Julia called to the woman getting out of the tech van. "Hey, Sonia. Our vic needs his phone. On the front seat of his vehicle. Okay if I grab it?"

"Don't call me a *victim*," Sam muttered, his gaze lingering on the bat.

"Sorry, Sam," Julia said, squeezing his hand. "Habit. You're *not* a victim. You're the hero here. You took Kirby down."

She felt Sam stiffen beside her. He tried to untangle his hand from hers, but she tightened her grip. She couldn't let Sam go. Not now. Not ev…

Her mind skittered away from that dangerous thought. Maybe, after what she'd said and done that morning, Sam didn't want anything to do with her. She wouldn't know until she was able to talk to him privately.

Until then, she needed to focus on washing the taste of fear out of her mouth. Making her hands stop shaking. Comforting Sam.

The tech dropped her gaze to Julia's hand, still holding Sam's. Raised her eyebrows, but nodded at Julia. "Sure, Carleton. Go ahead and take it. If I need it later, I'll let you know."

"Thanks, Sonia."

Unwilling to let Sam go, Julia tugged him in her wake as she hurried to the car. She grabbed his phone from the front seat, pulling it from beneath a bag of baseballs. A couple of them had spilled out onto the leather of the seat.

"We'll meet you at the station," Julia called to Jackson and Grimes as she was finally forced to let Sam go. She watched as he climbed into her unmarked, then she slid into the driver's side.

As soon as she pulled away from his garage, she began, "Sam, I am so sorry about…"

"Not now, Julia. Okay?" His voice sharp, Sam held up his hand. "Give me a chance to catch my breath before we get into any heavy stuff." Staring straight out the window, he clenched his hands in his lap. Relaxed them, then clenched again.

What heavy stuff did he mean? Did he think she was going to justify what she'd said to him that morning?

Maybe he did. How would he know otherwise? She'd talked to him several times today, but each time, she'd been all business. As if there had never been anything personal between them.

She'd hurt Sam. Possibly affected his game today -- she'd seen his stats on the phone app. Two strikeouts, one line drive and one double play. That wasn't the Sam Marini the fans were used to. She was horribly afraid that was her fault.

Worst of all, she'd turned him into a guy who didn't want to talk to her. At least not right now.

Her heart shriveled in her chest. She'd done this to him with her cold words and the abrupt, unfeeling way she'd broken up with him. She wanted to pour out her apologies and beg him to forgive her. But the guy who had been an open book was closed to her right now.

The only thing she could do for him was give him the space he needed.

And maybe reassure him that he'd done the right thing. That he hadn't had any other choice.

After she turned onto the cross street at the end of his block, she said, "I wasn't just blowing smoke back there. I meant every word I said. Derek would have killed you if you gave him a chance."

"Yeah, I know that," Sam said without looking at her. "I could see it in his eyes." He closed his eyes briefly. Opened them again to stare down at his hands, resting on his knees. "But I'm going to hear the sound of his arm breaking for a long time."

"Your mother and Don will hear that sound in their nightmares, too," she reminded him, reaching across the console to put her hand over his. His muscles tensed beneath her palm, but he didn't jerk away from her.

It was small comfort when she wanted to do so much more, but she'd take what she could get. Squeezing her fingers between his, she said, "You think Derek would have felt bad if he'd hurt you? He'd have been dancing a jig when I showed up. And then he'd have gone after me. I would have shot him to save you without hesitating."

Sam's deep breath echoed in the quiet car. He stared straight ahead and said, "I know you're right, Julia. I know I had no choice. But it's hard to wrap my mind around what I did. I broke a man's arm with a baseball bat.

"I used the tools from the game I love to shatter his bone. How do I deal with that?" He stared out the side window, his knee jittering beneath her hand.

"I get it, Sam. I do." She shifted on her seat, hoping her long ago but still-vivid memories would help him. "The first time I had to fire my gun on the job, I wounded a guy. He was threatening a woman with a knife, and I shot him in the thigh. The woman was okay, and the guy survived. But I puked my guts out into a dumpster when it was all over."

Remembering the sight of the blood, the scream from the man who'd collapsed to the asphalt of the alley, still made her queasy. Injuring another person was never easy, even if it was necessary.

Waiting at a stoplight at a busy street, she squeezed his knee once more before letting him go and putting both hands on the steering wheel. "I guess what I'm saying is that your regret about what you had to do makes you normal."

He shrugged. "I don't know about that. But I wasn't about to stand there and let him shove that knife into me." His fingers drummed on the arm rest on the door. "I guess I need to look at the bigger picture. Nick will get justice."

"Yes." She touched his arm as she turned into the parking lot at the station. She needed the constant reminders that he was with her. Safe. Unhurt. "I doubt either Derek or his father will be free anytime soon." She slotted her car into a parking spot, then turned to Sam. "Let's go in and get this over with. I need to wrap up this case and move on to other things."

Sam frowned and turned to her as he opened the door. "You catch another case?"

"Something like that." Sam was leaving tomorrow for a week-long road trip. She needed to make things right with him before he left.

* * *

Captain Francisco was waiting in the bullpen as Julia walked onto the floor with Sam. The way he hurried over told Julia that Grimes and Jackson had called into the station on their way to the hospital.

"You okay, Marini?" Francisco said, his gaze traveling over Sam.

"He's fine," Julia answered. Was he looking for holes, for God's sake?

"I heard Kirby had a knife. Did he get Marini's tongue?" Francisco asked her, one eyebrow raised.

Julia flushed. "No, sir. Sorry," she muttered.

"Julia's right," Sam said. "I'm good. Kirby never got close." He sounded weary. "Can Julia please just get on with it?"

She wanted to reach for Sam's hand again, but not in front of Francisco. It was one thing to tell her boss she and

Sam were seeing each other socially. That didn't mean she wanted to risk his rebuke by illustrating their connection in front of him.

"*I'm* going to take your statement," Francisco said. "Carleton's too close to the situation."

He glanced at Julia, as if daring her to object. When she didn't say anything, Francisco added gruffly, "You can sit in if you like, though, Carleton."

"Thank you, sir," she said, being careful not to inject sarcasm into her words.

They moved to a conference room. Julia started to take the chair next to Sam, then noticed Francisco's narrowed gaze. She moved to the other side of the table and sat beside her boss.

"Start at the beginning, Marini," Francisco said, turning on a recorder.

His voice flat, Sam went through all the details again as Francisco took notes. He interrupted to ask questions, and Sam answered in the same monotone. He shifted often on the uncomfortable chair, and kept his hands folded on the table.

The open, joyful Sam was gone, replaced with a closed off version who was impossible to read.

I did that.

Swallowing hard, she resisted the urge to move her foot toward Sam's. As much as she needed to be in contact with him, she didn't want to distract him. Francisco would notice. Her captain noticed everything.

When Francisco finally turned off the recorder, signaling they were done, it felt as if hours had passed since they'd sat down in here.

She glanced at her phone. In reality, it had been less than an hour.

She stood up and nodded to Sam. "I'll drive you home," she said quietly.

He opened his mouth to respond, but she gave a slight shake of her head. *Not in here.*

When they stepped back into the bullpen, Connor Donovan jumped to his feet. Walked over and punched Sam's shoulder. "I hear you hit one out of the park today, Baseball Boy. And in your own garage, no less."

For the first time since Julia had run into his garage, Sam smiled. "It was an easy one. The douchebag was moving a lot slower than a fastball."

"You've got a perfect 1.00 batting average against Kirby," Connor said happily. "Too bad you won't have the chance to get in another swing. The judge denied his old man bail. I'm betting Little Kirby won't get it, either. Especially after tonight. Looks like game over. No extra innings for the Kirbys."

Julia sank onto her desk and watched Sam's friends clustered around him. She'd wanted to cheer him up, but it looked as if the Donovans had that handled. Loneliness crept over her as she watched them all laughing and talking. It felt like the days after her father died, when she'd felt so isolated. So totally alone. Like she belonged nowhere.

Which was her own damn fault. She was the one who'd walked out on Sam. Hadn't pushed hard enough to connect with him at the ballpark and warn him about Kirby.

She could hardly demand Sam's attention now.

Quinn walked into the bullpen and strolled over to the group. "Just heard from Grimes," he said. "Kirby needs surgery to pin that arm."

Sam's smile disappeared, and Julia saw a glimmer of regret. "I hate that I did that."

"Hey," Mia said, elbowing her brother aside. "Don't second guess yourself. You had to defend yourself. And surgery? It's only fair, since Don had to have surgery."

She patted Sam's shoulder, and if Julia hadn't known how happy her friend was with her movie star, she would have leaped at Mia. Told her to keep her hands to herself.

"Don't know if you had a chance to talk to your mom," Mia continued, "but she brought Don home this afternoon. I talked to her a little while ago. She got Don settled, then went into the shop for a few hours. Said she had to calm everyone down." Mia shook her head. "She told me Don is going to work tomorrow. He can't do any of the repairs, but he can breathe over the guys' shoulders. Make sure they're doing things right."

A few of the other detectives and five or six patrol officers wandered over, and before long everyone was talking and laughing. Sam looked comfortable. At ease. As if he'd finally let go of the tension and regret.

As the cops began to drift away, Sam glanced around the room. Stilled when he spotted her.

He said something to the Donovans, who were the only ones still with him, then headed over to Julia.

"You didn't have to wait for me," he said. "I could have taken a Lyft home."

It hurt that he thought she wouldn't want to wait for him. Wouldn't want to drive him home. "I *wanted* to wait for you," she said. She suspected he could hear the sorrow in her voice. "I want to talk to you. Tonight. Before you leave for your trip."

Sam paled. Swallowed. Squared his shoulders, like someone getting ready to walk the plank, alive but already dead. "Okay. Let's go."

CHAPTER 31

Sam stared out the window as Julia drove to his house. Julia didn't say a word, and neither did he. But thoughts raced through his mind as they got closer and closer to his house. What could she have to say to him that she hadn't already said?

She'd told him she needed to get this Kirby case over with so she could move on to other things.

What the hell kinds of things?

Had the Kirby case been the only thing holding them together?

Maybe it had been. If she'd dumped him because she thought she'd been distracted and screwed up this case, as she'd said this morning, it wasn't looking good for a future together. Because another case would replace this one. Then another. As long as she was a cop, there would be homicides to solve.

He glanced at Julia, her hands gripping the steering wheel so tightly that her knuckles were white. Was she dreading this as much as he was?

Riding with her in this silent car, all the air sucked up by the tension swirling between them, was driving him crazy. He gripped the door arm rest, squeezing tight. As if it was a baseball he was getting ready to throw to first base. He wanted to yell *drive faster* at Julia. He needed to get to his place. Get it over with. Rip off the bandage.

Watch Julia walk out of his life once and for all.

The seats in this tiny car were too small for him. He shifted, unable to get comfortable. Traffic was backed up, and groups of people streamed across the street in front of her car. Damn it! Why hadn't she taken a side street? Avoided this mess?

Was she going to justify ending it with him? Tell him they were too different? That constantly being recognized when they were in public would be too painful for her?

Was he going to let her go?

Hell, no. When had he become the kind of guy who gave up at the first sign of trouble? He'd always fought for what he wanted.

He wouldn't let Julia walk away without a fight. It might be the biggest fight of his life, but he'd make sure she knew he wanted her in his life.

Finally she turned onto his street. Parked along the curb a few houses down from his. She got out of her car at the same time he did and waited for him on the sidewalk. She didn't meet his gaze.

As they passed through a cone of light from a streetlamp, he stared straight ahead. Kept a careful distance between them. He didn't want his hand to brush hers. Didn't want to touch her. Not until they were inside his place.

He didn't want to beg, out here on the street.

Out of habit, he looked around when they reached his house. Scanned the street, looking for a dark Escalade.

"He's in Cook County Jail," Julia said, putting her hand on his arm. Her fingers burned into his skin. The heat from her touch rushed through him like wildfire. "He didn't get bail. We're safe. It's over."

They still had that connection. About some things, anyway. "I know," he said gruffly. "It's just... habit, I guess."

"For me, too." Julia slipped her hand into his. "It'll probably take a while before either of us stops looking."

He clung to her hand as he fumbled with the lock on his door, hope stirring in the ashes of his dreams. Why would she take his hand if she was determined to dump him?

She kicked off her shoes, as if she planned to stay for a while, and walked into his living room. He stopped in the doorway, watching her mouth curve up as she studied the kids' pictures he'd had framed. "I love that you did this," she said, her voice low in the quiet of his house.

Shoving his hands into his pockets to stop himself from reaching for her, he said, "You wanted to talk to me?"

Julia turned back to face him, her expression uncertain. Wary, almost. "Sam, I'm so sorry for the way I walked out on you this morning. It was wrong of me to tell you we were through like that, without any explanation. Wrong of me not to tell you the whole truth."

"Are you saying you didn't mean it this morning?" he asked cautiously. "That you've changed your mind?" Instead of watching the hesitation in her expression, Sam stared out the window at the now-dark street, watching tree branches sway in the wind. They reminded Sam of himself and Julia, buffeted by forces beyond their control. "Or just that you did it the wrong way?" He wanted to hope. But he didn't want to be knocked down again.

"I... I wasn't prepared for what I felt for you," she said slowly. "I was scared. Terrified by the emotions you stirred." She swallowed, and he wanted to put his mouth on the ripple of her throat. "You make me vulnerable," she whispered. "The one thing I swore I'd never be again."

She'd said *make*. Like he still did. Maybe she didn't want it to be over, either. "I don't want to push you, Jules," he said, speaking too quickly. He wasn't sure if she was giving him an opening, but he'd take it anyway. "I don't want to say goodbye to you. We can go slow. As slowly as you like. We need to get used to each other when we're not looking

332

over our shoulders every minute. When we're not trying to hide a relationship Kirby could use against us. I won't rush you. I promise." The words spilled out of his mouth, tumbling over each other in their hurry to get out.

"Slow?" She took a step closer to him. "Sam, we haven't gone slow since the minute we met." She swallowed again. "I kissed you at Cilla and Brendan's wedding. After I'd known you for less than two hours. That's not me. I think before I act. About everything. But I kissed you that night."

"I couldn't stop thinking about that kiss," he confessed. "Best kiss of my life." His fingers twitched to pull her close and do it again, but he kept them in his pockets. "It's why I bugged Cilla and the Donovans about you. That's why I played basketball with them. They promised me they'd tell me who you were if I could beat them. But basketball was never my game. I've come close, but I don't have the moves.

"Truth? I was getting desperate. Ready to cheat so they'd tell me who you were."

She sucked in a breath. Shock filled her expression. "You let those Donovans kick your ass at basketball? More than once? So they'd tell you where to find me?" She took a step toward him. Stopped. "I know how they must have crowed about that. How that must have pissed you off."

He shrugged. *Yeah, it had.* "Worth it. I went back every week. I wanted to find you, and I knew sooner or later, I'd beat them."

"Sam," she said, her eyes glittering as she blinked too fast.

"But I can slow it down," he vowed. "I can. We'll pretend like the last few weeks never happened. We'll start from scratch. Date like normal people. Get to know one another."

Julia closed the gap between them. Took his face in her hands. Stared into his eyes. "Sam, stop. I don't want to start over," she murmured, her mouth so close that her breath feathered over his face. "I don't want to pretend like the last few weeks never happened." She drew in a shaky breath. Let it out. "I love you, Sam. I'm in love with you."

Oh my God.

He opened his mouth to respond, but she put two fingers over his lips. "It doesn't matter if you don't love me back. Maybe that will come. Maybe not. But either way, I needed to tell you. You've done all the heavy lifting in our relationship so far. You're the one who pursued me. You're the one who pushed. And the whole time, I was just as into you as you were into me, but I was too scared to show it. Too afraid of being hurt again.

"And because I was scared, *I* hurt *you*." She brushed her mouth over his, but pulled away when he tried to deepen the kiss. "The last person in the world I wanted to hurt. So it's my turn to step up. My turn to put myself on the line. My turn to give *you* the power."

Brushing her fingers over his mouth, his cheeks, his neck, she whispered, "Will you take me back, Sam? Give me another chance to get this right? Another chance to show you how much I love you?"

"Jules," he breathed, curling his fingers around her shoulders. "I lo…"

Her hand covered his mouth, her skin soft as silk against his lips. "Please don't say it," she murmured. "Not just because I did. I want to earn your trust. Let me prove that I'm in this. All the way."

"You don't have to earn anything, Jules," he said. He drew her against him, held her close enough to feel the rise and fall of every ragged breath she took. The thunder of her heart slamming against her ribs. Closed his eyes and buried his face in her hair.

He'd been afraid he'd never hold her like this again.

"You have nothing to prove," he murmured into her hair. "I think we both want the same thing -- to be together. In a real relationship. Not just a series of booty calls."

She nodded vigorously into his neck. "Yes, Sam. I want

a relationship with you. I want a lot more than just a relationship, but that's where we'll start."

Sam took a deep, shuddering breath. Let it out. For the first time since this morning, when he'd watched Julia walk down the hall at the Houston Hotel without looking back, the tightness in his chest loosened. The ache in his heart eased.

"It's been far too long since I kissed you," he said, bending to nibble on her neck. "Years. Eons."

"Way too long," she agreed, turning her head to find his mouth.

Jules kissed him tentatively at first, all hesitant lips and stuttering breath, as if she still wasn't sure he'd forgiven her. But as soon as he opened his mouth to her, she surged against him. Touched her tongue to his and kissed him with her whole body. One of her legs wrapped around his, trying to draw him closer. Her arms tightened around him as if she'd never let him go. Her hands combed through his hair. Fluttered over his face. Cupped the back of his head, holding his mouth against hers.

"Jules," he gasped, backing her against the wall. Pressed his aching erection into the vee between her legs and fumbled with the buttons on her shirt. "This is going to be over way too soon. I'll make it up to you. I promise. But I can't wait another minute."

"Me, either," she said, sucking his lower lip into her mouth.

When he couldn't get the buttons open quickly enough, he yanked on the front of her shirt, ripping it open. Buttons plinked on his hardwood floor, each tiny sound intensifying his arousal.

Instead of being horrified, Julia moaned into his mouth, a needy, impatient sound that had him lifting her into the air.

She wrapped her legs around his waist as her fingers fumbled with his belt. As soon as she'd undone the buckle, he whipped it off with a sharp crack, sending it skidding across the floor. He'd barely lowered his zipper when she pushed his boxer briefs down and closed her fingers around him. Tightened in a fist, making his hips jerk against her.

"Not here," he managed to say. "Bed."

"Can't wait that long," she muttered, letting him go as she shoved her own pants down, making his eyes roll back in his head as she wriggled against him, fighting to free her legs.

Once one leg was free, she grabbed his penis and guided him to the space between her legs. Shoved her underwear to the side and surged onto him. They both moaned as they joined together.

She gripped him tightly, her hands shaking, as he thrust into her. In moments he felt the flutter of her approaching climax. Felt his own orgasm bearing down on him.

"Don't stop," she cried. "Please." She gripped his shoulders hard, then screamed, "Sam," as she came around him.

He followed her over the edge, holding her tightly as he shuddered against her.

Eventually he slid down the wall, cradling Julia's body against his. Kissing her again, slowly and sweetly this time. Telling her with his kisses all the things she didn't want him to say yet.

Julia's face was pressed into his neck. Her chest heaved against his. Sam rubbed his hand over her back. Through her hair. Down her back again.

"Oh, my God, Jules," he managed to say. "I've never had real make-up sex, before, but it sure as hell lives up to its hype. I may never walk again."

She eased her face out of his neck to look at him. The tension and fear in her expression had been replaced by the fading red of arousal on her skin and a satisfied, dreamy look in her eyes. When their eyes met, she smiled, and it felt as if the sun had come out.

"You've only had fake make-up sex?" she asked, pressing a kiss to the corner of his mouth.

He shrugged as he ran his hands up and down her back. Both soothing and claiming. "I've never really been in a serious relationship. The kind where stuff matters. The kind where you fight and hurt each other. Where you have to talk through your problems and forgive each other."

Her eyes went soft. "That's what I want, Sam. Exactly that. I want us to be bound so tightly to each other that, even when we fight, when we yell and scream, we always work hard to get to the make-up sex. The amazing, rock-your-world, make-up sex."

He struggled to stand up, still holding her. "Let's take this into the bedroom. I have more making up to do."

She shook her head, and long curls of her hair brushed over his face. "I'm the one who has more making up to do."

Looping her arms around his neck and her legs around his waist, she kissed him again, a tender melding of lips and tongues and teeth. As he eased her onto the bed, she broke their kiss to smile up at him. "What are you making up for this time? Because trust me, you covered all the bases back there in the living room."

"Nice use of a baseball metaphor," he said, stripping off the rest of his clothes and dropping down beside her. As he peeled off her shirt and bra and removed the pants that trailed off one leg like a tail, he said, "You get extra orgasms for that. Also because I never got your underwear off. This time, I'm taking my time with you."

Laughing, she rolled on top of him, soft curls of her hair tickling his skin. "I'm the one who has more making up to do. So I'll take those extra orgasms and give them right back to you."

* * *

Hours later, Julia curled into Sam's side, burying her nose in his neck and inhaling his scent. She'd lost track of the number of times they'd made love. The number of orgasms he'd given her. But she hadn't forgotten a single one of the words he'd said to her. Or the words she'd given back to him.

"I have to leave tomorrow," he said, his voice scratchy and hoarse. He trailed his magic fingers up and down her back, making her shiver. "Road trip. I'll be gone for a week. I can't bear to be away from you."

"It'll go fast," she said, stroking his chest, letting the soft fuzz of his hair tickle her palm. "You'll have games every day. I'll have a lot to do on the Kirby case. And we'll talk whenever we can."

"I have one off day," he said. "Thursday. We'll fly to New York on Wednesday night, then we play the Mets over the weekend." He shifted against her, propped himself on one elbow.

She leaned back, her fingers drifting over the wrinkles at the corners of his eyes and the curl of his mouth. She wanted to hold the memory of the twinkle in his eyes until she saw him again.

"Can you get Thursday off?" he asked, stroking his hand down her side. "Maybe Friday, too? Fly to New York for a couple of days?"

She paused, staring at him, excitement rising inside her. She knew they'd both be busy this week, but she'd been dreading the separation, too. Especially since now they could focus on each other and not the Kirby case. "I have that weekend off," she said slowly. "Maybe I could take personal days on Thursday and Friday. I have a bunch of them banked."

"Could you do that?" he asked eagerly, threading his fingers through hers. "Fly out Wednesday night? Spend the whole weekend with me?"

"I'd have to talk to Captain Francisco. Make sure I clear it with him." She shifted to her side, facing him, running through the possibilities as she stroked her hand down his side. "If he can't spare me, maybe I can find another detective to trade days off with me."

She pushed him onto his back and rolled on top of him. "Are you sure that would work, though? I might tire you out so much you wouldn't have any energy left for your games," she teased. "I don't want to be responsible for Sam Marini going into a slump. Letting his team down."

"You've forgotten the wild card in this scenario," he said, lifting up to press a lingering kiss to her mouth. "My girlfriend will be watching. Knowing she's in the stands, I'll have my best games of the year." He flipped them again, putting himself on top. He stared down at her for a moment. "You've never seen me play," he said quietly. "I'd love knowing you were there at the ball park."

"I'll see what I can do." Her heart was doing silly, fluttery things in her chest, knowing Sam was so excited that she'd be watching him play. "But you're wrong about one thing."

His eyebrows twitched together. "What's that?"

"I *have* seen you play. I've watched you and the 'Cats on television."

He sat up abruptly. "And you've never told me this? You've been keeping this secret since we met?"

"Not since we met. Since we reconnected." She shrugged, feeling suddenly self-conscious. "If the game was on television and I was at home, I turned it on."

"Oh, my God, Jules! I love you so much."

He realized what he'd said at the same time Julia did. Both of them froze.

Then he sighed. "It just burst out of me." He cupped her cheek with one hand. "I know you didn't want me to tell you tonight. You had some crazy-ass idea that you needed to atone or something. I've known how I felt for a while, Jules. I kept it under wraps because I didn't think you were there yet. I didn't want to scare you off."

"Sam." She rolled out from beneath him, then crawled into his lap. Kissed him. "Don't ever be sorry for telling me that you love me." She took his hand and placed it on her chest. "Can you feel that? My heart's beating a mile a minute. Because you love me." She pressed a kiss to his mouth. Lingered.

When she finally broke away, she said, "And you're right. If you'd told me that a few days ago, I probably *would* have run. Because I was scared. Not because I didn't feel the same way.

"I love you, Sam," she said, nibbling at his ear. "Once the sun comes up, we're not going to see each other for four days. So why don't you tell me what you're going to do when I walk into your hotel room next Wednesday night?"

"I'd rather show you," he said, sliding down and stroking his tongue over one of her nipples.

"I'm all for show and tell," she replied, easing away and sliding down his chest. His six-pack abs. Going lower.

Later, as the sky lightened to grey, then pink, Julia snuggled into Sam's side, utterly exhausted. Completely happy. His steady breaths in and out ruffled her hair and made her shiver.

Nuzzling his neck, she whispered, "I love you, Baseball Boy. Forever."

EPILOGUE

Three weeks later

Clutching Sam's hand, Julia pushed open the door to the labor and delivery waiting room at the downtown hospital. The room was packed, and Julia stopped so abruptly that Sam grabbed her hips to steady himself. His fingers curled into her, reminding her of what they'd been doing when Brendan had called that morning.

"Took you guys long enough to get here," Connor said. He sprawled on a two-person chair, holding Raine's hand. "You're lucky that kid is taking his or her time."

"How's Cilla doing?" Julia asked, reaching behind her to entwine her fingers with Sam's. The urge to touch him, to keep him close, had only gotten stronger since the night Derek Kirby attacked him.

"Everything's moving along nicely, and Cilla is holding up like a trouper, according to Brendan." Joanie sat along the opposite wall, holding Don's hand. She glowed with joy. "My first grandchild," she whispered, smiling and crying at the same time.

"How do we get into the pool for boy or girl?" Sam asked.

All the Donovans and Marinis looked at him. Joanie and Don, Rose and Pete looked slightly shocked. Everyone else looked guilty.

"Uh," Connor began, glancing at his mother. He cleared his throat. "It's fifty bucks. Sex, day and time of birth. Since the day is pretty much a lock at this point, you have to ante up an extra twenty bucks apiece. Money is going to Bren and Cilla for some fancy stroller they want. Winner gets the first picture with the kid."

"Sign us up," Sam said, pulling a wad of twenty dollar bills out of his wallet, counting and handing them to Con. "Two entries, one for each of us." He turned to Julia. "You first."

Julia's lips twitched. Having a pool to guess the sex and time of birth of a baby would have horrified her family and their friends. But she loved the idea. Not only was it fun, but it was getting Brendan and Cilla something they wanted.

She glanced at the clock. Eleven-thirty AM. She knew nothing about labor, but she'd take a stab at it. "I'm going to say a boy. At three-twenty this afternoon."

"I've got a girl at four PM." Sam handed the money to Connor. "I'm feeling lucky today, too," he added.

He swirled his thumb over the back of Julia's hand, and she shivered. She turned to press a kiss to his cheek. "I feel lucky every single day," she said softly.

"Wow, Carleton!" Quinn sprawled in the chair, holding his wife Tessa's hand. "I had no idea you were such a sap."

Julia scowled at him. "And I had no idea you have the ears of a bat and use them to listen in on private conversations."

Quinn winked at her, looking pleased with himself. Julia suspected he'd bring up this moment again in the future. Torment her with it.

Julia winked right back. Several weeks ago, she would have been horrified at the idea of Quinn or any of her co-workers seeing her at a vulnerable moment.

Now? She looped an arm around Sam's waist and kissed

him again.

Everyone resumed talking, and Julia frowned. Something was missing. The usual din of a Donovan or Marini get-together. Then she realized what it was.

"Where are all the kids?" she asked.

"They're with Helen and Jamie," Rose said. "We were worried that they wouldn't be allowed in the labor and delivery waiting room. So the cousins will hang out together. We'll all go back to Helen and Jamie's place later and order some pizzas."

"That sounds great." Julia glanced at Sam. "We might not make it, though. Sam has a game tonight."

"Then you come by yourself," Rose said, tilting her head. "You're one of the family now. You don't need Sam as your ticket in."

Julia swallowed the lump growing in her throat and reached for Sam's hand. The first time she'd met all of them together, she'd been intimidated by the huge Donovan and Marini families. Chaos had reigned in Finn and Mia's house, and the noise and emotion were more than she was used to.

Now, though? She and Sam had gone to another family dinner, and Julia counted herself lucky every single day that she'd been welcomed into these two amazing families. Even though she was still a stranger to most of them, they made her feel like she belonged. Like they'd stand by her side no matter what.

Speaking of family... Julia looked around the room, frowning. "Where's Livvy?" she asked. She couldn't believe that her friend wouldn't be here when her sister was having a baby.

"She got called in this morning," Mac said. He held his wife Lizzy's hand. "One of the guys she's prosecuting was beaten up in Cook County Jail overnight. She has to deal with it. She and Ryan will get here as soon as they can."

As he spoke, the door burst open and Livvy and Ryan hurried in. Livvy made a bee-line for her mother. "How's she doing?" she asked, reaching for her mother's hand. "I'm not too late, am I?"

"Not at all," Joanie reassured her. "We're still waiting."

"Thank God." Livvy leaned against Ryan and closed her eyes for a moment. "I'd never forgive that ass... that idiot in Cook County if he made me miss my sister giving birth."

The door hadn't completely closed when it banged against the wall as Alex Jennings and his wife Gaby stepped inside the crowded room. Alex glanced around as he ushered his pregnant wife to the last chair. "We having a party in here or something?"

"Or something," Connor said to his fellow cop from the twenty-third. "We're glad you're here, but how did you know?"

"We had a prenatal thing at the hospital. The nurses were talking about the huge, loud family in the labor and delivery waiting room. Being a brilliant detective, I put two and two together."

"How's it going?" he asked. He curled his hand around his wife's ankle. "I'm already out of the pool, but Gaby has tomorrow. I'd hate to wish Cilla a long labor, but..."

"You shut your mouth, Alex Jennings." Rose Donovan frowned at him, but her eyes twinkled. "I don't want you cursing my Cilla."

"Yes, ma'am," the former Navy SEAL said meekly, biting his lip to hide his grin.

Julia reached for Sam's hand and pulled it into her lap. Leaned close to him. "Is it going to be like this when you and I are the ones in the labor and delivery room?"

Sam stilled. Tightened his hand around hers. Finally turned to study her. "Are you proposing to me, Julia Carleton?"

Was she? She swallowed as she stared at Sam's shocked expression. Maybe she was.

What had happened to her fear? Her wariness of commitment? Her reluctance to be in a relationship with someone in the public eye?

It had all vanished when she told Sam she loved him.

344

"What if I am?" she said slowly. Her gaze locked with Sam's. She loved him. She wanted forever with him. And she was pretty sure he wanted forever with her.

When he didn't say anything, she swallowed. "It's too early to talk about that," she said hurriedly. "We've barely started dating. I'm only getting married once, and we both need to be sure."

"I'm sure," Sam said, his voice low and gravelly, as if he had a lump in his throat. "And you can't take it back. You already asked."

"I didn't actually ask," she said, but her heart was racing and her chest felt two sizes too small to hold the happiness spilling out of her. "I was speaking hypothetically."

"About our hypothetical child. Unless you were thinking about being a single mother."

"No. Of course not. But…"

"Yes." Sam lifted her hand and pressed a kiss to her palm. "My answer is yes, I'll marry you, Julia Carleton."

"Oh, my God," Julia breathed. Was this what she wanted? A life with Sam?

Yes. More than anything.

She swallowed the lump swelling in her throat. "I don't have a ring," she said, running her finger over her father's signet ring. She stilled. "Wait. I *do* have one."

She tugged the ring off her middle finger and slid it onto Sam's pinkie.

Sam looked down at the ring. Touched it almost reverently. "Jules," he said softly. "I know how much this ring means to you."

"You mean more to me, Sam." Sam would always be there when she needed him. He'd always stand by her side. She could count on him, no matter what.

He swallowed, hard, then leaned over and kissed her. What started as a small brush of their lips deepened and grew, until Julia lost all track of where they were.

"Hey, you two, break it up," Connor said into the silence surrounding them. "There are impressionable parents in this room."

Julia eased away from him, pressing her fingers to her lips. Staring into Sam's eyes, wondering if she dreamed the whole thing.

Then Sam grinned. Holding her gaze, he said, "Julia and I are getting married."

There was an instant more of silence, then everybody spoke at once, their voices rising in a happy burst of sound. Joanie hurried over and reached for Julia, hauling her out of the chair and into her arms. "Welcome to the family, Julia," she whispered. "You and Sam are perfect together."

Everyone in the room hugged her. Hugged Sam. Questions flew at her from every side, until finally, laughing, Julia held up her hand. "The answer to all your questions is the same. *I don't know.* But I guarantee you'll be the first to know."

Everyone was still on their feet, asking questions, suggesting wedding venues and dates, when the door opened and Brendan walked in. Cradled carefully in his arms was a swaddled baby, wearing a white hat with a pink pom pom on the top.

"Hey, everyone," he said, and everyone was instantly silent. "Come meet Zoe Marini Donovan."

Both grandmothers rushed over, identical expressions of awe on their faces. "She's beautiful," Rose breathed.

"So alert," said Joanie, biting her lip as the infant gazed up at her.

"Grandmothers only," Brendan said, gazing down at his daughter with a completely besotted smile. "The doc said not to pass her around."

He placed the baby in his mother-in-law's arms, his hand lingering on the infant's chest.

"How's Cilla doing?" Sam asked.

"She's great." Brendan beamed. "Nearly broke my hand, but she was a champ."

Joanie handed the baby to Rose, then leaned over her shoulder to keep staring at Zoe.

Connor pulled what looked like a spreadsheet out of his pocket. Studied it for a long moment, then smiled. "Charlotte won the pool," he said happily. "We'll get a picture of the cousins together when Zoe comes home."

Connor folded the paper and returned it to his pocket. "Looks like the two-year-old outsmarted all the detectives in the family." He nudged Brendan, his eyes twinkling at Finn and Sam. "All the big shots, too."

Amidst the laughter and the talking, Julia fumbled for Sam's hand and clung tightly as she watched the family cluster around Brendan and Zoe, oohing and aahing over the newborn.

Zoe had been born into this amazing family. Julia would marry into it. But both of them would be showered with love for the rest of their lives.

Finding Sam had been a gift.

His family was the bonus she hadn't been expecting.

And now, their future children would never be alone, the way Julia had been. They'd have cousins, aunts, uncles, grandparents. An unending stream of love from people who adored them.

"Have I died and gone to heaven?" she asked, leaning her head against Sam's shoulder. "Or is it always going to be like this? Love and support and noise and laughter?"

"Pretty much," Sam said, curling his arm around her. "And you fit right in. The Donovan and Marini magic has rubbed off on you already." He nuzzled her hair. "And I love it. I love this new, bold version of Jules. The one who tells me she loves me. The one who asks me to marry her."

Julia twined her arm around Sam's waist. "I barely recognize myself."

"Not me. I knew this Jules was always there. She just needed a little push to come out of hiding."

He drew her over to a now-deserted corner of the room. "I'm a little concerned about something, though."

She swung around to face him, relaxing when she saw the twinkle in his eyes. "What's that?"

He leaned closer, so his mouth was brushing her ear. "How are we going to celebrate our engagement? I have to be at the ball park in less than two hours."

"I guess we'll have to wait until after the game tonight to get started." She nudged him with her hip, happiness engulfing her. "And that's exactly what it will be -- a start. Because I'm planning on a life-long celebration."

She turned and wrapped her arms around him, not caring that they had an audience. "Our future starts today, Sam, and I can't wait."

* * * * *

ABOUT THE AUTHOR

Two-time Rita finalist Margaret Watson published her first book in June, 1991. Since then, she has written thirty books for Silhouette Intimate Moments and Harlequin SuperRomance, as well as nine titles in the Donovan Family series.

Margaret's books have won or been finalists in many contests, including the Colorado Award of Excellence, Desert Rose Golden Quill, Holt Medallion, and National Reader's Choice.

When she's not writing, Margaret practices veterinary medicine. She lives in the Chicago area with her husband, three daughters and a menagerie of pets.

* * *

Thank you for reading Catch Me. I'm honored you chose one of my books, and I hope you enjoyed it!

- If you would like to receive an email newsletter when my next book is released, sign up at **www.margaretwatson.com**.
- Reviews help other readers find books they'd like to read. Please leave a review of this book at your favorite on-line retailer. I welcome all reviews.
- Please recommend this book to your friends and on discussion boards.

www.ingramcontent.com/pod-product-compliance
Lightning Source LLC
Chambersburg PA
CBHW050918250626
47155CB00001B/281